THE BEST OF
Penny Dread
Tales

Michelle,
I hope you enjoy
reading these as much
as I did collecting them!!

[signature]

THE BEST OF Penny Dread Tales

To Michelle—

Steam on!

Edited by

Kevin J. Anderson

&

Quincy J. Allen

WordFire Press
Colorado Springs, Colorado

ISBN: 978-1-61475-253-0

Cover design by Kathryn S. Renta

Art Director Kevin J. Anderson

Book Design by RuneWright, LLC
www.RuneWright.com

Published by
WordFire Press, an imprint of
WordFire, Inc.
PO Box 1840
Monument CO 80132

Kevin J. Anderson & Rebecca Moesta, Publishers

WordFire Press Trade Paperback Edition November 2014
Printed in the USA
wordfirepress.com

CONTENTS

INTRODUCTION

The *Penny Dread Tales* series can be traced back to a single conversation at MileHiCon in Denver in 2010. I'd just set my feet upon the path of becoming an author and was looking for writing gigs. The de facto leader of the local steampunk community was promoting both AnomalyCon (Colorado's primary steampunk convention) and her Internet radio show *RadioSteam*. We talked, and as a result of that conversation, she let me write what turned into two episodes for the show.

My interest in the burgeoning steampunk sub-genre was born. I'd grown up loving steampunk, even before the term "steampunk" had been coined. The old *Wild Wild West* TV show as well as works by Mary Shelley, Jules Verne, and H.G. Wells were all things I could claim as writing influences. But this was something new. Steampunk as it is today put a lot of interesting new twists into 19th century sci-fi, modernizing it into a palatable form of both aesthetic and social commentary that encourages all manner of cross-over.

That's probably what intrigued me most. I love cross-genre fiction. It's like they say, "There is nothing new under the sun." However, crossing sci-fi, paranormal, horror, mystery, western, historical, and everything else with the steampunk aesthetic is commonplace today. For a writer, I consider it to be fertile ground.

Add to that my desire to have another book on my table at conventions, and producing a steampunk anthology seemed like a logical course of action. I think *Six-Guns Straight from Hell*, published by David B. Riley in 2010, contributed to my decision as well. It's a mashup of paranormal and horror stories set in the Old West. I figured that if weird westerns could make up viable anthologies, then there was no reason steampunk couldn't. I sent out calls for submission, went through a surprisingly large number of stories, and was able to compile the first *Penny Dread Tales*, which was released at the first AnomalyCon in 2011. I must admit, I had no idea I would end up producing a second volume, let alone a fourth, but when I saw the interest, there was only one thing to do.

I really had no idea what I was doing, but as a result, a new *PDT* volume has hit the table (and the Internet) each year, with more and more people asking about the next edition. The books have garnered increasing interest over the past four years, so when Kevin J. Anderson asked me about letting WordFire do one of them, I was ecstatic. It was validation. I've been bumbling along in this writing career of mine for five years now, and to have someone like Kevin take notice was worth its weight in gold. During our initial conversation, I suggested a *Best Of* collection to him, which is what you're reading now.

The *PDT* series has been, and I hope will continue to be, a labor of love. It has also been one of the best learning experiences I've had since I set out to become a writer. *PDT* has allowed me to meet some amazing new people and extend my "writer's tribe" literally across the globe. It's been a most amazing experience.

I wanted to take an opportunity to thank each and every writer and artist who ever had enough faith in *Penny Dread Tales* to work with me. Not all of them made the *Penny Dread Tales* volumes, and only a short list made the *Best Of* collection, but every one enhanced my understanding and appreciation of what steampunk is and can be. I also wanted to thank Laura Givens for the first *PDT* cover, Nathan Lee for what was the original second cover, and Kathryn S. Renta for the new look of the *PDT* series as well as the covers for volumes III and IV. Finally, I can't thank Kevin J. Anderson and Rebecca Moesta at WordFire Press enough for helping make the Penny Dread dream (among others) come true.

I am supremely grateful and monumentally humbled by what *Penny Dread Tales* has become. I owe everyone who has ever been involved a debt of thanks I can only repay by continuing to do what I do. I'll try not to falter along the way.

— Quincy J. Allen

Iron Angel

Cayleigh Hickey

Deryn

I love dreaming that I can fly … until I wake up tangled in the sheets on my bed in the room that has been my home for the past sixteen years of my miserable, wingless life. Every inch of these walls makes me want to scream, so perfectly I've memorized them. The sprawling, luxurious bed my father built when I was six, with its dark, sweet-smelling wood and its gauzy white canopy; I want to tear it all to shreds and demolish the room that has been my prison.

The only small comfort I can find in glancing around it is in Corbin's drawings. They're everywhere, pinned to the walls, stacked on my nightstand, dangling from the ceiling. Pictures of me, of him, of the townspeople, of the forest that lies just outside my balcony but is as untouchable as the sky the rest of my race soars through on beautiful, glossy wings I'll never have. The pictures depress me sometimes, but they're nearly all I have, so I hold them close.

I've got Corbin's pictures … and Corbin. They're the only things that will ever put a smile on my pale, elfin face.

After waking, I lie in bed for long, tense minutes until I absolutely can't stand it anymore—until I know the sanity of walking will outweigh the agony of it. It takes a full quarter-hour for me to drag myself up and hobble, step by excruciating step, over to the balcony adjoining my room where I collapse against the rail, taking all the weight I can off my fragile legs. Even this, the most freedom I can have, drives an awful reminder deep into my heart. My balcony is the only one of hundreds that has or needs a railing, for a painfully obvious reason.

If anyone besides me were to fall, they'd have five hundred feet to spread their wings and fly to safety. I don't imagine flapping my arms all over Hell would offer much lift, and a soft landing it wouldn't be. My legs would shatter, even if my spine or skull didn't. Hell, my legs would crumble if I fell the ten feet to my living room. By design, my people are born with weak legs. We aren't supposed to need them much, after all—we're supposed to be able to fly. There's a few keywords there—*supposed to be*.

I'm an anomaly: twisted and malformed. I came into this world without wings and with nothing to compensate for the loss of them. I was sick—still am. My bones are even frailer than most—they're like glass. I can't walk faster than a crawl and could never run any more than I could fly. There's no going anywhere, no doing anything. My dad put together a ladder leading to the lower floor of my house, but only on a good day can I manage that, and I have very few of those.

I peer through the sturdy, utilitarian rail at the beautifully vast world sprawled out before me and contemplate screaming. It's positively gorgeous, all of it, and I can reach none of it: the trees that soar as high as my sister can, with their lovely, gnarled trunks a mile thick; the houses that wrap around them like chains, strung with moss and flowers that ooze colors so vibrant they hurt my eyes; the leafy canopy hanging overhead, fluttering in a breeze I can't feel this far down, offering tantalizing glimpses of clear blue sky, bits like broken eggshells. I can see a few of my people dancing with the clouds, their outstretched wings just as stunning as the torturous vista engulfing me.

Screaming seems all the more tempting.

"Deryn?" It's my mother calling, and I'm tempted not to answer. She'll find me within moments; I can't exactly hide anywhere. But I call back anyway, because I know how much she frets over me. She's convinced that I'm going to tumble right off of the balcony, even though the railing could halt a charging bull, and I'm not *that* clumsy. Weak, maybe, but plenty coordinated enough to keep my feet on the ground, exactly where I wish they weren't.

"I'm out here!"

She flutters through my room to where I sit, her feet barely grazing the ground I suffered over. My mother is ridiculously lovely: all long, lanky limbs and shiny red curls that I might've been envious of if I hadn't already been so distorted. As it is, my plain, dark hair is the least of my discontents.

"Good morning, sweetie," she says, leaning down to give me the lightest of hugs, afraid I'll break in her arms. I know she's being careful not to let her wings brush my skin, and part of me is grateful while the rest roils with irritation. They're huge and dark brown, with just the faintest dusting of white peeking out from underneath. They're elegantly beautiful, and they could've been mine. My sister got them. I got nothing.

"Morning, mom," I mumble back, making it more one word than two. I pull my arms back and tuck them tightly over my chest, crumpling bits of my silky white nightgown between my fingers.

"Do you want anything to eat?" she asks, crouching beside me so that that the tips of her pinions brush the wooden floor. "There's some stew leftover from last night, or I can make you something else ..."

She lets her voice trail off to leave the statement as a question. I answer with a gentle shake of my head and a noncommittal sound that could be taken a dozen different ways. My mother frowns, distraught by my sullenness. "Alright then ..." she struggles upright with a groan, her legs despising her for making them bear so much weight. She presses a feathery kiss to the top of my head. "Let me know if you need anything. Is Corbin coming by at all?"

I sigh, wishing she hadn't asked but knowing all along that she would. It wasn't like the answer wasn't the same everyday lately. "I don't know," I enunciate, trying to bang the idea into her head. "He might. *I don't know.*"

My mom walks away and leaves it there, and for that, at least, I'm thankful. A few weeks ago I wouldn't have minded her asking—a few weeks ago my answer would've been an undoubted, unshakable *yes.* It used to be that everyday Corbin would fall to my balcony with a huge, manic grin, a folder of sketches under one arm and a breakfast for two hanging from the other. I'd clamber out of bed to meet him. If it was a bad day, he'd come to me, and we'd sit in my room for hours eating and talking and laughing as he told me about the world, drawing pictures in the air with his fingers and on paper with the pencil that was forever perched behind his ear.

But now ... there are days when he doesn't show at all, and when he does, it's never for more than an hour. There's something different now in the way he carries himself, some sort of apprehension. Either he or I have built a wall between us, and I can't, for the life of me, tell how thick it is ... or if I can bring it crashing down if I just try hard enough.

Forty-five minutes I wait for him there, my legs dangling off into space through the gaps in the railing, my chin pillowed on my forearms, my eyes scanning the skies for any glimpse of his dark wings and hair. When my limbs start to fall asleep, I admit defeat and haul myself back inside, gritting my teeth through it all.

Corbin

Sarika is just about the craziest, most eccentric woman on or off the face of the planet, but she's the best bet if you're trying to hunt down something city-side. And my tall order of metal plating, pipes, motors and a dozen other gizmos is definitely up her alley.

She has everything you could ask for buried in the massive cave of wonders she calls home. She goes into the city, her wings glamoured from human sight, and trades with the best inventors she can find. She gives them magic secrets in returns for what they make from them.

There are people who hate her, who think she's meddling in the timeline of humanity, giving them things that are too advanced for them to handle. But everything she has works, and that's all I care about.

"What is it you're looking for this time?" she asks as she sifts through a heap of screws and bolts, tucking some away into the pockets of her apron and binning others. She's wearing men's trousers and a shirt that hang like a pillowcase over her bony frame, her white wings peeping from frayed holes. There's a pair of thick goggles perched atop her head, cushioned by her graying blond hair.

"I need another motor," I explain, casting my eyes around the shop. There's metal and glass everywhere, from twisted hunks of iron to delicate aluminum framework to decorative designs in silver and gold. "Lighter than the one you gave me last time."

Sarika bites her lower lip, centering the glasses that are eternally slipping down her nose. "Hmm, I'm nearly positive that was the lightest I have," she says, her brows knitting together with thought. "I'll look though. Maybe there's something hiding from me."

Clattering like a metal man, Sarika wades down the aisle, stepping carefully over fallen bits of shrapnel and weaving her arms through contraptions hanging from the ceiling, raw ideas made into wood and iron flesh: a long, thin tube with narrowed ends and flat, featherless wings poking from either side; a wire box with four wheels running along on air. These are things Sarika will show to the humans, things they will build long before they would've thought of them themselves.

Sarika is a million miles ahead of me, clanging through her workshop, and I have to scramble to catch up with her. She stops in front of a series of shelves, and I'm moving so carelessly that only a frantic pin-wheeling of arms keeps me from running right into her.

The shelves she's contemplating are packed full of gadgets and hardware of all shapes and sizes, twisted and smooth, fragile and sturdy. I can't count them all, but she runs her eyes over them with the air of someone glancing over a collection of books they know by heart. It sounds like she's murmuring something under her breath, but I can't make out anything concrete.

She lets out a triumphant breath, and her nimble fingers dart forward, digging out something about the size of a baby's head and about as lumpy. She dumps it into my open hands, and I weigh it tentatively, not daring to get my hopes up until my mind has fully registered the feather-lightness … and then those hopes soar right off.

O O O

When I alight on our front step, the first thing I hear after the rush of flying fades is someone arguing, her words pointed and tipped with venom. Fluttering inside with the bag of parts dangling from my shoulder I find my brother Bran in the middle of the living room. He's tall and intimidating, even slouching as he is, cowering in the face of a pint-sized, whip-thin fireball that looks like she could as much do damage to him as a fly could to a buffalo. Her twiggy arms cut through the air like knives, illustrating some grand point that apparently my brother can't get through his head.

"Well where the hell is he?" she rants, cutting off with disturbing suddenness as the creaking of the shutting door interrupts. Whirling on the tips of her toes, her skirts fanning out about her knees and her wild, crimson hair flaring around her pale, freckled face, she glares at me angrily. "*There* you are."

It's Arlette, Deryn's older, tinier, scarier sister. The woman that would hardly come up to my shoulder is overflowing with bloodlust, all of it directed straight at me. I don't dare say anything, knowing that she'll take the reins without any prodding.

"Where the hell have you been disappearing to for the last three weeks?" she shrieks, hands flying instantly to her diminutive hips. Folded at her back, the dark brown feathers of her wings are ruffling with anger. Only when she's this furious can you see any familial resemblance between her and Deryn. They have the same frown, the same quirk of wrinkling their noses and drawing their eyebrows together.

"What do you mean?" I ask, figuring that feigning ignorance is the best plan of action here ... acting like I have absolutely no idea whatsoever about the elephant in the room she's referring to.

"You know exactly what I mean," she says, shooting me full of glares. "You've hardly been to see Deryn in nearly a month. She's going to go mad soon if she doesn't have anyone to talk to!"

Now I know *exactly* what she's talking about, and I know that I would never consider abandoning Deryn to her miserable fate, but I can't figure any other way to get Arlette out of my hair. I'll have to feign cruelty, callousness, all the things I never, ever show.

I don't dare tell her the truth without knowing how she'll react. There's every possibility she'll stop me now, that she'll dash Deryn's last hope without a second thought. If she doesn't trust me enough, all she'll see is her sister in danger, and she won't stand for that. So I cross my arms and try on the most withering look I can manage. "I'm not her keeper," I say, trying to channel some of Arlette's irritation into my voice. She's got plenty to spare. "It's not my job to check in on her twenty-four-seven."

This stops her short. I don't know what she was expecting me to say, but it definitely wasn't that. "I …" There's a long pause during which her mouth closes and opens again, gaping like a dying fish. "Well then," she finishes with a huff, tugging at her skirt with fingers made clumsy by shock. I think she might be trying to smooth out some wrinkles, but if she is, it's a lost cause—she's just making them worse.

Hiking her chin, she glances over her shoulder at Bran who's staring like the idiot he is. She tosses him a terse nod before blazing past me towards the door. I doubt her bony shoulder clipping my upper arm as she passes is any sort of accident.

Arlette pauses at the threshold without looking back, fingering the doorframe. "I always thought you were a better boy than that. I guess I was wrong." Then she's gone, and Bran collapses onto the old couch, his long spider legs dangling over the end.

There's a strange look on his face, caught in a fight between anxiety and pain. "Thanks for not telling her," I mumble, knowing that he must've borne the brunt of Arlette's anger before I came and knowing exactly how hard that must've been for him. After all, he's been head over heels in love with her since he was a gangly twelve-year-old that hadn't yet grown into his height.

"No problem, Corbin," he breathes, running a big hand over his face, pushing back the long, messy fringe that just loves to fall in his eyes. He sends me a tired grin, and for someone like Bran who hands out his smiles like war rations, that means something. "I'm not *that* much of a sellout. Did you get the last part you needed?"

I bob my head, hiking the bag off my shoulder and ripping open the drawstring. My fingers search for the motor and find it easily, holding it out for him to see.

"It's twice as light as the other one," I say, unable to keep the edge of juvenile excitement from my voice. It is a very neat toy resting in my hands, even though the small knot of metal and gears may not look like much. "This thing might actually *work*."

There's a glimmer of madness in my brother's eyes to match my own as he hauls himself over, his eager fingers absorbing the motor's surface. He picks it up, weighing it in the palm of one hand. "It might," he whispers, every word drenched in disbelief. "It actually might."

Deryn

It's been a month now since Corbin's been here for any longer than a quarter of an hour. It feels like pixies snuck into my room in the middle of the night and sawed off the top of my skull so they could steal my mind. I used to always be scared as a child that they would do just that, and now it seems like the fear has finally become reality. I can hardly think anymore. Corbin was the one who made the world I hardly knew make sense, and now everything's gone wonky.

Arlette stops by to visit more, but it isn't the same—listening to my tiny, emotional sister rattle off stories—as it would be listening to my best friend do the same. Maybe you think I'm pathetic, going so crazy over something so small in the grand scheme of everything, but you have no idea. You don't know what it's like to be so completely imprisoned and have your link to the outside world severed.

You don't know.

Corbin

I can picture Deryn laughing at me as I truss up a stack of books like a present, my fingers fumbling at the knots they can't seem to manage. The thought makes me ridiculously sad. Even if I had a perfectly good reason for not visiting these last few weeks ... that doesn't make me miss her less. The build has needed my full attention, and I couldn't risk letting something slip or forgetting to take a sketch out of my folder, but still ... I wish she was here now, sitting on the end of my bed like I've sat so many times on the end of hers. Maybe, if this works, she'll be here before long. If she forgives me.

No, no, I *know* she'll forgive me.

The image of the smile that I *know* will break across her cheeks keeps my hands moving, dragging the books across the floor because they're too heavy for me to lift on my own. They weigh as much as Deryn does, or as much as I remember she did. Hopefully she hasn't put on much weight since then.

Bran walks in from outside to give me a hand, and together we manage to haul the ballast onto the balcony where my baby is waiting. It's not literally my *baby*, of course, but it might as well be.

It's been swallowing my blood, sweat, and tears for four weeks now, and consuming my mind for three times as long.

I can hardly believe that it's sitting here, in front of my own eyes, completely finished. It's beautiful, with wooden bones and metal skin, clockwork organs and a leathery smile.

They're the wings of an iron angel. They're Deryn's wings, or they will be: if they fly now, if they can bear the weight and keep on going. My people don't have any specific god like the humans do, but I send out a prayer towards the general vicinity of the sky, figuring that it can't hurt any.

"You ready?" Bran asks me, setting the stack of books in front of the wings and wiping his hands on his trousers, leaving greasy smears where his fingers were.

Bran was the one who was at my side every second, warning me away from stupid mistakes, advising on the shape of the feathers, the positioning of the motor and throwing in an extra bit of muscle when brute strength was needed. The idea might've spawned from my head, but he built the contraption as much as I did. I still haven't quite figured out how to thank him.

I nod and set to work affixing the books so there's not a chance they could fall if they tried. As I finish, I rise to my feet and flutter my wings a little, my toes just barely brushing the ground. Leaving one wing for Bran, I take the other, and together we lift it up and over the balcony's edge. Even though I know its weight down to the gram, it feels shockingly light in my hands, probably because Bran's taking more than his share of the burden, like always.

The books don't plummet, and neither do either of us, though the art of hovering level has taken on new difficulty. We manage though, and I'm the one that frees one hand to pull the motor's ripcord, setting it coughing and chugging with reassuring regularity. *It might work. It might fly.*

The wings, with their sculpted aluminum feathers, start to whisper back and forth, faster and faster, until Bran and I are ducking every which way to avoid been smacked upside the head. The motor is snarling like a living beast now, curls of smoke polluting the air.

"Ready?" I ask. I can see people peering out of their windows and stealing onto balconies to watch with huge, curious eyes. I hear children shouting and laughing, and I know they're pointing. Maybe they think we're mad. Probably they do, and probably we are, but I start counting down anyway when I catch Bran's nod.

"Three, two, one!"

And without another word we let go, our fingers uncurling at the same moment, our wings twitching in anticipation of a dive that's never necessary.

Because it flies.

Deryn

I'm lying on my bed on top of the blankets, my head propped up against the headboard, when my favorite voice breaks the non-silence of the forest at midday.

"Is the ceiling really all that interesting?" he asks, sending my neck snapping upwards. My gaze locks onto the entrance to my balcony where he's waiting. He looks just the same as ever, if a little wearier. There are darkish purple rings hanging under his sky-blue eyes, a pale undertone lurking beneath his sun-browned skin. His arms are hanging limply at his sides, his palms turned outward in a gesture of peace. The set of his shoulders is hopeful as he stands completely, utterly still, waiting for me to make the first move.

That move takes a minute, because first I have to work through the surprise that has flash-frozen my thoughts. It's been so long since I've seen him, I mean, *really* seen him ... like this. No walls wrapped around him, no apprehension hiding in his eyes. My instinct is to jump to my feet and fling myself into his arms, but even if I *could* do that without fracturing something vital, I'm wary. I have no explanation of his disappearance, and I'm not sure how angry I am with him yet. Maybe he had good reasons, but until he shares them, I think I'll stay right here, thank you very much.

"Not gonna talk to me, are you?" he asks. I know he's expecting no answer, so I give none. I just sit up a little straighter, folding my hands into my lap as I watch him, waiting. "That's okay; I didn't really expect you to." He takes half a dozen steps forward until he's barely a yard from me, approaching like I'm prey that'll bolt any second— as if I *could* bolt. That's almost funny.

"I'm sorry, Der," Corbin says, real pain and remorse saturating his voice, care weighing down his nickname for me, the one I don't let anyone but him use. "I've been really, *really* busy. I've been building something, and I couldn't risk you finding out about it until it was finished." He polishes off the sentence with a sweet, white grin, shocking my defenses. "It was a surprise; I didn't want to ruin it."

That brings a withering look surfacing from under my impassive mask. "I can't imagine any surprise that would be worth a full month of near-solitude." I shake my head, knowing he can't imagine, can't step into my shoes and see exactly what I'm getting at. No one could, so I can't really blame him for it. "I've being going insane here, Corbin. There are times when I think I already am. I can't imagine anything you could've made that I would have chosen over your company, had I known."

And I really, truly can't. Corbin's companionship is one thing I will never, ever be able to put a price on, because he has no obligation to me, and we both know it. He spends time with me—or did—out of a genuine like of me, out of compassion, and—I might as well admit it—there was some pity there, at the beginning at least. I would never even consider trading something as precious as his true, pure friendship away.

The smile he gives me is unhinged, the sparkle in his eyes just as strange. I wonder if he's joined my spiral into madness. "Of course you haven't imagined it," he says, not like I'm an idiot but with an irrepressible excitement that has me intrigued. "I'm the only one crazy enough to do it."

When he reaches out a hand to help me up, I take it without question. I don't know if anything could ever make me stop trusting him. I'd probably jump from a thousand foot cliff if he was right there beside me, fingers wrapped around my own.

Clearly pleased with my reaction, he takes nearly all of my weight as he leads me along. First, off the bed and onto my feet and then, more slowly, across the open floor. I can feel him pulsing with exhilaration, and it's got me shaking too.

I ponder and ponder what he could've possibly built, but I can't think of anything. He hasn't really given me much to work off of, except that whatever it is, it's insane and wonderful.

I realize that it's not just the two of us there when we're halfway across my room. I can hear a set of pacing footsteps that clashes with our own. And, if I listen hard enough, I can hear someone whistling,

13

low and soft, under his breath. I'm eighty-percent sure I know who it is when we cross the threshold, and then it jumps the extra twenty-percent to make it an even hundred.

Bran tosses me a wave and one of his rare smiles from where he's leaning against the rail. I make a move to smile back, but then the entirety of my attention is stolen away by something waiting just to his left: something amazing, something beautiful, something that tears a squeal from my gaping lips.

A pair of wings built from wood and leather and metal, covered in layer after layer of perfectly wrought feathers. The sun beats down, setting the edges aglow with light, turning the silvery surface to deep orange-gold, the color of phoenix wings. There are no words to capture the beauty before me.

I'm even more floored when I realize ... these are meant for *me*. I see the motor strapped to the back, and I know that they will fly, that they will bear me as they do so. This is Corbin's secret—he's been building me my freedom.

Before he can say anything, I spin around and pull him into the tightest hug my fragile arms can stand and press my lips to his in a moment of whimsy. "Thank you," I say, the words shaking as they fall from my mouth just as badly as the rest of me is. I think my mind's stopped working, because all I can do is say "thank you" over and over and over again.

Corbin is grinning at me, gentle color flushing his pale cheeks as he takes both my hands in his and leads me over to the where the wings are resting. They're even lovelier up close. My breath catches in my throat, and my eyes prickle with the forerunners of a flood, no matter how ridiculous I know that is. Why the hell should I feel like crying now?

"I hope you forgive me, Der," he says, watching from behind as he lets me go, lets me sink to my knees and explore every inch of his invention, my eyes wide and shimmering. I want words for this moment, but no matter how hard I search, I find none. "I figured it would be more special this way."

And I'm just giggling like an idiot, my hands resting atop the motor, the sun warm on my cheeks. "Can I fly?" I plead, beaming up at him and Bran who's lurking and snickering behind his shoulder.

Corbin laughs a laugh that morphs into a smile as he crouches down beside me. "'Course you can," he says, reaching around my hands so he can get a good grip on the leather backing. Bran joins him, holding onto the wingtips so that, together, they can lift it off the floor and maneuver it around to my back. I stand and spread my arms in anticipation for the straps that come up onto my shoulders, the whole thing sitting like a backpack. I bear as much of the weight as I can. Bran easily takes the rest so that Corbin can focus, tightening me into the harness until the leather straps are on the verge of suffocating me, and I have to tell him to stop.

Corbin nods at me and then at Bran, who tears at something attached to the wings. I feel my torso jerk, and the motor grumbles against my back. I cough as a puff of greasy smoke ventures down my throat.

Hands on my shoulders, holding me fast, Corbin appraises me with his eyes as the wings begin to flutter, growing lighter as they start to support their own weight. I hear Bran fumble out of the way.

"I tested these with some weight, so there shouldn't be a problem," Corbin says, each word slow and steady. "But if there is, Bran and I will catch you, I swear. We won't let you fall."

I bob my head, not in any sort of mindset to care about my own well-being.

He shows me a set of dials affixed to the straps. "This one will let you go higher," he explains, pointing to the larger one. "This one will drop you down," he adds, indicating the smaller. "You'll need one of us to come to a complete stop, okay?"

I'm just nodding and nodding, so eager to fly that I might shake my way right out of the harness.

"Alright then." Corbin lets me go and hops easily onto the edge of the railing, holding out a hand to help me up. I take it gratefully and stand there a moment, my bare toes hanging off into the abyss. "Let's hope this works so your parents and Arlette don't have anything to kill us about, yeah?"

I snort and flip up the big dial, my teeth chattering as the wings work so hard my feet are already slipping away from the wooden rail. I'm nearly hovering, and it feels amazing, but it's not enough.

I was born to fly, and instead I've been grounded all my life.

I throw myself off the edge, laughter torn carelessly from my lips as I spread my arms to catch just that extra bit of air …

And I fly free of my cage on iron angel's wings.

THE DIRGES OF
PERCIVAL LEWAND

Aaron Michael Ritchey

Doctor Davyss circled the skeletal piano and my beautiful automaton like an African lion stalking his prey. Around my basement chamber lay derelict parts of pianos and castoff brass gears. Crumbling stone walls leaked water from the street, and the ceiling's rough-hewn wood showed the soot from my candles and lamps.

No windows. A single door. No other means of exit out into the cruel streets of East London.

I stood by my slender mattress and watched Davyss pace. Both hope and horror left me breathless.

My benefactor smiled at me then returned to scrutinize the automaton, Christine, seated on her wheeled cart, her slender, gloved fingers resting above the ivory keys, motionless.

"Surely, your cabinet player staggers the imagination, Mr. Lewand, yet as I have said before, her playing is only adequate. What she lacks is that primal passion and vitality we feel pulsing through our veins."

"So you really do believe in …" I whispered, but could not finish the sentence.

"Blood," Davyss murmured, a dreamy look on his face. "Christine has bones of brass and sinew of rubber, but at her core she is empty. Where do our passions lie? In our blood."

The anxiety pressing down on my chest increased. I felt ill.

Davyss leaned forward, his clean-shaven face inches away from the porcelain mask covering Christine's clockwork head framed by a silk-spun wig. A gown covered the rest of her brass gears and wheeled cart. I had fashioned her to have a woman's curves, yet I made sure she retained her feminine modesty. I was proud that Christine's clothing was every bit as fastidious as Davyss' dress. Both were as well kempt as they could be.

"You say she sees the music as ones and zeroes," Davyss said. "That I quite believe, but I am resolved that she be less mathematician, more musician. Did you make the modifications I requested?"

"To the letter of your instruction," I returned, desperate to impress my benefactor.

Davyss eyed me skeptically. "Really. Including the burning of the black candle at 3 a.m. followed by the Latin incantation."

"Yes, just as you told me." I fought to keep my countenance blank. Such violent emotions stormed through me. Davyss' descent into the occult had made me question his sanity … and my own. He had a patient—a denizen of the London Hospital's mental ward—who claimed to be adept at the dark arts. This lunatic had led my benefactor down a path that had nothing to do with science, all in hopes of improving Christine's playing.

I hurried forward, always so obsequious—driven to please by a shrinking belly and a chilly bed. With a shaking hand I motioned to the strange black candle, half-burnt, resting on the piano. I then showed him the port at the base of Christine's neck, large enough for a single glass vial. "Through tubing, whatever liquid we add will mix with the automaton's whale-oil lubrication system. Although I have tried to keep my mind scientifically detached, I have little hope that this will work. My cabinet player is a machine. Hence, blood should have no effect on her playing."

"But you will humor me, yes?"

I nodded.

"Then we will give our thirsty girl a bit of your blood, Lewand."

I gulped. Such superstitious nonsense, fit only for women and primitives. Still, my debt shackled me to Davyss. I removed my coat and pushed my shirtsleeve up above my elbow. He unpacked needles, vials, and other medical supplies from his black bag.

Davyss' face was positively glowing. "If your cabinet player could but know the fiery passion at the heart of life, she could play to packed theatres, and your miracle could rise above the petty machinery of the Aeolios Company."

At the mention of my competition, I paled. "But surely, Dr. Davyss, the engineering itself could be impressive enough for you to invest further. Please ..." *I'm so very hungry*, I wanted to add. But I could not. Davyss was a man without pity. He expected results. At times I was honored to have such a unique relationship with Dr. Martin Marquavious Davyss. Other times, my connection to him felt like a morass, offering no escape save death.

Blood was what Davyss wanted, and blood he got. Moments later, he took a thick needle and without ceremony pressed it into my flesh. Icy pain churned in me as he twisted the needle to affix the vial until my own dear essence dripped out, leaving me even more lightheaded and nauseated. I had not eaten in days. All money went for parts and rent. I had even abandoned tea for the project.

Once the vial was full, Davyss pulled out the needle quickly, gave me cotton for the puncture, all the while buzzing with excitement. Odd, I had never seen him so full of what the French call, *joie de vivre*.

"Now, give her music to play." His voice blistered with expectation.

"Yes, but first, I must prepare the gears." From around my neck, on a simple chain, I held the key to Christine's heart. I took the key, found the aperture on the left side of her head, and slowly turned. Once her gears were wound, I inserted the vial into a slot at the base of her neck and snapped it into place. She was ready. "Now, what piece of music should I have her play?"

"It does not matter!" Davyss struck his hands together. A deep breath followed as if to calm himself. Then, casually, he said, "I understand that you think the stimulus of the music will affect this experiment, but I assure you, your wonderful simulacrum could play a child's lullaby, and we would instantly know if our efforts have been in vain or not."

So I chose Beethoven's *Piano Concerto Number 5 in E-flat Major*, a favorite of mine.

Gearing set, I gently pulled down the lever hidden under her hair. The cylinders inside of Christine began to turn, and through a slot in her back, I fed a thick piece of perforated paper. Machines could not read sheet music, and so I had created a language all my own, far more ingenious than my cabinet player's metal body. Each perforation on the page represented a zero, otherwise a one. The instant the sensitive cilia covering the cylinders discovered the first perforation, her brass fingers pressed down on the keys.

Both Davyss and I listened intently.

"Yes." Davyss hissed the word.

I had a sensitive ear, and yet I could not discern any difference. The notes came out in perfect time, but a machine could play perfect time, and each note was crisp and clear, but that too was a machine's forte.

She finished the first page and returned to her primary position, thumbs hovering over middle C. The paper emerged from her back and drifted to the floor. I pushed the lever to stop the cylinders.

Davyss shrugged off his jacket in a single violent motion. "Lewand, you have a scientist's blood, cold and logical. Do not think ill of that. To be so very levelheaded with such lazy passions is a gift. I would be such a man if I could. However, I am anything but."

He did not stop undressing until, to my shock, I saw the pale skin of his chest and arms.

Adding to my discomfiture, he wrapped tubing around his arm and stabbed the needle into a tumescent vein. Thick crimson oozed into a second vial.

He pumped his fist. "Oh yes, I believe that what our girl Christine will require is the very heights of animal passion. She is a machine. Dull emotions she would ignore, but not intense, primal feelings. Our girl is bloodthirsty, oh yes she is."

Jerking out the needle, he gave me the vial, warm to the touch. More blood gushed across his skin.

"Your wound, Doctor," I said, having to swallow my gorge.

He ignored me. "Replace your blood with mine. Give her the same song to play."

I rewound the key, to make sure we had the same parameters for this next experiment, then replaced the vial with Davyss' blood. I fingered the lever down and fed the same music into Christine's cylinders.

The same cylinders processed the same perforations. Her mechanics interpreted the same notes. Yet what a joyous difference! How can a zero not be a zero? How can a one not be a one? And yet, she was interpreting the mathematics so very differently.

My mouth dropped open. Such passion, such desire, I felt tears sting my eyes. I shamefully squeezed them shut.

Davyss had no such sensitivities. Tears stained his face and chest as he stood nearly naked in my apartment. His left arm was gloved in blood. I saw his mouth moving.

The paper once again spun out of the cabinet player's back to float to the ground. That's when I heard his quotation.

> *"... I've read, that things inanimate have mov'd,*
> *And, as with living Souls, have been inform'd,*
> *By Magick Numbers and persuasive Sound ..."*

He caught me staring. "Do not those words capture the very essence of your creation? Next Friday evening, August 31st, you will bring Christine to my estate. She will play for all of my colleagues, the best ears in London. In the meantime, my man will bring you more blood, and I shall make arrangements on delivering Christine." He reached into the pocket of the coat he had draped on the chair and removed a stack of pound notes. I took them, noting the bloody fingerprints.

I levered off Christine's mechanism even as my head swam. First, I was stunned that the occult was real. How else could simple blood have such an effect on my automaton?

Next, my engineering mind filled my head with questions. Would the blood last through multiple windings? How many iterations? Most importantly, how did it all actually *work*, and could I find the answer to that question in the realm of science?

The amount of study I had to do was staggering, all in a week's time before Christine's first official performance. I had only inscribed a few lines of music. Now, I had to encode an entire piece onto a rolling scroll so Christine would not be limited to short passages. That in itself would take me most of the week. More sleepless nights lay ahead of me. This time, however, I would labor on a full belly.

"You will be a very rich man, Mr. Lewand." Davyss beamed, and then his eyes seemed to glaze as he whispered. "I have always known that the vapors in our bodies coalesce in our blood, and thus, a frightened man's blood would be very different from a kind man's, or a savage man's. So much has been proven tonight. So much more lies before us."

His eyes met mine, and he returned to a more serene state. "You and I have started a journey, my dear Mr. Lewand. Where will it end?"

"Hopefully at a dinner table in a finer room than this hovel, my good doctor." I smiled. For the first time, I had spoken my true mind.

"Oh, yes," he said. The gleam was back in his eye. "We shall all eat our fill."

Perhaps I would have found his words and demeanor unsettling, had I not been so preoccupied with more mundane appetites.

O   O   O

As promised, more blood appeared on my doorstep. Davyss sent his man, a whiskered, laconic brute armed with a walking stick, more cudgel than cane, which he used with abandon on street urchins and prostitutes. I watched him beat them for his own amusements as he left my door, walking through the wet streets like a rampaging mammoth.

Some vials were marked with my benefactor's initials, MMD. Others had different initials, patients from the hospital, I assumed. He had sent along an anti-coagulant that kept the blood from thickening, though the vials were cool to the touch.

Each vial affected Christine in a different away. Most simply had little effect, like my own. Davyss' blood, as always, made her passionate, full of bright expectation, while only one other vial, marked RDS, affected her. With the RDS, Christine's playing became melancholy. Such a radical difference it was, I immediately sent Davyss a letter with my findings.

He responded that he would ensure I had the proper blood for Christine's first performance.

In amazement, in victory, I spent long hours running tests. Christine's passion, fueled by Davyss' crimson ichor, would last approximately two hours, during which she would play with such joy that I could scarcely keep from dancing. Then slowly her musicianship would degrade until she was once more a machine, plinking through notes.

I did my work, stuffed with beef and bread. I drank tea without ceasing. What is an Englishman without tea? I daresay, an American, and I had lived as such for many months, every farthing going to the landlord and for parts. However, one positive aspect of being poor meant I could not afford gin, which was a blessing, for drink was a danger to me.

The week passed quickly. Thursday evening I worked to put the finishing touches on Christine, adjusting the joints on her three-toed foot attached to a single brass leg, hinged at the knee. When I finished, she articulated the pedals on the piano perfectly.

Davyss had arranged to move Christine to his manor for her evening performance. It was just past midnight on that Friday when I heard a knock on the door.

It could only be Davyss or his brute, for I had no other visitors, no other connections. To my surprise, it was the former. His face was streaked with sweat, his eyes wild to the whites. He pushed three vials of blood at me, all three marked with the number one. "I was in the neighborhood," he said, rushing his words, "and I wanted to stop by. More blood for our girl. Tomorrow, have her play using these vials. It will be a triumph!"

With that he was gone, as quickly as he had come. Strange, shocking.

Why would he be out delivering blood, and why mark it with numbers instead of initials? And I found it hard to believe he was in the neighborhood. One who lives on an estate in West London does not simply find himself in Whitechapel.

Oddest of all, why were the vials still warm?

O O O

In the music room of Davyss' manor, I felt out of place. No one knew who I was. Lords, ladies, the rich and powerful, all ignored my cheap dress and balding pate as I stood nervously holding a wine glass that seemed almost magical. Whenever I looked down, it was empty, though I could have sworn moments prior, it had been full. I was becoming intoxicated, and that would not do. Christine and I had our work. Draped in a sheet, she sat expectantly at Davyss' grand piano.

Standing next to my creation, I attempted to eavesdrop more and drink less. Two topics of conversation buzzed about the room. People spoke of the Aeolian Company and the advancements they had made in the self-playing piano. The general agreement was that such a device might be superfluous. Who could not play the piano? Why have an expensive machine for such a task?

The other piece of conversation was far more sinister. The body of a woman had been found in Whitechapel, horribly murdered.

I recalled Davyss' strange visit from the night before but quickly discounted my suspicions. Sad to say, the population of my East End slum was not blessed with longevity. Death was common. At times, even welcome.

Mrs. Edmund Reid spoke in whispers, for this incident seemed different. Her husband was the Detective Inspector working on the case. "Inspector Reid was very tremulous when he came home this afternoon, and that is why he could not attend this exhibition. The horrid, unimaginable details of the crime have shaken my husband to his foundations. Is Whitechapel filled only with the bestial and the wanton?"

No, Whitechapel is mostly filled with the hungry, I wanted to say, but I refrained. A huge grandfather clock chimed four, and it was time for Christine's performance.

Davyss stepped out. "My friends and colleagues, brothers and sisters of Phoebus Apollo, today you will see a dream fulfilled. My dream, and the dream of my associate, Mr. Percival Lewand. Countless hours has Mr. Lewand worked to bring us this modern miracle. Not just an automatic piano, but an automatic piano with the sensitivities to move us as no other musician could. I present to you, Mr. Lewand and his creation, Christine." With a flourish, he tugged the sheet off the automaton. A number one vial of blood was loaded. Her gears were set. All she needed was the music.

I moved forward, not having the courage nor sobriety to make a speech of my own. Every eye in the room fell on me. I wheeled over a tall stand with a hook holding a long continuous scroll of perforated music. I triggered Christine's lever, then fed the first part of the scroll into her cylinders. As she played, the paper would unwind giving her an uninterrupted stream of ones and zeroes.

The music I had chosen was from the incomparable Liszt, his *Piano Concerto No 1*.

Sweat pinched my eyes. I had tested the blood from the number one vials briefly, and yet what if this time it did not work? If she failed to perform, I would be a laughingstock.

But Christine played, and played beautifully. So sad, so very sad, that soon no one was unmoved. Even during the more jovial movements of the piece, she played them with such a fragility and melancholy that I found myself on the verge of tears.

Once she finished, everyone stood to applause. A standing ovation! We were a success! An unbridled success!

After many minutes of shaking hands and basking in praise, Davyss pulled me aside and whispered in my ear. "Next Saturday afternoon I have a friend who owns a theatre. He wants Christine to play as a prologue to a guest symphony. Already people are asking if they can purchase a Christine." From his pocket, he pulled out several inches of pound notes. "Mr. Lewand, this is only just the beginning."

Smiles filled me like sunshine. "Will we be playing the number one vial again?"

Davyss leered. "Oh, no. Fresh blood. I know what Christine likes. The fresher the better, full of passion, lust, and a raw longing for life."

O O O

I was free to continue my experiments with the number one blood. I found that every song emerged from Christine's fingers brimming with melancholy, no matter what modifications I made. I gave Christine Beethoven's *Ode to Joy*, and her playing was anything but joyful. Where had Davyss procured such blood? And why had the donor been so sad?

Long hours I spent testing and encoding new pieces for Christine to play. All the while eating beef and drinking tea. I could not discern how the blood worked, but work it certainly did. I rejoiced in what I had created and what my benefactor had improved upon. I felt like a blessed Pygmalion, or a more fortunate Daedalus, destined for a seat on Mount Olympus!

Once again, Davyss pounded at my door in the very earliest of the morning hours on the Saturday of our next performance, September 8th. I had to wrestle myself out of my blankets to let him in. He had three vials of blood, all marked number two. His manner was far more subdued, almost peaceful.

"The number two should prove to have some interesting results," he said. "Interesting indeed."

"Since we have three vials," I replied, "I will test them, and then find suitable music."

He smiled. "It does not matter what piece she plays, as long as she plays with blood full of raw passion." With that, he disappeared into the gloom. Dawn colored the horizon.

I got to work right away. The number two made Christine's music rage. Even mellow, melodic pieces came out jagged and hateful. I chose a piece for her to play to match the furor in the blood. Chopin's *Nocturne in C minor, Op 48, No 1.*

Our next performance drew an even greater audience. The theatre owner was ecstatic. After Christine's wrathful playing, I found myself in the foyer near Mrs. Reid. "They have found another body in Whitechapel, murdered in a similar fashion." The woman's face was positively colorless. "My poor husband cannot sleep. Truth be told, neither can I, with this murderous madman on the loose."

I glanced up to see Davyss listening intently, a little smile playing on his face.

I could not wrest my gaze from my benefactor's self-satisfied visage. Suddenly I had an explanation for his strange visitations and the warm vials. The blood, number one and number two, it had come from the women killed in Whitechapel. And Davyss had murdered them.

Cold horror drowned me until my heart froze solid in my chest.

"Is there a problem, Mr. Lewand?" Davyss asked.

I shook my head, glanced away. Futile were my attempts to swallow all of the shock and loathing I was feeling. I could scarcely breathe.

O O O

For the next few weeks, gin rode on my back like a devil with a switch. Every time I thought to call the police or contact Inspector Reid, the devil would strike me. No escape. I would drown with Davyss in a swamp of blood. And still, whenever my Christine would play, I found myself moved because we had captured the lightning and sorrow and emotion of life. To experience such passion was only the turn of a key away.

Rarely sober, my mind began to play tricks on me. I would awake to hear Christine playing a piece, but no, that was impossible. She sat empty of music, no ones or zeroes for her cylinders to interpret, bathed in the blood of Whitechapel women.

One night I woke in the pitch black of my basement, a horrible notion filling me that something was very amiss. I lit a candle only to find the space in front of my piano empty. My first thought made me utter a syllable of despair. Someone had crept in and stolen Christine.

No. I found her in the corner, her three-toed foot soaking in the perpetual puddle that covered that side of my room. I wheeled her back to the piano, wondering why in my drunken stupor I had moved her. I dried her foot carefully.

Another night, I woke to the sound of her gears moving. This time, she was in front of the door, fingers reaching, toes pressing, playing at a piano that wasn't there until her gearing unwound completely. The music in her back was Chopin's *Funeral March*. I tightened the lever at her neck and adjusted her leg again. A malfunction in the knee hinge must have inadvertently pushed her to the door.

Our next performance was on Sunday, September 30th, and again, in a far larger venue.

I looked in the newspapers for another murder, but none came. I knew the reason. Davyss would wait until the evening before our concert to give Christine fresh blood. With my silence, I may as well have been murdering the women myself.

I still had some of the sad blood, filled with death's lamentation. Listening to Christine playing the number one, it was as if I were dying. Gin took care of that. Days of inebriation, two week' worth, and on September 29, I paced through my basement apartment, splashing through the rainwater there, beating dilapidated pianos with the leg of a bench, furious over my own avarice and cowardice. And still the gin beat me into submission with a switch of fire.

I waited for Davyss to come. I did not have long to wait. At midnight, the knock came on my door.

I flung it open, revealing the villain in his coat. This time, he had a small case filled with six vials, three marked as number three, three as number four. Two women had been butchered, all because I wanted to eat. Because I had vainglorious dreams of wealth and fame.

Our eyes locked.

Like the last time, he was mellow, his whole manner one of passive relaxation.

"May I come in?" he asked.

Wordless, I acquiesced.

Once inside, Davyss' voice came out even. "Mr. Lewand, you think that I am murdering women in Whitechapel so that Christine's playing will move the hearts of her listeners. Is that correct?"

I nodded, stifled a belch, though I knew he could ascertain my level of intoxication by smell alone.

Davyss smiled. "Oh, Mr. Lewand, that is not the case, I can assure you. At the hospital I have access to all types of blood. Do not let your imagination get the better of you." He paused. "And do not let alcohol become your master. You have worked too hard and too long to be locked up as mentally incompetent due to excessive intemperance."

"Is that a threat?" I asked, hardly breathing.

"Oh, no," he said, still grinning. "I would be doing it for your own good. As I have done for others who so desperately needed help with their drinking. Do you understand my meaning, sir?"

"I understand," I whispered. His lies did not fool me. The truth of his crimes whispered to me through the tormented notes Christine played.

He left me with the blood of the two Whitechapel women. I read about them in the newspaper later that day. They were killed just down the street from my basement apartment. The newspaper had a name for the murderer, a horrible name, part fairly-tale everyman, and part description of how he killed the women. He ripped them open. He was a ripper. A monster. And I knew his identity.

Yet, because of the qualities in the blood Davyss brought me, our Sunday concert went perfectly, absolutely perfectly. In an effort to keep our Christine novel, Davyss declared we would not have another performance until November. Let six weeks pass so that word of mouth could make Christine's next appearance the biggest, the best, and the most profitable.

Already, other pioneers of the self-playing piano, men such as Misters Wilcox and White, were asking Davyss to see Christine, but of course he refused them. As he also refused the Aeolian Company despite their offer of lucre. Christine was ours, his and mine, along with his deranged secret, which I could not tell a soul on penalty of incarceration in the London Hospital's insane asylum.

Six weeks until another murder. Six weeks until our next performance, on Friday, November 9th.

What could I do? Nothing. I drank gin. I listened to Christine play, not remembering what pieces I had given her. Impossible, that she could play without the perforated music, and yet, it seemed I would find scrolls of music in piles on the floor and her fingers still moved over the keys—her face only a porcelain mask, unmoving, unmoved, with the same blank expression I had painted on it.

I moved my cabinet player about nonsensically in my inebriation. How else could she travel to the door, to the wall, to the corner? One morning I woke with a start to find her looming over me, hands hooked into claws. I admonished myself as I moved her back to her place in front of the piano, thumbs above middle C.

Randomly, Davyss would come to listen to Christine play from the numbered vials. He would sit on a cast-off bench, eyes closed, and sometimes he would murmur from that poem, strange lines:

"What then am I? Am I more senseless grown

Than Trees, or Flint? O force of constant Woe!

'Tis not in Harmony to calm my Griefs."

Christine would begin a new piece, and he would pace, then stop, as if remembering some fine evening of love, then he would cry such anguished tears, then laugh. In my gin-soaked fog, I would watch him in loathing, wishing him out of my sight. Even so, he would bring me bundles of money, which I stuffed into a suitcase next to my bed.

Blood money. In every sense of the word.

O O O

Thursday, November 8th, the day before the performance, I was determined to stop him. I had kept myself away from gin in the morning so that I might be sober, so that I might go to the police and tell them the Ripper would strike again, that Dr. Martin Marquavious Davyss would strike again.

Every time I went to the door, I would turn back. I was shaking, delirium tremens a storm in my body. Would the police listen to me? Or would they have me sent to the insane asylum?

All day long, all night long, I suffered in my paroxysm. Christine would play, her fingers striking keys in a fury, but it was not music, it was madness. I would go to the door, she would stop. I would open the door, close it, and go back to pacing. And her playing would continue. Had I wound her gears? I must have. Did she have music to play? Of course.

One of Davyss' acquaintances had given me an unpublished piece of music by Camille Saint-Saëns, *Le Carnaval des Animaux*, or, *The Carnival of the Animals*. I had encoded it for Christine, and she would play it, ferociously, filled with the blood of the innocent slain.

Thursday night passed into Friday morning. I clung to sobriety, thinking maybe Davyss had lost his desire for blood and murder. No knock had come on my door. Had he given up his wicked ways?

At noon on that Friday, scarcely an hour before Christine was due to be brought to her evening performance, a knock sounded on my door.

Davyss. Carrying a satchel. He shouldered off his overcoat to reveal hands half-washed, still stained a pinkish hue. Dried blood flecked his entire suit of dress. Words gushed out of his mouth in a torrent. "Lewand, oh, Lewand, I cannot wait to see how Christine interprets number five, for she was, well, I had time. I could take all the time I wanted with number five."

He saw the ill abhorrence on my face.

"Oh, you had six weeks to come to peace with our arrangement. In that time, you never went to the police, so I think you can live with what I do for us. I am sure the gin helps. Do you want to hear the number five? Do you want to know what agony sounds like? What the desire to live sounds like? For I have it in these vials. That and the innards. Perhaps if we gave Christine this heart, oh, I know, nonsense, but the blood worked, and if the blood worked, so could the heart, could it not, Lewand?" He laughed, loudly, not waiting for my reply. "And that Robert Stephenson, that buffoon from the hospital, he is suspicious of me, but he is so addled, he has mistaken my name. He thinks Morgan Davies is the Ripper, not Martin Davyss. Ha, the fools, all scurrying around at my feet. I could go on with this project for years, Lewand, for years, free to delve like an explorer into the darkest regions of my own psyche."

He handed me the satchel, leather stained, seams dripping. Inside, lay the heart and entrails of a woman. And five vials of blood.

I went to my knees, sickened. I vomited onto my floor. Christine's thumb fell on middle C. A simple sound.

"What was that?" Davyss asked suddenly. "She has no sheet music to play."

He went over to her and touched Christine's porcelain mask. "What have I made you into, my dear? For now, truly, you are more than your gears. Do you have my same tastes? My same passions? What are you now?"

The automaton made no reply of course. She lifted her hands and returned, motionless, to her resting position.

"Lewand, the number five. I want to hear it."

"No." Trembling, on my knees, I finally rebelled.

He walked over to me, knelt, and from his nightmare satchel, withdrew a vial of blood. "Lewand, your squeamishness is unmanly. You and I are gods. And what of the harlots I kill? Hardly human, they are mere chattel for greater minds to use as we please."

Back at Christine, he inserted the vial. The roller stand stood behind her, loaded with *The Carnival of the Animals*, apt for what we were doing. Yet we were worse than animals—far from gods.

He touched the lever and my Christine came alive.

Impossible, impossible—

She whirled herself about, the wheels on her cart squeaking, and she latched onto Davyss with her left arm and pulled him off his feet and onto the piano's keyboard.

Her right hand rose and came down on Davyss' middle, ripping through his clothes, his skin, into his stomach. Blood geysered out of the man as he howled like swine in the slaughterhouse. His flailing arm knocked Christine's wig off her head; a punch struck her mask askew. With her right hand pinning him to the piano by his stomach, she lifted her left hand and ripped down through his shoulder, popping out the white ball from the joint. Her right hand moved further and fell between his legs. Her fingers clutched to rip his genitals from his body before falling again to transfix him to the piano while the left hand rose. Davyss gibbered nonsensically, squealing in a high-pitched whine until Christine clawed through his voice box.

Strangely, my horrified mind remembered the poem he had been quoting, the first line and the last.

"Musick has Charms to sooth a savage Breast ...

... *Why am I not at Peace?*"

I had to close my eyes. Still I would never forget the sight of Christine's hooked brass hands, trailing strings of bowel, her gloves torn to shreds, rising and falling in showers of offal and gore.

Then, music. She had chopped through Davyss' flesh until her fingers struck the keys, and I heard her play *The Carnival of the Animals*, muted by the blood, flesh and sinew. It was joyful. It was terrible. It was a song of vengeance now, and I dry heaved until she finished playing the final note.

I heard the wheels on her cart squeak. She turned on me with unseeing eyes, and yet I knew she saw me.

With a great sweep of arms, she rolled herself away from the blood-splashed piano, the three-toed foot clicking on the floor, pushing herself toward me. Her brass claws reached out, her mask, her gown, everything drenched in crimson.

I ran and reached the door ahead of her—slammed it shut in her face.

Still, the whisper of her hands, scratching at the door. Right on the other side. Brass fingers caressing wood. When had I last wound her gears? I could not recall. But she was beyond that now. Davyss had been right. She was now far more than her brass gears and clockwork mind.

All of my money, stuffed into the suitcase, lay on the other side of the door. I had to go back in. But I could not. The bloody number five had awakened an angel of vengeance inside Christine, something not of this earth.

Suddenly, such a clarity of mind struck me that I felt more lucid than I had for weeks and weeks. I had a plan. If I were quick, I could avoid Davyss' fate. If Christine had a distraction, I could dart in, grab the suitcase stuffed with money, and escape her punishment, one I deserved, and yet might avoid. With my fortune secured, I could change my name, maybe to Theodore Brown, a nice, common name. I could begin my work on the automatic piano anew, without the aid of the occult and the blood of Whitechapel women.

I waited. It began to rain. When Davyss' brute came to collect the automaton for that evening's performance, I forced a smile onto my face and gestured to the door.

"Inside, Christine is waiting for you. She is more than ready for her next performance."

THE TUNNEL RAT'S JOURNEY

J. M. Franklin

My name is Emily, although no one calls me that. Most often I'm referred to as "Tunnel Rat," and I don't know my last name, so don't ask. I was orphaned at four years old, and as a ward of the state I was trained to repair the steam tunnels that run under the city, heating it like a giant radiator. Occasionally one of the pipes will spring a leak, so I go in and seal it up. Sometimes they burst, and I can't fix that without getting burned, so I keep a close eye on my section of pipe, keeping it in good repair. The pipes are getting old though, nearly a hundred and fifty years old. It's hard to believe that humans took refuge from the ice above in this underground city only a hundred and fifty years ago. It seems as though we have been here forever.

There are murals throughout the city depicting landscapes of things I have never seen—things like the sky and mountains. The only wind I have ever felt on my face is the hot vapor of the steam. In these murals are large beasts that I have never seen and have no names for. The only animals I ever see are the rats that run the tunnels with me. Even three kilometers underground humans can't get rid of the rats. I know that somewhere in the city there is a rabbit farm, but I have never seen one. Small, quick to multiply and easy to care for, they are raised to feed the rich, so I have never tasted one.

Large solar panels mounted on telescoping towers are raised every day into the frozen atmosphere above. Flexible tubes carry hot water through the towers to prevent them from freezing. The solar panels collect the sun's energy and relay it to a machine in the gardens, which converts it back into sunlight to raise crops for the city. It has been said that this machine alone will ensure the survival of the human race through the ice age.

And that is what we humans are doing: surviving. I don't know what life on the surface was like, but I find it hard to believe that it was worse than this. I work ten hours every day to earn enough credits so I can keep my bed in the dorm and feed myself, and once a year I buy a new set of clothes. I have two sets, one to wash and one to wear.

Maybe things are different for those who have more money. The people with more—more food, more clothes, a real home—don't really seem to be all that happier than those without; they just seem to hide it better.

"Emily!"

The shout breaks me out of my thoughts. I look down at my tablet to stare into my boss's fat, angry face on the screen. "Yes boss! What'cha need?"

"Are you deaf? I've been talking to you for the last five minutes!" His red face grows redder. "There is a low pressure reading coming from a tunnel point six kilometers ahead of you and to your right. Go check it out!"

I double-check the seal on the pipe I have just finished before gathering my tools and rushing off to the next pipe in need. It looks like my day is going to get a little longer. I have already been down here for over nine hours, not that I have anything else to do.

By the time I finish my work and find my way back up to the city streets, I have put in nearly a twelve-hour day. I'm exhausted and hungry. I've traveled close to ten kilometers in the tunnel today, and now that I have emerged back onto the street, I check the map on my tablet to figure out where I am. I look up at the tall buildings surrounding me, their dark facades rising up to disappear into the ceiling high above. The ceiling of the enormous cave the city was built in is always kept in darkness, as if to imitate the night sky instead of reminding people they are three kilometers under what used to be called the Swiss Alps. My map says there is a steam train tunnel a block over.

I find a route map just next to the stairs that tells me I only need to take one train back to base. *Sweet!* I think happily. I go from one tunnel to another. Running down the stairs, I feel the ground vibrate from the approaching train. I make it without a moment to spare, stepping onto the car just as the engine releases a puff of steam and begins to move.

The car jerks and, thrown off balance, I bump into a man standing in the isle.

"Pardon," I say as inoffensively as I can.

Without a word he grabs my arm roughly, shoving me towards the back of the car. "Disgusting Tunnel Rat!" he spits after me. I don't have to look to know that he wiped his hand on his pants.

Now, I know that after a hard day of work in the steam tunnels I look like hell, and I smell no better. But for the life of me, I don't know why steam pipe workers are regarded so poorly. I mean, really, without us there wouldn't be any heat. Scientists long ago predicted the onset of the current ice age, and thankfully, technology had advanced far enough for them to do something about it. They drilled down to the earth's molten core, tapping the last heat source on the planet. Using that heat and the only other resources they had in abundance—ice and water—they built a huge system of pipes. Now the only power we have is steam and solar, and I am responsible for maintaining that power. So how is it that I'm treated like last week's garbage?

I manage the rest of the train ride without further incident and arrive back at base within a half hour. Unfortunately, my boss is waiting for me.

"Girl, in my office now!"

My boss' name is Karl, but I never call him that, just Boss. "I already sent you my reports, Boss. You should have them on your computer already."

"I have your reports. Sit your ass down!" Karl closes the door behind him. He sits down on his desk and shakes his head at me. "Where were you today?"

I'm confused. Karl can keep track of all of us tunnel workers via the tablets we all carry. He knows where I am every second of every day. "What do you mean? I was where you told me to be."

"I mean your head. How many times have I caught you daydreaming instead of doing your job? I'm beginning to lose count!" Karl crosses his meaty arms over his gold shirt covered in coffee stains, the buttons of his shirt straining to retain the paunch beneath it.

"I ... I ..." I sputter. I don't know what to say.

"Well, for wasting my time, I'm docking you three credits."

"What!?!" I cry. Three whole credits! I only make twenty credits a day!

"Now that I've gotten your attention, maybe you will keep your head out of the clouds." He reaches out and snatches my hard hat off my head. My long blond curls, released from their bonds, cascade around my shoulders. Karl leans over and taps his pudgy finger twice on my forehead. "Keep your head on your work!"

"I'm sorry boss!" I can't lose three credits! "It won't ever happen again, I promise. But three credits? Come on."

With a glimmer in his eyes, he says, "If there is some way you want to make up your time, I'm open to suggestions." He raises his dark eyebrows suggestively at me.

I pause, not wanting to answer or meet his gaze. Defeated, I say, "No, there is nothing I can think of."

He actually laughs at me. "Then three credits it is." His full laughter follows me as I quickly flee from the office.

I stop at the time clock and insert my account card. When the machine spits it back out there are only seventeen credits added to my account. I need ten to pay for my bed in the dorm tonight and four credits for my meals. I will either have to scrimp on dinner tonight or on breakfast tomorrow. It will have to be dinner. It is easier to sleep on an empty stomach than to work on one.

Leaving the building, I reflect on my conversation with Karl. I guess I shouldn't have been surprised that he finally noticed I grew up. At fifteen I have thankfully small breasts and narrow hips. I always wear baggy, gray trousers and a loose button-down shirt with a tweed jacket over it, and I always hide my hair, either under a hard hat at work or under a cap otherwise. When I was younger, I easily passed for a boy, but now, not so much.

Back at the dorm I stop by the office and pay for my bed for the night. I have been doing this every day since they brought me here so many years ago. I don't even know who "they" were. All I remember was someone in uniform telling me that my parents were dead and that from then on I had to earn my keep. That's when I was sent to Karl to learn my trade.

Getting in the elevator, I pull the gate closed and grab the wheel on the side of the door. The elevator works on a pulley and crank system, and I turn the wheel to raise the car up to the third floor. Home sweet home. There are forty beds on this floor, a row on each wall and a double-row running down the middle of the room. At the head of each bed is a locker. I pull out my key and grab my other set of clothes before heading to the washroom. Water is one of the few things that are free in the city; there are tons of it above us on the planet's surface. It's in the form of ice, but it really takes very little steam to melt it and send it running down into the city. In fact, a river runs the length of the entire city, ending in a huge reservoir. So, at least I get to bathe daily, and every day I wash out my dirty clothes and put on clean ones.

Once clean and dressed, I head across the street to the small diner, Millie's. Millie is a grouchy old woman who is never nice to anyone, but four credits gets you a bowl of soup or stew (whatever she has that day), a crust of bread and a potato. Unfortunately, I only have three. So, the stew it is.

"Here you go." Millie places the largest bowl of stew I have ever seen in front of me. I didn't know that she had bowls that big. When I look at her questioningly she snaps, "What? I ran out of normal sized bowls!" Like I said, she is never nice, but she never lets anyone go away hungry.

Davie, my only friend in the world, sits down next to me. A couple years younger than me, he is scrawny for a ten year old, but he swears he is at least twelve. He has big brown eyes and buck teeth that I keep hoping he will grow into. "What, no potato?"

"Karl docked me three credits for daydreaming." Davie is a steam tunnel worker too, so he is just as familiar with Karl as I am.

"No way!"

"Yes, way!" I answer back. "He told me to get my head out of the clouds. As if I've ever seen a cloud. As if he has either. I don't know why he thinks I'm daydreaming; it's not like I have anything to dream about."

Looking desperate to change the subject, Davie notices the giant bowl of stew. "That thing is huge! You know, we could share that."

Just then Millie appears and looks expectantly at Davie. He looks back at me before ordering two potatoes and another spoon. "I guess my day was rather uneventful compared to yours."

"I haven't even told you the worst of it." I get a wiggly feeling in the pit of my stomach. Maybe I shouldn't tell Davie about Karl hitting on me. He sometimes gets strangely protective, as if he could actually protect me from anything. But I tell him anyway.

"I'll kill him!" he yells at me, slamming his water cup down on the metal countertop. The entire diner stops to look at him.

I grab him by the shoulders hard. "Shhh! That's all you need is for someone to hear you threatening Karl. What would happen if you lost your job? What else could you do? He will fire you if he ever thought you could threaten him."

"Oh, whatever, Emily! As if I could really do anything to Karl. He outweighs me by at least a zillion pounds!" He shakes off my hands and slumps down on his stool.

Now I'm angry. "Don't you *whatever* me! You may be too much of a runt to do anything to him now, but Karl knows that runts grow up. And who's to say that you will always be a runt? You think Karl will keep you around knowing that you have a grudge against him? I can handle Karl; don't worry about me."

O O O

The next day Karl sends me to the furthest reaches of the tunnels. It's his way of payback for *"daydreaming"* yesterday. Not much of a payback. I focus my thoughts to the pipe at hand. It won't do for Karl to find me daydreaming again. I put my thermal goggles on and look at the pipe. It appears that the new gasket is holding just fine. It will take another day for the compound to cure completely, but as long as the pressure in the pipe doesn't spike, the seal will hold.

"Emily!" Karl barks from my tablet.

"Yes, boss?" I reply right away.

"There is a huge pressure drop in the pipe two tunnels over to your left and just point-two kilometers ahead. The pipe must have burst. I already have Davie in that area, but I think he may need some help. Get there quick."

Whatever personal faults Karl has, and they are many, the last thing he ever wants is someone hurt on his watch. Gathering my things, I switch to the map on my tablet. Each of us rats wears a locator beacon, and our positions are displayed on our maps.

Just as I stand up to go I feel a vibration in the earth under me. It is subtle, like the feel of a steam train going through the tunnels, but there aren't any steam trains in this area. "What the…?" I say out loud. It is over in a second, and though it disturbs me, I walk on to find Davie. I don't get far, only a few meters before it strikes again. This time the entire earth shakes, knocking me off my feet. I feel the earth beneath me shudder before I hear the hiss of the gasket I had just replaced rupture.

As suddenly as it started it stops. "Damn!" I swear as I pull myself to my feet. Reaching in my bag, I pull out a rubber clamp. I don't have any more gaskets. This will only be a temporary fix, but it is all I have. Pulling on my thick leather gloves to protect my hands from the hot vapor leaking from the pipe, I manage to get the clamp in place without getting burned.

"Emily!"

I hear my name being called from the tablet, but this time it isn't Karl's voice. It's Davie's, and I can tell that something is wrong. I run to where I left the tablet on the ground where I fell. The screen is dark, but I can hear breathing. "Davie?" I call tentatively.

"Emily," comes Davie's weak reply. His voice is shaky, and his breathing is heavy. "Emily, I'm hurt. My headlamp went out. I can't see." Hurt and in total darkness, Davie has to be terrified.

"I'm coming Davie! Hold on!" I command. I bring the map screen back up on the tablet and find Davie's location before racing off. *"Please"* I cry silently, knowing not who I'm crying to. *"Please let him be okay."* He is my only friend.

I reach him within minutes, but when I find him I'm repulsed by what I see. The left side of his face and chest look badly burned. Steam escapes from the pipe next to him. The pipe must have burst right under him. The burn on his face is red and ugly, and his arm and shoulder are already starting to blister. I pull my coat from my bag and wrap Davie in it. He screams when the fabric touches his burns, and, thankfully, he passes out. I've got to get him out of here. He doesn't weigh much, and I easily pick him up and throw him over my shoulder.

I pass an access tunnel on my way here, but there is no telling where in the city it would let me out. Once again, I pray silently to no one.

Emerging into the city, we are somewhere I don't recognize. The buildings here are placed further apart than I have ever seen, and each building is only three stories high and fifty feet wide at least. I have never seen such small buildings, and I can't imagine what they are used for. Each one has steps leading up to it and a railing enclosing an open area in the front, which contains several chairs and a low table.

As strange as things are, I don't have time to wonder. The map on my tablet doesn't show first aid stations, and Davie needs help fast. I take the stairs in one leap, even with Davie on my back, and try the door. It's locked. Desperate, I pound on the door and keep pounding until I hear movement within.

"Alright already! I'm coming!" A male voice says from within. I hear the sound of knobs turning and levers moving, and then the door swings open, revealing the oddest man I've ever seen. The first thing I notice is the strange hat on his head. It looks to be made of copper and has a magnifying glass attached to it hanging in front of the old man's eye. Also, there is some sort of tube wrapped around it, which appears to be attached to nothing. Spiky white hair sticks out from under the hat to frame a long and weathered face.

"Please, sir," I say in a rush. "Could you tell me where I am and where the nearest first aid station is? My friend is hurt."

"What is all this now?" he asks, stepping out the door and taking a good look at Davie on my shoulder. "Hmm, perhaps you should come in."

"Begging your pardon sir, but he needs help. If you could just point me in the direction ..." I try to protest.

"He does need help," the old man interrupts. "Now get your tail inside so I can give it to him!" The look on the old man's face is firm but not unkind, and for some reason I don't think I could have disobeyed him if I wanted to. I nod and follow him into the strange building.

"Here, put him on the sofa," he commands. I put Davie where he pointed. When I turn around the old man is gone, but I hear rustling from the other room. "Rose!" I hear him call. "Rose, get down here. We have company."

Company? Is that what he is calling us? Still, it is the nicest thing we have been called in a long time. A tiny, slim woman comes down the stairs at the far end of the room. She wears a long gray skirt and a white blouse with a high neck trimmed in lace. She has a round face with cheeks that seem to glow a rosy color.

Looking at Davie, she says, "Oh my, what have we here?"

"This boy," the old man says, coming back into the room, carrying a toolbox and without the strange hat, "is a most dreadful shade of red. I do believe, my dear, that he is also in a great deal of pain. Here, I've fetched your things for you."

"Good man," she says as she takes the toolbox from him and places it on another low table. It is filled with gauzes, bandages, needles, and vials of who knows what. She pulls out a needle and fills it from a vial.

"What are you doing?" I cry. "What are you giving him?"

"Please," the old man puts a gentle hand on my shoulder and guides me to a cushioned chair at the far end of the room. "Rose was a doctor before she retired. She knows what she is doing." The woman sticks Davie with the needle, and I immediately see him relax. She then pulls out some type of ointment and begins rubbing it all over his burns before bandaging his wounds. He doesn't stir once during the entire procedure. How does he not feel it? The pain must be excruciating.

The woman looks at me and smiles. She holds up a bottle and says, "Morphine," as if that explains everything. When my confusion doesn't end she adds, "Pain killers." My confusion only lessens a little bit. I know there are such things, but only the rich have access to them. Why would anyone give them to Davie? I also wonder what they are going to charge us for them.

"Well then, now that your friend seems to be resting comfortably, why don't you tell us what happened?"

The woman *tsk*s at him before I can say anything. "Where are your manners, Harold? At least bring the girl a cup of tea and maybe a sandwich. She looks hungry." Harold looks ashamed and hurries off to comply with the old woman. "My husband," she says to me, "he is a wonderful man, but sometimes he forgets his manners."

Manners? I think. I just burst in here, tossing an unconscious kid on her sofa, *and* I think she just saved Davie's life, and she is worried about her husband's manners. What kind of people are these?

Just then Harold comes back in the room carrying a tray of steaming cups and some small sandwiches. He places the tray on the table and gestures for me to help myself, but I hesitate. "How much?" I ask.

The two look at each other questioningly. "How much?" I ask again. "For the food," I add when they still don't seem to understand.

"We don't want your credits," Harold says. "Just eat. In this house, no one goes hungry."

So this is a house. I didn't really believe that they existed in this city. I knew that people who were better off had their own apartments for their own families, but I never heard of people having an entire building for themselves. "You live here? All by yourselves?" I ask in wonder.

"Yes," Rose answers. "Now, a few sandwiches and some tea won't hurt you any, so eat up." As if to prove to me that they are safe, she picks one up and daintily takes a bite. That was all the encouragement I needed. I grab one and gobble it down ... and then another. I am half way through my third before I notice they are both staring at me.

"Sorry," I mutter through a mouth full of bread and cucumbers.

"No need, dear," Rose assures me. "You just go ahead and finish. We'll wait."

Swallowing, I take a sip of tea before saying, "I'm finished."

Harold looks me over with a keen eye before he says, "You're a steam pipe engineer, aren't you?"

Engineer? That was a new one for me, but I feel myself nodding in response.

"You were in the tunnels when the earthquake hit?" Once again I nod. "That was how this young man came to be hurt?"

"Davie," I say. "His name is Davie."

"I am Dr. Rose Higgs, and this is my husband, Professor Harold Higgs. And your name?" Rose asks.

"Emily. My name is Emily. How long do you think Davie will be out of it? We really need to get back to base."

"Oh, you aren't going anywhere any time soon, my dear. The earthquake knocked out all the steam trains. Plus, the young man needs to rest. I would think the earliest anything will be up and running will be tomorrow."

"I have to get back. I can walk; it's not that far."

"It's at least twelve kilometers. It will take you hours to get back."

"But there will be damage to the steam pipes. There will be work to do, and I'll be docked if I'm not there to work. I can't afford not to work. They will throw my things in the street if I don't pay my rent at the dorm. I can't stay here!" I'm starting to get hysterical. What little of a life I have is about to be over.

"Come with me, Emily," Professor Higgs commands. Heading up the stairs, I follow him to the third floor and through a door into a giant laboratory. There are workbenches covered in glass beakers and copper pipes. Wrenches and saws are hung on one wall, and an acetylene torch sits in the corner. It is impossible to discern what the Professor is working on as half-finished inventions lay discarded all over the worktables. On the far wall hangs a giant information panel. All the panels I've ever used were touch screens, but this one has a strange keypad that the Professor begins punching with his fingers. A map of the city appears on the screen.

"Which dormitory are you living in?"

"It's on the corner of Dyott and Bainbridge, the Museum Dorm."

"I know that area. It used to be a great neighborhood back when the museum was still up and running." The Professor continues to press keys on the keypad as he speaks.

"The museum?" I'm not familiar with any museum in the area.

"The Museum of Human History was located only a few blocks from where you now reside. It housed many of our treasures from the days above. People could go there and learn about what it was like when we lived on the earth instead of under it." He looks up at the screen as a picture of the Museum Dormitory building pops up. "Here we go. Now we just need to transfer the credits for your bed."

"You don't understand; until I go back to base and collect my day's pay, I don't have the credits to pay for my bed." I don't know why I feel embarrassed; everyone I know is just as poor as me, everyone but Professor Higgs.

Professor Higgs doesn't hesitate; he just presses more buttons and says, "There you go. It's all taken care of. You are paid through the end of the week."

The end of the week! That was five days away! "I don't need your charity."

"Then call it a gift. Or if you would like, pay me back, but I can tell you that we really won't miss the money. Come. Let's get you settled in for the night."

"I still need to contact my boss. I need my job."

"Very well." He punches more keys. A photograph on the wall catches my attention. It looks like the city, only somehow different. The area above the city is blue, like the old murals in the steam train tunnels, and the blue seems to go on forever. "London," the Professor says over my shoulder. "This city is based on it."

"This was above ground?" I say in wonder. He nods. There were many landmarks in the picture that I recognized.

"What is the Judicial Center of our city was called Westminster Abby above ground. The Clock Tower was called Big Ben, and this here," he points to the largest bridge in the city, "was the London Bridge."

"How do you know all this?"

"My great-great-great-grandparents helped build our city. My grandfather was an engineer responsible for building the drill that was used to reach the Earth's core. My grandmother was an environmental scientist; she helped develop the machine that turns solar power back into sunlight, allowing us to grow food, even underground. I still have the original blueprints for the city."

Wow, no wonder he is so rich. His family helped ensure the survival of the human race.

"Professor Higgs?"

I turn to see a well-known face on the information panel. "Is that the mayor?" I ask incredulous.

"Yes," the Professor replies, nonchalantly. "Mayor Campwell," he addresses the screen. "What can I do for you?"

"I'm sure you know that we have indeed just experienced an earthquake of a magnitude that this city has never seen before, and while the tremor dampeners that our forefathers installed did indeed suppress the vibrations to the city, there has still been immense damage. Worst of all, the steam pipes in the solar towers have burst. Without heat the towers will freeze, and we will be unable to retract them, leaving the solar panels exposed to the elements. With the severity of the storms on the surface, it is only a matter of time before the panels are destroyed."

"Your Honor," Professor Higgs replies, rubbing his temples between his thumb and index finger, "my invention is only a prototype and has yet to be tested. There is no telling if it will actually work."

"I'm afraid, professor, that you will have a trial by fire. I'm trying to locate a steam pipe worker who isn't already working deep in the tunnels. Many of the pipes have burst, and already the temperature in the city is beginning to fall."

"One moment please, Your Honor." Professor Higgs turns to me after muting the screen. "Are you very good at your job?"

Uncertain as to what this is about, but very certain as to my abilities with a wrench and a steam pipe, I nod. "I'm the best!" I'm not boasting either; there isn't a pipe I can't fix.

"This could be dangerous."

I still have no idea what he is talking about, but I face danger every day. There are a million ways to get hurt down in the tunnels. I straighten my back, plant my feet and ball my fists as if to say, "Bring it on."

"Good." The Professor turns off the mute on the screen and says to the Mayor, "I seem to have found my own technician, Bill. I will see to preparing the ship and contact you when we are ready."

"Once again, Professor, this city's hope resides with a Higgs. We are counting on you."

With a sigh the Professor turns back to me. "Have you ever wanted to see the surface?"

"What!?!" I nearly feint right there. "Are you kidding me? Nothing can survive on the surface."

"That is what we are going to find out." He motions for me to follow him back down the stairs and out a back door. There, behind the house, stands an enormous warehouse with sliding doors that stand two stories tall. Professor Higgs seems giddy as he hops from foot to foot. "I have never shown this to anyone besides the Mayor and Rose. I hope you'll like it." With that he leads me through a much smaller door on the side of the building.

It's dark, and I can hear the professor fumbling for a light switch. "Ta Da!" he announces. The lights come on abruptly, the glare momentarily blinding me. I put my hand up to my eyes, waiting for them to adjust to the light. When they do I can't believe what I'm seeing. The thing is huge and gold and massive and … and … and I just don't have the words to describe it. "Here, come. Look at this." The professor leads me over to a workbench where he shows me yet another picture. This time though, I have no idea what I'm looking at. "They called it a tank back in the days above. It was a weapon of war. I have based my designs on it, but she isn't a weapon. See, while my machine has tracks like these, the gun barrel is missing from mine. And this machine ran on oil while mine is steam-powered. And my machine is much, much bigger!" His excitement obviously difficult to contain, he runs like a school kid over to the machine. He raps his knuckles on the hull. "Three-inch thick steel and copper-plated. Isn't she a beauty? I call her *Pandora*, because I know that I can get into a whole lot of trouble just by opening her hatch."

"And this machine can travel to the surface?" I ask.

"It's never been tested, but I have designed it to withstand the elements and insulated it against the temperature. I don't think she could stay on the surface indefinitely, but a day … yes … maybe even a week … long enough to repair the steam pipes in the tower."

"Yeah, but I can't repair the pipes from inside that … that … thing! And I will freeze to death the instant I step out of it!"

"No you won't. I have a suit for you. I'll show you." Turning a wheel on the outside of the ship, a hatch opens, and the Professor disappears inside.

I'm uncertain that this contraption can go to the surface, but that isn't going to stop me from checking it out. It's too cool! I find the Professor pulling pieces of a strange, bulky suit out of a trunk. It's so thick I don't think I will be able to move once I have it on, and it would be impossible to do precise work with the thick gloves. He pulls out a giant, bowl-looking thing that I guess would go over the head. It looks ridiculous to me.

"Once, man not only traveled the surface he flew through the sky. He even went beyond that, travelling out of our atmosphere. He used a suit like this one to protect himself from the vacuum of space. I believe that it will protect you as well."

"But I can't work in that thing. I won't have any range of motion or the ability to do precise work."

"If we can get to the towers before too much heat is dissipated, then it should be warm enough for you to remove the suit once you are inside the tower. We just need to get you in there."

As we spend the rest of the afternoon going over blueprints of the towers and studying maps of the terrain, the Professor's strange hat reappears from someplace. The tube, it turns out, is a straw, and he sips tea through it non-stop. The Professor tells me about an access tunnel that actually leads to the surface but had long ago frozen over. Thus he designed the gun turret on *Pandora* with a super-sized drill.

Just as Rose declares that food is ready, Davie wakes up, which makes perfect sense if you know Davie. His burns aren't as bad as we initially feared, and the burn cream worked wonders. He hardly has any pain. When we tell him all that has happened, he insists on being part of the expedition. "It won't hurt to have an extra hand," he argues, and he's right. Luckily, the Professor has another suit.

O   O   O

Less than twenty-four hours after the earthquake hit, Davie and I find ourselves sitting in the cockpit of Professor Higgs' contraption as he "*fires her up.*" The cockpit is a conglomeration of dials, buttons, and levers, and I'm not certain that the Professor knows what they all do.

"She runs mostly on steam power," the Professor announces, "but the instrument panel is powered by solar-generated electricity just like all tablets. Hydraulics work the track, but it's the constantly expanding and contracting of water vapor that generates the power." With that he throws a lever, and *Pandora* surges to life, jerkily pulling herself forward along her tracks. The city disappears behind us slowly, and the Professor guides *Pandora* through a large tunnel in the rock. I have never been outside the city before. I have never seen the rock walls of the cave that sequester humankind deep within the earth. I know that we are underground, but it is quite another thing to come face to face with the boundaries of human existence and then surpass them.

It isn't long before we encounter an enormous door that looks very much like the door to a safe. I recognize Mayor Campwell standing with several others at a control panel to the side of the door.

He waves to us and then punches a code on the door. The vault door opens slowly, with the groan of hinges that have not moved in at least a lifetime. Behind the door the tunnel continues, and we pass through out into the unknown. The tunnel begins to slope upwards, and then, after nearly a kilometer, we encounter a wall of ice.

"Here we go!" Professor Higgs throws the switch that starts the drill, and I can see the bit begin to spin. It makes an awful wail when it connects with the ice, but it works. Slowly we push through the ice. "Another kilometer or so of this and we will reach the surface."

With a splintering crash the ice ahead cracks and shatters as *Pandora* breaks through to the surface. It doesn't look at all like I had imagined. In the pictures the Professor had shown me the sky was blue and light. Yet, all that I can see in every direction is gray and dim. White flakes drift in the air, tossed about on gusts of wind. There is nothing appealing at all to me. The look of disappointment in Davie's eyes mirrors my own.

Checking the readouts on the screen, Professor Higgs adjusts our course and takes off across the vast plane. I hope he knows where he is going. More importantly I hope he knows how to get back.

"There …" he points as a looming structure emerges out of the gray fog. "Each tower is nearly a hundred square meters, and on the top of each tower are five solar panels, each twenty square meters in size. It appears that this tower is partially retracted."

"How can you tell?" Davie asks.

"I can see the top of it. When it is extended, it stands nearly two kilometers high. We have to find the entrance point, get you two inside to fix the pipes and then move on to the next tower. There are four towers. Suit up."

I never thought we would even make it this far. The thought of going out into that frozen wasteland scares the crap out of me. I can tell Davie isn't so keen on it either. We shrug at each other. What else can we do? Without the solar towers we will all die anyway.

Professor Higgs pulls *Pandora* to within three meters of the tower. Pressing a button, he shoots a harpoon out of *Pandora's* hull, which imbeds in the side of the tower. A cable attached to the harpoon now stretches from the hull to the tower.

"Attach your safety lines to the cable. The wind is so strong out there it could blow you away. Don't release your safety line until you are both inside the tower. I have installed temperature gauges on the wristbands of your suits, so you will know if it is safe to remove them." Professor Higgs gives us the thumbs-up sign before pushing us into the hatch and sealing the inner door behind us.

With a deep breath, I release the outer hatch, hook my safety line to the cable and take my first steps onto the planet's surface. The white ground gives a few centimeters under my weight, but it holds me. It is only a few steps to the tower door, which, as we suspected, is frozen shut. I am prepared; I take my mini torch from my bag of tools. It takes a few minutes, but I get the door open relatively easily. Once we are both inside, we remove our safety lines and close the door. There is another inner door, and once through that, we discover that it is indeed warm enough to remove our protective suits. Now, it isn't warm by any means: 5° C by our gauges. We each wear thick woolen clothing and heavy gloves. Hopefully, it will get warmer the closer we get to the pipes.

I pull up the schematic of the steam tubes the Professor has downloaded onto my tablet, and we are able to locate the access tunnels without incident. The tubes are different than the pipes that run under the city. These are flexible, but the basic principles of how to fix them still apply. Davie and I are in our element as we silently set about checking for leaks and ruptures, making repairs when we come across them. It takes nearly two hours to check all the tubes, but satisfied, we head back to the *Pandora*.

The next two towers go just as smoothly as the first. The last, however, takes longer. Many areas of the fourth tower have already begun to freeze due to the loss of heat. Davie and I have to use the torch to break through the inner tower door as well as the access tunnel door. An entire section of tubing has split down its length. We have excess tubing aboard the *Pandora*, and I have to wait for Davie to return with it. As I wait, I explore a bit. I find a hatch in the ceiling of one of the tubing chambers. It's frozen, so I put my suit back on—I have no idea how cold it is on the other side of that door—and use my mini-torch to open the hatch. Crawling through I realize that it is much colder on this side. My suit's gauge says it's -15°C. I think this is an observation area. Two of the walls are made of thick glass. I can see the *Pandora* waiting below. If the fog wasn't so thick, I think I could have seen forever.

I close the hatch behind me as I return to the tubes. Davie has returned with the extra tubing, and in no time we will be back on our way to the city. The repair is easy, but since it is such a long length of tubing, it takes both of us to fix it. Thank goodness Davie is with me, otherwise I would have needed the Professor to help me. We test the last seal for leaks before re-pressurizing the system.

No sooner is the system back up and running than a vibration shakes the tower. The entire structure seems to move. I grab the tablet just as the Professor pops onto the screen. "What's happening?" I ask.

"I just got word from the Mayor. The city engineers want to test the towers before we return to the city. We can't leave if they aren't fixed."

"They're fixed I tell you!" Davie comes to stand next to me, nodding his head in agreement.

"They won't listen to you! Hell, they won't even listen to me! They are extending the towers. You just have to hold on. Clip your safety lines to something and hold on!"

I motion for Davie to follow me. If I am going to be two kilometers in the air, I want to see what it looks like up there. I push open the hatch I found to the observation room and crawl through it, turning to help Davy behind me. Looking out the window, it's hard to believe that we are moving. The fog has intensified, and all we see is a wall of gray. But as we ascend further up into the sky, the gray begins to lighten. Suddenly, the wall is pure white. And then it happens. We break through the clouds and the air is clear.

We sit atop a bed of clouds, and the sky above is the most brilliant blue. A bright yellow orb hangs on the horizon, turning the edges of the clouds pink and orange.

My first sunset.

I can't breathe. I forget to breathe. I have found my dream; and I know that I will dream of this moment again and again for the rest of my life. I feel Davie touch my arm. He is as awe-struck as I am. We are the only people alive who have seen this wonder. My heart fills with a joy I have never known. After today we will never be just "tunnel rats" again.

The Professor's voice comes over my helmet com. "It worked! Now let's go home!"

THE CUTPURSE FROM MULBERRY BEND

Gerry Huntman

I want you to teach me how to pick pockets," the girl said, intensity flaring in her cultivated voice and brown eyes.

"Whoa, girl, what makes yer tink I have that craft?" the gang leader replied, surprised at the young stranger's impetuousness. He was enjoying reading the tattle in the *Manhattan Enterprise* and soaking in the spring sun on the steps of 21 Baxter Street, lovingly called by the locals as *Grand Duke's Theatre*. The address was considered no more than a dive bar by others, but it was his job to make sure the Baxter Street Dudes weren't interrupted, and to be the eyes and ears of the Boss for this section of Mulberry Bend. He never hesitated to crack skulls when push came to shove, but the little girl—*surely no more than fifteen*—took him completely by surprise.

"I've been watching you, Mr. O'Rourke, and I know you work for O'Gilvy. He's the top dog in the Five Points, and especially here in The Bend, so you must be pretty good. There's something I've got to do, and I need some help. I reckon you're the best man for the job, and I can pay."

Now Seamus O'Rourke was doubly taken aback. He took off his well-worn spectacles to take a proper gander at the girl and realized she was small for her age and more like eighteen years old. She wasn't a local by any account. She wore a dainty pink dress modestly to her ankles, only slightly soiled by the streets, and her face was clean and tanned, signifying that she came from the west, for all the locals who lived in the slums were pasty-faced, if not jaundiced and pock-ridden. She had a way with words that signified tutoring, possibly in one of those refined New England Girls Schools.

For a moment Seamus wondered what sum he would make if he introduced her to Madame L'Orange, or whisked her onto a steamer bound for the Far East, but something about the child caused the Irishman to pause. He wasn't sure if it was the intensity of her voice and gaze, or whether the fine lines on her somber face spoke of some solemn, if not tragic, tale. Her dark brown hair was long and tied back as was the custom with the young women of today, and she wore finely crafted gold earrings set with small rubies. Seamus was genuinely surprised she didn't have them ripped from her ears by now. *She's capable.*

"Young lass, it ain't wise to speak suchlike in the open. Yer've my attention—why is a girl from a good family traipsin' about in Mulberry Bend? Where's yer escort? Why would yer want to learn a scabby occupation like pickin' pockets?"

"I lived in Arizona … got caught up in the Chiricahua War … most of my family was killed. Lived in New Mexico with my uncle and aunt over the last two year—"

"Jesus, Mary'n' Joseph!" Seamus exclaimed. "I've read in the papers 'bout that bloody conflict with Geronimo an' all." He recalled reading about how Geronimo and Juh got hold of accelerator rifles and grenade launchers, which caused a lot of grief for the Federals as well as the homesteaders. Many people died at San Carlos. It took General Crook and his fleet of dirigibles filled with the latest firepower to turn the tide of the war. They bombed settlements, killing many warriors as well as their families, to clip Geronimo's wings.

He studied the girl again and realized why her face hadn't smiled in years. She was a war orphan. Seamus O'Rourke pitied her, an emotion he rarely experienced.

On mentioning "Geronimo" her face grew sterner than ever. "I have money, Mr. O'Rourke. I just need to know how to pick a man's pocket."

"And why, child?"

"General George Crook retired recently, hurt in the line of duty," she spit venomously. "He has something I want."

"Saints alive! Yer wantin' to pick the pockets of a war hero? In broad daylight? Do yer even know where he lives?"

The girl glanced to her left and right, to make sure there were no eavesdroppers, and whispered, "I've been told he walks down State Street and spends time at The Battery each morning. He also has a few companions … bodyguards. I need to get past them."

Seamus couldn't believe what he was hearing. A young girl, obviously from a good family, wanted to steal from a national hero and escape capture. It was lunacy, and yet it warmed his heart. This girl had pluck and determination that seemed to have no peer.

The gang leader was about to ask the girl's name when three rough looking men came into view, and on spotting him, tramped quickly in his direction.

"Who are they?" the girl asked.

"Trouble. They're from the Rummugger Gang, and I'd say they're wantin' to settle a score with me." *And this is only goin' to get worse when the Brooklyn Bridge is opened*, he mentally noted.

Seamus lifted his right hand and made a sign to Slim Bill across the road to urgently fetch some men. He considered running but had to show these shites who was running the Five Points.

"Girlie, stay clear. When it's over I'll give yer a hand with yer mark." He felt for his trusty Colt in his pocket.

The three intruders caught the Irishman's full attention when they broke into a trot and pulled out truncheons and knives. They meant deadly business, and he realized he wasn't as prepared as he wanted to be—*looks like the Colt's in order.*

The girl suddenly rushed toward the three in a blur. It caught the Rummuggers by surprise, but they shrugged her off as inconsequential and continued their charge toward the gang leader.

Seamus pulled out his bowie knife, deeply concerned over the strange girl. He couldn't use his gun for fear of hitting the girl.

Before he could take two steps, the girl deliberately dived sideways to the road, while swinging her right leg into the shins of one of the assailants. There was an almighty crack as she inexplicably broke both of the man's legs—he crashed to the cobblestones in screaming agony.

The other two men skidded to a halt, shocked at what had occurred. The girl was already back on her feet, hitching the left side of her dress up to her waist. Part of her left upper leg sprung out, revealing metal and whirring cogs, and she reached in and pulled out a long, deadly knife. She switched it to her right hand and marched toward the men.

The remaining Rummuggers stared at each other in disbelief and closed in on the girl for no other reason than self-protection. Seamus stood back, rooted to the spot by the sheer insanity of what was playing out before him.

In the blink of an eye the girl jumped for the right hand assailant, moving so fast she was impossible to follow. The thug swung his truncheon like a veteran, but it was blocked by the girls left arm, echoing the familiar sound of hollow metal. She swiftly buried her foot-long blade into his stomach, retracting it as quickly while turning to face the last man.

The remaining Rummugger lost heart, and scampered away.

She turned to the gobsmacked Seamus, wearing the same sober visage as she had before, as if nothing had happened. "Can you show me how to pick pockets now?"

He nodded and quickly led her away from the carnage.

O O O

"Who are yer?" O'Rourke asked, after the unlikely pair had settled in his apartment, accessed via Ragpicker's Row.

"If I tell you, will you help me with my task?" she asked, shyly.

"Of course. I owe yer, girl. Yer probably saved me life. First, tell me, what's yer name?"

"I'm Isabella Johnson. My father was Jebediah Johnson—he was an engineer, and inventor. So is his brother, Aaron, who took me in after—" She gulped, showing a sliver of emotion for the first time. "My father married an Apache, and he chose to live near the reservation. It was easier to live that way than to be treated like dirt by the white settlers, and almost as badly by the Indians who lived on the reservation.

"Dad didn't meddle in the war, and most folk understood why he didn't take sides, but the war came to us, and our home.

Geronimo holed up nearby, and Crook's dirigibles came and started to bombard everything, and everyone. One bomb hit our home and blew it apart." Tears welled in her eyes. "I don't remember much except a bright light and terrible pain, and then darkness.

"I woke up in Crook's army hospital. My left arm and both my legs were blown to bits. I had other injuries but they healed quick enough. My uncle came a few days later and took me to New Mexico where he and my aunt cared for me. It took a long time, but Uncle Aaron made me a clockwork arm and legs. Clockwork mechanics is what he is best at, and he made a lot of money from it."

Seamus realized then what he thought to be a miracle, was instead the wonders of modern science. Everyone had heard of clockwork machines, and in the British Empire the rich had servants made from machinery, known as automatons.

"Tell me," he said, "what is it that yer want to do? What is it that Crook has that makes yer want to nick it from him?"

She shook her head slowly. "This is the one thing I can't divulge, Mr. O'Rourke. The one thing. Please, show me how to get to General Crook so I can take what must be claimed."

Seamus stared long into her eyes and found them unwavering; her willpower was made of the same stuff as her limbs. "Righty-o, Isabella. How long do we have? Pickpocketin' is like any craft, it takes years an' years to perfect, maybe months if the student is talented and young."

"I want to take what's owed to me tomorrow."

"What?" he cried out in dismay. "Impossible. Yer can't learn the techniques, the readin' of people's actions, the deftness of the fingers, the lightness of the touch, the slittin' of pockets and purses without a sound ... yer just can't learn that in a *day*!"

"Then ... then how can you help me?" she asked, for the first time her voice faltering.

"I can get one o' the best to do it for yer ... not a problem," Seamus said, relieved.

"No, I have to be the one to do it." What little light that was in her eyes, darkened like storm clouds.

He ran his fingers through his beard in frustration. "Then it's impossible. The best I can offer is to have some o' the lads cause a distraction—then you can do yer best. I've seen yer run, girl, yer won't have a problem gittin' after the deed."

"Alright," she said, with her usual subdued tone, although the Irishman could detect a hint of buoyancy, "tell me your plan."

So he did.

O   O   O

State Street was busy with human traffic and carriages, both horse and steam driven varieties. O'Rourke wanted to witness the caper, having had a feeling deep in his guts that it was going to be a remarkable morning. The trouble was he wasn't sure it was necessarily going to turn out happy for the girl. He stood some distance from the point where Isabella was going to mark General George Crook.

As he waited, he thought about what motivated him to support such an odd girl, beyond what he owed when she had beaten the ruffians. He ran his fingers through his beard again, and his steely blue eyes unfocused, instead swiftly travelling time, punctuated by the wasted opportunities where he could have settled down and had children—even possibly a girl with such pluck as Isabella. A trace of moisture was quickly blinked away and he smiled. "You old softy," he muttered.

The plan was simple, and one used by the most experienced pickpockets in the city. In fact, the caper went back centuries, to the Old World. It required a team effort. He had two experienced boys and a young mother with child in tow work with Isabella. The baby would cry at the best moment for the caper, which would cue one boy, who was positioned on the perimeter of the point, to shout "Mark!" at exactly the same moment another boy would run in the opposite direction from where Isabella would approach Crook. Between the baby crying and the two boys distracting the party, Isabella would have the best chance to grab what she can. It would then be up to her to scamper off into the side streets.

An uncomfortable feeling of uncertainty was mounting in Seamus' stomach, and yet there was also a thrill. He genuinely wanted her to pick the general's pocket without being seen doing it. He wanted her to pick his pocket like a professional. *Like father, like daughter.*

Isabella approached the group head-on with close to perfect timing, while the others moved to their designated positions. George Crook was in the center of the group, deep in discussion with a hanger-on, a leather satchel slung over his shoulder. O'Rourke smiled.

To the Irishman's continued admiration, Hattie got the baby to cry with immaculate timing, and very loud indeed. People's heads turned from all points on the street within fifty yards. A few steam carriages stopped. Young Sam cried "Mark!" as if he was trying to attract a friend's attention while Freddy the Cutpurse's running distraction commenced. It easily carried to Isabella's attention, and for the first time since meeting her, Seamus noticed something akin to a satisfied look on her face.

Isabella easily closed in on Crooks. Out of plan, she moved in front of the general, directly facing him. She whispered something and he laughed, extending his hand to condescendingly pat her on her shoulder.

Her clockwork hand shot up and grasped his upper right arm. Crook yelped in pain, and the entire street heard a bone break. Two bodyguards, who were finally focused on what was happening to their charge, grabbed her and tried to pry her loose from the general, but to no avail.

She laughed as her upper right leg opened like it did the day before with the Rummuggers.

The bodyguards, forgetting decorum, punched her—one hit her arm and fell backwards with an injured hand. The other punched her in the side, which caused her nearly to collapse, but her clockwork arm held firm.

The bystanders who were near her stepped back, shocked at what was happening and afraid of the strange contraption coming from her leg, boldly outlined through her dress. Isabella quickly lifted the folds of cloth with her right hand, revealing several sticks of dynamite secured in the hollow of her leg. A small switch was conspicuously placed on top.

A few bystanders shrieked in panic but most of the people who were near her—Crook's bodyguards and entourage—were oblivious to what she had concealed within the metal limb.

A bodyguard tried to clip Isabella on her chin, but in mid-flight she flipped the switch.

Seamus saw that satisfied expression again—oh so briefly—and it was tinged with a mix of profound sorrow and resignation.

The explosion was tremendous, reminding the older folk of the War, and yet most of its damage was confined to a short range around the point of detonation. Isabella and Crook were no longer to be seen—they literally disintegrated, scattering over hundreds of yards. A few of the guards fared no better. Other men lay dead or dying on the street. Body parts were scattered everywhere. A large number of bystanders received minor cuts, only a few died from their wounds. O'Rourke was knocked off his feet, and a piece of metal was lodged in his upper right arm—he later discovered it was a small bronze gear.

O O O

In the dusty aftermath of the explosion, a wounded Irishman worked his way back to Mulberry Bend, wondering why Isabella chose to kill herself. Tears ran in rivulets down his whiskery cheeks. *Yer took what ya needed to take, girlie, but God Almighty at what a price.*

He wore Isabella's bronze cog on a chain around his neck for the rest of his life. He no longer judged a book by its cover, and furthermore, he no longer had any business with Madam L'Orange or the Chinese traders.

THE GREAT DINOSAUR ROUNDUP OF 1903

Laura Givens

12, March 1903

My Dearest Bess,

I take pen in hand to inform you of the possible untimely death of your brother, Pete. I know for a fact he loved you dearly and regretted all the things he said that last time in Wichita. He was drunk that night, and a man will say stupid things when in such a state. I am still here in Wisconsin—a town called Milwaukee—with the Wild West show and will send his last wages and belongings as soon as old Buffalo Bill settles accounts. I'm certain Pete would want your mother to have them, so please see that she gets them.

I say possible untimely death because Mr. Tesla says, strictly speaking, Pete died a few million years before he was even born. Be that as it may, he was still alive the last time I saw him, though his situation seemed dire enough. Bess, sit yourself down, and I'll try and explain, as best I might, just what happened and how Pete wound up trying to break a dinosaur with a Bowie knife.

Well, it all started with the two of us finally getting some time off so we could take in the local culture of the fair city of Milwaukee.

You'd think that getting massacred at the Little Big Horn twice a day plus an extra matinee on Sunday wouldn't be all that hard, but it gets to you after a while. Me and Pete got a little happy before one show and decided that maybe Custer should win that night—just as a change of pace. Now, the way it works is the Indians ride around us shooting lots of fake arrows at us. We troopers wear padding under our outfits that those arrows stick into, and we stumble around dying heroically. These city folks just eat it up. That particular night we just stayed up, getting shot at until we both looked like a couple of porcupines. Finally, one of the Indians, big old son of a gun called Cold-Wind-In-Spring, dismounts and stomps over, picks Pete up by his shirt and throws him at me. We both go flying right onto General Custer—Bill Cody himself—who gets up and starts whacking us with his hat and using words that I shall not repeat here. So, we had us a week off.

Now, Milwaukee makes some mighty fine beers, and just to be neighborly, me and Pete had us a few more than might normally be considered temperate. Well, we got into a sort of roping match to see who could lasso and hogtie this yahoo in a funny uniform and helmet. I won, and Pete was about to use a cigar as a branding iron when we were accosted by a horde of men in funny helmets. To make a long story short, that yahoo turned out to be a policeman with no sense of humor at all, so we got us a night's lodging in the local calaboose. The next morning Cody shows up to throw our bail. With him is this real refined gent in a three-piece suit, spats and a top hat. That was our introduction to Mr. Nicola Tesla, inventor of the time machine, among other things.

After he got us outside Bill, blistered our ears for a spell. He finally finished up by saying that if we weren't the best damned straight-up trail hands he had ever seen, he would have let us rot. Luckily for us, it seemed he needed us for a special deal he was working with Tesla. Bill had met the man ten years earlier at the Chicago World's Fair, and they hit it right off. Mr. Tesla had him an idea about something he called "time travel," and they had set up a secret base up there in Milwaukee where land was cheaper. Bill had fronted the money for the whole operation because, it turned out, he'd loved something called "archeology" since he'd met some fella years ago digging up dinosaur bones out west somewhere.

With this here time machine, me and Pete were going to go back a few million years and round up some critters called *Tyrannosaurus rex* for the show. Bill is always lookin' for new exotic acts for the show. If we refused to help, we were informed we could spend the next sixty days in the jug and be left stranded in Milwaukee. Cody had us by the short hairs, so we were in whether we liked it or not. Tesla explained it all to us in detail, and I understood not a word of what he said. He is the only man I've ever met more in love with his own voice than Bill.

After a while Pete kind of warmed to the idea and allowed as how it might be fun. You will recall that your brother's idea of fun also included riding your Pa's prize bull through town in hat, spurs and the suit God gave him on his birthday. I remained skeptical but enjoyed the Havana cigars he had offered us.

Traveling through time turns out to be loud and flashy but not as uncomfortable as you might think. Tesla had set up the whole shebang in an abandoned brewery, with big old machines with dials and electric lights and wires everywhere. Strangest of all was a whole line of poles with lightning climbing up and down them, made my hair stand right on end. One wall had a huge rolling metal door set to roll up and down like a curtain. Right up against it was a great big cage with three sides tall enough to hold a two-story house.

The plan was that we would ride out through that metal door, and on the other side would be those rexes and other such critters. Then we'd herd them back into the cage, the door would drop down behind them, and we'd have us some dinosaurs. There was a smaller escape door on the side of the cage that me and Pete would be let out through. It sounded simple enough. Bill gave us pictures of what the rexes looked like and told us that if we couldn't find none of them we should get a three-horned varmint called a Tri-ceratops. So, we said we'd keep a look out.

I was on a fast little pinto pony, and Pete had him a roan he was particular to, both top-notch cow ponies, but the noise and lights had them plum skittish. I've never enjoyed riding a rearing horse, but I understood that pinto's point of view. When that big old door started `rolling up, I thought they would go loco. I certainly felt the urge myself. Up till that moment, I hadn't actually believed what little I could understand of Tesla's explanations. I fully expected that when that big old door raised up I would see the woman selling flowers we had passed coming in. We'd all wind up looking a mite foolish, and that would be an end to it. But there, on the other side of that door, looking like something out of a picture book, was a jungle all hot and humid, alive with sounds that hadn't been heard on this earth in millions of years. Pete's horse reared up on its hind legs, and Pete let out a whoop of pure joy. He set off at a gallop into the forest primeval. Against all good sense, I lit out after him.

Bess, you know how they say the buffalo herds used to be, going on and on as far as the eye could see? Well, that's what this was like, but not just one kind of animal, no, there were critters of every shape and description grazing everywhere or lolling around in watering holes and rivers. It was so pretty, Bess, I wish you could have seen it. We rode around for a while, trying to find us a rex, to no avail, so I suggested we have us a little picnic and see if we couldn't maybe catch one of the little ones running around on two legs ... lure him in with a biscuit and grab him. I pulled out some chicken legs and fresh biscuits, while Pete produced a bottle of whiskey. Whatever else I might have thought of your brother, I always admired his priorities.

We got to toasting one thing and another, and Pete fired off a couple of rounds just to celebrate our not being in jail. I guess he must have winged one of the big old leathery birds that kept flying overhead, because it suddenly dived at us like an owl looking for a mouse lunch. I rolled back and grabbed my pistol, just managing to snap off a shot as that vulture snatched Pete's hat—almost took his head along too, just for good measure. I must have stung it though, because it lit out, wanting nothing else to do with us. We finished off those chicken legs fast as we could, so we could get back to the job at hand.

Every now and then as we ate, one of these cute little critters— looked like a salamander walkin' around on two legs, bright red, about three-foot tall—would get curious about us. None, however, was enticed to come very close by the food we offered. Then, just as we were about ready to ride, one little guy came right up to Pete and offered him his lost hat. That big bird must have dropped it, and this salamander was sharp enough to know to bring it back to Pete. On an impulse I grabbed him up and clutched him to my chest, him squawking and struggling to get free. He was handful, but we finally got him quieted down, Pete making soothing noises. I was trying to figure out how best to transport him when we heard a blood-curdling screech and saw something jump from the undergrowth and land a couple of yards away. It was another salamander, but this one stood a good six feet tall and had a spear clutched in one paw. He had a real determined look, and his other paw was ready to draw a bone knife from the woven belt slung round his torso. I dropped the little one and put my hand on the butt of my gun, not drawing it for fear of making things worse. There was no telling how many more might be out there. We stood there, eyeball to eyeball for a good minute, the little one cowering behind his daddy.

It was then that Pete put himself between us and made a big show of putting his hat back on and waving back at the youngster. Then, in a stroke of genius, he took a swig from the bottle of whiskey and offered it to that big old salamander fella. Hesitantly, he took the bottle from Pete and sniffed it real good before tipping it back just like Pete had done. It was a mite comical the way he let out a big old belch and started blinking real fast. Well, he took a second swig and then tried to hand it back to Pete. Your brother motioned that he should keep it.

That red devil lifted Pete's bottle and let out three blood-curdling whoops, and three more salamanders dropped out of trees. Well sir, the daddy started makin' all kinds of clicks and barking sounds. We'd both been around Bill Cody long enough to recognize a speech when we heard one—even if we didn't know what was being said. At the end of his remarks, we all sat down and passed that bottle around till it was bone dry. Then, without so much as a by your leave, they hopped up, whipping around fast as lightning, and were gone into the trees, leaving the bottle lying on the grass.

Me and Pete stared at each other a moment, and then we both started laughing like jackasses. After we had laughed ourselves dry, we crawled on our horses and got down to some serious rex hunting. Fun was fun, but we still had us a job to do.

Eventually Pete got bored and started cutting out critters from this group of duck-billed critters with horns on their crests. He was herding them right and left, plying his trade so to speak, when all of a sudden he ran smack dab into a greenish brown wall with four legs

65

and three horns. He had found us a Tri-ceratops!

Now, neither Bill nor Mr. Tesla had mentioned how bad tempered one of these things might be. It started swinging its head around right and left, gorging and throwing duck-things all around it. It was about to have a go at Pete, but I rode in through the herd, whooping and hollering and blazing away with my Colt. The bullets didn't hardly faze that critter none, but I had distracted it enough that Pete could get to a safer distance. Once we had the beast confused with our fancy horsemanship, we just kept at it, riding in circles and putting ropes on him till we figured we'd plum tired him out. He was big but none too bright, and I started to think of him as just another really cantankerous steer. Just as we thought we had him, that three horned devil gave one last huge jerk of his head and sent me and my pinto flying towards the trees. I got up, rubbing my back and using foul language.

Spying my Winchester on the ground, I determined that maybe I could make a larger caliber impression on that son of a buck with the right tool. All of a sudden, from behind me, I heard a roar and a high-pitched squeal that ended abruptly. Turning slowly, I saw four horse legs flailing in the air, and where its body should have been all I saw were long, pointy teeth and two eyes straight out of a nightmare.

That picture we had been given by Bill was off in several minor details. If this was a Tyrannosaurus rex (and I had a suspicion it was) it wasn't some slow, tail-draggin' oaf like in the drawing. This thing looked fast and mean as a scorpion on a hot rock. The teeth looked a lot bigger than in the picture, too.

Old three-horn took one look and tore off like a bat out of Hell, pulling Pete right off his roan, dragging him through the dirt and ferns. I ran over, grabbed the reins to Pete's horse and was in that saddle faster than a flea on a hound. The one bright spot in all this was that the Tri-ceratops was heading right in the direction of that time-travel door, so I took off after him. Glancing over my shoulder, I saw that the rex was crunching away on his pinto lunch. Nonchalantly, as he chewed, Mr. Rex was studying all the action with his eyes. After a few minutes of hard riding, I spotted the Tri-ceratops standing there breathing hard. In the distance ahead of him, I saw a dark square on the horizon that I knew had to be the time door. Missing from the scene was any trace of your brother. I made my way carefully around the heaving brute, fearing what grisly remains I might find on the mouth-end but was puzzled when I found nothing. I had no idea where Pete could have gotten to.

Then I heard a whump in the distance, followed by a second and a third and so forth, each one getting louder and closer together. Suddenly, I saw that rex barreling at me, crashing through the undergrowth like a runaway freight train. Three-horn took off like a shot, heading straight for the dark patch. I am ashamed to admit that my pony and I froze right there on the spot. I thought I would soil myself when that big old monster stopped right in front of me and opened wide, letting out a roar that could have stripped paint from a barn. All of a sudden something dropped right out of the branches overhead, landing on the varmint's back. It was Pete, clothes all shredded and covered in mud and leaves, somehow still wearing his hat. He lifted that big old Bowie knife of his and plunged it into the critter's hide. Pete let out howl and held on for dear life as that lizard tried to shake him off. Roused from my stupor, I put spurs to that roan and went off like lightning after the Tri-ceratops.

It must have been a strange sight for those boys back in 1903: having a three-horned mountain barreling at them, followed by a screaming maniac on a strawberry roan who was trying to get away from a big old dragon weaving from side to side, the dragon ridden by a laughing madman.

The Tri-ceratops went right through the big door and proceeded to tear through that cage like pages from a Sears & Roebuck. That critter started smashing machines and lightning poles to beat the band. By the time I rode through there were people running everywhere and explosions like it was the fourth of July. I thought it the better part of valor to get out of there fast as I could. As I made for the cage door, I turned one last time, and through the fireworks I could see Pete still on the other side of the big door riding that wheeling, bucking Tyrannosaurus rex, with Pete waving one hand in the air and singing the *Yellow Rose of Texas* at the top of his lungs. Just before the smoke got too dense to see, I would swear I saw a spear hit the beast right under one of its tiny arms. I heard three loud whoops as I was unceremoniously shoved through a side door and out onto an overcast Milwaukee street corner.

Once we were out, that building started shaking and tearing itself apart. It finally just up and imploded into itself with a big old whump of air. By the time the volunteer firemen showed up there wasn't much left to see. Men in white coats gave statements to bewildered policemen as I sipped a beer offered to me by an understanding soul. Nicola Tesla was off to one side, covered in dust and debris, scribbling madly in a notebook that was now charred slightly at the edges. Buffalo Bill sat hunched up on a curb, hat in hand, crying softly for his lost dreams of dinosaurs at a dime a head.

So, my dearest, Pete is gone. The professor says he will rebuild his machines one day—Bill says not with his money he ain't. So rescue seems out of the question. The common sense thing to assume is that your baby brother is long gone, a meal for monsters. But Pete was never one much for common sense. I lay awake some nights wondering if, somewhere back in pre-history, Pete didn't manage to bust that rex after all. If so, then maybe my old partner has managed to start himself the world's first and only dinosaur ranch. Never count a cowboy out till he's six foot under, that's what I always say.

Hug the children for me. I will be home from my travels in the spring.

Your loving husband,

Sam

American Vampire

Keith Good

Part One: Bandito

1913

I

He craved death. Each bone-stubbled carcass, each spike of irradiated grass growled at the dark inside him. Days stretching to weeks, he entertained the fantasy that, like him, these plains would die forever. It was a cruel thought. Flickering lizards—little candles of life—and summer cloudbursts snuffed his macabre fantasies. He could never die, and the world would only live.

He pulled the pamphlet from Rosie's saddlebag only to put it back. He'd arrive soon. Hypnotized by the chuff of Rosie's pneumatic horseshoes, he fell into a dream. Denver City sprouted from the shimmering heat, woven from light and fog. He and Rosie trotted its familiar High Street, a squat warehouse on their left. Its hand-carved sign declared:

Metalwork & Horseshoeing
L.M. Smith, Prop.

In this false lucidity, he pulled Rosie's reins toward their former home. She ignored him, instead breaking into a brisk jog. As all good things do, Denver City died. He tried to ask "¿Que es esto, Rosie?" but weeks without water left his voice dead as the surrounding plains.

The question proved superfluous; a black speck squirmed on the horizon, too big for brush and too small for buffalo. Another horse—and another rider—lay 500 yards ahead. He swung an arm behind him and let the safety off his rifle … just in case. Rosie, her sight superior, her attentions inexhaustible, recognized the speck and upped her pace. The Rider obliged her enthusiasm and sat firm, hand to gun and his eyes on the growing shape.

As in most matters, Rosie's judgment proved correct. A horse stretched across the earth, missing most of a foreleg and bested by the cruel heat. A bandito slumped against the horse's neck, pot-bellied and bloody-mouthed. Rosalina broke to a thundering gallop, the tubes grafted to her hooves screaming steam. Too proud for bit or saddle, the Rider tugged her mane to maintain his seat.

"Whoa, chica," he croaked. His words did nothing. Rosalina put the greasy outlaw under hoof and reared back to deliver vengeance, but a forceful pull on her mane felled the blow wide. The mare stomped murderous intent, snorting and spitting. The Rider, minding his grip lest he end up on the brick-hard ground, whispered in Rosalina's perked ear.

She settled, and the Rider, rifle in hand, hopped to the ground. The bandito slouched in the shade of his dead horse, gnawing a grisled femur. Yellow blisters and the blackness of encroaching death dotted his book-leather skin. Blood mottled his cheek, flies landing without reprove on eyelids, nose, and cheeks.

"¿Hablas íngles?" The Rider trained his rifle on the bandito, custom scope flickering a red dot between heavy-lidded eyes.

The bandit laughed and tossed the femur away. "No. I sprecken zee Doitch."

"Get smart with me again and I'll relieve you of your brains." The Rider punctuated his warning with a kick to the bandito's ribs. "You one of the Banditos Rouges that held up the Union Pacific last week?"

"What if I am? You a law dog?"

The Rider lowered his rifle. "If I'm a dog, then you're the bitch, bandito." He turned from the wretch and whispered in Rosie's ear. She snorted, putting a rare smile onto the Rider's face. He pulled the small book from Rosie's saddlebag and secreted it to a pants pocket.

"Today is the luckiest day of your life, amigo. The way I figure, your boys are whoring in Santa Fe by now. Rosie here will take you to them." The Rider took a canteen from his hip, emptied half into the aluminum tanks on Rosie's haunches and tossed it to the bandito. "Take it easy with the water and you'll live."

The bandito laughed.

"You're gonna give away your horse and your water in the center of hell? Gringo, you'll be dead by sundown."

"Doubt it." The Rider slung the bandito by his collar over Rosie's back. "Thinking ain't your strong suit, bandito. You leave the logic to me. Consider yourself fortunate—I'm in a charitable mood. That only happens every two hundred years or so." The Rider pointed to the rectangular metal case strapped to Rosalina's hind. "Whatever you do, don't open Pandora's box. Hell's inside."

With a swift slap, Rosalina and the crusty bandito set off into the plain. He bounced as if strapped to a bucking bull. The boots grafted to Rosie's hooves hissed pressurized steam, driving hydraulic rods to the ground in concert with her gallop. The machine amplified her speed tenfold.

"What the hell kind of horseshoes is these?" the bandito roared, voice heavy with the echo of distance. Within seconds Rosie and the thief plunged under the horizon. The Rider thought of the noose awaiting the gullible bastard and flashed another rare smile.

The sun needled exposed skin, fighting a battle it could never win. Alone again, he pulled the book from his pants pocket and put it back. Denver City congealed out of the haze. He stood at the arched door of his old workshop, the damned machine just beyond. Decades wound back like the gears in his pocket watch.

The Rider walked through the arch and into a daydream, shuttled from 1913 New Mexico to the floor of his workshop, at the end of the High Street in Denver City, 1861.

Part Two: Compañera

1861

I

Electric dragons roamed the warehouse. Birthed from copper and steel obelisks, they flew to the center of the shop, leaving a wake of sapphires. He shoveled one last load of compressed coal into the boiler's mouth and stepped back. His conglomeration of magnets and locomotive parts conducted a beautiful symphony: coal fire from the boiler shot compressed steam to each of the four magneto towers, forcing the magnets across copper screws that pulled electricity to the domes atop each column.

Above the boiler, insulated from its hellfire by layers of Comanche fabric, sat a crystal dodecahedron twelve inches across. The dragons swarmed a filament ascending from the box and plunged inside.

Protected by crystal and glowing with electricity sat a human heart. Each snapping dragon made it dance. The man stepped to a small dial atop the boiler and nudged it clockwise. The pistons increased their intensity. Sparks flew faster, stronger, until one dragon chomped the tail of the next into continuous arcs of power. Electrons sputtered from the machine, condensing an electric cloud over the man's head.

He lowered black-tinted goggles and peered at the heart glistening inside the crystal box.

The heart beat. It was alive.

The man fell to his knees and cried in savage ecstasy. Electricity rained over his hands, his eyes, until his veins ran blue, flesh indistinguishable from the cloud above him. The dragons, weary of their mechanical master, ransacked the shop. They exploded vials like glass bombs. They kindled errant papers and wood like struck matches.

Even for one who cannot die, the chaos proved too much. Frantic to save the machine, to preserve the two tons of steel and 78 years of toil, he lunged to the copper kill switch glinting from the boiler. The machine shrieked in agony, bleeding molten steel. The pistons halted, the steam fizzled and died.

The familiar dark draped over his eyes. In the haze between life and death, the man saw a strange beast—maybe imagined—roaming his workshop. A chimera of water and flesh doused the shop, squelching the hungry fires. The water-beast hovered to where the man lay, stooped down to his face. He opened his mouth to speak, but the curtain of consciousness dropped, plunging him again into the unfathomable abyss.

II

She perched on a charred stool, his rifle bouncing across her knee. "You should be muerto." She was as dark as the room, only eyes and teeth, her hair tangled to bare shoulders.

"True." It still hurt to speak. He coughed ash and propped to his elbows, pain cramping his every muscle. Most humans he read like children's rhymes: all definition and subtext gleaned from a simple once over. This black wraith, however, was obtuse—indecipherable. She wore rags but had the air of an oil baron.

"Who are you?" he asked.

"The chica that saved you from the ashes." A slender cigar bounced from the corner of her mouth, ruby ember conjuring peacocks of smoke that strutted and swirled above their heads.

"That's a fifty-cent cigar you're chomping." He made incremental movements in the low light, inching forward while looking stationary.

"Esta cigarillo es mia." A steely cloud rolled from her mouth. "The way I figure, you owe me for saving your skin."

"My skin needed no saving."

"Tu máquina, then." She tossed her black hair to the mass of steel, copper, crystal and magnet behind them. He gave the machine a once-over: it seemed intact, cogs and wheels still in the right place. The worst damage afflicted the crystal heart—a crack ran top to bottom, saline solution dripping to the floor.

"Fair enough." He pushed elbows to palms, sitting up in the low light. "If that Oro Cubano pays part of my debt, what more do I owe?"

Her eyes sparked with bemusement. "When the Law shows up, you tell them I'm not here and you never saw me." She looked to the arched doorway across the workshop. Her attentions foolishly divested, he jumped from the floor, stole the rifle and trained it between her chocolate eyes.

"Chica," he snorted, "Law ain't piss next to a malo like me." He swung the barrel skyward and boomed a shot into the rafters. "I despise humanity. Pray tell why I shouldn't blast your head clean off and bury you under the floorboards with the rest." His finger flexed against the trigger, rifle nestled into his shoulder.

"Easy," she snorted. "No soy humana. Soy monstrua." She bared her incisors and growled.

"A monster?" He lowered the gun a shade.

"Mi madre was a slave in El Paso. Una dia, a pack of banditos rode in; slaughtered her master like the puerco he was, burned the house and plundered its stores. It would have been a blessing if they'd burned mi madre with the house, but they were coños without compassion. They cut her face, stripped her naked and took turns. Twelve banditos, one after another for days. When they got bored, when she stopped fighting, they rode away, left her for dead. The law came in after and sold her to another puerco. Nine months later I arrived … she died soon after."

She stared past him into a dark corner of the warehouse. "Soy una monstrua: half bandita, half negra. In this country, a Mexican half of three-fifths ain't shit." The woman looked to the barreled ceiling and whispered smoke.

"Alright." He swung the rifle point to dirt and leaned his elbow to its stock. "What's the law want with a monstrua like you?"

"The sheriff of this town mistook me for a sporting bitch. I told him my honey wasn't for sale, but the coño slapped me around and stole the poke I wouldn't sell. When he was done, sleeping like a baby, I took a set of butcher shears and—*snip!*" she mimed cutting with her fingers, "Sliced off his tiny little pene. I was out the window and down the street before he realized the blood was his."

He had no choice but to laugh with her, sap the electricity she generated. He hadn't laughed in centuries; the ease of his smile and the helium bubbling his chest surprised him—joy was a luxury he thought long dead.

"Fine." He tossed the rifle onto the girl's lap. "The Cock-Butcher of Denver City can stay in my shop as long as it would have taken me to rebuild the machine she saved. Two months sound fair?"

"Sí." she answered with a firm nod.

"¿Como te llamas, senorita?" he asked, striding to inspect his damaged machine.

"Rosalina." She quit the stool and followed.

"Get a wrench, Rosalina. We have some repairs to make."

III

The law hobbled in 24 hours later, comical in an ill-fitted waistcoat, waxed moustache and frayed bowler. His accessories—a gauze diaper and sapling crutch—proved too much for the Blacksmith's sense of humor. Only practiced self-discipline (and molars gnashing his tongue) kept his laughter at bay.

"Now, John, I heard of cowpokes asking whores to diaper them, let them suck the tit, but honestly, I didn't peg you as the type."

"Where is she, Blacksmith?" The sheriff's voice was more cry than command.

The Smith put on a cocksure smile. "I'm sorry, but of whom are we speaking?"

"The mulatto who tried to kill me, that's who!"

"I heard she only tried to geld you, John."

The Sheriff struggled to stay upright, sweating and out of breath. The strain of argument nearly felled him. He took a few breaths and swallowed before starting again in a calmer voice.

"We know she's here, Blacksmith. We ain't found her tracks out of town, and we checked every dern building. Hand her over so she can hang for what she done."

The Smith showed the sheriff his upturned palms, absolving himself of sleeved aces. "As much as I'd fancy any dame that snips off your prick, I regret to say I haven't seen her."

The sheriff stood fast at the door, blood dribbling down his diaper. Seeing him not easily divested, the Blacksmith, palms still out, stepped aside and waved the law in.

"You and your boys are welcome to nose around the shop. I should warn you though," he pointed to the mass of blackened steel behind them, "I'm experimenting with electricity. I'd hate for any mortal accident to befall you."

The Sheriff righted himself as best his gnarled groin would allow, face scrunched with skepticism. Trickles of sweat arched his convex jaw, quivering at each of his three chins. With his non-crutch hand, the Sheriff removed his bowler—blonde wisps matted to a bald head—and mopped his flop sweat with a sleeve. Bowler back in place, he unleashed a heavy-hearted sigh.

"I suppose she ain't here."

"Very good," the Smith replied.

The Sheriff nodded—bookending their interaction—and the Blacksmith swung the massive oak door. It slammed into the jamb with a resounding thud.

The Smith turned to face the waiting dark. "Don't think he'll be back."

IV

Rosalina proved an inexhaustible fountain of questions. Had the Smith known this from the start, he may have shot her and been done with it.

"¿Que es esta máquina?"

Her first query came before the diapered law. The Smith was walking a slow circuit of the contraption, hands clasped behind his back, head swiveling, when the reserves of Rosalina's restraint evaporated, exposing a vast bed of curiosity.

His first thought was to be glib—to say, "Metal and glass," but the girl had saved the machine. She'd earned enough currency to purchase a few answers.

"It is a mechanical heart," he said. "The four magnetic towers convert steam power to electricity, which then flows to the central chamber. At the right frequency and power, electricity revivifies the heart inside the machine."

"¿Una corazon maquinal?"

"It mimics the function of your own heart. Your body metabolizes food into small parcels of electricity which move your muscles and beat your heart."

"It looks like a torn up train to me."

He turned around. As requested, Rosalina stood behind him, wrench at the ready.

"Yes ...." Again the Smith found himself smiling. "Excepting the magnets and crystal, the machine's components were ... borrowed from the Southern Pacific 2224."

"They just gave you a train?"

He resumed his diagnostic circuit.

"A rifle between the conductor's eyes can be an invaluable bargaining tool."

"How do you know Spanish? You don't look like no Mexicano to me." Rosalina spoke between savage mouthfuls of potato two nights into her stay.

"In my youth I was an explorer, a Privateer," the Smith said, swirling the food on his plate. "I spent years in the southern reaches of the American continent with a group of buccaneers."

Rosalina's eyes bulged, contrasting her dark face.

"In your *youth*? You're barely older than I am! Gringo loco!" She petered into a disbelieving chuckle, amusement glinting her eye.

He flattened his mashed potato Matterhorn with the brunt of his fork, leaving a great grey plain. "Yes ..." The Smith cleared his dry throat. "I suppose it only seems like many years ago."

"What were you looking for?"

He shrugged his shoulders. "Vida."

"How do you know so much?"

Rosalina interjected during an explanation of magnetism and electricity, placing a hand on his forearm. He was surprised at the softness of her palm, the light kiss of her fingertips. Like a spooked rabbit, he hopped backward. Rosalina's arm hovered before folding gently over her bosom.

"It would take ten lifetimes to gather so much into one head, gringo."

Her observation elicited a single surprised word from the Smith "True."

V

It took the Blacksmith thirteen days to repair his mechanical heart. He hadn't considered the value of extra hands until he had Rosalina. She fused fresh copper into cracks, calibrated magnets, helped patch and refill the crystal box. No precaution was overlooked. Both the Smith and Rosalina donned rubber gloves and smocks to insulate against the electrical maelstrom. Buckets of water, four for each tower and six circling the heart, sat ready.

Rosalina wore excitement in flush cheeks. She stood at the boiler's mouth, a shovel of fuel ready. Her wards were the fire and the kill switch. Her head followed as the Smith made a final pass to inspect their repairs. Satisfied, he took three brisk steps to Rosalina and whispered in her ear.

"Esta es el tiempo, señorita."

Before he could remove himself, Rosalina swept in and planted a kiss on the Smith's cheek, warm and full of the life he envied.

"For luck." She winked and heaved the first shovel of coal into the boiler. Fiery teeth gnashed the fuel. Her back turned, the Smith rubbed his cheek where Rosalina's lips landed, hoping to trap her lingering heat.

The machine groaned.

"More!" The Smith mimed shoveling coal. Rosalina scooped a mountain of briquettes—eyes clenched and arms trembling with strain—and heaved toward the furnace. A surge of raw power rewarded her effort. Pistons driving, the towers moaned steam. Lubricating oil squished obscenely, accumulating at each tower's base.

Satisfied all was within operating parameters, the Smith again mimed Rosalina to feed the boiler. The coal drove the machine to frenzy. Pistons pumped violent lust, hungry for more. The towers quivered, copper screaming against steel. The workshop floor shuddered under the machine's primal force. Vials and test tubes clinked a ghostly dirge. Rosalina clenched her eyes, certain the vicious coupling would kill everything.

But the machine quieted to a low hum. Equilibrium achieved, the earthquake shivers lessened. A laden hush fell. The hum matured into a buzz, and Rosalina felt the hairs on her arms stand on end. She turned to the Smith, saw him grinning at the southeast tower.

Pearlescent electricity squirted like heavy water, morphing through the blackness. The Smith, one final time, thrust his fists forward and tossed them left. One last shovel of fuel.

Rosalina tossed in the last of the fuel and slammed the boiler door. Ropes of glistening light shot from the towers, weaving over the machine. Rosalina raised a gloved hand and watched as electricity ran over her fingers and down her hand.

Then came an encore to the show she'd witnessed two weeks prior; the ropes and globules congealed to steady streams of blue fire, arching from towers to the central heart. This spectacle, now that Rosalina understood the machinations, resembled a dance. Electric arcs fed by the grunting towers grew in stature and quickened their steps until, at center, illuminated by an oceanic glow, the heart partnered in their dance.

The shimmy was life itself. Rosalina looked to the Smith. His rounded shoulders bobbed, arms and legs slack, utter relief softening his face.

His joy, however, soon died. The scene continued as it had before; the electric dragons grew bored of their restraints and fled. The Smith rushed to the machine's heart and began finessing the control knob, but the dragons refused their orders, eager to explore the shop.

Rosalina put her palm to the emergency stop, awaiting an order she knew wouldn't come. The Smith's face slackened in defeat as raw electricity exploded vials. He watched his heart twitch a St. Vitus' Dance beyond his control. Entropy advanced, great snakes of blue lighting pillaging the shop. Sparks tumbled from the heart itself, attacking the Smith. He offered no resistance. He only fell to his knees, hands cradling the violent heart in its crystal shell.

Rosalina would take no more. With hell closing in, she slammed the copper emergency stop with all her might.

VI

The Smith fell to despair. He existed only in dark recesses of the shop, staring at nothing, eyes unfocused. His reverie plunged deep, his isolation colder than Rosalina thought possible.

The machine became proxy in her desire to nurse the Smith. Rosalina checked every inch of copper, steel and crystal and repaired all trauma. She swept away the ash and dust. Only minor burns remained as badges to this second failure. The Smith, meanwhile, seemed a statue, eating and relieving himself only once exhaustion had pulled Rosalina to sleep.

Six days on, Rosalina's patience broke. The last traces of day glowing through the workshop, she put a gentle hand to the Smith's shoulder. His cold demeanor seemed to manifest physically—chilling her fingertips.

"Cheer up." She put her lips to his ear. "Esta es temporary."

"Don't," he growled.

Rosalina disobeyed, massaging his shoulders and back, her hands sliding lower with each pass, eventually finding his chest. His muscles softened under her hands. She lingered, playing gentle notes over ringlets of hair.

"I can take your mind from here." She nuzzled his neck.

"Please—"

Rosalina squelched his protestations and swung onto his lap. Eager hands yearned down his torso, ripping buttons from his shirt, her lips exploring the topography of his clavicle. With a playful tug the tails of his shirt pulled free and fell to the floor. He sat barechested and bowbacked, Rosalina astride him.

"Please." His nasal, desperate plea did nothing. Rosalina's kisses traveled south, trekking his mountains and valleys.

Then, in a burst of animal sexuality, heat flowing from her in great rolling waves, Rosalina clawed his belt, tearing the sliver buckle from leather.

"Now comes the real fun, gringo." Her fingers dove under his pants into tufts of pubic hair.

But he did not react—could not react. He sat petrified on the stool, face to the sky. His skin would not warm under passion's flame. Like so many other times in his life, days and years gone, the Smith wished with all his might that he could just die. He scorned himself for even thinking it—hope was a bankrupt enterprise.

Rosalina, eyes alight, apple cheeked and lips flush with anticipation of kisses yet to land, reached down and felt the Blacksmith, flaccid. Cold. Her playful smile fizzled with the sunset. She recoiled as if bitten, limp member peeking from his fly.

"You a fairy? You like boys?" She cut the Smith with a cutlass gaze.

"No," he said, "No … it's—"

"Porque soy una monstrua."

He moved in to grasp her, smother her fires of self-loathing. She welcomed his embrace with a flurry of body blows—open palms and knuckles to his cold heart.

"You're not the monster, Rosalina. I am."

She broke into sobs on his shoulder.

"I'm the monster," he repeated.

They stood in the advancing shadows, her body rocking against his, the Smith attempting to soothe her false inadequacies with soft words and softer caresses. Rosalina looked up to him, red eyes trying to read his face. A million questions flew through her mind—inquisitions, accusations, expeditions to the core of this man, but all she could ask was "Porque?"

His answer was simple and profound. "Porque." He took her hand in his, and stepping back, placed her palm over his heart.

The infinite questions received answers; why he rarely ate, why she spied him awake at all hours of the night, his vast knowledge and why he'd put so much of himself into that damned hulking contraption.

The Blacksmith had no heartbeat.

"It stopped beating two thousand years ago," he said, barely a whisper.

Rosalina's mind raced with horror stories whispered around dying fires in the slave quarters. Their macabre words bubbled to her lips.

"¿You …" she stammered, "¿Vampiro?"

The Smith released Rosalina's hand. It stayed fixed to his chest, probing for some hint of life.

"Vampire?" The Smith looked to the ceiling. "Vampire—yes. It's been some time since anyone has used that term … But yes, they used to call me 'vampire.'"

Rosalina cupped her hands around her neck.

"¿Quieres mi sangre, no?"

The Smith pried Rosalina's trembling hands from their protector positions.

"The stories are exaggerated. I did experiment drinking human blood, but never from living necks." His fingers played down from Rosalina's hands. "Wrists are much easier to drain—less splatter."

His ill-advised attempt at humor only fanned Rosalina's fear. Feverish shivers wracked her body, her gaze elusive.

"I'm not alive but I can't die." he swept errant coils of hair from Rosalina's face. She flinched but dared not move. "I am every monster history has ever imagined, impotent in every way."

Her terror a poison, the Smith broke from Rosalina toward his machine. He stroked the crystal box, gazing at the dead heart inside. It shimmered like a carefully wrought gemstone, beautiful but without intrinsic value.

"Years ago I discovered lightning could make cobbled corpses walk again. So this collection of magnetized ore and locomotive parts is my attempt to create and harness life. I hope to revivify my shriveled heart so I may finally die in peace."

Rosalina shook, crumpled onto the floor, trying to reconcile reality with the man-shaped monster before her. She steeled herself, pushed the panic down so she could again speak.

"How?"

"Like so many of the events in my half-existence," the Smith spoke in a voice as distant as his origins, "my genesis is more myth than history. The truth is I can no longer remember. Myth says I was, at the dawn of human civilization, a rake and a thief—condemned for coveting that which was not my own. In my final moments, I asked another, one much greater, to save me my fate. I expired and was laid to tomb, only to wake in the blackness, neither alive nor dead.

"Had I known the curse for which I begged, I would have gladly died for my crimes.

"I spent generations debauching, reveling in excess, devil-may-care to the consequences. But each passing year brought diminishing joy, fading happiness. All things human and good evaporated, leaving me an empty shell, a zombie cursed to roam the earth.

"I turned my energies to death, spent centuries spreading famine, plagues, pestilence—secreting help to those who joyed in sorrow and pain. I led holy conquests. I built the gears of war and oiled them with the blood of the innocent. Always in the hope—silly hope—

that the next wave of death would carry me with it. I sparked revolutions, kindled wars, burned homelands until all was ashes and death.

"In my máquinaciones, I found the greatest tools of death were not powder and steel, not blades or pandemic illness, but the hands of man. Ensconced in the European mountains, I set about the task of creating the ultimate weapon—human life.

"Needless to say—undoubtedly you've heard the gothic tales— I succeeded. Made a pariah, I fled here, following stories of rocks which draw electricity from metal. Hoping to spark life in my own bosom, I manufactured this ... this monstrosity."

He turned from the limp heart. Rosalina sat cross-legged on the floor, staring at him like an attentive schoolchild before the lecturing head master.

"My machine has twice proven a failure. Electricity alone cannot endow life. I failed to realize that even cobbled corpses contain ... for lack of a better term ... the vitreous humor of soul—the essence of life, a substance foreign to this mass of steel and magnets."

His words melted the doubt frosting Rosalina's bosom. She pushed from the floor and strode to him. With memories of sunlight dancing over her skin, Rosalina took his cold hand.

"If you are cobbled from myths, perhaps a myth is your answer."

The Smith looked to her—eyes brimming with curiosity and surprise—and gave an almost imperceptible nod.

"Travelling monks tell tales of a spring at the heart of a volcano." Rosalina spoke in low musical tones. "Legend says one of their number, wandering the southern ridges of the Sangre de Cristo Mountains, fell to ambush by a warrior tribe. They gave chase, arrows flying. This monk's escape brought him to the lip of a volcano. There, an arrow hit true and sent him tumbling into the mountain's bowels. Figuring the interloper dead, the natives quit their chase and offered prayers of sacrifice to their god.

"Badly wounded and expiring of thirst, the holy man prayed to his Savior. He swooned, and in his dream he saw a vision of the Savior weeping over a lame lamb. The monk awoke to find a fountain of purest holy water at his feet. He bathed and his wounds were healed—he drank and was thirsty no more. He emerged from the mountain with new life."

The Smith did not respond. Countless times he'd tried to quit the vice of hope. Against the warnings in his head, infected by Rosalina's inexhaustible vigor, the Smith nodded.

"Yes." The word was a magical incantation, transubstantiating the Smith into pure hope. "Yes." He felt centuries of weight being lifted from his body with each repetition until he felt he would quit the dreary Earth forever. "Yes," he whispered, "yes."

VII

Claire huffed, uneasy hooves dancing in place over the dark earth. The cloud-mottled night camouflaged all but the white lozenge on her muzzle and the glint of her queer metal boots. She moved in uneasy bursts, apprehensive of the steel grafted to her legs.

The Smith sat bareback. One hand on her neck, he made a final once over of the machinery strapped to Claire's flank. The cylindrical water tanks were full, the metal box over her tail secure—waiting. Most important, two thick glass bottles—carefully wrapped and wrapped again—lay nestled in the luggage pack behind his seat. His rifle, scope extended and ready, lay across Claire's neck.

"So I follow the mountains south?" He asked the dark.

"Sí," the dark answered. "Take the east fork when the ridge splits in two. The volcano is at the southern end of that ridge, north and east of Santa Fe."

"Claire and I will return no later than sundown tomorrow. It would be in your best interest to stay in the shop until then. There's food and water in the cabinets."

"¿Mañana?" the shadow retorted. "Gringo, it's a day and a half just to get there."

"You don't worry about that." Mischief put a smile on the Smith's face. "I work in horseshoes the same I do hearts, señorita."

He spurred Claire, shooting horse and rider into the unfathomable dark. Steam hissed from Claire's horseshoes with each step, shooting them into the southern wilds like a bullet from a rifle. As the city melted into earth behind him, the Smith heard a valediction whispered from the dark:

"Adíos."

Claire's satisfied breaths fell into the rhythm of hissing steam and drumming earth, and the darkness swallowed them whole. Without landmarks to measure time, it seemed horse and rider floated through a vast black nothing. Regrets and fears materialized from the black and orbited his aching head, night's aether a superconductor for the old scars.

He had vowed long ago to quit hope. Hope was a child's story, a fairy tale, something he'd long outgrown—a wretched invention, hope, always fungible, never dried up, photosynthesized with the slightest glimmer of sunshine. He most despised the pious hopeful, yet there he was, riding into hope's waiting trap.

A dome of sun soon lazed over the horizon, reluctant to quit dewy sleep. A cone of earth cut through its pink glow. Claire, sensing their proximity, pushed to a sprint. Morning's full bouquet—the sky all hyacinth, rose, and dandelion—found horse and Rider at the volcano's base. The Rider shielded his eyes and surveyed for a route to the top. The steam boots, far too dangerous on fragile volcanic soil, he toggled off.

"Well chica, what do you think?"

Claire toed the mountain's skirt, neck craning to the apex. Having made the appropriate triangulations, she leapt to the volcano's face. The monk's myth proved popular—a few yards up the west face, Claire and the Smith found a trampled footpath. The trail spiraled to the volcano's cone.

Following the feet of countless pilgrims, horse and rider crested the mountain at noon. On their heavenly pedestal, the world seemed a child's toy below. Black earth yawned to his left, a downward path catching glints of noonday gold. Claire pawed the rock, testing its composition and hardness.

"Well, Claire, that's enough sight-seeing. Let's begin the end."

With a pat to her neck, Claire started forward. Her forehoof jerked, hesitant to contact the inner face of the volcano. The Rider, impatient with the prize so close, spurred Claire downward. She lurched into the volcano, front hooves exploding the loam. Desperate for a foothold, Claire bucked, throwing the Rider into the Earth's bowels.

The volcano buffeted the Rider with bone crunching blows as he fell. He flailed his arms, desperate to stall his descent, but the volcano gave no quarter. His falling dream came to crescendo with a sonorous crunch as his skull split like a summer melon. He tasted iron, smelled roasting almonds and his consciousness hemorrhaged blackness.

VIII

He woke to perfect black, roused by the dirge of midnight crickets. The Rider turned his head—burning pain!—and met Claire's unblinking eye. She lay breathless beside him, flies diving like falcons to the blood curdling from her deformed rear knee.

"Oh, chica," he rasped. His body prickled, molten needles darning his tattered flesh.

Pushing to hands and knees, he saw the silver pool ahead. Palms squished wet earth as he crawled forward. He inhaled, smelling only the iron tang of water and dirt. Cupping the liquid in trembling hands, the Rider drank and waited. He pressed a hand to his heart, anticipating.

Nothing.

Fooled again by hope.

"Just dew in a crater." He stroked Claire's muzzle with a dripping hand. "My apologies, girl." The dew sunk into her hide, trickled into her open mouth.

Claire flickered like a firefly, skin slick with luminescence. Her flesh melted to pure electricity, illuminating a shattered skeleton. The Rider shielded his face; Claire burned to rival the noonday sun. Light coursed through her body, eroding the fractures to nothing. With a sucking gasp, Claire whinnied. As if ordered by the horse, the heat and light dissipated, leaving only the cold night.

A horse stood before him, alive and well, both Claire and not Claire. The same white lozenge covered her face, but now her hide was the light brown of coffee with cream.

"Claire?" He stared at the familiar and foreign creature. The horse splashed muddy earth, rebelling against her old name.

"Okay." He searched for a name befitting one stubborn enough to spurn the reaper. "How about ... Rosie?"

The horse turned to profile, presenting mount. Rosie it was.

He reached into the pack strapped to Rosie-née-Claire and found the two glass bottles miraculously intact. He baptized them in the pool and gathered the blessed water.

He held a bottle to the night sky, saw the universe dancing in its waters. Retrieving his rifle from the ground, he strode to Rosie, and careful to pack the bottles in layers of cloth, saddled for the journey home.

IX

The Rider's return to Denver City seemed instantaneous. Excitement and hope shrunk miles to meters. It was as if he traversed a tabletop map: the Sangre de Cristo Volcano and Denver City pinched together by a Titan's fingers. His mind ran the improved experiment; a thousand times he watched aqua vita goad life from his steel heart.

When Denver City broke the horizon near midnight, his stomach dropped. Onyx tendrils of heat rippled into the dark. Buildings stood in silhouette, outlined in a blood-red flicker. The Rider reached back to the box on Rosie's flank and spurred her on. He passed his shop, smoke and fire belching from its open door. Bloodlust echoed from the town square ahead.

A stumbling drunk confirmed the Rider's fear. "The whore is deaaaaaaaaad!" he sloshed an empty bottle of Bourbon, took a slug and kissed the ground.

Without thought, the Rider unlatched the box. Spring-loaded, its metal sides blossomed like a mechanized flower. Two Gatling guns, each the size of a forearm, flipped out and clipped into stays at Rosie's hip. They spun with a sound like rattlesnakes ready to strike, driven by the rods pushing Rosie's gallop. For good measure, his free hand cradled the rifle, ready to damn Denver City to the Hell he knew so well.

The square opened before him, lit by makeshift bonfires, drunks and puritans dancing like Pagans. Their false idol hung from the gallows at center, her head bowed and feet dangling.

Rosalina.

The woman—the one thing connecting him to the living world—was dead. Damn that sheriff. The Rider's last stores of pity evaporated in the searing heat. Teeth gnashed against his tongue, desperate for any feeling at all, the Rider toggled the safety.

The machine roared, spitting death and hellfire without aim. A cloudburst of blood and brain rained from the heavens. Man, woman, or child—the Rider didn't give a damn who crossed his path. The mob's drunken song morphed into panic. Revelers fled for their worthless lives, splashing through rapids of their kinfolks' blood.

He leapt from Rosie at the gallows, rifle in one hand and knife in the other. The horse ran laps around the square, pumping hot lead into those too drunk or stupid to run. Amidst a chorus of moans and blood slick breaths, the Rider stepped to his fallen angel, knife ready.

"Stop." The voice behind him was strengthened by the click-clack of a shotgun cocked. "I knew you were hiding that filthy whore. Your noose is nex—"

The Rider spun and gagged the sheriff with three rifle hits. His torn jugular a fountain, his shit-for-brains exploded out the back of his skull, and a poppy blooming over his heart, the law staggered back. He opened his mouth to speak, but his dying words drowned in a sea of blood and bile. Another shot blew off what was left of his head, and the sheriff folded over his knees and fell.

With the workman attitude of one driving railroad spikes, the Smith strode to the corpse and fired. The Smith shot his breech empty, reloaded, shot empty, reloaded, and shot empty again. The Sheriff's blood ran dry, his body perforated and torn like used paper. Ammunition exhausted, the Smith threw his gun and ran to his dangling compañera.

He sawed the rope until Rosalina's weight fell to his cradled arms. Her body against his, the Smith leapt from the gallows, and a bottle of liquid pulled from his horse's flank, sprinted from the square.

Will-'o-the-wisp fires roamed his shop, seeking mischief in dark corners. Kicking dust and ash, the Smith carried Rosalina to the waiting machine. He swept away the false heart and lay his idol in its place. The Smith plunged a filament through Rosalina's breast, giving electricity a direct line to her heart.

"For hope." Pulling cork from vial with his teeth, he dribbled the liquid over her bosom and into her mouth, swilling the dregs. The push of a button fired the boiler, and shovels of coal stoked it to fury.

Machine roaring, the Smith ran to his sideboard and impaled himself with a second filament. He lay next to his love, watching electricity twist down the filaments like ivy down a signpost. Each spark pulled him piano wire tight. He burned from inside out, his guts a desert. Blackness closing around him, he turned for one final glimpse of Rosalina. In the flash before total black, the Smith saw her glowing heart, its beat strong and steady.

Part Three: History & Myth

1913

I

The two-story house sat centered in his rifle scope. A white-washed picket fence guarded its verdant yard from the surrounding plain. He swung his scope left and saw three horses in an adjacent corral. The one colored like coffee with cream turned its white-lozenge face to the scope and whinnied.

Farther, maybe a mile past the house, stood a gnarled Joshua Tree, its tarantula shadow long in the setting sun. From a low branch swung a lifeless form. Little more than a smudge in his sights, the Rider snorted to see the greasy bandito's Karma paid out.

He lowered the rifle and approached, watching three girls bounce through the yard. Sweat and dirt splotched their chestnut skin, their white dresses matted with play.

Grandchildren, he thought.

His approach pulsed a wave of excitement through their game. Like magnets to iron they crowded the front gate, waiting in silent expectation. Damn if their chocolate eyes didn't look familiar.

With a forced smile slashing his skin, he pulled the small string-bound book from his back pocket. "I'm looking for the author of this story. Miss de los Santos."

He held a thin collection of parchment pages, folded lengthwise and bound with loops of twine. A flowery border bloomed over the cover curled and yellow with age, title and attribution printed in ornate text:

American Vampire
By Rosa de los Santos

The tallest of the three girls, upon seeing the tract, turned to the farmhouse behind. "¡Mama! Un visitor! ¡Tiene tu novella!"

The door swung open, dark save a ruby ember and feathers of smoke

"¿Que quiera, visitor?" Her voice had changed, gravelly with a patina of age, but the notes were unmistakable.

The Visitor crossed the threshold into the yard, scattering the girls back to their game. He held the book, his history, in outstretched hands. "I have something I'd like you to sign."

"Let me see." She strode from the darkness and took the tract. The Visitor gasped. Sixty years had only managed to age her twenty. The thin lines in her face only highlighted her beauty, traced her laugh, pointed to her chocolate eyes. As she turned the pages in her hands, the Visitor saw the hangman's necklace scarring her jaw line.

"You've torn the last chapter from my book." She spoke without looking to him, voice steady. "You've redacted poor, stupid Rosalina waking alone—hunted like a dog for more than a decade for a massacre she had no part in. You've torn out the epilogue where she outlives her children, her grandchildren. She ends up a filthy monster in the end, just like that bastard Blacksmith."

The Visitor took her shaking hands, put them over his still heart. "Rosalina." He dared touch her chest. Her rebellious heartbeat made him shiver. "Rosalina—"

"No." She stepped back, disengaging the Visitor's icy grip. "Anymore, Rosalina is just a character in a book."

The woman produced a pencil from the folds of her wrap and scribbled the book's cover. She finished with a flourish and threw it back to her Visitor.

For the briefest of moments, made even smaller by his unending life, their eyes met. "Rosalina," he said.

Her gaze hardened, jaw clenched with inexhaustible anger. She stepped back into the shade of her home and slammed the door, her final word terse and stinging.

"Adíos."

The Visitor looked down to the salutation penciled on his tract: "History and Myth are the same tale, told differently—Rosa."

The girls, witness to the scene, could no longer dam their questions. Inquisitive voices sung in chorus, the jumble of *quieras* and *mamas* forming an incomprehensible and beautiful round.

The Rider put his fingers to his lips and whistled. His horse— the only true Rosie now—jumped the corral fence and ran to his side.

With a tip of his hat he mounted the horse. He flung the book into Rosie's saddle pack. Its pages curled around a small vial of luminescent water. He turned Rosie east, toward the spilled ink of night, and without taking pause to look back, spurred her on. The Rider galloped toward the blackness, ready to pen another chapter in his miserable and infinite fiction.

LASATER'S LUCKY LEFT

Quincy J. Allen

With an annoyed scowl setting the exposed part of his face into deep lines, Jake Lasater slowly returned his hot Colts to the holsters at each hip and waited for the thick white veil of smoke to clear. He let out a long, resigned sigh and winced as he rubbed the shallow gash in his right sleeve and bicep. That's when he noticed the black shuriken sticking out of his left arm just above the elbow. He pulled the irritating little weapon out with a jerk, dropped it on the ground and realized that the fingers of his right glove were now sticky. Holding his fingers up to his good eye, he saw a yellow residue, like honey or pinesap. It coated the dark leather in a jagged pattern that matched the shuriken points. He gave his fingers a sniff and regretted his curiosity straightaway, turning his head with a jerk. The stuff smelled like a cross between snake oil and horse piss fermented in a cheese cellar too long.

"Tricky Tong bastards," he muttered with a sour, southern Missouri drawl. He aimed his curse like a pistol at the four, silk-clad bodies lying in the muddy alley between him and the bright daylight of Sacramento Street. He'd seen men in the street go running when the shooting started, but they were already starting to walk by as if nothing happened. Chinatown was a rough place where people minded their own. On top of that, everyone knew that the San Fran Marshals would take their own sweet time to check things out in that part of town—if they came at all.

Lasater kneeled and wiped his fingers on the crimson shirt of the dead gambler who'd started the whole thing, trying to remove the sticky resin. "And here I thought we were friends, Po," Lasater said to the corpse as he rolled it over and looked down into a still, muddy face. All four bodies were clad in red silk, which meant they were part of the Tong. "And you have your boys try to poison me?" Annoyed disbelief filled Lasater's voice. "San Francisco is not at all what I expected."

Lasater reached beyond Po's body and picked up his short top hat from where it had fallen during the fight. Miraculously, it had landed on the one dry spot for twenty feet in both directions along the alley. With a muted whine of clockwork gears from his legs, Lasater stood, brushed the dust off the brim of his hat and adjusted the silver and turquoise hatband so it was straight once again. "You're lucky you didn't muss up my hat, Po, or I'd have to kill you again, damn it."

Lasater gave an irritated shake of his head and pressed the top hat back into place. As it settled over his wavy dark hair, a relieved smile broke up the irritated scowl. He'd had the hat made special back in Kansas City only eight months ago. The inside of the brim had a small inner notch so that it fit snugly around both his head and the skin-tight leather strap that held his left ocular in place. The intricately hinged, brass-set lens was as dark as pitch and blocked out most of the light. The whole thing was set into a steel plate that covered a quarter of his face from cheek to forehead, and the steel had been riveted to the leather band that wrapped around his head and tied at the back. He'd worn the thing since he was discharged from the Union Army back in '64.

Amputations were common in the Civil War, and like so many others, Lasater had left a fair amount of flesh, bone, and blood in that hot Army tent after a Reb canon did its job on him. When the bandages had finally come off his face, the Army docs discovered that, along with everything else, the canon round had made his left eye permanently dilated. Even low light hurt him, but Tinker Farris, at the expense of Lasater's inheritance, had fixed him up pretty well in all quarters. Lasater was actually more of a man now than when he started. He took his discharge and what little money he got for the amputations and headed West to find his fortune and forget about other people's wars.

Kansas City, Scottsbluff, Santa Fe, Denver, Fort Hall—he'd gambled his way across the territories and done pretty well moving from one saloon to the next, one poker game to the next. He'd tricked, bribed, and shot his way out of or through a number of fiascos along the way and never once landed in jail, but the Central Pacific line pretty much ended in San Francisco, so here's where he ended up. Unfortunately, the four bodies in front of him now meant that this latest fiasco was just getting started. It also meant he'd have to leave San Fran in a hurry when all was said and done. He had mixed feelings about that. He'd been there only a couple of weeks and even made friends with Hang, Po and a few other members of the Tong. He didn't ask about their business, and they didn't meddle with his. It was all poker between friends. Right up until he walked away with all those winnings.

It had actually been five men who had come up behind him and "urged" him into the alley at the point of a dagger in his back. The fifth, the one with the big scar running down his cheek, neck, and under his collar, had run off with the bag of winnings Lasater dropped in the mud to distract the thieves. That's how he got the drop on them. When their eyes followed the bag, his Colts sailed free and sang their song. He'd accumulated the bag's contents in a particularly long and lucrative poker-game over at Hang Ah's saloon around the corner, and eight hundred dollars in paper and coin plus a fair amount of gold dust was not something he planned to just leave behind. He only had a few coins in his pocket, so the bag was pretty much his whole stake.

Lasater walked out of the alley, his black boots squishing through the mud, and stepped into the bright, morning sunshine of Sacramento Street. Hang Ah's was just a block up and across the thoroughfare. Scar's muddy footprints made a beeline straight for it, so he made a path of his own, following in the footsteps of the Chinese thief and reloading his Colts as he went.

It was still early morning and between mining shifts, so Lasater barely had to weave his way between the migrant residents of Chinatown to get to Hang Ah's. A rainbow of brightly colored silk and patches of drab cotton walked up and down the street, with every man sporting a long, black queue either down his back or wrapped around his neck. He didn't see a single woman amidst the workers. Lasater, at six-foot, could see easily over the pointed hats and silk caps that covered most every other head. A white man in Chinatown was an uncommon enough sight, and with his left ocular looking ominous and his dual shooters looking even more so, the path in front of him seemed to open up all by itself. That is, until one of those new-fangled mining rigs stepped out onto the street from the gaping warehouse doorway of Qi's Emporium of Wondrous Power.

Its power plant grumbling, the machine was at least twelve feet tall, and its brass and steel carapace glinted in the morning sunlight, looking all the world like a Chinese god of war. Riveted plates housed a steam-driven powerhouse that drove four, multi-jointed legs *hiss-stomping* out into the street. Its massive, four-toed feet squished and sucked through the mud, and the joints clicked and clanged in an unlikely rhythm as it turned towards Lasater and began walking forward. It had two partially retracted arms attached at the shoulders, and its elbows bent around massively hinged joints. Glinting brass hydraulic pistons gave the limbs life, pushing and pulling as the thing moved, and at the end of each arm were great, clam-shaped scoops that could close and contain at least a cubic yard each.

Lasater recognized it as one of Miss Qi's diggers. Qi was the only tinker in Chinatown and also the only woman he'd seen treated as an equal by the men there. The diminutive little woman, dressed in bright blue coveralls, was folded up into a cockpit at the belly of the great beast, enclosed in a brass cage. Her long dark ponytail flipped and flopped behind her as the thing clunked down the street, and her dark goggles hid jade eyes and most of what Lasater considered a truly beautiful face. Her co-pilot was perched in a similar cage atop the thing, and his job was to operate the great arms during work.

Lasater stepped aside as the machine walked by, tipping his hat to the woman. She smiled and nodded her head towards him, a magnificent smile shining from within the cage. Lasater's heart ached for the memory of that smile. He'd spent an evening playing cards with Qi—she was a hell of a card-player—the previous week, an evening that ended with Lasater waking in her bed. It was a night he would never forget, but they'd both agreed that no future was possible. She was committed to her work, and he was the consummate rolling stone. Lasater watched the digger make its way down the street, a wistful smile upon his face, and then turned back to the task at hand as Qi turned her machine around the far corner.

He strode the last twenty yards through the mud, stepped up to the doorway of Hang's and pushed in the red, swinging doors. As the doors swung closed behind him, he looked around the saloon for any clue as to where Scar went. Aside from the bright red and green paint here and there, plus a few gold dragons decorating the corners, it looked like most saloons he'd been in. Although the room didn't get quiet, the chatter that he'd heard from the other side of the doors dropped down a bit as sidelong glances from the men inside identified him. He spotted a few elbows make their way into other men's ribs and saw a few hand-covered whispers, but he had no idea what was said. For mid-morning, the place looked as full as a white man's saloon on a busy Friday night. Chinatown was funny that way. The mostly male population was crammed in like dynamite in a crate, and they worked in endless shifts, so there was a non-stop cycle of workers coming in and out of damn near every building.

There were still three mahjong games going on that had started the night before. The only other cowboy in the saloon was at one of them. He was a black man, his ebony skin standing out amongst the lighter skin of the Chinese, but he had wavy, shoulder-length hair and piercing, tan eyes, which told Lasater he was mulatto in some way. His clothes, what Lasater could see of them, were tidy—not new but well kept—with a blue button-down, a gray on black paisley vest and a black handkerchief tied around his neck. His dark hat dangled to the side of his chair, and Lasater thought it might be a Union cavalry hat, which meant they'd both chewed some of the same dirt back in the war, and the cowboy was probably a Buffalo. The tan of a heavy, weatherworn duster draped over the back of the chair peeked out from behind him when he leaned forward to flip a tile. Lasater didn't recognize the cowboy, but when those tan eyes looked up, the two cowboys exchanged knowing nods and smiles that can only be understood between those in a minority amongst the majority—cowboys and Chinese respectively in this case.

Groups of Chinese men flowed over the inside of the saloon, with the drinkers wearing smiles and the opium smokers looking sleepy. Lasater spotted Hang standing behind the bar in black silk. The small Chinese man with streaks of gray in hair and beard glanced at him and then turned his eyes quickly to the glass he was cleaning.

A guilty look flickered across the saloonkeeper's moon of a face, and the short proprietor pretended not to notice Lasater by turning away from the front door. Lasater crossed the room in big strides, stepped up to the bar, reached out a black glove and firmly turned Hang towards him. Hang flowed with the motion and then threw up an innocent smile.

Hang spoke brightly through a thick, Chinese accent. "Mister Jake! How good it is—"

"Hang, let me set the tone for ya ..." Lasater interrupted, cutting Hang's pleasantries off with steely fatigue. Hang's eyes widened just a shade, and he clamped his mouth shut. Lasater plucked the glass out of Hang's hand, set it on the bar and grabbed a bottle of whisky. "I've been up for eighteen hours straight." He poured a healthy shot into the glass. "I'm tired, sore and bleeding." With a jerk, Lasater threw back the shot and set the empty glass back on the bar. "It seems as if Po, *your* friend and mine, was a sore loser."

"Mister Jake," Hang blurted, "you don't think that I—"

"I don't know what to think here, Hang. But let me tell you what I do know. A man in red pajamas just come running in here with a big bag in his hands. *My* bag."

"I don't know what you're—" Hang blurted, but his face spoke volumes.

"You have a shitty poker-face, Hang, and the guy's muddy footprints lead right up to your front door." Embarrassment filled the round face. "Hang, you still owe me thirty-five dollars from that card game last week. Thought I was too drunk to remember, did ya? I like to keep a few outstanding debts around town to call in for rainy days." Lasater leaned in a few inches to make his point. "And it seems as if it's raining, now don't it?" Hang's eyes shifted nervously between Lasater's good eye and the black lens wrapped in brass of his left. "I'd be willing to forgive the debt if you let me know where that fella went ... you know, the one with the scar from here to here?" Lasater traced a line from above his right eye down to his collar with a black-gloved finger. He stared at Hang with his one good eye and narrowed it down to a sliver. "Or ..." he placed his hands on the Colts at his hips and then opened them, suggesting the alternative of loud and bloody conversation instead of the polite kind. "I'd much rather have this conversation without heating up my

Colts, if you catch my meaning. Now where did he go?" Lasater wasn't the kind of man to shoot people in cold blood, but Hang didn't know that for certain, and the mahogany-gripped Colts were worn enough to tell a tale of crowded cemeteries.

Lasater was one hell of a card player, and he could see calculating going on behind Hang's wide eyes. The saloonkeeper was probably trying figuring out who was more dangerous, Lasater or Scar, but Lasater picked up something else working in Hang's eyes ... It looked like scheming.

Lasater watched the worry slowly evaporate off Hang's face, replaced with something resembling resolve and perhaps a little venom mixed in for good measure. The salooner motioned with his head, the dark braid hanging down the middle of his chest doing a little dance over the black silk. Hang spoke slowly. "Through that door." Lasater turned to see a red door under the stairs at the back of the saloon. He knew the stairs led up to the singsong girls above, but he had no idea what was behind the red door. During the poker game he'd seen a number of red-clad fellas coming and going through it, which meant that the Tong was probably down there in numbers. "Go down two flights. At the bottom, go through the black door, down the long hallway and through another door. You will probably find him there."

Lasater turned back to Hang with a calculating eye. "That's a short road, Hang. Rest assured, I'll be able to find my way back if it turns out he's not there ... or someone else is. I'll see you soon." Lasater walked off without another word, made his way to the door, opened it and stepped inside.

Hang pulled a red rope hidden behind the bar, which disappeared through a hole in the floor, tugging it with three short pulls, two long and a short one. "Perhaps," Hang said under his breath with vicious intent as he watched the red door close on Mister Jake Lasater.

The spiral of worn wooden stairs creaked under Lasater's boots, and he made his way down them as quietly as he could. The faint, warm light of an oil-lamp shone up from the bottom of the stairwell. One rotation of the spiral presented him with a dark hallway that stretched back underneath Hang's saloon. Lasater could smell the opium and hear the occasional giggle or moan coming at him from the dimly lit hallway of red curtains that faded away from him through the thick smoke. Another rotation brought him to the bottom and a black door. Lasater put his left hand on a Colt, the other on the doorknob, and opened the door slowly.

The hallway beyond was well lit with a lamp set on either side, each lamp set between a pair of doors along both walls. He picked up a scent of jasmine incense and old blood. Jasmine was something he'd never smelled before coming to San Francisco, but soldiers who lost limbs in Army tents never forgot the smell of old blood dried on wood and canvas. Lasater walked down the hallway and tested each door, finding every one locked. There was a door at the far end of the hall with a small iron bracket on each side bolted into the doorframe. There was no mistaking that the door could be barred from this side, but there wasn't a plank lying around to drop into the brackets. Pulling the hammer back on the Colt, Lasater took a deep breath and twisted the doorknob, pulling the door open slowly and looking in with his good eye. He didn't know what he was expecting to see, but the room beyond wasn't anything he would have thought up, even in a bad dream.

The swinging door carried with it an even stronger smell of dried blood, and he could see lines, splatters and splotches of deep brown on the pine floor and walls beyond. The room had eight walls, about eight feet high and fifteen on a side, and in the middle of each was a lantern with a big, hinged lid. Under each lantern was a door just like the one he'd opened. Here and there the smooth pine walls were dotted with the splintered wounds of what could only be bullet holes. Lasater could see a railing going around what was clearly a fighting arena, and from the looks of it, these boys played for keeps. He didn't see anyone on the upper level, but Scar was on the far side of the pit wearing black silk instead of red, and he held a slim sword in each hand. Courage and rage filled Scar's face, and the flush of blood set off the pale line running down his cheek, looking like a white bolt of lightning in the flickering light.

Scar slowly moved into a fighting stance, his body twisted to the side, one sword held high the other low, both points aiming directly at Lasater's heart. The bag was just behind Scar, lying on the floor, and all Lasater could do was look Scar in the eyes and sigh. He took a look at the half-inch planks of the door and doorframe and shook his head as he stepped into the room.

Clearly Lasater wasn't the first gun-fighter to end up in that arena. "Y'all must think I got sawdust for brains," Lasater concluded, chewing off each word like it was gristle. Stepping further into the arena, he slowly closed the door behind him with a mean smile on his face. The Colt rose up and out like it was on rails, the silver runes along the barrel glinting in the lamplight and the barrel now making a straight line between Lasater's good eye and Scar's head. Scar's eyes got wide with a healthy mix of fear and hatred. "Seems I'm gonna hafta' make a point, Scar." He slowly lowered the hammer, dropped the pistol to his side and slid the Colt back into its holster.

The sound of a wooden board sliding into the brackets on the other side of the door sprouted a smile as wicked as a demon's across Scar's face, putting another kink in the white line running down his cheek. Lasater talked over his shoulder, never taking his eyes off Scar. "Don't go far, you hear me, boys? I'll be with you in a minute." The gleeful laughter of two men splashed through the wood from behind the door.

Lasater raised his hand and rotated the outer lens of his ocular. The eyepiece was actually made up of two lenses, both nearly clear by themselves but polarized. When they were cross-wise to each other, they looked black and kept out virtually all light, but when they lined up just right, they allowed light to go through normally. As the outer lens clicked into place, Scar could see Lasater's closed eye and the pink ripple of burned scar tissue around the eye-socket. "Fair warning, Scar," Lasater said slowly. "You push that bag to the middle of the floor and step away; you just might live through this. If not ... well, I might just have a surprise or two for ya." The grin never left Scar's face.

"SHU KAI!" Scar shouted. There was a metallic clank from the eight lanterns on the walls as the shrouds dropped down and the light disappeared. Black folded in on both men, and Lasater never heard Scar dodge left and start silently snaking his way across the arena. Most men would have drawn their pistols in the darkness and shot into the inky black hoping to get lucky.

All Lasater did was open his left eye.

His right eye was vainly trying to adjust, but his left, fully dilated open, used what little light was coming from under the door behind him. Lasater was a statue, a monolith in the darkness. He watched and waited as Scar zagged his way like a cobra. The swords rose into the air as he approached. Lasater had to admit, the man never made a sound. He was quiet right up until Lasater pulled a Colt and filled the room with a dull clap of thunder and one bolt of lightning. The slug caught Scar dead center in his chest, and he went back like a rag-doll, hitting the boards with a loud, staccato thud. The swords took a few bounces before coming to a clattering rest well outside of Scar's reach.

Lasater stepped up to the downed man who was making harsh, sickly-wet choking sounds as his lungs filled with blood. Even to the last, Scar fought for life, but it wasn't enough. As Lasater stepped over him, Scar made one last gurgling cough and then a death rattle left him still and silent. The Colt slid home once again.

"I warned you," Lasater reminded the corpse without looking at it. His boots thudded across the wooden floorboards as he made his way to the money. He grabbed it, tied the pull-strings around his gun-belt and went back to the door he'd come in through, this time moving almost as silently as Scar had. Lasater stood to the side of the door, out of the line of any fire that might come through it, and placed his left hand on the door. The knob twisted easy enough, but the door didn't open. It moved a fraction of an inch and came up to the bar that had been dropped in place. Lasater was finally pissed off and finished with warnings. He stepped in front of the door and flexed his legs, just barely hearing the gears of Tinker Farris' handiwork do what he told them. His clockwork legs were several times stronger than the real thing had been, and Farris was, after all, a complete genius. Lasater pulled both Colts out, stepped back and then gave a mighty kick at the barrier before him.

Wood splintered and steel brackets tore free from their housing. As the door few open, the man standing just on the other side went flying. So did the sawed-off shotgun he'd been holding. The second man watched his buddy sail by and reached for a pistol, but Lasater's Colts shouted at him twice, and he spun into a wall, dropping to the floor in a lifeless heap. Lasater didn't even wait for the other to reach for the shotgun. Two more shots rang out, and the man stayed on the floor.

Lasater took a minute to reload each pistol, watching the hallway in front and listening for anything from the room behind. When both pistols were ready, he marched back down the hallway through the door and up the stairs. As he passed the opium hallway, he heard nothing and, guns leveled, was careful to step past it quickly.

Lasater's Colts came first through the red door at the top of the stairs, and there wasn't a single set of eyes in the saloon not watching him. Everyone was Chinese. Most eyes were filled with surprise, some with awe. Hang's were filled with rage, and Lasater's Colts never shifted away from the saloonkeeper's head. The only sound in the room was Lasater's boots walking up to Hang. He holstered one Colt and left the other one cocked and pointed at Hang's face.

With eyes as cold as an undertakers, Lasater reached into his pocket, pulled out a twenty-dollar coin and threw it at the Chinese salooner who caught it with a fast-moving hand. "That's for the mess I left below. Just so you know, I'm leaving San Francisco, and I ain't never coming back. I'll be on the next train for San Jose and parts east. This better be the last time I see you, Hang. If it ain't, I'll be throwing lead at you instead of gold. You understand me?"

Hang's face was frozen with a glare that told Lasater everything he needed to know. He backed out of the bar, backed down the front steps and then made his way down Sacramento Street amidst the throng of Chinese workers who were going to and from their shift changes. Lasater wove his way through the men as quickly as he could. Just as he reached the end of Sacramento Street, he ran smack-dab into Miss Qi.

Her goggles were perched on her forehead, and her ponytail draped over her shoulder, making an ebony cascade down her left breast. The image brought Lasater back to their night together, only then there weren't blue coveralls between him and her pale skin. She looked at him with those pools of jade that many a man had lost his heart in, and he smiled, taken once again by the beauty.

Lasater pulled his hat off, wrapped his arms around her and kissed her—a long, passionate kiss that got her arms around him and even got her left foot up in the air behind her. The kiss was long enough to make every man for ten yards stop and stare. Whispers filled the street. Finally, slowly, regretfully, Lasater released her.

"You are the sweetest little lady I've ever tasted." She smiled, knowing what was coming. "I'm off, Miss Qi. It's not too likely I'll be back San Fran way, but I wanted to tell you that I'll never forget you, and I'll take that last kiss there to the grave. I can die happy now." He gave her a wink with his good eye, and she placed a hand delicately upon his bearded cheek.

"Nobody knows the future," she said in a smooth Chinese accent. Then she winked back and stepped past him, walking briskly to her shop. Neither of them looked back at the other.

Lasater made a beeline for the train station, keeping an eye over his shoulder to see if any red pajamas were following him. He never saw a pair. He had to wait three edgy hours at a saloon next to the station, waiting for the train to San Jose. The place was full, and plenty of men and women were coming and going. Back to the wall and eyes peeled, he even saw a handful of Chinese men go by. Some of them noticed his hands slide to his Colts, but nervous glances and blank stares were all they gave him. Not one seemed to be interested in him, which was how he hoped it would be till he made it to San Jose.

He figured that if he could just get on a zeppelin he'd be home free, but San Jose was the closest place for that. The big earthquake a couple months earlier brought San Francisco's original landing platform down like so much kindling. Word had it they were taking their sweet time rebuilding it to make it pretty and expand it to be a stop between the U.S. and the Orient. There were ferries to cross the bay, but Lasater wasn't one to cross open water if is life didn't depend on it. His artificial limbs were more anchor than anything else in liquid surroundings, so a short train ride to San Jose and then a zeppelin from there was his best option.

He figured fifty-fifty odds or worse that Hang would come after him. The salooner had lost face, there was no doubt about it, and what little Lasater knew about the Chinese, they didn't take to that sort of thing very well. With a zeppelin between him and Hang, he could put San Francisco behind him forever, and good riddance.

While he waited, several of the barmaids tried to convince him that they could make a tumble upstairs worth his while, and under normal circumstances the money in the bag still tied to his belt would have been burning a hole through his pocket. With each lady prettier than the last, he politely declined, ordered another glass of water and shooed them on their way. He at least had the decency to pay a dollar for every water, which was ridiculous. Whisky was only four-bits, but he wanted them to know he appreciated the attention.

He heard a whistle blow outside and made his way cautiously out of the saloon. The Number 13 chugged its way through the midday sunshine, billows of steam and smoke pouring into the sky. It took twenty minutes for the passengers and cargo to be off-loaded, and then Lasater boarded his assigned car. They didn't have any private compartments left when he'd gotten his ticket, so he had to make do with sitting on the far side of the car in a corner seat away from the platform. At least he'd be able to keep his eyes on both doors from there.

After thirty minutes of boxes and people getting loaded onto the train, a long whistle split the sunshine, and someone shouted "All aboard!" from just outside the car behind him. Folks shuffled into their benches on the train, and the car was nearly full. Lasater smiled at the mix of people who were coming out of San Fran. Most of the passengers looked like upstanding couples, men dressed in tails and paisley vests and the women on their arms in bright, billowing dresses full of lace and sporting huge bustles and matching parasols. There was a smattering of grizzled, smelly miners whose new clothes and untrimmed beards spoke volumes.

Lasater had seen a handful of such coming out of Sacramento when he was on his way in weeks before. The gold rush brought plenty of men who lived harsh lives on the brink of poverty. Some of those—the smart ones Lasater thought—would quit while they were ahead after hitting a major load and head back home to buy farms or cattle. The dumb ones pissed their dust and nuggets away like sparkling rain at saloons and whorehouses around the boomtown, staying just one step ahead of broke.

He saw a tinker in a fine black suit and bowler step on to the train, wearing a pair of gold and silver goggles to beat all. Even Tinker Farris' rig hadn't been as impressive. They had a half-dozen lenses swung on each side and a dark pair swung down over his eyes to keep the sun out. He had a beautiful black woman on his arm dressed to the nines in dandelion yellow, and Lasater picked up a darker pattern of lines and characters on her cheeks and forehead that said *witch* to anyone who knew the difference. It was pretty common for tinkers and witches to team up, and the woman who had worked with Farris was the one who'd given Lasater's limbs the life and strength that had gotten him out of so many fixes.

Lasater heard a couple of grungy miners a few rows up from him whisper "Yank" and then proceeded to comment on the woman's color in less than polite terms ... and they weren't quiet about it. The man with the bowler gave them a sidelong scowl as he helped the woman into her seat.

Lasater wet his whistle and started in on *Battle Hymn of the Republic,* aiming it right at the backs of the two miners to remind them who won the war. Lasater had given plenty in the name of freedom and the abolition of slavery, and he took every opportunity he could to remind Rebs of it when they spoke their mind on the subject. A dozen heads turned to Lasater, most smiling. The bowler nodded to him in thanks while the miners glared at him from twisted, craning necks. Lasater winked at the men and stopped whistling as his good eye narrowed down to a slit and he didn't flinch, didn't give them any quarter.

"Ain't no room for Rebs no more, you hear?" Maybe it was the good eye looking mean and not giving up. Maybe it was the black lens looking wicked. Maybe it was that no one spoke up for the two miners. It was probably all three, but both men's glares weakened a bit as they turned their heads and went real quiet. Lasater just grinned.

"Last call for Sacramento!" a man yelled from outside their car. The train whistle blew three times hard, and there was the sound of steam blowing somewhere up ahead.

The mahjong-playing cowboy from Hang's was the last to enter the car. Lasater tensed as he watched the cowboy step a few rows into the car, spot an open seat and start to turn around to plop down into it. At the last second he paused, turned his head and eyed Lasater. A friendly smile spread across his face, and he waved at Lasater who returned it with a nod as the cowboy straightened and started walking back through the car. His spurs chinged across the weathered floorboards, and Lasater gave the man a thorough once-over. He was a little shorter than Lasater with a single six-shooter on the left hip, making him a southpaw. He wore faded blue jeans with trail-worn boots sticking out the bottom. The tan duster covered the paisley vest and blue button-down, and the scarf was still in place. Ancient saddlebags that looked like they'd seen better days dangled in one hand, almost scraping the floor, and there was a faded "U.S."

on the flaps. He had on a faded, blue cowboy hat that definitely belonged to a Union cavalry officer before years of sun and rain turned it into just another way of keeping the weather off. There was a subtle bulge on the inside of his right forearm under his duster that said *hide-away*. Lasater wondered if it was a pullout or one of those fancy, spring-loaded rigs that shot the small pistol into his hand in an eye-blink.

"I see you made it out," the cowboy said, sounding like New Mexico.

"'Peers that way." Lasater sized up the man like he was sitting across a poker-table. "I noticed you weren't there when I come up."

The cowboy cast a questioning glance at the empty space next to Lasater. Lasater made it clear that he thought about it a second and then nodded.

"Much obliged," the cowboy said as he settled down into the seat with enough space between them to show respect. Then he leaned back and relaxed like he was at home. "Well, soon as you went through that door Hang barked something in Chinese to them boys sitting at my table. They jumped up like they was on fire and went running out the back door quiet as a couple of panthers. Hang come over, picked up their money and told me pretty clearly that the game was over. My mamma didn't raise no dummies, and my daddy taught me when to fold a losing hand. I grabbed my money and walked outa there quick as you please. I felt bad and all, but I don't know you mister, and there was a whole lotta them and not much of me." He pulled the blue brim down over his tan eyes and folded his arms across his chest.

"No hard feelings," Lasater said with a trace of warmth. "You played it smart. No shame in that."

The cowboy peeked an eye out from under a blue brim. "Seems like it all worked out anyway, didn't it?"

"I reckon. But this shit may not be over." Lasater ran his fingers over his goatee thoughtfully and stared out the window.

"You figurin' they might come after you?" He lifted his brow and followed Lasater's eyes out into the hot sunshine of the station.

"My mamma didn't raise no dummies, either," Lasater said, and they both chuckled.

"So what the hell was that all about, anyway?"

The train whistle announced Lasater's story, and he started in on it just as the train lurched and they headed out for San Jose. Lasater started at the beginning, with the poker game. He was prepared to finish the whole thing, but he heard the cowboy start snoring about halfway through, so with a shrug, Lasater pulled his hat down over his one good eye and followed suit.

O   O   O

The lurch of the train as it came to a stop is what woke them both up. The sun was just going down, but the remaining daylight left people enough to still see by. The gas torches of San Jose were on but not really doing much besides looking pretty. Along with most of the other folks, the cowboy stood up quickly and grabbed his gear. Lasater spotted a ragged, pale friction-scar chiseled into the dark skin of the cowboy's neck, the bumps and ridges pink under the handkerchief. He raised an eyebrow, wondering if the cowboy was wanted somewhere.

The cowboy saw Lasater looking and figured out what was up. "Don't worry, mister. This don't mean there's a bounty on my head somewhere ... at least not that I know of. Some boys down in Texas didn't fancy me courtin' a white business girl who had a room above the saloon where I was drinking. There was a ruckus, but the sheriff broke it up and let me be. Seems he fought for the North. Them boys caught up with me the next day a half-day's ride outside of town. They figured I belonged in a dogwood tree."

"Damn," Lasater said, shaking his head in disbelief but knowing such things happened throughout the territories and states alike.

"It worked out though. They didn't tie my hands ... wanted to see me squirm up there ... and it seems the boy tyin' the knots of the noose didn't know how. The rope let loose of the saddle-horn it was tied to, and I dropped down in the middle of 'em. They were all real surprised when I come up with one of their pistols in my hand."

"Did you kill 'em?" Lasater asked.

The cowboy paused, not certain of what kind of response he might get if he told the truth. He took a deep breath and figured he'd just go ahead and spill it. "Just two of 'em. The ringleaders figured I didn't have the guts to pull a trigger ... or they figured I wasn't fast enough. They looked at each other and went straight for their guns … pretty stupid, really … so I shot 'em down. I had the three left over strip down to their skivvies and sent them on their way."

Lasater laughed and then sobered a bit. He looked the cowboy dead in the eye and said as serious as a heart attack, "You should have burned them all down."

The cowboy gave Lasater a thoughtful look. "The thought crossed my mind, I gotta admit. That worked out too, though. I headed off towards El Paso, five horses in tow, and the sheriff come up behind me a few hours later. At first I thought he was after me. He asked me what had happened, and I told him … showed him the ring round my neck. He knew them boys pretty well. He said he was impressed I didn't kill 'em. Told me to be on my way and not look back … just never come back … less trouble that way, you know?"

"Yeah, I can see his point. Folks are what they are, I suppose, good and bad," Lasater agreed.

"I reckon. Anyway, that's where this come from." The cowboy moved the handkerchief back in place.

"You headin' to a saloon?" Lasater asked.

"Naw. I gotta go get my horse and the rest of my rig. Gonna find a stable. You got a horse?"

"Unh-unh." Lasater lifted one of his pant legs revealing a golden, metallic shine underneath. "Both legs. I'm just too much of a load, even for a Morgan. I'd feel guilty putting my golden ass on some poor horse."

"Is it?" the cowboy asked a bit surprised. He had to be thinking how far up the gears went on Lasater's bottom half.

"What?"

"Golden," the cowboy specified as he turned towards the door at the end of the car.

"My ass?"

"Yeah," he called over his shoulder, grinning.

Lasater lifted his hat and rested it far back on his head, looking up at the cowboy. "No. From the thighs down … and before you ask, I still got my gear. Still worked last time I checked." They both chuckled.

"You headed to Sacramento?" the cowboy asked over his shoulder.

"Yep,"

"Me, too. I'll see you on the zep then, much as I hate getting on those things. I want to put as much distance between me and San Fran as I can."

"Hey," Lasater called, and the cowboy stopped. "I'm getting a compartment on the zep if there are any left. You're welcome to tag along if you want. There's plenty of room."

"No shit?" The cowboy's face held genuine surprise.

"No shit."

"Much obliged," he replied and tipped his hat to punctuate his thanks.

"I believe the Sacramento run kicks out at nine tomorrow morning. Meet me at the platform at around 8:45. I'll finish my story on the way up."

The cowboy smiled. "You got a deal, and I'll try not to fall asleep this time." He winked, hefted his saddlebags and started walking out.

"You better not, I might take it personal."

O   O   O

After loading his horse into the big cargo bay of the zeppelin's gondola, the cowboy met Jake precisely at 8:45. As a result of the earthquake, the platform was a hastily built, forty-foot tower with ramps and stairs to allow both passengers and cargo to be loaded onto the towering zeppelins that came through San Jose to parts north, south and east. Both men stood on the main platform and were mid-way along the gondola's length underneath the massive tan bulk of the Pacific Line's zeppelin airliner the *Jezebel*. They were lost in the gargantuan shadow of the triple cigar-shaped envelopes high above that covered most of the station and a fair portion of San Jose. Passengers passed by the two men who stood examining the hull of the airship and the great rotors spinning slowly set in five pairs on each side of the gondola. Two massive clamps, looking more like claws, anchored the zeppelin to the boarding platform that stood thirty feet above the dusty main street on the eastern edge of San Jose.

"You ever been on one of these?" the cowboy asked, his eyes and feet shifting as he pondered the uncomfortable prospect of getting on board the airship. He ran a hand along the smooth burgundy hull of the gondola that ran almost the length of the envelopes. The lower half of the gondola was dedicated to cargo, while the compartments above were for the passengers and crew.

"A few times ... when I had the money ... mostly trains, though. Sure beats eating trail dust for days or weeks on end." Lasater leaned against the hull and looked at the cowboy. "You?"

"Just once. Military transport from Oklahoma to Virginia. The 10th Cavalry got shifted from patrolling the Cheyenne to assisting some of the forward Union positions during the war. I'll tell you, that ride scared the hell outa' me. I'll take Cheyenne over thunderstorms in one of these anytime."

"You were with the 10th?"

"Yessir," the cowboy said proudly.

"Y'all have a hell of a reputation," Lasater said, genuinely impressed. He'd figured the cowboy was probably with the Buffalos, but the 10th was something special.

"We did what we had to," the cowboy said quietly, and he got a distant look on his face that spoke of heroism and fear and regret.

"From what I hear, y'all did a hell of a lot more than that."

"Well, truth be told, maybe us Buffalos had a bit more at stake than the rest of you Yanks."

"No doubt," Lasater conceded, "but I'm not just talking about the war ... out on the plains ... facing the Cheyenne and Comanche. Like I said, y'all have a hell of a reputation."

"Thanks, mister."

"None necessary. You earned it."

The cowboy was quiet for a while, running his eyes over the great, floating bulk of the zeppelin above him. "Come on. Let's get to that cabin."

"After you." Lasater ushered the cowboy up the last flight of stairs, their spurs jingling and boots thumping. They bumped together as they stepped through the portal and made their way down a narrow aisle between benches packed with travelers, and the cowboy gave Lasater a curious look.

The interior of the zeppelin was done in smooth walnut, and every window, handle and accent was polished brass. Both men had to weave their way through affluent travelers, including a few families, the children laughing and darting around haphazardly like frightened fish in a pond too small for their numbers. Lasater reached the end of the narrow corridor and faced the last door on the right.

"This is it." Lasater opened the door and motioned for the cowboy to step in.

"Damn! This is a hell of a lot nicer than that military transport." He walked between the two richly padded benches done in red velour and looked out the wide center window set in a row of three. As with the rest of the gondola's interior, the wood was a pale walnut, and all of the fittings and frames were polished brass. A shiny, brass hand-crank at the top of the window called to him, so he grabbed it and started turning. The middle window started sliding up in its frame, letting in the warm, fresh San Jose morning air. He took a deep breath and looked down at the town spreading out before him. The cowboy grinned like a kid at a carnival.

"I'm glad you like it," Lasater said with a smile in his voice.

"I really do appreciate it, mister. This is about as nice as I've ever seen."

Lasater stepped into the cabin and grabbed a brass handle set a few feet above the middle cushion of the right-hand bench. With a gentle tug he pulled and swung down the recessed bed. "There's one on that side too, you just pull on this lever, see?" He patted the down pillow to see how soft it was. "Nicer than a Kansas City hotel."

"Yeah. Pretty slick," the cowboy said, turning fully to face Lasater. "Don't take this wrong, mister, but I gotta ask you a question."

Lasater lifted the bed back into place, pulled his hat off and sat down, leaning his head against the window and stretching his legs out across the seat. He hung the hat on a hook above his head. "Why am I being so nice?" he offered, beating the cowboy to the punch.

"You nailed it. I ain't never done nothing for you, and when a deal seems too good to be true, it usually is." The cowboy sat down across from Lasater and hung his own hat on the hook above him, but he sat facing Lasater with a look of curiosity tainted with a blurry haze of mistrust. "What I owe you for all this?"

Lasater smiled. "Not a thing. I consider it paid in full, and I sorta still owe you."

"How the hell you figure that?" Disbelief filled the cowboy's voice.

Lasater tapped his right leg with his knuckles. "These."

"Hunh?" The cowboy couldn't have looked more surprised if Lasater had told him that the sun was made of honeydew.

"The battle where I lost 'em. I was tore up bad enough to be left for dead … in fact, the white boys in my regiment did just that. There was Rebs coming over a hill after that canon volley tore me up … well … from where I lay screamin' and bleedin' on the grass … all I seen was the backs of a bunch of blue coats and the bottoms of their heels. I figured I was all done, you know? Gave it up." Lasater raised a gloved hand and rubbed the side of his face as he thought about the battle. "The Rebs musta' been about forty or fifty yards away, running and whoopin' and hollerin' like they was about to win the war. All I could do was stare at 'em. Then we all heard it. Horses … a lot of 'em … They burst through the trees off the left flank of the battlefield. Forty or fifty riders … black as night and the sweetest sight I ever seen." Lasater closed his eyes, remembering. "They came straight for the Rebs … and they didn't make a sound. They held their fire, they didn't yell … there was just the thunder of them horses … they were black too. The cannons let into them, and some of them fell, but not one of them slowed down. The Rebs had time to get into lines and started shooting, and they dropped a few, but you know most of them boys couldn't hit shit when the heat was on. Then those Buffalo Soldiers opened up … they dropped most of the first line with their first volley, from horseback I might add, and then half tore into the Reb infantry like dogs into a carcass while the other half rode up that hill and took the cannoners apart piece-by-piece." Lasater smiled, reliving something he still couldn't believe. "In the middle of it, two of them Buffalos, they saw I was still moving, so they dropped off their horses, grabbed me and pulled me outa' there, quick as you please and got me to the doctors. I never saw 'em again. Never thanked 'em." Lasater sighed and sniffed a bit, barely controlling his emotions. "Without a doubt, I'd be dead if it weren't for them. I figure my life is worth a hell of a lot more than a few days in this thing, so you just enjoy the ride, you hear?" He never opened his eyes.

The cowboy looked at Lasater for long seconds, looking for words but coming up short. "Don't know what to say, mister."

"Don't need to say nuthin'."

The sound of the gondola rotors revving up filled the morning calm and broke the silence that had taken up a perch between them. With a gentle shift of weight rearward, the zeppelin pulled away from the ground slowly and began a gentle ascent away from San Jose. Then they heard the whoosh of the big propellers at the back of the ship kick in, sending them sailing into the air with a lurch. A church steeple in the distance disappeared from view through the open window, and the zeppelin banked around in a long curve, pointing its nose toward the well-risen sun. The cowboy slid up to the window on his side of the cabin and cranked that one open too, sniffing in the fresh air and watching a flock of birds fly by at eye-level. As the birds disappeared behind the gondola and out of view, headed for the coast, the cowboy finally broke the silence.

"So ... uh ... where's the head? This morning's coffee is looking to make a getaway."

Without opening his eyes, Lasater pointed towards the door. "You'll find a pair of 'em fore and aft, one pair just around the corner from our cabin, and the other all the way back past where we got on board, just this side of the dining cabin."

"Much obliged," the cowboy said and stood up.

"And remember to put the seat down when you're finished." He punctuated the directive with a chuckle. "There's proper women-folk on this crate, and we wouldn't want to offend their delicate sensibilities, would we?"

The cowboy let out a guffaw. "Don't you worry, I'll be sure to tidy the place up for 'em." The cabin door closed on their laughter, and Lasater folded his arms in his lap. After a few minutes he dozed off into a light, dreamless sleep.

It was the cabin door opening that woke him up, but he didn't open his eyes. He didn't even open his eyes when he heard footsteps come in and approach him. When he heard the second set come through the door, he opened his eyes and his right hand was already moving towards his pistol, but it was too late.

In the span of a heartbeat, three things happened. First, Lasater spotted Hang Ah in a black, coat-tailed jacket over a red paisley vest, the ensemble topped by smoldering eyes shadowed under a short bowler hat the same color as the jacket. Hang held a long dagger in his hand that was closing in on Lasater's face. Second, a shuriken thrown by the man behind Hang hit Lasater in the right arm, and the poison that coated it instantly paralyzed his arm, causing the limb to drop down uselessly at his side. Then, as he reached with his left hand for the pistol on that side, another shuriken hit home and his left dropped motionless to his lap. By that time the dagger was inches from his face, and he could even see small nicks and scratches in the polished steel.

Lasater looked down at both motionless arms and shook his head. "I was hoping I'd seen the last of you, Hang," he said calmly. His breath fogged the blade as he spoke. "I figured friends could walk away from a mess like that and just go their separate ways. Guess I figured wrong."

Hang spoke quietly, his accent making it that much more difficult for Lasater to understand. "Honor must come before friendship, Mr. Lasater. So, yes, you did." Hang's eyes narrowed down to slits. "*Gravely.*"

Lasater nodded his head and tried to fix an 'I've learned the wickedness of my ways' look on his face. Then he slowly leaned sideways and awkwardly adjusted his position so that his back was against the seat cushion rather than the outward-facing wall. The dagger maintained its inches-away position, keeping pace with Lasater's good eye, but Hang did not otherwise hinder his prey. "So, umm … what happens next?" Lasater asked. He tried to rub his itchy nose on his shoulder, but he couldn't quite put the two together with the numbing poison in his arm. When Hang made no move to help him, he wiggled his nose like a rabbit sniffing to try and make the itch go away. The motion did at least prompt a reaction from Hang and the assassin standing silently behind him. They both got subtle smiles as they watched Lasater suffer.

"What happens next, you ask?" Hang finally replied. His smirk turned to a beaming smile of pure delight. "Why, we wait." Although the dagger never moved, the rest of Hang's body appeared to relax a little, and the assassin's shoulders actually lowered slightly as he leaned back on his heels. "Are you familiar with the ancient Chinese proverb on patience?"

Lasater's features drifted into a desert of sardonic boredom. "Can't say that I'm familiar with any Chinese proverbs, Hang. Why don't you enlighten me?"

Hang's tone took on a taint of formality, like he was quoting scripture. "One moment of patience may ward off great disaster. One moment of impatience may also ruin an entire life."

"Hunh ..." Lasater blinked his eyes a few times, not really getting where Hang was going with it. "That's really interesting and all, but I think you lost me there."

"What I find interesting is that the reverse is also true."

Lasater drew out his response, as if he were talking to a lunatic, "Right ..." Before he could add anything, the cabin door opened and the cowboy stepped in.

"Run for it!" Lasater shouted, trying to warn the man off. Lasater was the only one in the room who was surprised.

"Why would I want to do that?" the cowboy asked as he closed the door quietly behind him.

Lasater felt the bottom of his stomach drop out. He wanted to kick himself for not seeing it coming. He was normally such a good judge of character, but he clearly missed the mark with the cowboy.

"So you sold me out, did you?" Lasater accused through gritted teeth.

"It certainly appears that way, don't it?" the cowboy replied like he was talking about the weather. He stepped past the Chinese assassin, and just as he was behind Hang, he winked at Lasater with a serious look on his face. "Guess it's like them Buffalo Soldiers you was talking about before ... this old Buffalo's gonna be your undoing." The cowboy put his back to the windows and faced the assassin. "You catch my drift, mister?"

Lasater looked at the cowboy with steely eyes. "I believe I do. You know how I hate them Buffalos. You go right ahead and do what you gotta do." Then he turned his face and stared down the Chinese Tong boss who held the dagger. "You sure you don't want to rethink this, Hang? Last chance." Hang and the assassin chuckled at the impertinence of a man about to die. "Well, Hang, I guess this is it." And then Lasater did something that actually widened Hang's eyes with surprise. Despite the poison, despite the dagger, despite being outnumbered three to one ... he smiled, and it was a mean, bloodthirsty smile. It shook Hang, if only for a moment, and the Tong leader licked his lips and swallowed.

The kick from the cowboy hit the assassin square in the balls and lifted him up off the floor a couple of feet. The boot took the wind out of the little killer with a grunt of pained air blowing out of his lungs. Lasater's left hand flashed in a motion too fast to follow, the gears of his artificial left arm screaming like the peal of a falcon, and it wrapped a leather glove around Hang's dagger-hand and squeezed. *Hard.* The cowboy was grabbing the assassin before he came down and pushing him towards the open window with a twist of his body. Hang yelped like a little girl as the bones in his hand were crushed against the steel hilt of the dagger. He tried to thrust, but his hand moved forward only a fraction of an inch. With Lasater's shoulder against the wall, Hang would have had to push like an ox to get Lasater's arm to give way. The assassin went sailing quietly out the open window, still gasping for air.

It was Lasater's turn with smoldering eyes. "I gave you every opportunity to walk away from this, Hang. Bent over backwards to do it. But I'm not spending the rest of my life looking over my shoulder for red pajamas. *Good bye.*"

Lasater tightened his hand, the gears within protesting at the resistance, and then all three men left in the cabin heard Hang's fingers snap, pop, and crack like kindling as they were crushed to splinters. Hang screamed, his face contorting into agony and his other hand coming around to grip the broken one. Lasater released the crushed, useless fingers, and the dagger slipped through them and stuck in the floor, point down. His hand darted to Hang's begging throat, and he squeezed there too, popping Hang's eyes out as the air was cut off and blood started to swell in his now-crimson face. Lasater stood up, lifting Hang clear of the ground, and with a twist, he flung Hang's flailing body out the window to sail screaming through the clear air down into a rushing river hundreds of feet below. They never heard him hit.

With an annoyed look on his face, Lasater pulled the shuriken stuck in his right arm out and tossed it out the window. Then he slowly sat down and ran his hand over the numb, lifeless dangle of his right arm, hoping that he'd be able to use it soon and the that poison didn't have more in store for him. He let out a long, resigned sigh. "Damn it, Hang. I thought we were friends."

The cowboy sat down across from Lasater, reached out slowly and pulled the shuriken from Lasater's left arm. He had to tug quite a bit, and it finally came free, but he looked at Lasater with the unspoken question painted across his face.

"Rubber," Lasater replied. "Over brass. It feels more natural when I brush up against people, but not by much. Is that how you knew? When we got on the zeppelin?"

"Yep ... figured it was something like that." The cowboy leaned back and smiled, waiting for the next question.

"So, they paid you to set me up, did they?" Lasater asked, a bit of irritation creeping into his voice.

"Yep." The cowboy's smile was broad enough to get a horse through.

"And you telegraphed from San Jose?"

"Yep." His smile grew to deliberately infuriating.

"You get paid up front?" Lasater asked without taking the cowboy's bait.

The cowboy's face took on a more serious shape. "Half, but I figured it paid in full from the beginning."

"How do you figure?"

"Better to see 'em coming when ya got help than not see 'em comin' at all." The infuriating smile was back.

Realization dawned on Lasater's face. "So you set *them* up."

"Yep." The cowboy's features softened into one of camaraderie, the kind that only the minority can share amidst a majority. "I figured if you were able to make your way out of that hole back at Hang's, well this would be no trouble at all if you had just a little bit of a leg-up."

"That's a damn good point," Lasater said, smiling. He paused for a bit and then added with narrowed eyes, "And you didn't mention all this before because...?"

"I didn't want to scare ya." The cowboy grinned like the devil himself.

Lasater sighed. "Next time ... go ahead and scare me," he suggested a bit tiredly.

"Actually, when I sent the telegraph to them from San Jose, I didn't really know what sort of fella you were. If you'd turned out to be a Reb at heart, well I'da maybe just turned my back and let you fend for yourself. I never did get your full name."

"Lasater. Jake Lasater, outa' Missouri."

"Montgomery McJunkins," the cowboy said. "New Mexico. But my friends just call me Cole—don't ask why." Cole paused and stared down at Jake's left arm. "That's quite a left you got there, Jake."

"Yep. I'm lucky I got it. It's got me outa' more fixes than I care to think about. Where you headed, Cole?"

Cole smiled at the use of the friendly moniker. "Colorado. Figuring to try my luck on the other side of the Rockies."

"Poker?"

"Yep. Had my fill of mahjong ... and San Fran."

"First beer's on me, Cole."

SINKING TO THE LEVEL OF DEMONS

David Boop

Deputy Matthew Ragsdale considered the sheriff's badge mocking him from the desk of his dead boss. He swore it even laughed at him, but then realized the sound came from his daughter Trina playing back by the jail cells. His wife Sarah, hovering anxiously near his side, took a tentative step closer and laid a hand on his arm.

"What are you going to do?"

"I don't have a choice."

Water pooled at the corners of Sarah's eyes but refused to become actual tears.

"You can wait for a new sheriff from Tucson, or marshals from Denver."

Matt thought about that, but the longer they waited, the more likely Jimmy Kettle's Claw Rock Gang would come back to town. They were satiated on blood, alcohol, and women for the moment. But how long would that last?

His mentor, Sheriff Levi Fossett, had laid out what it'd take to bring the outlaws down. A plan that would put Kettle in his grave with little risk to either of them.

Too bad the Claw Rock Gang had gunned down the unarmed man outside of church. Fossett's body cooled in the freshly covered grave. Sarah, Trina, and he still wore their Sunday best, all three having just attended the funeral. As the reverend spoke his words about death and resurrection, the town folk looked to Matt, and their eyes asked unspoken questions: "Are any of us safe?" or "Are you man enough to stop the madness?"

He stood in the sheriff's office pondering that very same question. He'd been like them, when his family first moved West on the first expansion. His father, a trader, was one of the original settlers of Drowned Horse. Matthew's strict upbringing carried over into a love for law and order, a love Sheriff Fossett picked up on and nurtured.

Trina emerged from the back and sidled up to her daddy. She hugged his leg, her ever-present rag doll he'd made for her hanging from her tight little palm.

"Someone has to." He picked up the badge with conviction. "No. I have to. I have to finish Fossett's work. I know the plan."

The plan wouldn't work just by himself. Deputy ... no ... *Sheriff* Matthew Ragsdale would need help. However, he wouldn't get it from most of the men in town. The outlaws had terrorized the locals going on two months, and more than a few had died standing up to Kettle and his gang of fiends. Leaving the town unprotected while he rode to Flagstaff didn't bring him any comfort either.

He didn't need many men. One more should do it.

o o o

Adoniram G. Craddick nearly swallowed his mouthful of square nails when the newly christened sheriff poked his head around to the back of his business.

"Ram."

"Shaywiff."

Matt stepped into the room. "Now don't start that shit up. Don't matter what title they hang on me. We've been on a first name basis since we married sisters. That's what? Going on ten years now."

Lanky, but not skeletal, Ram righted himself to his full six-foot-three frame. He examined the project he was abandoning, and then gave his guest his full attention. After setting down his hammer, Ram spit the nails into one hand. The other he offered to Matt.

"Yeah, I s'pose I'd never get used to calling you that, anyhow. Offer you some lemonade in the parlor? Sadie just made it this morning."

Matt looked down at the item Ram had been working on. "There isn't a rush on that, is there?"

"That?" Ram indicated the coffin. "Nah, just planning ahead. With the Claw Rock Gang around, it pays to have stock."

The statement stung Matt visibly, and Ram quickly backtracked. "I mean, not that it'll always stay that way. I'm sure they'll get their comeuppance before long."

Matt removed his Stetson and stared at the rim. "Yeah. Sorta why I needed to talk to you."

Drowned Horse's undertaker raised a wary eyebrow at his best friend. "Sounds like I might need to make that drink a bit harder." He opened a clay urn and pulled out a small flask. Ram blew off what Matt hoped was only dust. "Whisky?"

O O O

Claw Rock hadn't been named because it looked like a claw, or a hand, or anything remotely claw-like. It got its title from the gouges outside the red sandstone cave. Word had it the Apache dragged prisoners into the cave and slaughtered them; a brutal tradition dating back before a single settler set foot in the area.

Kettle and his men chose to hole up near the *Wiipukepaya*, the tribe that moved in when the Apache left. The gang traded food and money to the Indians for the right to claim the cave as their own. Starved and desperate as the *Yavapai* Nation had become, they didn't care if one group of white men killed another. While the natives still considered the area sacred, Matt had a sneaky suspicion that the Wiipukepaya knew what everyone else suspected; the U.S. Military hovered just on the other side of the horizon, planning to drive them from their homes just as they had the Apache.

James "Jimmy" Kettle was a former military man. Despite the informal nature of the outlaw life, Kettle ran patrols that walked a perimeter around the Claw Rock at night. They patrolled in pairs, each watching the other's back. So, Matt and Ram moved as a team, with the notion of taking out both guards lest one get off a shout.

There was enough of a moon out that a posse would've been seen moving through the brush, but two men crawling stealthily could be missed. The odds were still in their favor.

"I'm not so sure 'bout this, Matt," Ram said in a whisper, "I'm more used to buryin' dead men, not makin' them."

"We need to take out four, maybe six men to get to the place we need to be," Matt returned the hushed tones. "If this works, then the town's safe."

"If? You didn't say nothing 'bout no 'if'!"

Matt pushed his brother-in-law's face into the sand because Ram's voice crept up more than the sheriff thought advisable. Directly into Ram's ear he whispered, "Shush! They'll hear." He let the man's head back up and Ram spit sand from his lips. "There is always ... how do those generals say it? Oh, yeah ... a margin of error."

The undertaker shot daggers at Matt.

The sound of approaching footsteps signaled the men to roll in separate directions, positioning themselves on either side of a small mound. While Jimmy Kettle might be smart, his men were not so much. They followed a well-worn path around the rocks which made it easy for Matt and Ram to lay a trap.

As soon as the outlaws stepped into the snares, the lawmen pulled them tight, tripping the guards. Matt and Ram were on them before they could call out. Bringing the butt of their six-guns down decisively on the patrol's heads, the lawmen knocked them out quietly.

"See?" Matt badgered, "That's two we didn't have to kill, Deputy Craddick."

Ram huffed. "Don't call me that."

The next set of guards' pattern would take them too close to the cave's entrance to risk any sort of protracted attack. Fortune had it that they'd stopped by a large rock to roll a smoke. Matt and Ram slipped rags over their mouths and slit their throats. They fell without a sound.

Ram stared unblinking as their blood stained sand and rock.

Matt whispered, "These men raped two of the Sagebrush's whores, beat them bloody and left them for dead. That's no way to treat a lady, even one who sells her body. Every man in Kettle's gang has blood on his hand. If we end their reign tonight, the blood on ours might just be justified. Ain't this worth it to not have to fear Sadie's gonna end up raped or worse?"

Ram shot back, "Yeah, yeah. That's how you got me out here in the first place, damn snake oil salesman that you are. I just never had to take another man's life before. Give me a moment."

Matt gave him all the time they had to spare. Ram must have come to terms with his problem, because he helped drag the bodies behind the rock.

The late Sheriff Fossett covered everything in his plan, including spots to get an unobstructed view of the entrance of the Claw Rock cave. The height of the opening was easily thirty feet tall and curved out like a shell in the sand. The rock itself had a plateau above it where two more guards watched the grounds. In front of the cave an area had been cleared of rock and debris becoming a communal meeting spot. Nearly a dozen men milled around a cook fire, acting bored.

That bothered Matt, as they'd most likely be riding back into Drowned Horse soon.

Kettle's gang held a gallery of wanted men, each more mean than the next. One in particular stood out; a black man the likes of which Matt hadn't seen around those parts. Stocky and wearing a stove pipe hat, his ears were pierced with bone. The man stared into the fire like it contained a whore dancing on a stage. Seeing something he apparently didn't like, he spat into the fire pit, got up and entered the cave. He didn't reemerge, which gave Matt the willies.

Ram exhaled long and hard. "I think that's a black magic man. Like the witch doctors you read about in adventure magazines."

Matt asked, "How do you know?"

"I'm an undertaker. We know the people in our trade. Voodoo men from Louisiana, like him, specialize in death; creating it, worshiping it, fighting it."

"Fighting it?"

Ram shivered. "It's said they know death's face, and when he comes for you, a Voodoo priest can scare him away."

"Why would Kettle have one in his gang?"

"Scare people. Keep his men in line. Who knows? It gives me the creeps, though."

"Me, too. Let's get this over with."

They made their way around the back of Claw Rock and scaled up the side thanks to a series of stacked rocks. The guards stood there, looking out at nothing, paying no attention to the lawmen approaching their backs, their complacency a result of Kettle's dark shadow. Who'd have the cojones to attack such an evil son of a bitch?

Keeping their hats tilted low, Matt and Ram spoke in turn.

"We're here to relieve you."

"Yeah. Boss wants a word."

The guards turned without a concern in the world.

"You're earl—" one started to say, but the sheriff shoved a knife through the bottom of the outlaw's jaw, pinching his mouth shut and driving the tip into his brain.

The second guard, however, was quicker and caught the undertaker's hand before it could plunge in. They grappled and it became quickly evident Ram was outmatched.

Matt moved up fast to wrap an arm around the man's throat, silencing him.

The guard was strong and, despite being outnumbered two-to-one, he held his own. He pushed backwards, dangling Matt over the rim. The sheriff looked down briefly at the campfire below him, but God's mercy kept anyone from looking up. Ram pulled them back from the edge. Matt tightened his chokehold, but the burly bad guy showed no signs of surrender.

The outlaw let go of Ram, twisting the undertaker's knife out of his hand in the process. He swung it wildly at Ram, driving him back toward the opposite edge. Suddenly, he turned the knife around and stabbed Matt's arm. The lawman let go with a holler and dropped to the rock. Changing targets, the outlaw looked to send the blade right through Matt's heart when a gun went off and a red geyser spurted from the guard's forehead. The sheriff rolled out of the way as the dead man fell forward.

Moving fast as lightning, Matt grabbed a bundle of dynamite from the satchel they'd brought along. Ram did the same with a second bundle. They placed them where Fossett had predicted an explosion would bring the whole cave down.

After lighting the fuses, they hopped down the backside like mountain goats. Kettle's men made it around the bend in time to see the duo reach the trail. Bullets bounced against stone. Matt and Ram retreated, doing their best to keep cover between them and their pursuers. They returned fire as often as they could.

The explosion, when it came, took the top off of Claw Rock like a volcano. The lawmen didn't get as far enough away from the blast as they wanted, and they hit the ground hard. Dirt and gravel sprayed over them. Matt came up first, spitting sand from his mouth. Ram rolled on the ground, laughing.

The round-up didn't take long. Most of the Claw Rock Gang had gone inside seeking cover, not expecting the whole entrance would come down around them. According to the surviving crew, Jimmy Kettle, including his Voodoo man, had been inside when the explosion sealed the cave. No one was coming out of that alive.

Matt's satisfaction in seeing Fossett's plan through to the end kept a smug grin on his face as they escorted the remaining criminals off to jail.

O   O   O

Drowned Horse gave Matt and Ram a hero's welcome. Music wafted from the Sagebrush Inn for the first time in weeks. The owner, known only as Owner, made the first round of drinks on him, and both men felt duty bound to imbibe.

Sarah and her sister Sadie, upon hearing of their men's return, came rushing over and lavished both lawmen with a public display of affection. Embarrassed, Matt blushed, but Ram jokingly asked Owner if he and his wife could use one of the rooms upstairs.

"You takin' to this deputy stuff, after all?" Matt ribbed.

Ram gave his new boss a mischievous grin. "If it's all free beer and taking down men like Kettle, then hell yeah, I'll be your partner." He held up his hand as a warning. "Part time, at least. Still got a business to run and all."

Matt handed over a tin star he'd grabbed while at the jail. "Let's make it official, then." He settled the crowd and spoke loudly. "Today we saw the last day of the Claw Rock Gang and the first day of Deputy Adoniram G. Craddick, my brother-in-law."

The Sheriff pinned the badge on Ram's pocket, and the crowd whooped and hollered. Sadie gave her man a big kiss. Sarah lifted a sleepy Trina onto her daddy's shoulder.

"Now, take good care of our town while I'm escorting these ne'er-do-wells off to trial, 'kay, Deputy?"

"Sure thing, Sheriff."

They slapped each other on the back, and all was right with the world.

O   O   O

Sherriff Matthew Ragsdale returned from Flagstaff two days later to find what was left of Ram dead in the middle of the street.

Blood splattered the area surrounding the body like the pattern on a Navajo blanket. Matt scanned the street to find pieces of Ram scattered to and fro; a rib over by the water trough, a foot near the porch to Mrs. Harris's clothing store. As close as Matt could guess, a pack of coyotes had ripped his deputy apart. He couldn't understand why the body rotted in the center of town.

There were signs of chaos, overturned chairs, broken windows. The town appeared as it did after the Claw Rock Gang went through it. The town's padre approached Matt with a message that turned the Sheriff's blood to ice.

No one was to touch Ram's body on orders from a very much alive Jimmy Kettle.

Before the Father could explain further, Matt rushed home to find his home ripped asunder. He raced through the three rooms and to the back yard. There were no signs of his wife or child.

At Ram's funeral parlor, an inconsolable Sadie tore at him as soon as he stepped through the door, alternating between beating Matt and trying to gouge his eyes out. Visiting nuns from the church managed to get her restrained.

"What happened? Where are Sarah and Trina?"

The holy women crossed themselves, and Sadie composed herself enough to speak.

"This is all your fault. If you'd done left Kettle alone, he would have bothered us for a while, and then moved on when he saw there was nothing else for him here. But no! You had to play the hero and you just had to drag Ram along. Wanted to make a big name for yourself, didn't ya? Bigger than Fossett. Bigger than God! Look where it got us!"

He grabbed her shoulders and shook his sister-in-law. "Where. Is. My. Wife?"

"They took her," one of the nuns began. "Unholy creatures."

The other one picked up with, "'And it is said in the last days, the dead shall rise and walk the earth.'" She pointed at Matt. "You've brought on the apocalypse, Sheriff. Kettle has unleashed demons. He is in league with Satan! And it's all because of you!"

Matt looked at Sadie. "What is she talking about?"

Sadie wept. "Kettle came back into town. He had men with him. His gang. Some were alive. Others …"

Not understanding, Matt asked, "He brought dead bodies with him?"

"Walking corpses they were. Their souls are in Hell, but their bodies still moved, possessed by demons!"

"Sister, there is no—"

"Tell that to the dozens who saw them, Sheriff! Tell that to the priest who soiled his cloth. Tell that to your brother-in-law!"

"They came at Ram and he fired," Sadie interjected, "He kept firing, but they wouldn't go down. T-they weren't alive. They swarmed him, about six of them. He k-kept fighting as they tore his body apart." She sobbed. "Kettle told us to not touch the body. That it would be a lesson to us all. Not even death would stop him."

Matt thought back to what Ram had said about the Voodoo man. There had to be a connection. Could he really bring back the dead? Even just their bodies?

"Sarah and Trina. What happened?"

She could barely get the words out. "H-he took them. Left a message for you to come to Claw Rock, alone. Or he'd kill them."

Matt turned and double-timed it from the funeral parlor.

Sadie followed him to the porch. "You bring her back! Even if you have to die, yourself. Don't come back without them! You hear me, Ragsdale? Don't show your face in this town again if you don't bring them back!"

The words echoed in Matt's ears as he loaded his saddlebags with more guns than he thought wise to carry. He had no plan for his return to Claw Rock, only a target.

He stopped by the Sagebrush. No music wafted through the rafters. Men huddled over drinks. Women consoled each other, dabbing eyes. Most of the town was in attendance.

"Who's with me?"

No one would meet his eyes.

"They've taken my family. *Your* families will be next." He spoke slowly, but forcefully, "Who is with me?"

Frank Chalker, the town's blacksmith, spoke up, "We've seen what happens when someone rides with you, Sheriff. Best you be off, now. Go."

"Cowards!" Matt spat on the floor. "You let them walk into our town. Beat our women. Kill good men. Take whatever they want, including a child. And you won't lift a finger to help? You hide, afraid for your lives. What kinda life is that?"

Another man called out. "Kettle's got demons or something riding with him now. We can't fight that!"

Matt moved around the back of the bar where Owner kept a Bible. He grabbed it and flung it hard down on the counter.

"You tell me, in this book you all profess to believe in, where it says evil is stronger than good? Anybody?"

No one spoke, nor moved, nor barely breathed.

Disgusted, the sheriff went to the front door. With his back to the crowd, he removed his badge and tossed it away.

"Y'all are dead to me. Dead as those things Kettle calls men."

O   O   O

Matt moved forward through the brush much the same way he and Ram had the other night, painfully putting into perspective why he was back there so soon. The patrols were no longer two men marching side by side, but one undead creature that used to be a member of the Claw Rock Gang.

Their milky white, sunken eyes never blinked.

Matt tracked them from Fossett's lookout as they moved slowly in formation. He spotted the two he and Ram had killed by the flapping neck flesh and then counted six more in various states of damage and dismemberment; from missing arms to crushed skulls. Not all the gang had been killed, several still living outlaws could be seen. Those among the still living were Kettle's Voodoo priest and Kettle himself.

Matt discovered the walking corpses didn't hunt by sight or smell. When he'd taken a step towards one, it turned slightly. Stepping back, it returned to its original position. Step forward, turn. Step back, return. He deduced they must have a sense for the living, as if his beating heart drew them. That changed his tactics.

Sadie said that guns had little effect, but Ram had a Remington while Matt brought his father's Sharps Big 50. He considered what the walking corpses would do without their heads.

Somebody behind Matt kicked a rock, so he rolled and drew. A Wiipukepaya scout held his hands up to show he wasn't armed. Matt uncocked his sidearm with a sigh of relief. The scout motioned for Matt to follow, and the former lawman figured he had nothing to lose.

O O O

The late afternoon sun always made the red rock of the area glow, as if the heat absorbed by the stone monuments was released back into the world.

Matthew Ragsdale walked right up to the villain's camp unarmed. He hadn't set two feet into the area before he was set upon by living corpses. He wasn't attacked in any way, just subdued and led forward. He tested their grip on him and it was if his arms were in irons.

Matt took in the scattered rocks that circled the front of the cave. Blood and scratches coated the many of the large boulders.

A devil's laugh bounced off the red sandstone walls of the cave. "You're late."

Kettle's granite form stepped out from the darkness of the cave. Built like a lumberjack, Kettle's muscles appeared ready to burst from the seams of his shirt. He cinched his belt closed as he approached Matt. "I've already finished. I expected you to hear her screams when you arrived and do something stupid." He grabbed Matt's chin and tilted it up. "I really wanted you to do something stupid."

Understanding the implications of Kettle's words, Matt lurched at the outlaw, pulling with everything he had to break free. His futility brought amusement to Kettle's face. The former lawman cursed and foamed at the mouth.

"You cocksucker! You're a dead man! You hear me? If you hurt her in any way, I'll rip your balls off with my bare hands!"

Kettle moved to a chair that sat waiting for him on his imaginary stage. "Oh, she struggled at first, mind you. But I think by the second time, she quite enjoyed it. Turns out she'd only been with boys, not a real man like myself."

"Sarah! Sarah! I'm here! Where is she you fucking monster?"

The outlaw made a motion, and two of his living gang went into the cave. Moments later they dragged Sarah Ragsdale's partially conscious body out. Her clothes were torn, and when they dropped her in front of Kettle, Matt could see blood on the inside of her leg. She made little choked sobs, and her husband couldn't tell if she knew what was happening anymore.

"Oh, my god! Sarah. Sarah!" Tears of futility ran down Matthew's cheek. He shook them free and glared at Kettle. "You goddam bastard. If you touched my daughter in any way …"

The Voodoo man followed shortly after Kettle's men, pushing Trina forward. He had hands on her shoulder and steered her until they stood beside Kettle. Cheeks stained from crying, Trina held her rag doll tight against her chest, like a cross to ward off evil.

"I haven't done anything to the girl, yet. She's too young. After you're dead, I plan to sell her to a whore house. Once she bleeds, I plan to be the first one to taste her flesh." Kettle gave a pensive look. "I wonder which one will be better? Mother or daughter?" He glowered over Matt. "I'm sure it'll be your daughter. She'll be fresh, unspoiled. And after she watches what I do to her daddy, obedient!"

The two locked eyes, testing the seriousness of the other's will; hatred radiating off their bodies like the desert in summer.

As if to accent the tension, thunder rolled in the distance. To the north of their position ran Oak Creek and from there the trail up to Flagstaff. A storm rolled down the mountain.

Everyone alive could taste death in the air. Gang members, licking their dry lips, backed away from their boss, the Voodoo man held tighter to his charge, and even the walking dead seemed nervous.

Matt gave first. His head dropped to his chest and in a voice, barely over a whisper, he pleaded, "What do you want? I'll do anything. Just let them go."

Kettle leaned forward. "I'm sorry. What was that?"

"I said, 'You Win!' Take the damn town. Take whatever you want. Take me, my life. Just let them go!"

The madman stood. "I don't need your permission for that, Lawman! I never did. What I need now is payback. You tried to kill me. Nearly succeeded. All I want now is revenge."

"Then take it. Do whatever you want. Beat me senseless. Kill me in the most spiteful way you can imagine. Just let them go."

Kettle scanned his two hostages. "No, I don't think I will. Your wife will recover and I think I can get some more use out of her before she's unable to walk. And I already told you what I have planned for your little girl. No, I think I will kill you, just as you suggest. Slowly. Painfully. And all the time, you'll know that I have your family."

He walked up close to Matt again and said, "I nearly lost all hope in that cave, you know. Luckily, I had my witch doctor with me. He didn't like being trapped any more than I did."

To accentuate the point, the Voodoo man slid his hands closer to Trina's neck.

"He brought my dead men back to life. Controls them now, he does. They don't feel pain like we do. Dug us a nice tunnel out. Of course, Claw Rock has a few more claw marks in it now."

Matt's face took on a strange mix of confidence and satisfaction. Kettle took a step back, his brow furrowed.

"So, the Voodoo man controls the corpses, huh?" Matt asked.

"What?"

"Your lease's been revoked, Kettle."

Matt gave a whistle that was answered by two whooshes as a pair of arrows flew in. One struck the Voodoo man in his upper torso. He fell back against the rock, releasing Trina. The stocky man staggered, but kept standing. Matt cursed it wasn't a killing blow.

The second arrow hit the walking corpse to Matt's right. The charge that burned on it was small and the fuse short. The explosion that followed had just enough to blow the once living killer apart. The creature on Matt's left didn't react at all, still holding the former lawman tight. With one arm free, Matt tried to escape, but the death grip remained.

Kettle ran to where Sarah slowly got to her knees. The gang leader yanked her up and held her like a shield in front of him, one meaty arm wrapped around her waist, his pistol drawn and poking her in the side.

More explosions could be heard, as the Wiipukepaya took out the walking abominations.

"Call them off, Sheriff! I'll kill her! You know I will!"

Awareness returned to Sarah face. Her eyes darted wildly, finding her husband. Shame, anger, and pain marred the face that once only showed him love and laughter.

Matt reached a hand out toward her.

Sarah mouthed, "Save Trina," and then reached back to where Kettle's Apache knife pressed against her back. She fumbled it free from its sheath and, cocking an arm behind her head, cut Jimmy Kettle from ear to jaw. The outlaw threw Sarah down, holding his free hand to his gushing face. Snarling, he fired three shots into Matthew Ragsdale's wife.

Noise stopped. Matt could no longer hear the cries as Indians appeared everywhere to shoot the living and dead members of the Claw Rock Gang. He couldn't hear the moans as the walking corpses attacked, shrugging off damage and ripping warriors apart.

All Matt could hear was the blood pumping through his ears as his wife's arm dropped limp and lay there motionless. He barely noticed when the Wiipukepaya chief chopped his jailer corpse's arm free from its body. Suddenly released, Matt ran to his wife, clinging to the hope that he'd find a spark of life there, but finding none. He pulled her to his chest and cradled her.

Sound returned as Trina called to him.

"DADDY!"

Wildly he searched. Kettle was gone. The monsters fought the Yavapai warriors, one corpse to five warriors, and the corpses were getting the upper hand. Their number seemed to increase and Matt swore he caught a fallen Indian rising out of the corner of his eye.

Just in time, Matt saw the Voodoo man dart into the cave with Trina.

Not wanting to be distracted any further, Matt searched for a gun, knowing his grief would have to wait and, upon finding a fully loaded Colt, set off after his daughter.

O O O

The tunnel extended farther down than Matt would have expected. An escaping flicker of light below meant Matt would also need a torch to follow them. He found a lantern with busted glass, but still contained oil. He lit it, hating the fact that it'd make him a target.

A dozen feet. Two dozen feet. He lost track how far down he went. The path opened up on a cavern easily as big as the Sagebrush. Stalagmites and stalactites made a cobweb of stone throughout. In the center, a locomotive-sized pit yawned.

"Dad—" The word was cut off, but a decidedly male, "OW!" followed it.

The Voodoo priest stepped out from behind a pillar, shaking his hand. Trina looked scared but smiled when she saw her father. The black man took a knife and pressed it against Trina's collarbone. The wound in his chest still seeped, but he didn't show any signs of slowing or passing out.

"Let her go, and you get to go. Simple as that." Matt had the borrowed gun drawn, but both he and the Voodoo man knew he wouldn't pull the trigger. Matt changed tactics. "What do you want?"

With a decidedly Creole accent, he said, "Your head. You done left me in a hole to die. Now I'm gonna leave you in one to die. I dunna care about da girl. Kettle can have her, or da reds. I jess wanna see you jump in dat hole over dere. Den I let da girl go."

"My life for hers? You swear?"

"I swear."

Matt walked over the edge and peered over. It was blacker than a starless night. He kicked a rock and never heard it hit bottom. He turned to say goodbye to his daughter when a large explosion rocked the ceiling above.

The Voodoo man smirked. "I lay a curse on the whole area. Any who die around here come back as zhombie. Da reds be killin' da living, dey come back. The zhombies be killin' da reds, *dey* come back. Hope everyone got enough boom powder."

Another explosion and one of the stalagmites near the black man fell to the ground, forcing him to move Trina and himself closer to the pit.

Matt seized an opportunity. He dropped his lantern, extinguishing it, then drew and fired, knocking the torch from Voodoo man's hand and down into the abyss.

"And I hope you can see in the dark."

The room went black. Matt fired a second shot at the spot where he visualized the black magic wizard to be. The man cried out in pain, but Matt didn't hear a follow-up thump indicating he'd been killed.

"Trina! Crawl to me, baby!"

The former lawman fired twice more. Once to find the Voodoo man in the flash, the second to shoot that direction. He missed, but he caught Trina moving toward him. Matt crouched down and crab-walked her way. A clink of metal hitting stone reverberated through the cavern, and Matt realized his enemy stabbed the ground in hopes of piercing the girl.

Two bullets left, Matt thought.

He fired once more, finding the villain poised to bring the knife down on Trina's back.

Matt leapt forward, covering his daughter. The weapon entered near his left shoulder blade. In agony, he twisted, pulling the Voodoo man over him. They wrestled, rolling one way and then the other. The blade tore its way out causing Matt more pain as his flesh ripped.

Matt lost track of where the pit was until his leg crossed the rim and hovered over the chasm. A moan reverberated through the cave, and it wasn't one of theirs. The shuffle step of one of the undead told Matt the Voodoo man had called for reinforcements.

"You hea dat? Dat's death coming for you and your little girl."

Matt got his legs under the larger man and donkey-kicked him up and over his head. The Voodoo priest sailed into the pit and Matt said, "Not if you die first."

Matt had no less than a breath to enjoy his victory before he heard his daughter.

"Daddy! Help!"

"Trina!"

He had no idea where they were. He scrambled around until he found the lantern and relit it. The zombie held Trina and stood poised in mid-action near the edge, like its last orders were cut off. Terrified, Matt cautiously moved closer to his daughter. The zombie was one of the guards he and Ram had bled.

"Easy now, big boy. Don't do anything you'll regret." Not that talking to it would help the situation. To Trina, he comforted. "It's okay, sweetie. Just hold your hands out for daddy. I'm coming to get you."

Bravely, she extended her arms, rag doll fisted in one.

"I need both hands, honey. Can you let Miss Molly go for a moment?"

She hesitated, unsure what to do. Slowly, she nodded and released the doll.

The zombie stepped off the edge.

Matt dove for Trina, but he wasn't close enough. Their fingers grazed and he watched her vanish into the black, a scream taking his heart along with it.

Matthew Ragsdale wailed, his anguish magnified by the cave's echo. He rocked back and forth, rag doll clutched tightly to his chest.

O O O

The zombies stopped moving upon the death of their master. The remaining Yavapai dismembered them with no problems after that. They followed it up with a purification ritual. The smell of burnt carcasses filled the air.

Matt's original Indian scout pushed the former sheriff's shoulder flesh together and field stitched it closed. He wrapped a bandage about Matt's neck and torso and told him that he needed a doctor to sew it properly back together.

But Matt didn't acknowledge him. He walked to where he'd left his horse and mounted. By the time he'd gotten to Oak Creek, rain fell in sheets. Oblivious to the cold, Matt let it numb his body as a partner to his soul.

The trail rose steeply the farther up the trail he rode, becoming increasingly treacherous. Much to many a traveler's surprise Arizona wasn't all dessert, and the path Kettle took had killed many who were unprepared. Matt found spots where Kettle's mount slid in the mud. Within a half hour, two sets of tracks, man and horse, were barely visible.

Not much else was in the torrential downpour. Matt dismounted and grabbed his rifle and two pistols. He wacked the horse's butt, and it went back down the way they came. It wasn't five minutes later the former lawman moved out of the way to let a second horse come down the trail.

Kettle was close. Even through the rain, the increasing dark, Matt had a sense of him, as if their fates were tied.

A shape moved ahead. Too small for Kettle. A river otter heading down to the swelling creek below.

A blow sent Matt to his knees. It'd come from the rocks above. Two fisted. Hard. It landed on the lawman's shoulder—his bad one, and Matt roared. The next strike came from a boot to his back, and Matt went all the way to the ground. He felt the stitches in his back pop free. Blood would flow. Matt didn't have a lot of time.

He rolled to his right in time to miss being shot. Matt kicked upwards and knocked the wet gun from the outlaw's hand. He kicked again, boots landing on Kettle's gut and forcing him back a couple feet, just enough for Matt to get up.

Kettle drew the long Apache blade and squared off with Matt. Sarah's wound to his face no longer bled, but it burned red across a wet, angry face.

"Don't 'spose there's much to say at this point, is there?" Kettle asked.

Matt drew his Bowie, much shorter than the one the outlaw wielded.

"No. I reckon there ain't."

They circled each other, gauging their mettle, neither at their best.

Matt went low, hoping to gut the larger man. Kettle tucked in, barely avoiding the knife, his own swing taking off Matt's hat. Matt jumped back as Kettle kicked forward, but took the boot to his shin. It stung, but not bad.

Kettle bull-rushed Matt, slamming into him before the former sheriff could get his knife positioned. They hit the side wall together and air escaped Matt's lungs. In retaliation, Matt brought up his knee as hard as he could, hitting close enough to a sensitive spot that Kettle rolled away. The larger man swung the blade around and Matt ducked in the nick of time. Matt's blade connected with Kettle's leg, sticking in and coming out bloody. The outlaw grunted, but managed to slice across Matt's right arm.

They stepped back from each other. Bleeding and woozy, they staggered, trying to stay upright.

Lighting struck a tree a ways from them. Matt, facing that direction, was momentarily blinded by the flash. A dark shape moved towards him. Matt dropped his knife, using both hands to grab at Kettle's blade arm. The force was too much and he could feel Kettle's blade pierce his left side down to the bone. The sharp pain brought inhuman strength. Matt rammed his good shoulder into Kettle, forcing them both to the ground.

The weight of their drop caused a chunk of the trail to drop off into the ravine below. Matt had Kettle's arm pinned to the ground, but the other was free to land punches to Matt's kidney.

The gorge hung next to them, and Matthew Ragsdale had a momentary flash of Trina as she fell into the darkness. Rage strengthened him as he twisted the outlaw's arm, forcing him to drop the knife. Matt rained blows on Kettle's face, one after another, after another. Kettle's nose and jaw broke. His teeth cut Ragsdale's hand as he pummeled the defeated man's mouth. Kettle held up his hands to defend himself, but nothing stopped the onslaught.

Ragsdale pictured his wife's eyes the moment before her death. He recalled the way his heart sank when he found his best friend laying in the street. The fear in Trina's eyes. His own failure to save all of them.

He didn't notice as his and Kettle's bodies slipped closer to the muddy edge.

Kettle got out a garbled, "Stop!" just before they both went over.

They landed on a lower level of the winding trail. The former sheriff propped himself up along the wall, forcing himself to his feet. Kettle clawed his way to standing.

Jimmy Kettle, drawing from reserves no man should have had, spun with a hold-out gun in his hand.

Ragsdale, gun still on his hip, drew at the same moment.

Thunder muffled the gunshot, but the blossoming bullet wound in Kettle's chest proved Ragsdale the quicker draw. Kettle wobbled for the moment, and then toppled over the edge. The former sheriff watched him plummet three hundred feet into the raging waters of Oak Creek, swallowed whole and gone.

Ragsdale sat, the deluge doing nothing to fill the well inside him. Nor did Kettle's death seal the hole that was as big as a locomotive and as dark as a demon's soul.

O O O

Frank Chalker pounded the glowing-red horseshoe three more times before dropping it into the water to cool. It'd been three months since the end of Jimmy Kettle and the Claw Rock Gang, and business had finally picked up.

Oh, sure, there were still rumors about Drowned Horse being the place where the dead roamed free, but the town had always been the stuff of scuttlebutt and gossip. A new sheriff had been expected for days, but that was bureaucracy for you.

It was fine, though. Peace reigned over the town—a pleasant change.

"Pa? Mom wants you in for dinner."

"Be right in, Nate," Frank called to his son.

Chalker thought about his boy. The kid hadn't taken to smithing, yet, but he had one hell of a dead-eye when it came to hunting. Maybe he could get the boy interested in making rifles instead of railroad spikes and they could expand the business.

Chalker and Son Weaponry. It had a nice ring to it.

The sound of a boot scuffing the dirt came from the entrance to the workshop.

"Almost done—"

When Frank turned, his blood ran cold. He dropped the towel he had been cleaning his hands off with.

"Sheriff Ragsdale."

No expression showed on the man's face.

"Not Sheriff anymore. Y'all seen to that."

Frank held up his hands. "Matt, listen …"

But the man didn't seem to be in a listening mood. He drew a pistol and aimed it at the blacksmith's chest. Frank caught a glimpse of something tied to the belt opposite the holster.

A rag doll.

"It wasn't my fault. T'was none of our faults, what happened to your family. Kettle, he had monsters. How do you expect …"

The man cocked the gun.

"Be reasonable, Matt. This isn't what your family would have wanted."

"They're dead. So is Matthew Ragsdale. So are you and every man who stood by and let Kettle leave this town alive."

The gunshot drew Nate from the house in a sprint. The man, gun still drawn, reflexively brought it around until he saw it was Chalker's kid.

Nate spotted his father's body and ran to it yelling, "Pa! Pa! Pa!"

The man tracked the boy, deciding whether to cover his tracks. He'd hoped not to be seen so quickly. He chose to holster the gun and walk away. Nate called after him, tears in his voice.

"Why? Why?"

The man stopped. "Revenge. Isn't it always?"

The boy cradled his father's head and between sobs asked, "Who are you?"

The man tilted his head so he could peer back over his shoulder.

"Tell everyone a vengeful spirit has returned from his grave. Tell them …

"The Rag Doll Kid is coming."

Vengeance

J.R. Boyett & Peter J. Wacks

As I write these words, I ask you, dear reader, to suspend all judgment. Suspend your judgment not just of me, but of those whom I have hunted. The story that I have to tell is one for which I am not proud, nor do I find pleasure in its telling. You may consider me a hero or a villain, but I tell you now that I am neither. It is a story of my rise to prominence in death, and of my fall into obscurity in life.

o   o   o

I can recall approaching the Airship, with its ribbed lift bladder and brass woven canvas bulging to contain the pressure of its contents, glowing with a ghostly reflection of gas lights from the city below. A soft breeze caught the edges of my cape as I crossed the gangway, and a wave of melancholy touched me. I remembered … many things. Such things as would haunt most men. Those distant lights, yellow and blue, flickered and danced, thousands upon thousands of lives stretching out below, reaching out to the river several miles distant. I could almost imagine the lights to be manifestations of spirits, the anima of those whom I have known, both living—and dead.

In the blink of an eye it passed. All the troubled thoughts of a troubled man had come and gone like the force of galvanism. Turning from the midnight vista, I took comfort in the solid weight of my cane's handle. The ease with which my satin gloves glided across the surface of that silver reminded me that those days were gone. No longer did I wear the wool of a traveler; no longer need I concern myself with the vagaries of weather. No, I had left the wilderness behind me and with it the sources of those memories. I considered myself retired, accomplished—a man of dignity—learned and traveled. I was, after all, the preeminent scholar in my field and Professor of Supernatural Mythos at the Queens College in Yorkshire. I know now that I was a fool. One does not retire. The Hunt never ends.

Here, over one hundred feet above the surface of the streets, I could hear a firm echo with each step taken. The air itself held the chill of an autumn night, but I would be loath to see a man of my station exhibit weakness to such things, and so my cloak fluttered behind me as we walked. I walked that gangway with a steady pace. Upon reaching the crest, I paused. Tucking my cane beneath my arm, I unfastened my cloak, handing both it and my hat to the attendant. I cannot recall what was said, even now. I had come to think that such things were below me, trusting in my host, in his hospitality, and that was all that mattered. I was followed immediately by my wife and my youngest sister, near two decades my junior. Following the death of our parents some years prior, we had come to be all that remained of our family, with me her guardian. Looking back now, I can see clearly the design of this, but again …

No. I have a story to that must be told.

It was for my sister that we had come to this place, for she had met a man of some stature in society, a man whom I had come to believe may be worthy of my dearest sibling's hand. Ilyena—with her golden hair and her natural poise—she was everything that a woman of our class ought to be. Detached and aloof to the proper degree, she was far from prone to flights of fancy. In fact, while relaying some tales of my travels, she had come to admonish me for what she had believed to be very Münchausen embellishments. Yet mention of one Harold Ruthven had been known to render her into very unladylike bouts of giddiness.

Harold Ruthven was a Scottish industrialist who had made a name for himself in the Eastern Provinces. While his businesses were diversified, he had acquired a small fortune by cornering one market in particular. Labor. I had investigated this man, and as I should. Harold Ruthven was not only a man of culture whose line could be traced to the aristocracy, but he was also a man who had successfully navigated the world of business. With his connections and successes he could not only provide for my sister in the manner that she deserved, but he would also allow her an opportunity to elevate her social status. Yes, I felt Harold Ruthven to be a good match for my dearest sister.

But wait, a story must begin at the beginning, and though this is *a* beginning, it is not *the* beginning. For you see, my dear reader, I am not innocent in this matter. I am not the victim that you may wish me to be. No. For I know now that what happened on that voyage happened because of my ignorance, because of my arrogance: the arrogance of a man of science. I am as much to blame for their deaths as I am to blame for *his*. I know now that what I had taken for a monster was anything but. The beast of *magic* which we had sought to study was anything but that which our study of the lore had led us *wise* men to believe. For you see, my dear reader, we are all a part of a family. As I sought to provide for mine, so he sought to avenge his. But I get before myself. I must first describe for you the events that brought us to this sad affair.

In those early days, I fancied myself learned. My colleagues and I were recently graduated from University. Schooled as we were, we had begun to dabble in the occult. We did not do this for reasons of fetish, like so many, but as a matter of intellect. Having studied well the world of man, we were drawn to the uncertainties offered by the practices of superstition. We left our universities and, taking advantage of our station, we became adventurers. We believed in science. In the visible truth of a hydraulic piston, a steam engine, or the myriad other miracles of everyday life.

It was the folly of youth, calling ourselves adventurers and thinking we ventured where no others had. The generations of mythos should have been treated with the same respect and reverence as our professors' volumes. Instead, we treated each new case with frivolity and skepticism. We responded like the Brothers Grimm to each tale of horror, to each rumor of beast.

A modicum of redemption may be found in knowing that our earliest pursuits found nothing to discredit our views. Unfortunately, we never thought to question our dismissals. We failed to ask the most basic question of epistemology; we assumed our skepticism to be superior and never bothered to examine it or the premises upon which it was based. This is the truth of arrogance, the truth that led us to the events of that fateful day.

As I have previously mentioned, my colleagues and I were students of the world. We had debunked the horror of the *Magi of Liverpool*, exposing the trickery of mirrors and clockwork for what it was. Just as easily we had established a purely rational explanation of the *Kraken of Ballybrack,* showing the mechanized monster for what powered it. Despite these early successes for science, we had come to face the very real truth that some mysteries were beyond our understanding. There was a village of the damned, Dalmigavie if I'm not mistaken, in which the occupants had disappeared with not a trace left behind. After nearly a month of investigation, our only discoveries were an etched wall, diagrams, and obscure references to a something called *Cthulhu.*

We followed any rumor on our grand quest for the truth. Visiting backwater villages, we came to know the squalor of the masses, eating their food and bearing witness to their poverty. How naïve we were to think that such things made us wise of the world. In truth we were just spoiled aristocrats living off of the success of our predecessors. We spoke with the people and studied their superstitions. Often we discounted certain attributes or drew correlations between one mythos and another, but to our credit we did study. Though we may have dismissed the lore, we at least listened to everything. Being the scholar that I am, I had taken careful notation of our investigations. In fact, it was this approach which served as the basis for my many publications on the subject, and which later secured my post at the Queens College.

Following this pattern we found ourselves in a small village in the hills some miles outside of Lesko, in Poland. We were drawn to this region by the tales of an *Oupire*, which, according to local legend, was a reanimated corpse. The regional mythos indicated that the body contains two souls, the lesser of which remains in the body after death. The theory was that this lesser soul could, on occasion, reanimate a corpse that would then act in many ways as an animal. I can tell you now that this is only partially true.

On the morning of our third day in the village, the day in which we had planned to depart, we were surprised by the presence of another visitor. His name is not one that I can repeat. The first reason for this is that I swore never to reveal that knowledge; the second is that despite all of our time together, I am not certain that he ever revealed to me the truth of his name.

We knew him then only as Markus. He had come to this village for the same legend we had heard of. He revealed to us that he was a hunter, not a scholar, and that his purpose was quite different from ours. He sought to kill that which we sought to study. Naturally, we were both attracted to and repulsed by him. While accompanying him would allow us a unique study, how could we take seriously a man who believed so foolishly in such things? Nevertheless, it was an opportunity we could not pass up.

O   O   O

Along our travels he revealed to us a contrivance he termed a shotbow, which he informed us had been crafted by his own hands. Along the barrel and stock I recognized many engravings derived from ancient and holy practices; each one was a ward against evil or a petition for protection. There were others which were foreign to me and which I suspect were barbarous in origin. It was the front of this weapon, however, which I found the most curious, for it bore a well-worn and aged handle, hammered of iron into the form of our Lords symbol.

When asked, he joked in a most unchristian fashion that one could best combat the living dead by harnessing the power of that which was once dead but yet lives. With this, he had a clockwork assembly feeding several hardwood stakes with silver heads and brass capped ends into the barrels, a short blade of silver that bore the very same engravings as the bow, two vials of blessed water, and incensed oil for burning.

It would not be incorrect to say that we had thought little for this man or his precautions. My fraternity and I had decided that we would accompany him on his *hunt*, if only for the academic opportunity which it presented. Despite his warnings, we were certain that there existed a perfectly natural explanation for the stories that we had come to hear. Perhaps this so-called *Oupire* was a mere hermit with the misfortune to have lost his faculties. Though, I must admit that a part of me had been made wary by his admonitions.

He had certainly viewed us as the spoiled aristocrats that we were. I recognize now that my affection for his warnings resulted solely from the surety of their declaration, pronouncements that were uttered with a certainty I had not known since University. He spoke to us like a professor ... and we mocked him for it. A part of me suspected at the time, and I am now certain, that he had been fully aware of our highbrow chides. We had taken his lack of response to such things as a sign that he lacked comprehension. I have come to recognize that he responded as a wise man would to children who could only learn a lesson in the hardest way. Pray that the world never arrives at a time that it is standard for its peoples to assume lack of intellect or wisdom due to linguistic barriers, as we did. A sad world that would be.

Early on the day of his hunt, we gathered in the stable yard. The soft autumn sun was made softer yet as it was filtered by a thin fog. Some nights I reflect upon this expedition, and I fancy that the fog clung to my skin in a most unnatural way. I know this to be false, but still, I fancy the image. We left the inn and village behind, and even the most boastful of us had sense enough to hold his tongue. For all our talk and exuberance, there was a part of us that must surely have known what was to come.

We traveled that day and camped early in the hills, building a small fire to stave off the shadows and boiling tea to warm our blood. While we brought to boil a broth, our companion busied himself drawing glyphs upon the trees. Determined to make the most of this venture, and intrigued as I was by grimoire, I copied each glyph into my notes and accompanied them with notations of purpose and origin, at least insofar as my guide could answer. I know that my fraternity viewed this with mixed emotions. On the one hand, I was doing as we had sought out to do, but on the other, I was encouraging this man's deviant ideology. Regardless, they held their tongues.

The following day brought with it a silence we felt in our bones. Even the birds kept their songs unsung that day. Our companion told us that we felt the touch of the *Oupire*. He pointed to marks upon one of the trees, which he claimed was sign of the *Oupire's* presence, though I must confess that all we saw were the scratches of a small animal. I felt as if we had been pulled into a gypsy's lair and fallen victim to her sleight of hand. We were beginning to experience a collective paranoia, one for which we knew not the cause.

We rode in silence for most of the day, with an occasional comment from our companion regarding some obscure lore or another. While I took notes, my fellows brewed upon his words in quiet solemnity. Tension among my fraternity increased as the day passed. I could tell that Niles in particular was becoming increasingly dissatisfied with the circumstances in which we found ourselves. He railed at each mention of the occult. I can see now that we had each committed intellectual sin; we had allowed ourselves to derive our conclusions before we had examined the evidence; and in doing so, we had denied any evidence a chance for consideration. Our travels had become a game to us, and we no longer conducted ourselves as scholars.

Our companion continued as if unaware of the pensive silence hanging over us. He would pause occasionally to sniff the air or examine the terrain. Several times he would remove a strange device, which he claimed measured energies. Comprised of several rings, brass and silver in construction, one inside the other and each free standing, it would spin and spin. Sometimes a ring would stop and reverse its order, or rotate to spin in a new direction. I had assumed the thing to be a trick of magnetism, but each time he would study it with care, and then nod as if the answer to his unspoken query was clear.

Mounted upon the back of a Dun in his worn, high colored coat, he made a strange image. The wide brimmed hat hid his eyes in shadow, but on the occasions in which I could see them, I had come to reconsider my previous evaluation. The glint in his eye, which I had earlier taken to be a sign of disturbed obsession, appeared new to me in the light of our second day together. He looked less like a man crazed and more like a man focused. I came to realize that day that he reminded me more and more of my father's gamesman. I was dismayed to find that I had somehow come to respect this man, if only marginally.

Vengeance

It was shortly after this revelation that he stopped once more to sniff the air and to measure energies. Engrossed as he was in his task, he seemed not to have noticed when Niles raised his objections. We had all known that he would, at least those of us who knew him, and I suspect that our companion had known as well. When the tirade was complete, our companion spoke firmly but softly. I can remember his words well, for the effect that they had.

"Silence, you fool. *It* is close." The authority of those words echo in my head still. Niles' face reddened, and he began to object, but he had not the time. Before he could speak another word, bedlam descended upon us.

Wilson was the first taken. The small glade in which we sat upon our horses was suddenly darker, as if a preternatural twilight had descended upon us. A shadow reached to him from an outcrop of granite—and he was gone. Pistols were drawn, and the air was soon filled with smoke. I confess my own inaction, for which I can only blame cowardice. I sat on my horse and watched in shock as the shadows danced around us. Of our party, the only one to remain calm was our companion. He watched the shadows from his saddle with steadfast alertness. As he held the shotbow in his right hand, he used the left to withdraw a vial of water from within his coat.

Niles, jaw still hanging open from his outburst, was the second to be struck down by the beast. What I know now to be one attacker had seemed then to be several. Distracted by the shadows, it pounced upon him from behind. The speed and ferocity of it lifted him from his seat and threw him through the air. Our companion was faster than we and had quickly trained the beast in his sights, for what good it did. The monster had used Niles' own horse for cover as he dashed toward his next victim, Rufus. Before we knew what had happened, Rufus, whom I had bunked with at college, was gone as well, hauled away into the shadows. I could hear his screams in the trees ... they ended abruptly. Niles, still alive, whimpered at the base of a tree. He was holding his cartography monocle like a pistol, waving it at the air in front of him. We would later conclude that he struck the tree and broken his collarbone.

Then our guide spoke to me. He was not afraid, nor was he weakened by what had happened. "Steady, lad, and rally to me." They were simple words, but they invoked such confidence that they broke

150

the spell of fear that had engulfed me. I noticed then that I had, out of instinct, been controlling my startled horse. It pranced in fear, whereas my guide's horse stood fast. I tried to calm my horse as I urged him beside my guide. He gestured for me to back up slightly, and I did. We sat there for what seemed to be several minutes, my guide watching the trees while Niles whimpered in pain.

When he moved again it was almost too quick for me to track. He spun in his saddle like an adder and slung an arc of water. As I looked to my right, the beast was rebuffed in midair. It had come for me, but now it fell to the ground as if it had struck a wall! I could see that it was man, or that it at least resembled a man. With alacrity that I have come to associate with its kind, the beast sprang to its feet. It clearly intended to retreat to the shadows, but it was met instead by silver-headed stake shot from my guide's first barrel. It screamed and hissed as the silver burned its flesh, smoke rising from his wounds. It fell to the ground and, barring its fangs, rolled to its back, scrambling backward as if to seek refuge in the shadows. My guide was already on the ground, dismounting while I had been watching the *Oupire*, and as the thing hissed, a flash of light forced another shaft of silver and wood into its flesh.

My guide dropped both the gun and the vial. Drawing that wide silver blade, he approached the beast with speed, though still showing caution. It cowered on the ground as if already defeated, alternating between bouts of hissing and whimpers of pain. I can recall being on the verge of urging my guide to finish the thing, when it suddenly pounced. It displayed a speed I had thought impossible. From prone it sprang up and forward in one motion, a blur of viciousness imposed over the dying sound of its last pitiful whine.

My guide was not as foolish as I would have been. He had known the deceit of the *Oupire* and waited for the attack. His reaction was clean and final. Hunter moved forward a fraction of a second before the beast, sweeping the blade in an upward arc as his left hand reached out to brace his other wrist, pushing his entire body's weight into the attack. The first slash hit the beast in the chest and stopped him in his tracks, ripping through the flesh of the beast's torso and unleashing a gout of reddish black blood. The second slash, delivered so smoothly that it seemed to come at the same time as the first, severed the *Oupire's* head.

As it fell to the ground, its limbs twitched. My guide wasted no time. He revealed the flask of oil and removed its stopper, emptying the flask upon the creature in front of him. Retrieving the shotbow, he cranked a cogwheel concealed below the stake feed belt, and the two barrels rotated, revealing a smaller diameter third one. Out of his pocket he produced a strange looking oversized bullet, similar to a shell from a fowling piece, painted red. I would later learn this was still called a shell, but was modified from the particular weapon called the shotgun, used mainly in the Americas. He loaded it, leveling the weapon at the *Oupire*.

After saying a brief prayer for the lost soul, he fired the weapon one last time. The contents of the shell entered the body and burned as if imbued with some magic. He would later teach me a recipe, a mixture of two metals, which when set on fire could not be dowsed. As it burned the chest of the beast, it lit the oil. The body moved for several minutes as the oil reduced it to ash.

After tending to Niles' injuries, we were able to recover the bodies of my dear friends. We could not retrieve the horses and resigned ourselves to walk back to the village, using the two remaining horses to carry the wounded and the dead.

This is how I became a hunter. I spent many years with my mentor, playing the role of both scribe and squire. What I learned I recorded, and in the years since I have published much of what I saw. I knew well enough what to withhold for the sake of the skeptic, and I was ever cautious to present my material within the realm of myth and tradition. Nonetheless, my work stands as the surest source regarding such matters, and it was due to the sheer depth and detail of my writings that I was offered a Professorship at the University.

Niles returned home, but died two years later. His body mended rapidly, but his mind was never the same. He kept to himself, hiding in dark rooms, eating scraps, and seemed unable to formulate coherent sentences. It was the night that his doctor and I were discussing moving him to Bethlam Royal that he took his own life. I now suspect that he had been encouraged to do so by an occult voice.

O O O

And this brings us back to the night in which I first met the Scottish industrialist. Upon boarding the vessel, Master Ruthven greeted us immediately. His exuberance at our presence was palpable. I can recall with stark clarity the processes of my mind in that moment. The familiarity of his features and the warmth of his smile bestowed upon me the inclination to greet him warmly, as a friend many years unseen; and yet, I can recall a hesitation, that warning of my base instinct which was quickly discarded by my higher functions. I recall that my hidden mind gnawed at my awareness. There was a hidden glint in his eye, the danger of which was at such odds with the warmth of his smile.

That dichotomy should have frozen my blood, but all I could see was the smile. It haunts me still, in my dreams. Giant, it looms above me. Even in this retelling, I find myself drawn to the charm of it, a magic that defies the meaning of the word. I have often wondered if the moth knows the danger of the flame, if perhaps something deep within it compels an attraction which it knows to be fatal. If so, then I was, that night, a moth.

He took my hand warmly and greeted us aboard his ship. I had taken his excitement as a sign of his devotion to my sister. There were cracks in his façade. His anticipation was well contained, and for that I mistook its meaning, its focus. Darkness I had been taught to penetrate with my gaze instead blinded me with its light.

After greeting us at the gangway, we were received in the vessel's grand hall. The ship itself was an eastern continental design, which I presume he had acquired during his ventures in that region. The ornamentation was heavily gilded, statuary and filigree interlaced across the visible areas of the ship, all designed to conceal the pipe works and gearing that an aristocrat's Air Yacht required to sail. It was an odd ship to see in the West, but the exchange of such fashions was not unheard of, and I could identify no less than four cultural influences in his décor.

The areas we traveled were all well lit by gas infused lamps, the piping seamlessly concealed within the walls and filigrees. It occurred to me that the quality of craftsmanship indicated a wealth greater than I had uncovered, but I reasoned that he had levied his business assets and had the vessel rebuilt to his personal specifications. My eyes took in the splendor as we departed. The ship shook a bit, swaying as the lift bladders vented steam to push us forward and up. The weakness I had felt when we embarked returned, and though I gripped my cane, a wave of dizziness overcame me, and I grabbed a rail, waving my wife and Ilyena forward.

"Go on ahead, I shall be with you shortly." They said something else, I am not sure what, but when I once again protested the group left me to regain my composure. Busy fighting the sudden sickness, I never noticed the assailant sneaking up behind me. A sharp pain flared across the side of my neck, and I felt warmth spreading across my shoulder. The injury awoke a fire in me, and I spun around, smashing a fist into the reaches of the wall above me, grabbing what was inside. Standing before me was a beast. One of *them*. I grinned at it, allowing the rage in me to come forth. Attacking me had been a mistake, and I would make sure it was the last it made. It paused, sensing that it had shifted from hunter to prey.

A scream echoed from behind me, curdling my blood. My sister's scream. I jerked the pipe in the wall out while smashing the lamp above me with the silver head of my cane. Cut off from the gas flow, the lamp died, along with the other lamps along the entryway that had been powered by the line I pulled.

Though I am a man of science, I will give luck its due, especially here. The lamp managed, with its last flicker, to ignite the stream of gas coming from the ruptured pipe I was holding. The explosion filled the hall, rippling through the air away from me, consuming all in its path and igniting the Oupire. However, the shockwave did not treat me so well. I was thrown off my feet, bouncing along the corridor like a football at the toes of a guttersnipe.

My constitution was near the limits of my lifestyle. I had not exercised in far too long, and there is only so much a body can take. One of the pursuits of the natural philosopher has always been improvement of the constitution. Some went in the direction of Sir Newton, becoming closet alchemists attempting to distill the elixir of life. I have found that where the body fails, the mind can push on. I struggled to my feet, leaning on the wall for support until I reached the stateroom. Blood covered the handle.

When I entered the room my fears were confirmed. Ilyena, my sweet sister, lay motionless upon the top of his desk, my wife crumpled on the floor. My vision darkened. All I could see was my sister's body.

He had lain her out as though she were his trophy. I could feel my skin tighten, and in the corner of my eye I could see that his eyes bore into me. Inside I raged with pain, but I refused to show it to him. Raising my eyes, with my resolve steeled, I began to walk.

My sister, my poor sweet sister, lay between us, discarded and forgotten in the necessity of the moment. No, not forgotten. Never forgotten, merely set aside. As much as I wished to throw myself to her, I was a hunter; a mountain cat facing a bear. I was outmatched, outwitted, and unprepared. My foe, I recognized him now for what he was, had succeeded in trapping me on his ship. With nowhere to run, I was to watch as he playfully destroyed everything that I loved.

As I stepped to the side of the room, he remained still, standing on the other side of the desk. Waiting for me to advance. A small smile flitted across his lips while his eyes followed me. He had the presence of a confident beast, lazily awaiting my move. We both knew who had the advantage. I could stalk all I wanted, and he was just enjoying the show. My only chance—yes, I had one—I could not undo the touch of death, but I could avenge. I had one secret from him. Something science could not explain, and of which I had never written.

I brought myself to the edge of obstructions. All that stood between us was twenty feet and the corner of his desk. A few more steps and he would have a clear line to me. I dared not give him that chance. I wished to tempt him with it, nothing more.

So I stopped. "Why have you done this?"

His response was, "To lament my brother. You helped the hated one slay us like beasts, yet we are not. We feel. We love. We speak. And the man you followed and idolized cut us down like so much meat."

I blinked. He was trying to get under my skin. Into my head. "You dare act like a civilized man? You hunted us long before we returned. I never would have known you existed if not for your unprovoked attack."

His fist slammed down on the desk. "It is the law and the lore! You come onto our lands, and you are ours. The peasants warned you!"

So many years of scholarly pursuit, yet I make the mistake of a first year. I had forgotten the lore that the locals taught me, so caught up in the existence of the *Oupire* as I had been. Too late to go back and check my notes for a scholarly argument. My family was dead, and I was not far behind. Wetness made a line down my cheek. Apparently I didn't have long before the damn of emotion was to burst, if the lone tear was any indicator.

Do you see now my dear reader? Do you see how I am to blame for our deaths? It was that night so long ago, when we had first known the fallacy of our wisdom. As I had killed his kin, so he would kill mine. For years he had stalked us, watched us. He had fallen upon our unsuspecting families, striking at our connections to this world. Did he seek to drive me to the same end that I suspect he had driven Niles? Yes, I believe he did. He had hoped to madden me, to strike such grief into my heart that I would gladly welcome death.

He taunted me and prodded at me, and when I should have been at my weakest, I let him see it. I let my pain show and allowed myself to look once more at her cold corpse; her lifeless eyes set within her pale face. He moved faster than most men could follow. To most he would have seemed a blur. Even I could barely see it happen. In my brief moment of revealed weakness he had crossed the distance between us, his hand had reached out to my throat, and he had revealed his nature with his teeth. But my training had taught me to anticipate this, even to provoke it.

Was he to grab me, would he kill me, or would he torment me some more? I recall this thought dimly gracing the edges of my mind. To be honest, my dear reader, I do not know the answer. His hand never reached my throat; his teeth never met my flesh. His eyes, those luring orbs, had held rage. I can remember seeing it in the corner of my eye as I looked at my sister's corpse. How I wished that she had been there to see what I had done.

I stared at her as his hands clawed at my arm. When he gurgled, I turned to him. Those horrible orbs … did they hold fear or surprise? I do not know. His hands left my arm and began to grope the blade that had pierced his neck. I looked over that blade and met his eyes. The inscriptions upon my blade, holy etchings from a dozen world Mythologies, glowed a faint blue, and his blood had begun to ooze down its length.

I stared into his eyes as the life passed from them. He tried to speak but could not. My blade, hidden within my cane, had pierced the center of his throat. He expunged his final breath, and with it a splash of blood. It caught me in the face, but I did not care. I had won, but at a horrible price.

My left hand still held the cane from which I had drawn the blade. As quick as he was, I was prepared. Pushing against the exposed cog on the head of the cane's shaft, a micro-hydraulic fired and the opening shifted slightly as the cog raised. I flipped the cane around, and tapped the open end against his chest. There was a flash, then he and the cane caught fire. I dropped the ruined cane shaft and released the blade, groggily watching the single red shell roll across the floor. The pressure switch in my cane was only good for one shot, but sometimes that was all you needed.

I had learned well from my mentor, letting my instincts take over when my brain could no longer make decisions. Ruthven had mistaken me for a human, when in truth I was a hunter. My feelings, my fears … nothing can stand between me and my hunt. And the hunt never ends. I watched the Oupire burn as the fire slowly spread across the room.

In the end I was a coward. I chose a few seconds of flight and a swift end over staying with my sister in the fiery airship. Just a few steps to reach the window, then the ground rushed towards me, delivering a swift end.

O O O

To my demise, as Ruthven had mistaken me, so too had I mistaken him. In all my travels I had never claimed to know everything, or even to learn all that there was to know of the subjects of my studies. I still maintain that for everything I learned, there was much more left undiscovered. You see, as my cane had hidden my attack, his blood had hidden his. I know now that it was the blood which had led to my death, for in the hours that followed I had awoken unharmed. I began to rant about things that even I knew to be madness. I had died. Why had the world forced me to live? My ravings did not go unnoticed. In my state I was aware of some small things. I knew for instance that I had become a suspect in the deaths of my family and of my host. After all, I was mad, was I not?

o o o

And now, dear reader, you know my tale. You have seen my demise and the price of my arrogance. And yet I live still. For how else could I pen these words? What I failed to know then, what I could not have known, was the true touch of the Oupire. My torment was not to end with my life. Upon my deathbed passed my first soul, but awakened by the Oupire's blood, my second soul arose. The soul of a hunter is tenacious at best. It would not allow me to die. As I have said before, "the hunt never ends."

So read.

Follow the works I have written, the clues laid therein. Find a way to destroy me, to deliver my soul—if you dare. I await you dear reader, where they have sequestered me and my supposed madness at the Bethlam Royal. I await you in Bedlam.

THE NOONDAY SUN

Vivian Caethe

The noonday sun shimmered across the black land as mirages smudged the border between earth and sky. Places like this in the New Mexico Territory bred ancient stories and whispered dark secrets. Hazel could imagine obscure tales hidden in the sharp-edged volcanic rock and the winding tunnels that yawned like open mouths to swallow the sky.

She rode into Cibola on the day after her twentieth birthday, getting fewer stares than she had anticipated. The rumors about the town—that it was cursed with a plague, with monsters, with witches—had drawn her to it. There had been rumors of "lloronas," vampire-like creatures endemic to the area. As a monster hunter, it was her trade to seek out such places.

The streets were empty, and only a few women watched from their windows as she rode down the empty main street. The only motion came from the dust that puffed around Rocinante's hooves as they came up in front of the saloon. She searched each of their faces, hoping she would see Dulcinea's.

The heavy sound of Rocinante's hooves on the packed dirt echoed through the empty streets. If a curse hung over this town, there might not be that many folks left to wander around during the day. The silence stretched as the afternoon faded the wooden storefronts to silver, the adobe walls to gold.

Reaching the center of town, she dismounted from her Belgium draft horse and stretched. Rocinante was the biggest horse she'd ever seen, and stood close to seventeen hands. He gave her room to hide behind as she checked her powered armor's fittings, ensuring the long ride hadn't jostled anything out of place. Rocinante permitted her to pat him affectionately as she tied him in the shade.

Looking up, she read the sign above the door, "Small Comfort Saloon." She snorted. If lloronas owned it, the comfort would be solely theirs. She loosened her guns in their holsters and pushed open the swinging doors.

The brothel's interior cooled Hazel's sunbaked eyes as she glanced around, her hands resting casually on the butts of her Schofields. What sort of saloon in the Territories was empty at noon?

The short, mustached bartender looked up when she entered. "Something to drink, miss?"

"Whatever you have." She took off her hat and placed it on the counter next to her. The bartender poured her a shot from an unlabeled bottle.

As she toyed with the shot glass, she dearly wished she could take off her duster, but the sight of her armored exoskeleton in a new town tended to have one of two predictable results: she became a freak show or some trigger happy fool'd decide she needed to be relieved of the exoskeleton on principle. She wished she had a penny for every time she heard, "What's a pretty lady like you doing with all that metal?"

Of course, they didn't ask when they saw her legs. Polio had been her greatest curse and her greatest blessing. Without it, she never would have donned the exoskeleton nor had the courage to become a monster hunter. She had heard of monster hunters growing up, but who hadn't? Tales of Sheriff Pat Garrett had kept her riveted for weeks. She still felt the small twinge of jealousy at the thought of his adventures hunting the werewolf Billy the Kid.

The wilds of the West teemed with monstrous creatures. The string of forts that ran up and down the Rocky Mountains were testament enough to the danger. She had traveled to Arizona to hunt chupacabras attacking ranchers' cows, gone to the rough country of Colorado to look for sasquatches that threatened the mining operations. And now she had come to New Mexico, the land of enchantment, the heart of monster country.

"What brings you to these parts?"

Hazel looked down at the empty shot glass then glanced to the open door to the kitchen where an edge of skirt could be seen. "I'm looking for an old friend, picking up work as I go along."

"Are you a mercenary?"

"Sort of." Hazel allowed a wry smile to crack her face. "I'm more of a bounty hunter, but I don't aim for men."

"I've heard tales of folks like you. You go after the monsters." The man had a strange gleam in his eye. Could that be hope?

"Yeah." Hazel smiled. "You seen any monsters around here?"

"Cibola is too small to be a town." The man looked away. "And the People protect us."

"The Indians?"

"Their mesas surround this area and the land is sacred to them. They wouldn't let monsters live here."

"But you've heard stories, haven't you?"

"Would you like some breakfast? I'm the best cook in Cibola. But I don't get to cook very often. Most of the men drink their dinners."

"You didn't answer my question."

The man's jaw set stubbornly. "The People protect us. There's nothing wrong. It's just a sickness, is all."

"Sickness?" Hazel asked.

He sighed. "There's been stories about witches that attack the men in their sleep. Some of them have gotten sick. The People won't come into town until they've passed or got better. Most of them don't get better."

"And then they die," Hazel said. His story sounded familiar enough to confirm her suspicions. There were lloronas here. Her attention went back to the skirt in the kitchen. It wasn't like such creatures to hide. They were bold, sensual. "Who's hiding in the kitchen?"

The edge of a skirt twitched and Hazel exchanged a glance with the bartender. She stood, putting her hand on her right revolver. "I feel compelled to tell you, sir, that I do not much care to be spied upon. Nor do I take chances in my profession."

"Come on out, niña." Juan sighed.

The girl that stepped from the kitchen looked like Dulcinea. Hazel hid her reaction. There was no use in getting her hopes up.

"You don't look like one of them," Hazel said.

The girl flushed. "Just because I live here doesn't make me one of the employees."

Hazel opened her mouth then realized they were talking about two different sorts of things. She had forgotten this was a brothel as well as a saloon.

The girl recovered her composure. "Who are you looking for? Your old friend?"

"An old friend of mine. We grew up together, but my family ... well, it's not a pretty story."

"If you don't mind, I'd like to hear it." The girl seated herself at the bar at a safe distance from Hazel. "It's been awhile since I've heard a story from a stranger."

Hazel took a breath, hurt by the implication that she was a stranger. Perhaps she had been wrong after all. "Well ... like I said, I grew up on a ranch in Texas. Our cook had a little girl, only a couple years younger than me, and we used to play together." Hazel took a sip of coffee. "My father, well ... he wasn't a very good man when it came to women. My mother shouldn't have been surprised, but he made some overtures at the cook after her husband died. My mother got wind of it and was out for blood. She would have had the woman whipped, you see. The cook wasn't white like my family; she was from south of the border, somewhere in Mexico."

Hazel paused, looking at the girl out of the corner of her eye. She was caught up in the story, but without a flicker of recognition. After a moment, Hazel took a breath and continued. "Well, I warned the girl and her mother. T'wasn't right what my father had done, what my mother was going to do. My friend and her mother escaped in the middle of the night, headed out for the Territories before my mother could get the hands riled up. My mother was as bad as my father. She was just better at hiding it."

"So you've come out here looking for your friend and her mother?" the girl asked.

"I heard she might be out here, might be in trouble with all the monsters here," Hazel said. "Heard about the curse here too, like I said. Figured if nothing else, I'd get a bounty from the railroad. They don't like it when there's interference at their depots."

The girl nodded. "What was your friend's name? Maybe I've seen her around town."

"Dulcinea," Hazel said. "Her name was Dulcinea."

Shocked, the girl's expression turned from curious to bewildered. "If I'm her, I don't remember you at all."

Hazel shrugged, trying for nonchalance. "I figured it was a long shot."

"No, it's not that." The girl shook her head, dark tresses spilling over her shoulder with the motion. "I don't remember anything. I don't ... I don't even remember my mother's face."

"I'm sorry," Hazel said, her throat constricting. She swallowed and spoke again. "If you think ... you might be her. I can tell you about your mother if you'd like."

The girl nodded shyly. Hazel sat on the stool next to her and took her hand, marveling at the softness against her own rough skin. "She had a smile that could light up the night. She had the most beautiful accent; it made everything she said sound like music. I remember sitting in the kitchen with you, listening to her sing as she made empanadas, both of us just happy to be there and hoping to sneak one or two."

Dulcinea laughed softly. Hazel continued. "She was always singing, smiling. She was the most beautiful woman on the ranch, and your father was madly in love with her. They used to walk around the pasture at dusk, holding hands and watching the stars come out."

"Your mother ... you look a lot like her." Hazel took a breath. "You have her hair. It was always so soft and long. She used to let us brush it at night, after your father died."

"Did you miss me?" Dulcinea asked, then blushed. "I'm sorry, I didn't mean ..."

"Of course I did. I wouldn't come looking for you if I didn't." Hazel smiled. She owed the girl a debt, for what her family did to her and her mother. It was more than forcing them to flee, it was forcing them to flee in the middle of monster territory.

"What are you doing here?" A woman's voice intruded.

Hazel looked up to see a pale woman standing in the hallway. She stood, her hand going to her guns. The woman advanced down the stairs. Her skin was deathly pale, and she wore a nightgown even though it was well past noon. "Who are you? Get away from her!"

"Sarah, it's all right. She's my friend." Dulcinea moved so she stood between Hazel and the woman. "We were just catching up."

Another woman came down the stairs behind Sarah. They could have been twins. "Get away from her, Dulcinea. You don't have any friends."

"Rachel, it's all right." Dulcinea's smile wavered.

In these parts, creatures like these women were called lloronas, foul creatures that preyed on the men of the Southwest. She had suspected when she heard of the curse ailing Cibola, but there was nothing like confirmation staring you in the face to get the blood boiling.

She unsnapped her holster and eased one of her Schofields out with her left hand. Juan had disappeared into the kitchen, and Dulcinea should have as well. If she needed to, Hazel could push Dulcinea out of the way and bear down on the two lloronas.

"Dulcinea." Hazel pitched her voice low, even though she knew that the creatures could hear her. "You need to get out of here. Get into the sunlight."

"But, this is Sarah." Dulcinea turned to Hazel. "Sarah and Rachel are my guardians."

"Go!" Hazel shoved Dulcinea out of the way. The girl gasped and stumbled. Sarah lunged down the stairs toward them. Claws grew from the woman's fingers as she slashed at Dulcinea. Hazel blocked and pushed Dulcinea further toward the door. The llorona's claws skittered across Hazel's exoskeleton, tearing gashes in her leather duster.

"Monster hunter!" Rachel spit. Fangs distorted the woman's mouth as she made a grab for Dulcinea. The girl screamed and tried to scramble out of the way. Hazel didn't have a good shot, not with the girl dithering about. Instead, she swung the butt of her Schofield into Rachel's nose with a crunch. The creature snarled and spit again. Black viscous blood spattered across Hazel's duster, sizzling where it struck.

She couldn't take on both of them and keep Dulcinea safe at the same time. Growling in frustration, Hazel holstered her gun and pushed the girl toward the swinging doors. Sunlight would protect them. She could come back for the monsters later.

Stumbling into the blinding sunlight, Hazel pushed Dulcinea forward until they were free of any shadows. Tied by the entrance to the saloon, Rocinante stomped dangerously. Hazel pulled her guns and pointed them at the dark entrance of the saloon.

Dulcinea bit back a scream and pointed down the street. Looking, Hazel cursed softly but vehemently.

Dead miners shambled down the street toward them, still clothed in their funeral best.

"Come on." Hazel grabbed the girl's wrist and dragged her to Rocainte. She felt more than saw Dulcinea's gaze on her arm, on the metal of her armor.

Letting go of Dulcinea's hand, Hazel took hold of the reins and murmured to the stallion as he fussed. Reluctantly, Rocinante knelt before them. Glancing back down the street, she mounted quickly, flashing metal in the sunlight. Dulcinea stepped back, her eyes on Rocinante's hooves. Hazel held a hand down to her. "Get on and hold tight."

She yanked Dulcinea off the street as the massive horse stomped, baring his teeth when he saw the creatures. Hazel smiled and murmured, "All right, Rocinante. Let's go."

The once-men turned toward them, sniffing the air. Hazel called over her shoulder, "It'll only be a moment before they catch wind of us. We will outrun them for now, but their mistresses will join them at nightfall."

She felt Dulcinea's grip tighten around her waist as Rocinante tensed and charged. The immense horse barreled down the main street toward the once-men. The last time Hazel had fought creatures like this, they had swarmed at the slightest motion. Rocinante could outrun them, but only if they got through the horde first.

Behind her, Dulcinea hummed a song that tickled the back of Hazel's memory. Rocinante seemed to feel something from it, his charge became smoother, his strides longer. He barreled into the once-men, trampling them as Hazel fended off their grasping hands. Fingers turned to talons by death grasped and grabbed, trying to find purchase on Hazel's duster.

Dulcinea shrieked. Hazel glanced back. One of the creatures grabbed her skirt, winding its talons into the folds. Flicking her wrist to extend the knife in her armor, she twisted in the saddle and cut through Dulcinea's skirt. The girl gasped and flinched, but the once-man fell back, the scrap of cloth clutched in its hand.

And then they were through. The once-men shambled after them, but they were too slow to catch Rocinante.

Outside of town, the stallion's hooves thudded into the desert, casting up puffs of sand into the late afternoon light. Hazel guided Rocinante into the wilderness where she hoped they could find a place to make a stand for the night.

As they rode, a thunderstorm gathered above the mesas. Lightning struck the heights, flashing through the dimness of the clouded afternoon. Within minutes, the clouds opened up and rain drenched them.

O O O

"Where are we going?" Dulcinea asked as Hazel slowed Rocinante to a halt.

"We needed to get away from the town, away from their power base." Hazel dismounted and glanced around. "But now, we need to find a place to hunker down for the night. There has to be somewhere around here where we can make a stand."

Hazel glanced up at the girl and her eyes met Dulcinea's. She found herself blushing, of all things, as she noticed that Dulcinea's wild hair cascaded loose down around her shoulders. She swallowed against the sudden dryness in her throat.

There was no chance that she would remember.... Hazel shook her head and held her hand up to help the girl down from the horse. It wouldn't be right. Dulcinea had been through so much. It would be too much to ask.... She glanced around. "There's a cave over there. We can seek shelter for the night and figure out a plan in the morning."

"Can I help?"

"Not with him." Hazel busied herself with picketing Rocinante at the mouth of the cave. They had just been friends, childhood friends. There was no way that Dulcinea could have the same feelings.

She glanced at Dulcinea and had to quell the sudden urge to take her hand. Instead she rummaged in her saddlebags and pulled out a torch. Dousing it with alcohol, she struck a flint and lit it. Glancing at Dulcinea, she led the way into the cave.

Although it was summer, the cave was freezing, the stalactites covered with the sheen of ice. Hazel shivered, feeling an unusual cold settle into her bones. It had to be at least thirty degrees colder in the cave than it was outside. An uneasy feeling settled into her stomach, and she used her free hand to unsnap her holster. Caves were always the homes of unpleasant things, but she had little choice.

The stalactites glimmered in the torchlight and the silica in the walls reflected the torchlight. She glanced at Dulcinea and wished she had taken the girl's hand. She was pale with fear. "Are you all right?"

"This is one of the sacred places," Dulcinea murmured. "We should tread carefully here."

They built a meager fire with what little wood they could gather and sat on either side of it. Swallowing down her emotions, Hazel watched the girl curiously. What was it about this girl that had interested the lloronas? Why hadn't they taken her already?

"They'll follow me, won't they?" Dulcinea's voice was barely audible over the sound of the crackling fire.

"Maybe an hour until sundown and another while they're on our trail. They can travel as fast as a horse." Hazel undid the latches at her shoulder and began to disassemble her exoskeleton. Drenched by the rainstorm, she needed to make sure that none of the parts had been compromised.

"But what are they?" Dulcinea asked.

"The lloronas? Closer to the Rio Grande they tell the stories in the night." Hazel rolled her shoulders to ease the strain of carrying the exoskeleton all day. "They say the first one was a poor woman who was very beautiful. One day a Spanish lord came to her and began to court her for her beauty. She grew to love him, believing that he loved her in return."

Dulcinea watched, wide-eyed, as she cleaned and inspected her exoskeleton, taking it apart in segments and putting them aside as she determined they were sound. "When it became public knowledge that he had gotten a child on her, he disavowed her as a witch, claiming that she had seduced him in the night."

Checking the engine that rested on the structure that covered her spine, she was glad to see that the creatures hadn't pierced the protective cover over the batteries. If they were compromised she wouldn't be able to move, much less fight. "After the child was born, he stole it and threw it into the Rio Grande to hide the evidence."

Hazel began reassembling her exoskeleton, latching on the legs first before assembling the rest of the machine over her body. She strove not to be self-conscious about her withered legs. It never bothered her when she was in her armor, when she felt whole and strong. But now, now she was exposed, vulnerable. She kept her eyes down, finishing the story. "The bishop and his priests arrested the woman. They stripped her naked, examined her for marks of Satan and then declared her a witch for the blemish she had on her back. The next day they burnt her at the stake."

She stood and stretched, the pistons hissing slightly as she made sure her legs were settled into the braces. The cold and damp hadn't affected them, but she would probably have to replace the gaskets soon. Dulcinea's voice was hushed as she asked, "But what caused the lloronas?"

"After she died they threw her ashes into the Rio Grande to rid themselves of the stain of witchcraft." Hazel flicked her wrists up to eject the daggers from their sheaths, making sure the mechanisms were clear of grime. Retracting the knives, she checked her revolvers. Releasing the barrel latch, she flicked both open one handed and made sure that they were loaded. Flipping her wrist back up, she closed them and reholstered them with one motion. Perhaps a little showing off was forgivable. "La llorona rose from the river that night, a vengeful creature who wanders the banks of the river crying for her child. The lloronas here, your guardians, are the descendants of that creature. Whether or not that's what actually caused them, they're attracted to places of misery and injustice, preying on the heartsick and the lonely."

"The lloronas …" Dulcinea took a breath. "Why has no one stopped them?"

"It's likely no one knows what the problem is. Or no one has the wherewithal to hunt them as I do." Hazel shrugged, now fully encased in her armor. "I don't suppose the two there were preying on anyone but the mining men. Two are powerless, comparatively harmless in the grand scheme of things. Three is too many for a small town like Cibola. They would leave the town, bringing sickness with them to every place they visited. When there are three, no one can stop them."

"I don't understand. Why did they need me?" Dulcinea rubbed her hands on her skirt. "And why did they wait?"

"Because you are the child of sorrow," Hazel said. "They couldn't take you until you became a woman, filled with the desires of a woman. I don't know why they waited as long as they did."

"But they never told me. They kept watching me with the men, but they had to know. That … they had to know I …" Dulcinea's gaze was riveted on the floor. "If they wanted me to be one of them …"

Hazel barked a laugh. "You thought they would ask? They run a brothel for a reason. They take what they need from men without permission or consent."

The silence of the desert above was broken by an eerie wail. Hazel watched as Dulcinea shivered. "What is it?"

"I've heard that wail before … I … I was so afraid. My mother sang to me." Dulcinea looked up, her eyes moist. "I can remember her face."

Hazel smiled briefly, but before she could say anything, there was another wail, closer this time. She crouched at the mouth of the cave, blinking against the darkness. Of all the monsters she had fought, creatures like lloronas were her least favorite. Most other monsters had the courtesy of at least sometimes attacking during the day.

She heard them coming. The soft sound of footsteps on sand, the crunch of dead men's boots on pumice. She unholstered her revolvers and held them steady at her sides. "They're here."

They'd only have one chance to get the upper hand. She didn't like the odds. Two against two was fair odds. Two against a score or more made things a little more complicated. "Stay here. Keep the fire going. It should keep them at bay."

"All right," Dulcinea said in a small voice. Hazel glanced back and gave her a quick, reassuring smile. Or at least she hoped it was reassuring.

When she exited the cave, she looked around, trying to adjust her eyes quickly to the moonlight. A shape darted across the moonlit desert to her right. Hazel tracked it with her revolvers and fired. The other came from the left and she fired at that one too. A high-pitched shriek split the air, and she smiled in grim satisfaction. It wouldn't stop them for long, but it sure felt good to score a hit.

Then the monsters were on them. The dead men walked forward, as unstoppable as a force of nature. She slashed out at the llorona as it passed, then turned to the men.

Her first shot caught one of the men in the torso, it kept coming and she thinned her lips in irritation. So it was that kind of gunfight. She shot him in the head and dropped him.

Another blur to her right and Hazel holstered her right hand revolver. Twisting her blade free, she struck out. The llorona was faster than it looked and dodged the strike. She spun to follow it and fired with her left revolver, missing by inches. The barrel flash lit the creature's features, teeth sharp and silvered.

The llorona leaped on Hazel, trying to claw and slash through Hazel's exoskeleton. The creature was horribly fast, faster than she had anticipated. But these creatures were after more than just food, driving their desperation.

As the llorona snapped at her, she caught its face with one hand and squeezed, feeling the bones bend under the augmented strength of her exoskeleton. With her left arm, she blocked a claw and fired her revolver, once, twice. She had one bullet remaining in that revolver, five in the other.

The llorona's body buckled with each shot and Hazel could smell the rotten stench of its blood. Shrieking again, the creature tore itself free from Hazel and tried to dash to the cave mouth.

"Oh no you don't." Hazel leapt after her, her armor providing the burst of speed she needed to grab it by the hair and yank it back. She fell on top of the creature and plunged her knife into its throat.

The llorona writhed and knocked her off with inhuman strength. Wrenching its head, it tore free, leaving most of its hair in her grip. Dropping it, Hazel pulled her other revolver, firing the last shot from her left-hand revolver into the creature.

In the moonlight, the llorona looked nothing like the beautiful women in the saloon. Bleeding from her wounds and missing most of her hair, she was a bedraggled, skeletal creature. Feinting right, she dashed left, making for the cave entrance. Hazel shot the few remaining bullets in her right revolver and holstered it to give chase.

Hazel skidded down the loose sand to the cave's mouth. Even in their damaged state, the lloronas were swifter than she was in her exoskeleton. She pushed herself to go faster. Dulcinea was down there. She should have left the girl a revolver.

Down in the cave, the creatures circled the fire, their features lurid in the firelight. Hazel reloaded as fast as she could, trying not to think of everything that had gone wrong. As she slid the special silver bullets into the Schofields, she exhaled, calming herself.

Dulcinea stood transfixed as the creatures neared her. She walked forward, reaching out to them. To the girl, they weren't monsters, they were the women who raised her.

"No!" she shouted. "Leave her alone."

"No," Dulcinea echoed, more softly. The lloronas eyes shone and they held out their hands to the girl.

"Come with us, Dulcinea." They spoke in unison, their voices echoing in an eerie harmony. "You belong with us. We are your mothers. We are your sisters."

Dulcinea stopped walking forward. She shook her head. Hazel tried to get a good angle on them, but they kept circling the fire, moving closer to Dulcinea with every step.

Frustrated, she holstered her gun and ran forward, grabbing the closest one. The least damaged of the two, vaguely recognizable as Rachel, snarled and turned. Its fingers elongated into claws that raked across Hazel's face. Despite the pain, Hazel kept her grip on the llorona and snicked out her blade, ramming the blade up and into the creature's heart.

Sarah dashed around the fire to Dulcinea, its movements impossibly fast. If she hurt one, the other became more powerful. Hazel slashed at the llorona through the fire, drawing blood black as ichor.

Grabbing and pulling Dulcinea's hair roughly, Sarah snarled. "None of that now."

A weight landed on Hazel's back. She stumbled and turned. Rachel scrabbled through her thick duster, tearing large rents in the leather. So close, the llorona's stench made Hazel gag and cough. The cloying smell of decay insinuated into her lungs as she tried to shake the creature off.

With a horrible snapping noise, she overbalanced and fell backwards. Rachel jumped clear as she landed. Her head fell back and hit the ground with a sharp crack.

Out of the corner of her eye, she saw Rachel throw something metal to the floor of the cave. Her battery pack.

Sneering, the llorona returned to its sister. "Enough of this."

Hazel cursed and rolled over, her head throbbing. Dulcinea stood with the two creatures. One of the creature's mouths opened more than was humanly possible, rows of teeth ready to latch onto Dulcinea. The girl's eyes were wide, unseeing as the creature opened its mouth wider.

Hazel raised her heavy arm and tried to grab for her guns. Without the battery's power, her limbs were weak under the weight of her armor. Thinking furiously, she tried to come up with a plan. Whatever she did, she needed to do it fast and without power.

The lloronas' thralls would be coming after them soon enough. One thing to try then.

Hazel raised her revolver, heavy without the support of the pistons. Her arms shook as the creatures leaned in toward Dulcinea; the humming sound they emitted grew louder and louder. They had paused, as if caught in honey, the tableau before her apt to break at any moment.

The gun was heavy, her arm was heavy. Her heart was heavy. If she died here today, it would all be for nothing. Dulcinea would still be dead, the monsters would have won. If only ... She raised her gun, aiming as best she could.

Before she could fire, the creatures' voices sneered in her head. "You would kill us when the men of this land would do the same to you? You think we wouldn't notice? The way you protected her? The way you looked at her?"

"No," Hazel whispered, the sound jerked from her lips. "No. She's my friend."

"She'll think you're a monster like me, once she learns of your desires. She'll run from you like she ran from me."

"No." But what if it was true? What if Dulcinea despised her?

"You think you hunt monsters? You are a monster." The sibilant hiss of the words tore through her lassitude, giving her strength. She might be a monster, but she fought monsters for a living.

"I don't eat people." Hazel fired, once, twice. The recoil nearly dislocated her shoulder without the power of her armor to dampen it. The muzzle flared as she fired again. The creatures turned toward her, their distended jaws open, their shrieking laughter cutting through her like knives.

"She'll think you're a monster." The creatures laughed, a gurgling, bubbling sound through the holes in their chests.

She aimed one last time. Two more shots.

Blood black as sin spurted from the creatures' heads, the impact of the bullets tearing their skulls apart. Dulcinea screamed and tore her hands from theirs. Mutilated, half of their faces missing, they still clawed at her. Hazel slumped to the ground, worn out. They wouldn't stop until their corpses were burnt and their ashes scattered to the winds.

With wide eyes, Dulcinea looked at the creatures before her, her eyes wide with memory. Hazel forced the words free. "Remember, Dulcinea. Remember your mother's songs."

Haunted, the girl looked at her for a moment, before turning her gaze to the creatures that fought against death, slowly rejuvenating before her. She folded her hands in front of her and closed her eyes.

"Duérmete mi niña, duérmete mi sol, duérmete cariña, de mi corazón." Dulcinea's voice was high and sweet, soothing the lloronas' gurgling shrieks. "Esta niña linda, que nació de día, quiere que la iglesia, por la Virgen María."

The creatures screeched louder as she completed the simple round. After the last words echoed through the cave, one of them, Hazel thought it might have been Sarah, fell to its knees and keened.

"Duérmete mi niña," Dulcinea walked around to the other side of the fire, continuing the round, "duérmete mi sol, duérmete cariña," she held out her hands to the monsters, "de mi corazón."

Both of the creatures turned to her like hounds on a scent. Slowly, as she continued singing, they inched towards her, ignoring the fire. "Esta niña linda, que nació de …"

The creatures followed Dulcinea's voice, crawling and scraping into the fire. The flames licked up their bodies, burning blue when it touched their blood. Kneeling, Dulcinea lowered her voice, almost murmuring the words, "… quiere que la iglesia, por la Virgen María."

The fire consumed the lloronas, burning them until they could no longer make a sound. The flames burned blue, and then green, dying out as they ate the final scraps of bone and ash. When there was only dust left, Dulcinea stopped singing. In the absence of the comforting sound, Hazel felt like crying.

With an effort, Hazel rolled up to a sitting position and looked around. The creature had torn the battery pack off, but if the safety detachment had worked, it might still be undamaged. If she could get to it, she could repair it. Then she could leave. The creatures were right. There was no point. Compared to Dulcinea, she was a monster.

○   ○   ○

With Dulcinea's help, she was able to get her exoskeleton back together. She avoided the girl's gaze. She had heard what the creatures had said. She had to know. Hazel was surprised that she hadn't left already.

Then she remembered the once-men. They would still be outside, and without the control of their mistresses, they would fall apart, but it could take days, if not a week. They needed to be dealt with.

Hazel shrugged her shoulders to settle the battery pack in its place. She would have to take it all apart later to repair it, but for now it would serve. Reloading her Schofields, she glanced at Dulcinea. "We'll need to take care of the once-men. Do you have a song for that?"

"I think ... I think so." Dulcinea smiled tentatively. "You'll be with me?"

"Always." The word left Hazel's lips before she could stop it. Wasn't this what she had wanted all these years? To find the friend her family had wronged? It was just ... She firmed her lips. "Let's go."

They slowly walked up the short ascent to the mouth of the cave. Night had fallen further, deepening toward midnight. The moon still illuminated the desert floor where the once-men shambled between the scrubby plants.

Hazel unholstered her Schofields and waited. After a moment, she turned to Dulcinea. "If you're going to do something, I would suggest you start now, before they smell us."

Dulcinea swallowed and nodded. She folded her hands in front of her and closed her eyes, taking her time. Hazel shook her head slightly as she watched the once men sniff the air. There wasn't time, but Hazel knew she couldn't force the girl to remember. Cocking the hammers back on her revolvers, she interposed herself between the creatures and the girl. She would have to reload at least twice, three times if she wasn't lucky.

"A … a los niños que duermen, Dios los bendice, a las madres que velan, Dios las asiste." Dulcinea's voice, hesitant at first, grew and resonated through the desert. "Duérmete niño, duérmete niño, duérmete niño, arrú arrú …"

The last turned into a lonely sound that echoed like a coyote howl off the mesas in the distance. The topography of the desert bowl conspired to amplify the girl's soprano. She opened her arms, holding them out to the once-men who turned toward them.

"A … a los niños que duermen …" Hazel fired, once. "Dios los bendice …" twice. "A las madres que velan," headshot. "Dios las asiste," headshot.

"Duérmete niño, duérmete niño, duérmete niño, arrú arrú …" Hazel emptied her revolvers into the crowd of once-men. As she reloaded, she glanced up and saw the creatures falling, one by one. The lullaby, cascading from Dulcinea's lips, sent them to their final rest. Even the ones nearest to them collapsed, their drive for human flesh quelled by the song.

The song was over. The once-men littered the desert, their arms flung toward Dulcinea and Hazel. They would not stir again. Hazel holstered her revolvers. "Come on."

O   O   O

The hour passed beyond midnight and into the earliest morning as they rode back to Cibola. Dulcinea held onto Hazel, shivering in the cold desert wind. Sensing Hazel's mood, Rocinante didn't tarry but rather allowed himself to be encouraged to a canter that ate up the desert sands beneath his hooves.

Silent, the empty windows of the town watched them reproachfully as they returned to the saloon. A light in the window greeted them, and Hazel glanced at Dulcinea warily. Who would be waiting for them?

She dismounted and helped Dulcinea down from Rocinante's broad back. Dulcinea took her hand, shaking her head as Hazel flipped the snaps off her holsters. "Juan."

Hazel nodded, remembering, but she didn't let her hand off her gun. "We don't know if they got to him too. We have to make sure that the curse has been lifted."

Pushing the doors aside, Hazel led the way into the saloon. Dulcinea refused to let go of her hand, so she used the contact to keep the girl behind her. With her other hand, she pulled one of her revolvers, holding it close to her chest, half hidden behind her tattered duster. "Juan?"

The bartender stepped out from the kitchen, a shotgun in his hands. He trained it at Hazel, his eyes dark. "Did you kill them?"

"I did." Hazel met his gaze.

"Did you burn their corpses?"

"Yes."

After a moment, Juan lowered the shotgun. "I thought that no one would come, that no one would be able to save us from them. And the niña?"

"I'm safe, Juan." Dulcinea stepped out from behind Hazel. "She saved me."

Juan put down his shotgun and walked to embrace the girl. "Mi corazón. Your mother would be so proud of you."

"I think she would be." Dulcinea's smile lit up her face. She turned to Hazel. "Please, accept my thanks and what hospitality I can provide."

"I ..." Seeing Dulcinea's hopeful expression, Hazel discarded half-formed thoughts of leaving in the night, of riding away, as far away as she could. There would be time to run away later, once she was sure her armor was intact.

Dulcinea led her up to one of the rooms and leaned against the doorway. "What you did to save my mother and I ... I owe you for tonight as well."

"I did what I had to," Hazel said, taking off her exoskeleton piece by piece. She didn't care if Dulcinea saw any more. She couldn't be any more of a monster than she already was.

"You think I listened to them, don't you."

"Of course you did." Hazel placed each part of her armor on the bed next to her, as neat as a skeleton.

"I don't ... you're not a monster."

Hazel shrugged out of the harness that supported the battery and swung it around to examine it. "Look at me and tell me that."

"You're not a monster." Dulcinea came and knelt next to Hazel, forcing her to meet her eyes. "Not for your armor, not for your legs, not for your heart."

"Do you remember?" Hazel looked away, her hands tightening on the straps. "Do you remember anything?"

Dulcinea helped her place the harness to the side and took her hands. Looking up into her face, she smiled hesitantly. "No. But if you'd like ... if you would like to tell me about it, I would....Would you stay and tell me the stories?"

"Stay here?" Hazel looked at her. "You would want me to stay?"

Hazel could feel Dulcinea's heart thumping through the pulse in her palms. "There are still stories to tell. And I think I'd like to make this an inn. With the town growing ..."

Hazel's heart pounded in the silence as she trailed off. She dared not interrupt.

After a moment, Dulcinea continued, looking down. "We could ... we might have use of a marshal. You haven't claimed the bounty yet. And I would hope ... maybe we can make some more stories." Dulcinea hesitantly reached forward and brushed a strand of hair out of Hazel's eyes. Her fingers brushed lightly against Hazel's cheek.

Hazel took her hand and met her eyes. She had not expected this. Not here. She had expected to find her friend at some point, maybe. That she would be happy to merely know that she was alive and well. And now ... She smiled, vulnerable yet hopeful. "I would love to."

INDUSTRIAL MELANISM

Aaron Spriggs

My Gravitationally Propelled Articulated Cleansing Coil don't have to be fed, clothed, housed, or rescued," Salesman said. He was overweight, and his clothes were disheveled, making for a poor first impression.

"Not now. I'm un-stucking an apprentice," Master Sweep said, shoving past Salesman.

Stuck in the chimney, Apprentice Sweep had gotten careless in his hurry. He just wanted time to wash the trees and wasn't thinking about the task at hand. Now, his knees were pressed into his chest and he couldn't move, barely able to breathe, arms stretched out above him, and the bricks taking their pound of flesh from four sides of his body. All the apprentices learned how to crawl up the inside of a chimney, inching their way up like a caterpillar, pressing their back against one wall and leveraging hands and knees and elbows against the other surfaces.

Careless climbers brought their knees up too high, or they got tired and let their bodies' slump down too far. Getting wedged was serious in the compressed space, which was usually only slightly wider than their shoulders.

Master Sweep stood on the lawn, ordering his cadre of apprentices about. Young boys, soot stained every one of them, were on the roof and in the house, working. It was bad form to have a lad stuck in the chimney. Hurt productivity for the day.

A small boy brought a bundle of clothes to Master Sweep. "Master Sweep, sir, here's his clothes. They was folded all neat and left by the fireplace."

"Well, put 'em back. He'll need 'em again once we've got 'im out of the chimney."

Salesman stepped up again to continue his sales pitch. "Here's my little darlin' right here, Master Sweep." He held forth his cleaning apparatus. It was a metal spring two feet long covered in thick warthog bristles. The spring, or coil, had small, articulated points along its entire length, allowing for slight movement while maintaining a general spring-like shape. One end of the coil enlarged and contained the clockwork mechanism which, when wound, caused small twitches and jerks of the entire coil.

Holding it for Master Sweep to see, Salesman pressed on with his commercial. "You wind it here," and he indicated with a grubby forefinger the winding key, "and then you drop it down the chimney from the roof. The little rascal does the rest of the work on its own."

"I said not now, and I meant not now," Master Sweep said.

"But the lads know what they're about, Master Sweep, sir, and they ain't got the knowing you do for improvements; innovations," Salesman said. His smile didn't waver.

Apprentice was having a harder and harder time drawing a breath, and spots were floating about in the chimney with him, though truth be told, he figured they were only in his eyes. They were the first things he'd seen in several hours.

He missed cleaning the trees. After cleaning chimneys all day, it was nice to sneak into the park with his scrub brush and pail of water and clean something living, and work while standing up, clothed, breathing fresh air.

Many chimneys were so small the chimney sweeps had to remove some or all of their clothing to fit. It didn't do well to have buckles or buttons snag on brick or sloppy mortar. Sometimes the boys just needed that much less size to fit, plain and simple.

When Apprentice Sweep had to remove his clothing, it reminded him of seeing insects molt. He shed his outer layer, exposing a new layer, just like a caterpillar. Apprentice Sweep would neatly fold his shed clothing and leave the bundle sitting by the fireplace, under the cloth shroud which protected the house from soot billowing everywhere as he cleaned.

"Master Sweep!" one of the boys on the roof hollered down to him. "Master Sweep, he's not grabbin' the rope no longer."

"Is Apprentice still awake in there?" Master Sweep asked.

"Don't know. Still can't see him, but the rope he had grabbed, he ain't grabbin' no more."

"Sprinkle a little water down on him and see if he says anything."

Scrubbing the trees, returning them to their pale grey color, almost white, that's what Apprentice enjoyed. The coal dust permanently stained the cracks in his skin, especially his hands and around his fingernails. He liked it though, on himself; made him look like a statue of sorts. But the trees, they shouldn't be soot stained. So, on days he got five or six chimneys cleaned, he'd race back to the workhouse and get his pail of water and come to the park.

A young boy, one of the youngest, came out of the house and approached Master Sweep and Salesman. "Sir, poking him with needles doesn't get him to complain no more."

"Well then, stop poking him. It isn't helping him, now is it?" Master Sweep said.

"No sir, Master Sweep, it isn't." The boy went back inside.

"How old was he?" asked Salesman, indicating the lad which had just left.

"Probably six. That's about the earliest I can apprentice 'em. Any younger and they're too weak to do any damn good scrubbin', but they do fit in there good at that age."

"And you get seven years out of each of 'em before they're old enough to quit?" Salesman asked.

"Yep, seven or eight, sometimes nine. Most of 'em don't count so good." Master Sweep winked at Salesman. "But by then they're starting to get too big to fit in the chimney. Most flues are only nine by twelve."

"True that, true that. Nine by nine, some. And that's why my Cleansing Coil is better than any apprentice. It can fit—"

"Leave off," Master Sweep said and turned to his scattered apprentices. "Hey! Get the mason chisel and hammer. We may need to go in through the chimney wall for this 'un."

It was funny, scrubbing the trees, having the coal black water run down his arms, collect at his elbows, and soak his coat. The water rarely reached his armpits. While scrubbing, every once in a while, a sneaky moth would get flushed off the tree. Most of the moths where dark and speckled and hid on the tree in plain sight. Sometimes, though, Apprentice noticed pale grey, almost white, moths, but they stood out and were easy to see; at least, they were easy to see before he scrubbed the tree. After cleaning the tree, they blended in on the clean bark.

Sometimes Apprentice felt like the black peppered moth after crawling out of a chimney, soot covered and blending in with all the coal dust.

Mallet and chisel in hand, one of the older boys was suspended off the roof by ropes, to the point where they thought Apprentice was stuck inside the chimney. He had just started chiseling.

"That's the way; good lad." Master Sweep was still directing from the lawn. A small crowd from the neighborhood had gathered, but, being English, they kept a respectful distance and stood on the other side of the iron fencing.

"So, Master Sweep, would you care to give my Cleansing Coil a try tomorrow?" Salesman asked.

"Perhaps, but I don't see how it gets the corners clean."

"With its twitching and such, and long bristles. It reaches all the corners the whole length of the chimney."

"An' what does it do when a bit of scrapin' is needed?" Master Sweep asked. "The apprentices take a scrub brush an' a scraper for the pitch. What abou' the pitch?"

"Um, well, my Cleansing Coil is easy and fast, and can be used more frequently than a boy, so the pitch won't have time to build up into no hard resin," Salesman said. He smiled large, proud of himself for thinking of that on the spot.

One day, while Apprentice scrubbed, he saw two gentlemen collecting butterflies. They had sweep nets, killing jars, pins, and cork boards. Dressed fine, their speech was musical to Apprentice's ears, even if he didn't understand all the fancy wordings.

"And see here, this pale pigmentation is pre-industrialization," Sideburns said.

"Good show. Yes. We need more of those to complete the range," White-gloves said.

"This post-industrial coloration, or, as you've so cleverly termed, 'Industrial Melanism' is going to be all anyone is talking about. But tell me again, they are not being dyed by the soot, correct?" Sideburns asked.

"Quite right, old chap. It appears individual moths come in two varieties in their population; the black morphotype and a white morphotype. Before all the soot in the air, the white morphotype was dominant while the black morphotype was easily eaten by birds."

"Yes, yes, I see that now. But now, the trees are soot covered and their bark is black," Sideburns said.

"Yes, you've got it. Now that the trees are black, the minority morphotype has become the dominant individual in the population, and the white peppered moth has become the staple in birds' diets around here," White-gloves said.

"I'm through, Master Sweep!" the apprentice called down as he handed the brick to another boy.

"Good job. How's Apprentice doing?" Master Sweep asked.

"He's not moving, sir!" The boy had his arm buried to his shoulder in the whole he had just made. "I'm shaking his head but he's limp!"

"Keep at it then! Make the whole large enough to get him out," Master Sweep said.

"What do you do if Apprentice is dead?" Salesman asked.

"We've got to get him out alive or dead. Can't go around leaving dead boys stuck in chimneys, now can we?"

"It's a harsh life for ones so young, in'it?" Salesman said.

"It's a harsh life all over, in'it? Somes die by the cough. Their lungs can't take all the dust. Some get stuck and can't breathe. Every once in a while, a chimney fire ain't out and the pitch catches and burns 'em to death, but that don't happen all too often. Most though, most put in their time, and make it to journeyman."

Industrial Melanism meant stained sooty black. Apprentice knew that much from their fancy talk. Once he was done apprenticing, putting in his time, he hoped to join the navy or dirigible brigades. Apprentice wondered if his 'industrial melanism' would clean off well enough to make him look proper while in uniform. White gloves would hide his marbled hands, and uniforms were cleaned and pressed, but what about his face? Was he stained for life?

"That's it then." Master Sweep and Salesman watched the constables haul off Apprentice's body. It looked smaller, being so still. The rest of the apprentices were quiet; a rare moment in their lives.

"Bring your Cleansing Coil around tomorrow and we'll have a crack at it. You know, Salesman, I can get 9d a bushel for my soot. That thing better clean as well as my boys can."

"Oh, it will Master Sweep, it will," Salesman said, smiling and nodding.

One of the older apprentices, scowling, approached the two men. "What of us, Master Sweep?"

"What of you?"

"If you go and get these fuzzy springs doing our jobs, how are we to eat? We still owe you years of work?" His thin arms were folded across his narrow chest.

"Have no fear, and don't give me none of that smart talk. I knows what's best. Who's the Master Sweep here?"

"You are, sir." The boy looked down, not making eye contact, but he didn't unfold his arms.

"Now, if you were to use yer head for somethin' other than holding a hat, think on this. Who's going to lower these coils down into the chimney? Hmm? An' who's going to collect the soot when all's said and done?"

The apprentice looked back up, his arms sliding to his sides.

"I still needs me my apprentices. Now get back to the workhouse and get our supper ready, this day's been longer than most."

"Shorter for some us, Master Sweep," the apprentice said, running off.

Today, the Sun Sets in the East

Peter J. Wacks

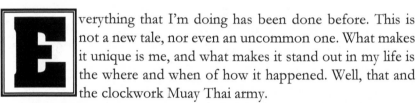verything that I'm doing has been done before. This is not a new tale, nor even an uncommon one. What makes it unique is me, and what makes it stand out in my life is the where and when of how it happened. Well, that and the clockwork Muay Thai army.

Let me start with an introduction. My name is the Hummingbird. The name I was born to isn't so important, when compared to the name I've earned.

So what kind of name is the Hummingbird? A damned fine one, by my reckoning. Most men might take offense at a name that, which at its most basic means faster than the human eye can track. Can you imagine it? Walking into your local saloon and having the girls squealing "hey, hummingbird!" to you? Tiny and fast, that's me. I take my pride where I find it.

Truth be told, though, I got the name for my gun slinging. I'm a small target, only five-foot-eight plus skinny as a boy, and I can draw my Colt, shoot six separate targets, then reholster in under two seconds. That's with my left hand. Now, I'm right handed, but for a long time I didn't have a right arm to sling with. I lost it to a piece of artillery in the last year of the Great War when I was nineteen years old. I didn't get it replaced till I was a man of twenty-six, a good ten years ago.

The standard replacement arms you see in the West tend to be big bulky things, all clockwork and pistons, and about twice the size of a normal limb. I went to the Orient for mine. Some clever Chinaman combined clockwork with this needle thing they have in the East called acupuncture. That's the arm I got me. The plate that attaches to my arm covers my shoulder and chest, from my neck all the way to the bottom of my ribcage on the right side. All told, there are one thousand, four hundred and twenty needles stuck into my body under those plates. Each one connects with a little metal thread to internal workings in my arm. All those little threads lay over each other and make mechanical muscles, which are a sight stronger than a normal muscle.

So, instead of clockwork and steam inside me, I have a few cogs for articulation and all them little wires laying over each other, coated with overlaying little steel plates for skin. They call it dragon scaling. The healing and learning to use the thing took a lot longer than I expected at that age. Afore I was allowed to have the arm put on, I had to spend a year doing this funny moving thing they call Tai Chi.

I figured at first it would drive me crazy, me being The Hummingbird and having to move so damned slow. But there is a peace to be found in it, at the center. In being so slow, I found out how to be even faster. Of course, once I got the arm, I took another two years of training afore the pain stopped and my body didn't hurt no more.

The way my teachers said it, I was a master of that path by the time I left, but I reckon there ain't no such thing as a true master of Tai Chi. Got pretty good with my fists though, and I keep my hand in it, practicing every day, learning, getting better.

I paid for my arm by bounty hunting. Didn't matter none that I was in the Orient, they still have criminals there. Where there is crime there is always a lawman willing to put good money down to not have to do the dirty work of catching outlaws their damned selves. Which finally gets me away from rambling about my past, and brings us to the present. I had plenty of money saved for my return to the West, and was just awaiting a few last things I had commissioned. I had to run down a last few bounties for the cash to pay for them.

Most of my work came from the police hub in Guangzhou, known by us Gwailo as Canton. Guangzhou is about a three- or four-hour ride inland from Hong Kong, or about twenty-five minutes on an airjunk. Now, I do a lot of trading and buying in Hong Kong, but Guangzhou is the administrative seat of the province, so it's naturally where I get my work and pay from.

I chose to avoid the Offices of Colonial Secretary in Hong Kong. The Brits charge you once to get assigned to a bounty, and then charge again, a private fee straight to the Secretary's pocket, once you brought a bounty back in. The Chinese just care about getting the criminals brought in. Regardless, the two cities being so close was damned convenient, and I generally stuck close to them. I liked saving the time of long rides all over.

Why not just take the airjunks between the two? Well, I suppose that cutting down the trip to half an hour or so would be nice, but it didn't seem worth the cost of three Pesos for just a couple hours saved. I refuse to carry Wen, since you have to string a thousand of them together to get any value. Instead, I carry mostly Pesos. Pesos are made from silver, and for the last decade or so lots of the Chinamen had been favoring them like me. They have a high enough silver content that you can get value for a Peso near anywhere in the world.

My thoughts were definitely on Pesos that day, hoping that I'd get lucky enough to find a bounty worth twenty or thirty of them and help pay for the guns I was having custom made in Hong Kong. My Colts are great shooters, but with how fast my right arm reacts, they just can't rechamber rounds as fast as I can shoot them.

So with my thoughts on a new pair of pistols, I rode up to the Magistrate's office and dismounted, letting my steed run the stable yard while I walked inside. The building was tall for the area, a full five stories, but still built with those curvy roofs Easterners seem so fond of.

I walked in, tipping my hat to constable Baojia, an old friend here at this office, while he bowed slightly to me and flashed a pearly-toothed smile. I flicked the brim of my Stetson, eyeing Baojia. "You're smiling friend. You have something good for me today?"

"We see, Gwailo." He grinned again. "Is two thousand Peso bounty." He raised an eyebrow at me.

Well. Ain't that just a bitch? Two thousand is some good money, and highly irregular. Usually, the Chinese government paid in Wen, and I'd have to take them down the street to get them converted to something less bulky. I sucked in a breath between my teeth and thought. Two thousand was also some mighty dangerous hunting. "Alright. Give me the details."

Baojia raised an eyebrow and tossed a folder onto the counter. Great. I never did get none too good at reading. I sighed pointedly, getting my message across, and scooped up the folder. Flipping it open, I painfully made my way through the reading.

Hm. Chang Yao Jin, also known as Tiger, was at large. I had tracked him down about six years ago, when I was a lot less careful, still full of the vim and vigor of youth. Last time I had missed bringing him in, though. I ran down all his hideouts, but someone else got to him first. Looks like he had escaped from a prison in Nanning. Well, no wonder 'twas so much money to bring Tiger in.

He was too well connected, with a network stretching from Hai Noi, Annam, all the way down to Bangkok, Siam. I grinned a bit. This was gonna be fun. Over the years he had been caught fourteen times, with bounty hunters rustling out five of his six biggest hidey-holes. Now me, I got lucky. I found two of his hidey-holes, but he was already caught when I showed up at the first one I'd decided to check on.

I glanced up to Baojia. "Yup. I'm reckoning I know where he is. How many other people you got on this?"

"Six, Gwailo. All good boys from China." "Good boys from China" from Baojia meant scumbags from around the world, hiding here hunting bounties instead of getting caught themselves at home. I had earned his trust by the simple expedient of being honest with the man and not getting arrested myself.

"Mhm." I showed him some teeth. "That's why you're handing it to me, eh? Cause none of them as is tracking Tiger has a shot in hell of bringing him in for you."

Baojia looked sternly at me and snorted. "Good Chinese boys! They succeed!" He leaned close to me. "I have five hundred Wen bet on you, Hummingbird. You go now. Go get him."

I patted my friend on the shoulder then walked out, glancing at the file again. Baojia had left a handwritten note scrawled on the backside of the bounty sheet that said Khon Kaen. 'Twas the same thing I had been thinking. Khon Kaen was the one place Tiger had that no other bounty hunter had ferreted out yet. I pulled the wanted poster from the rest of the paperwork, shoving that one page in my pocket.

Walking out to the stable yard the warm morning sun greeted me, promising a beautiful day of travel. I grabbed my nag from the yard, shoving the rest of the paperwork in my saddlebags, and rode around town for a while, making sure I wasn't being followed.

It's a pesky necessity, but when you pick up a bounty, there's plenty of vultures out there who'll just tail you, let you do the work, then steal the catch as you bring them in. Afore you get to asking, yeah, I learned that one the hard way. I was twenty-nine, and should have known better, but now I have a nice scar on the back of my head to remind me to beware of vultures.

Once I was sure that no vultures were on me, I headed down to the port to catch an airjunk to the kingdom of Vientaine, which bordered Siam right near Khon Kaen. 'Twas a much faster route than junking all the way down to Bangkok. Siam had been getting pretty industrial since about the same time the Great War was over in the States, but the junks pretty much all flew in to the capital, then you had to train ride anywhere else in the country. Right now, my fastest route would be Vientaine and a couple hours ride south. I pulled my reins up, riding carefully into the port. There was a lot of foot traffic for the flights today.

Airjunks are a mighty feat of engineering. Over in the States and Europe the airships are basically sailing vessels with balloons and a couple clockwork-powered propellers on them. Massive steam engines fill the aft decks, piping hot air up to the balloon bladders. While the philosophy is basically the same over here, the execution of them isn't.

The sailing junk has one massive segmented sail at the front, whereas the flying junk has two that are rolled up along the side, and two tiny ones up front. Once the lift bladder starts to pull the ship up into the air, the two sails snap out and get all rigid, like a pair of bat wings. The main bladder vents hot air, and the ship literally glides through the air. It has twin propellers attached to either side of the back of the hull, but much smaller than the side ones used in the West. The whole thing is powered by clockwork and steam, which makes a mighty smooth and fast sail through the skies.

The particular airjunk I boarded was red, with a dragon painted on the hull above the wings. As my nag trotted up the gangplank to the main deck, I glanced left, then right, again, one last check to make sure I wasn't being followed. I wasn't. I paid the chunayaun, he's the fella that takes money for the ride and is so called because he works for the bank, not the ship, and trotted my horse to the stable at the back of the junk. I reined her in amongst the half dozen or so other horses and took up leaning against the back rail of the airjunk where I could keep an eye on the rest of the riders.

Mostly 'twas business folk all huddling up at the front, talking to each other about the various dealings they'd be having in Vientaine or Siam. But one fella stood out. For one, he was Nipponese instead of a Chinaman, and he stood a solid five eleven, maybe six feet tall. He was wearing a kimono that was such a dark grey as to almost be black. Even with the silk robes draped over him, you could tell he was built heavy on muscle. His skin and face looked young and strong, but there was just a hint of silver at the temples of his close-cropped black hair. On his left hip he wore a katana set, and on the right, none other than my favorite pistol, a Colt Peacemaker.

That in itself was a bit of a surprise. The Peacemaker had been around for about ten years or so now, but since it was a U.S. government pistol mainly, 'twas a rare sight to see. I had a sinking feeling I was gonna be seeing more of this gent in Siam. Spend a few years hunting bounties, and sure enough you'll learn to spot the other folk who do the same.

The airjunk trip was mainly uneventful, and I spent the better portion of it watching my friend at the front. If you think you're gonna go at odds with someone, I highly recommend taking the time to learn how they move, if the opportunity provides itself. I had plenty of opportunity, as most of the trip is just sailing the skies over the south China Sea, and even the bit where we pass over the pearl cliffs of Hainan is near enough the straights that it's over in just a couple of minutes. Since I took the express to Vientaine, we didn't even stop in Ha Noi.

What that means to a man staring down at the scenery is lots and lots of mountains covered in jungle, with the occasional rice paddy field cleared out by the folks driven off the flatlands and fighting for a bit of peace on their piece of land. Soon enough, 'twas all over, and we were landing in Vientaine, at the airyard on the southern outskirts.

I waited at the stable on the junk, letting my nag nuzzle on my hand whilst I patted her head and allowed for all the business folk to get off first. When you're in another man's house, you respect his rules. These folk who constantly rode back and forth on the airjunks paid the bills for the ship's captain, so I felt 'twas only right to respect their travels afore my own. The Nipponese fella did the same, waiting by me with his horse.

We both mounted up and headed off the airjunk together, though I let him lead the way. Once we were out of the yard, French soldiers checked our papers, careful to not let us grubby mounted folk get their snappy white and blue colonial uniforms dirty, then cleared us on our way. Personally, I'm rather fond of the French, what with all that fundraising they're doing to build us Americans a big ole statue dedicated to freedom and liberty. I've seen pictures of her head on show in Paris, and it's mighty impressive looking. Plenty of folk around the world don't like them though. Most people felt that the only thing worse than the French colonial empire was the British royal empire. Heh.

Regardless, me and the Nipponese fella soon left the French and Vientaines long behind, trotting silently next to each other as we made our way down from the highlands into Siam. As each road split off, headed to other provinces, it became more and more clear that we had the same destination in mind.

I smiled to myself, rocking back and forth with my nag's movement, enjoying the silence with the stranger. Since neither of us had spoken yet, we could still enjoy each other's company and not fret the accounting that was most likely coming. Despite being in the lowlands, we were still surrounded by dense green foliage and a beautiful day, though 'twas coming close to evening. I figured we'd roll into Khon Kaen proper around dusk. After that it should be easy enough to track Tiger down, since Khon Kaen City was more a collection of small villages than a proper city.

My travelling companion grunted, pulling some dried meat out of his saddlebags whilst slowing down. I nodded in return, slowing with him, and pulled some bread, cheese, and a skin of tea out. We stopped and dismounted for about twenty minutes or so, sharing our foodstuffs in silence.

Once we had packed up and were getting ready to ride back out, the tall fella looked at me thoughtfully then grunted. "Inazuma."

I chewed on that for a moment then nodded. "Hummingbird." What with that out of the way, we both mounted back up and rode out towards Khon Kaen.

Afternoon passed into dusk, and purples and pinks started to lace the sky, with the sun still a half a hand or so over the horizon. We rode into Khon Kaen and immediately noticed something wrong. The streets were empty, dust and leaves blowing gently in the wind. Silence like a graveyard stretched across the town. I glanced at Inazuma. He was warily scanning the streets and empty windows as we rode forward, looking for some sign of life where there weren't none to be found.

I clicked my tongue, slowing my nag from a slow walk to a complete stop. Inazuma stopped next to me, and I pointed down the long main street to the town center, a couple hundred yards away. There were about twelve bodies, each nailed down to an X made of two crossed pieces of wood. I recognized four of them as other bounty hunters that worked my neck of the woods back in Guangzhou.

I dismounted, tethering my nag to a post in front of the building next to me, and let my left hand hover over my pistol while Inazuma dismounted. It didn't need saying between us that we were allies now, at least until we managed to get out of there in one piece with the bounty. The eerie silence was growing heavier as the sun finally touched the horizon, splashing the village in reds and oranges.

I glanced at Inazuma as he finished tying off his horse and cocked my head towards the center of town. Whatever the hell Tiger had done to this place, 'twas time to go find him and figure out what was going on. Inazuma grabbed the sheath of his katana with his left hand and let his right hand hover over the handle, much the same way I did with my Colt.

We ghosted down the red streets of the dead town, careful to stick close to the buildings till we got to the center of town. I started checking side streets to the left, making sure we were clear, while my new friend did the same to the right. There weren't a trace of anyone or anything here. What the hell?

I glanced back around and realized that Inazuma was staring at the furthest hanging man from me. He shook his head and sighed. That'd be the second most noise either of us had made this afternoon. I couldn't see the man he was looking at, since his back was to me, so I walked over to stand beside Inazuma and get a better look.

Oh, hell. There was Tiger, all trussed up. He had managed to get himself dead by the looks of it. I couldn't see any obvious reason for his death, but his chest was completely still, without the slight motion of someone trying to hide breathing. So, he was real dead. I sighed and pulled the wanted page out of my pocket. Always best to double check. A quick double check showed me that the man in front me was the same as the crude drawing on the page. Damn it. He was worth two hundred dead, rather than two thousand alive.

I nudged Inazuma with my elbow while staring at the corpse. "Two hundred pesos dead for me. You?"

He pulled a similar sheet from his kimono and glanced down at it. "Two fifty in Tokyo. Extra travel not worth it. We bring to Guangzhou. Step back."

I obliged the man, giving him a bit of space. Eighty pesos for two days work, after travel expenses, was some handsome wages. Even though I had been looking for two thousand, I weren't gonna spit on the eighty. Inazuma drew his sword damn near as fast as I draw my Colt, slashed the four bindings holding Tiger's body up, and resheathed in one motion. Damn. The man had style. Tiger's limp form slid to the ground.

He motioned for me to carry the body and started scanning the area. My hackles went up at the same moment. Something was watching us. "Not yet. I feel it too."

I glanced briefly at him as another thought occurred to me. "Besides, when we do take him, ain't gonna be me lifting. He's gotta outweigh me by a hundred and change." 'Twas true too. Tiger was about six feet and looked like he weighed upwards of two hundred and fifty pounds. All muscle and plenty of it.

Inazuma nodded. "Fair, gaijin." He was interrupted by the ground shaking. 'Twas one good rattling, like one of them giant Buddha statues had just taken a step nearby. Then there was a second tremor, but this time with a huge thud sound that seemed to come from all directions at once. Then another, and another.

I desperately scanned the surroundings, but there was nothing to be seen out there. I could feel it in the ground's shaking though, so

I opted to go with feeling. I took a slow, deep breath, closing my eyes, and extending my senses into the ground. As my thoughts cleared, everything slowed and I could feel it. The tremors were coming from about a hundred very heavy footsteps all in tandem. What was worse, we were surrounded.

Clomp. Clomp. Clomp. Whatever they were, I could feel them getting closer. I opened my eyes back up, standing up straight. "Get ready, Inazuma. They're gonna be visible soon."

He nodded, getting into his fighting stance. One foot slid back, angled outwards from his body while the other stayed in front of his mass. Both knees bent as he centered his weight, and his right hand crossed in front of his body to hover over his Katana handle. His head dropped and he tilted it to the side. I was impressed—he looked ready for business.

I got into my fighting stance too. I leaned casually against the recently emptied X that'd held Tiger and started cleaning out the gunk under my nails. Some might say that it's a bit of a cocky stance, but I've found that action flows stronger from a relaxed body than a tense one. My tai chi lessons taught me that.

We were both ready for a fight, but I don't think either of us was ready for what came around the corners and flooded the area around us. Clockwork men, monstrosities of brass and steel with steam whistling out of their joints, surrounded us. A clean hundred. They clomped to a stop a dozen yards away, poised with their fists in front of them, level with the foreheads of their featureless faces. Each of them was balanced on one foot, with their other leg pulled up in front of them.

Now, I've only been to Siam a couple times, but I recognize the pose they were in. Muay Thai is a vicious sport, and one of the bloodiest fighting forms I've ever seen. "Well. Ain't this gonna be fun. You wanna do this fifty each?"

Inazuma laughed, the first emotion I'd heard in his voice. "Tiny gunfighter, but big heart. Bullets will be a waste though. You have a blade?"

I shook my head. "Naw. Don't reckon as I need one." I pulled the leather gloves I was wearing off, exposing the dragon scale steel on my mechanical arm. Adjusting the brim of my Stetson, I watched the mechanical men. "Whaddya suppose they're waiting for?"

Inazuma tilted his head to the other side. "I wonder … let us try experiment." He cleared his throat and spoke loudly. "We take Tiger now."

The Automatons all took a step forward together.

I glanced around in surprise. "Well ain't that interesting? Maybe third time is the charm. You grab Tiger, I'll clear a hole."

Sure enough, three mentions of moving Tiger was the magic number. The automatons charged forward at us, the closer ones running and the further ones flipping through the air. I launched myself to intercept the ones closest to me. As I closed with the first one, a snap kick came barreling towards my head. These suckers moved fast, but I was in the calm zone, and they weren't half as fast as me.

I let my body flow in a circular motion, catching the kick with my metal hand and twisting. The leg ripped off at the hip seam, cogs flying everywhere. I let it drop to the ground as I finished the circle, bringing my hand up in a slicing motion that tore through its body. As the torso came apart, I realized what was about to happen just in time to roll to the side, landing on my back. Whatever steam engine drove these things, I had shattered it. The thing exploded, taking out two more of the mechanical fighters.

A metal foot stomped down, narrowly missing my head, and I came up at the thing's groin, using my metal arm to shred it. Three seconds or so had passed, and I already had a second to take stock. Glancing over, I saw that Inazuma was keeping up with me, elegantly sliding through the bodies pressed around him, that katana flashing like lightning as it arced back and forth. Oops! Shouldn't have stopped to gawk, he was two up on me now. I grinned and got back into the fight, launching myself forward at the next group.

I took a kick on my fleshy side, tucking into it to try to absorb the blow. It still hurt a bit, but it bought me a second to drive my right hand into the mechanical fighter's chest. I jerked my arm as hard as I could, flinging the automaton over me into a pack of four more of them, right as it exploded. An elbow caught me across the chin, and I felt the skin part. Letting the force of it move my body instead of resisting, I flipped through the air, catching another fighter's head and twisting as I landed. It came right off, and I tossed it to the side, turning back to my previous assailant.

A kick hit me square in the center of my back. As I flew forward, my gut landed right on the knee of the one in front of me, and I realized that the heads on my opponents were just for ornamenttation. Didn't matter that I had taken off the head of the one behind me, the machine had still put one right into me. The fighters were all controlled by whatever that engine in their guts was. An elbow came down into my spine, and as I watched my Stetson bounce onto the ground. I decided that I'd had just about enough of these things.

I rolled off the thing's knee where I was bent over like a child ready to receive a spanking, spinning on the ground as I twisted my way back up to my feet. Imagining an invisible ball between my hands, I spun it around as the rest of my body moved. My fighting buddy ducked briefly into my fight while I was recentering, and his katana slashed through the mechanical body in front of me. Inazuma spun back away from me, having dispatched the immediate threat.

Everything slowed further, until 'twas almost comical looking. I shook my shoulders, bouncing from foot to foot, then cracked my neck a bit to loosen up. My fists came up into a loose boxer's stance, and I watched the horde of fighters coming towards me. This is where I earned my name, time and again, in the zone where the whole world but me was moving nice and slow.

My fists flashed as automaton after automaton tried to swarm me. They flipped through the air towards me, metal feet, elbows, knees, and you name it all trying to smash into me. I floated through it all, impersonating my namesake, flashing from automaton to automaton like a hummingbird darting between flowers for nectar. Torso after torso was ripped to shreds under the lightning fast hammering of my right fist, while my left hand deflected the incoming blows and my body moved on its own in a liquid dance of avoidance.

The whole fight was done afore the sun had finished setting, leaving piles of metal and cogs strewn about the town square.

I bounced from left to right again and let my fists fall open at my sides, shaking my hands. Time sped back up, and I retrieved my Stetson. I brushed some dust off it and looked up to Inazuma, grinning. "Fifty one."

He nodded and sheathed his sword. "I am impressed. Unarmed and you still destroyed them faster than I."

I flashed a cocky grin. "I figure that there ain't much difference between fifty one and forty nine. Though I did pause for a break ..." He looked around the square, taking in the hanging bodies and destroyed clockwork army. His gaze finally lit on the prone form of Tiger. "You figure it out too?" He asked me.

"Ayup." I walked over to Tiger and planted a foot squarely in his ribs.

He grunted in pain and curled up to protect his ribs, hallow eyes staring at me.

"Nice little game friend. But it's done." I pulled out the wanted page, studying it. Something was bugging me. The hairs on the back of my neck rose, and on instinct I pulled my Colt and shot twice. The first shot took the Peacemaker right out of Inazuma's hand as he pulled the trigger, making his shot go wide. The second shot took the head off the prone Tiger, the fake, revealing the mechanical workings inside.

I kept my Colt leveled as he nursed his injured hand. "Just so you know, Tiger, the picture I have coulda' been either of you." I held up the wanted page. "It's hard to see if he is from China or Japan."

He nodded once. "Very well done." Now there was a surprise. He sounded British now. "I am a man of honor, believe it or not. I will go peacefully with you. But I will break out again, and we will talk once I do."

I raised an eyebrow. "Forgive me if I keep the pistol on ya anyway. What the hell is with you sounding like you're British now?"

He laughed. "Of course you have questions. Shall we head to Canton? I'm eager to escape again, as I have business to finish. I'll be more than happy to explain on the way, provided I have your word it stays between us alone."

I agreed, so we packed up and rode out of town, leaving a mass of spare parts behind us. Gettin' him back was easy enough. He turned out to be good to his word and didn't try to escape. We spoke a lot on the trip to Guangzhou, and I actually rather liked the fella. We learned a lot about each other, including that the fast, if silent, friendship we had shared on the ride to Khon Kaen was the real deal.

He did explain some of his past. He had been born to a Samurai gone Ronin who had been killed by his old Daimyo. A family from the British consulate had adopted him at the age of four, and

Inazuma had spent his life living as a British citizen, but studying the ways of his homeland. I discovered that Tiger was a con game. He would claim responsibility for crimes that were unsolved using the name, then collect his own bounty. Escaping from prison only drove up his bounty each time, and he had amassed a small fortune gaming the Chinese police.

I did ask him what had happened to the citizenry of Khon Kaen, and he was nice enough to fill me in on how he was good friends with the adjunct of the town, and the local government had helped him set up the whole bounty hunter trap. Each of the hunters he had drawn into the trap had bounties on their heads in other countries except me, which was why he had followed, then assisted me in the trap.

Also, true to his word, he broke out of prison within a couple weeks of going back, only this time he showed up at my lodgings. I made it a point not to swing by the constable offices in Guangzhou. What can I say? I liked the guy. These days we travel together. Someday I'll make it back to the States, but for now I'm enjoying my adventures. It's a funny 'ole world we live in, and that's for sure, but I wouldn't have it any other way.

THE WEATHER GOD

David W. Landrum

Du Mu touched the warm bronze statue of the Weather God. He did not touch it out of reverence. He did not believe in gods of any kind. Yet his gesture held a small touch of sentiment that was a little like faith. If anything saved them from the upcoming foreign invasion, it would be the Weather God—not this one, but the one Shao Jiazhen had assembled—the one that rose above the bay where the European and American troops planned to disembark. He turned when he heard a jingling of bells that told him Ling, his chief serving woman, had come into the room.

She bowed.

He spoke first. "They have arrived?"

"Yes, my Master."

"Please show them in."

She bowed and left.

He waited, his curiosity mildly aroused. Warriors like those that he had read about in the old romances hardly existed anymore. He often wondered if they ever really had existed and to what degree they had been invented just for the sake of story. Yet this man had impressive credentials. And everyone knew of the Princess. He put his hands behind his back and waited.

Du Mu tried not to show astonishment when his guests came into the room. The man, Chen Hao, looked as if he had walked out of an illustration from an adventure book. He was tall, wore his hair long, and had broad shoulders and sinewy hands. His very stance suggested energy and focus. He wore a black tunic, black trousers, and boots trimmed with silver. In accordance with their agreement, he carried no weapon.

Beside him—and, once again, it seemed she had materialized from a fantasy novel—stood the astonishingly beautiful Princess Jing Li. She wore a white dress with gold trim, her hair tied in a long sweeping braid. Tall, trim, with strong arms and wrists, she also suggested alacrity in the way she stood. Her eyes, beautiful and seductive, scanned the entire room in one motion.

They both bowed.

"Welcome," Du Mu said. "I am honored to have you in my home."

"The honor is surely ours," Chen Hao said. "Allow me to introduce my fellow warrior, the Princess Jing Lin."

She bowed again. Du Mu fought his curiosity and the impulse to stare. He had heard of Jing Li, heiress to a small but prosperous kingdom along the northern coast. The British and Italians had financed a revolt there, set up a puppet government and turned the capital of the kingdom into a port access for the good—and for opium delivery. The Princess led an army and drove them out. The foreigners suffered such heavy losses that they had never tried to avenge their defeat. They had not come near the place after the sound beating she gave their troops and the Chinese mercenaries they had hired. Her father had retaken the throne. The Princess then devoted herself to fighting against the foreign invaders who had established themselves other places in China.

"I have not met her, as I have met you, Chen Hao, but she is certainly welcome. We all know her story and are amazed at her skill in war and her devotion to her homeland. Shall we remove to the next room and have tea?"

They followed him to a rich but modestly decorated chamber. A servant opened the doors. Other servants escorted them to their seats and poured tea.

"Was your journey prosperous?"

"It was difficult. The revolt has disrupted things—travel no less than other matters. Brigands and self-proclaimed toll agents roam the highways. More than once we had to … *educate* the gangs and the militia we encountered."

Du Mu sipped his tea. "The land is ill. If we can rid it of foreigners, it will heal. You know the foreigners are under siege in Beijing. We have them surrounded, but their firepower is considerable—and the Boxers are not well-trained soldiers. Our soldiers have confined the international force but not overcome it. They can't last forever, though. They will eventually run out of food. Units of the Imperial Army are on the way. Of course, as you know, their governments are sending re-enforcements. Their ships are drawing near. This is the reason you and Princess Jing are here."

They drank in silence, waiting for Du Mu to continue.

"I have hired you to free a prisoner the foreigners have taken. His name is Shao Jiazhen. He is an inventor who studied in Europe and in our own universities. He has assembled a weapon that will destroy the foreign fleet and enable us to force the contingent in Beijing to surrender."

"Did they capture him to prevent him from using the weapon?"

"They don't know about his skills or the weapon. They don't even know he is a scientist. When our soldiers forced the foreigners into the embassy compound, they seized anyone who looked like they might have money or prestige and imprisoned them. He was unfortunate enough to be out walking, dressed in his best clothing that day. They are threatening to kill the hostages—keeping them as a final negotiating chip, I think. At any rate, only he knows how to activate the weapon."

"What sort of weapon is it?"

"The weapon—as I am able to understand it—draws on the power of the sun and earth. It creates disparity and is able to generate a tsunami. In the same way the divine wind destroyed the fleet Genghis Khan assembled to conquer Japan, this weapon will destroy the iron ships of the Western intervention force."

"You have seen it work?"

"I have. Only he knows how it operates. He must be rescued to launch the weapon."

Du Mu drained his teacup.

"I am skeptical," Chen said, "but you aren't paying me to sit in judgment on the weapon's feasibility. You're paying me to free its inventor. What do you know about where he is?"

"We know he is in the American quarters. Other than that, we know nothing."

"That's something to go on, at least. We'll undertake the assignment immediately. How soon will the foreign fleet arrive?"

"Four days."

"I will see to the supplies. Jing needs rest. She was up last night in vigil to the goddess she worships, so if you could arrange for a place for her to sleep, it would be appreciated. We will leave this afternoon. It's eighty miles to Beijing, so we'll start out this very night to get there in plenty of time."

Du Mu bowed and summoned the servant to escort them, Jing to a sleeping room and Chen to the guard barracks where he would select food for their trip. Chen had just finished loading their packs when a frantic servant came to him to report that the Princess had been poisoned. He rushed to the atrium where Du Mu and a man he took to be a physician stood over the pale figure of Jing, who sat in a chair.

Chen took her hand. She looked up at him.

"Close call," she said.

"Someone poisoned her pillow," Du Mu put in.

"I'm all right," she assured them, though she looked faint and her breathing was uneven. "When I put my head down, I caught the scent of almonds and knew it was poisoned with cyanide. Fate and the mercy of the Goddess Kuan Yin spared me."

"Fate barely spared you," Chen said, his eyes angry.

Du Mu spread his hands. "I don't know what to say. Shame overbears my soul."

"Assemble your servants," Jing Li said. "I want to see everyone who would have had access of that room."

Du Mu ordered the assembly. Jing seemed stronger now. "Chen," she said, "please fetch my uniform. It's hanging up in the room. Only the pillow is poisoned. If you don't touch it, no harm will come to you. Du Mu, is there a chamber where I might change, that modesty be observed?"

He led her to a small room. Chen brought her clothing. He could hear the household assembling in the atrium. He noted that Du Mu seemed uneasy, fearing, no doubt, that his guests would blame him for this treachery. After a while, Jing emerged dressed in loose-fitting black pants and a black smock. She looked more stable. Her color had returned and her breathing was even.

"Are the servant assembled?"

Du Mu nodded and led them to the atrium.

His guards had rounded up everyone—cooks, grooms, the gardener, the house servants; and then they themselves lined up in rank. Chen and Jing stood before them. At a nod from Jing, Chen stepped back. She stood in front of the assembly for several moments, saying nothing. The servants, already frightened, looked more and more anxious. Finally, she walked to the end of the line and went slowly down the rank, scanning every face. At the end of the line she stopped and turned on her heels. She paused and then walked up to a young servant girl. She stood a moment, looked at Du Mu, and said, "This one."

The blood drained from the girl's face. She collapsed. Jing caught her.

"Bring her to the reception hall," she ordered.

Four soldiers seized the girl. By now she had regained her senses. She sobbed and pleaded as they dragged her off. When they came to the threshold of the reception, she vomited. The soldiers pushed her to her knees in front of Jing.

"Look at me," she said. The girl lifted her terror-filled eyes. "Why did you try to kill me?"

"Mercy, my Lady," the servant girl wept.

"There may be mercy for you if you speak truthfully. If you keep sputtering, I'll order your master to have you crucified. Now answer. Why did you try to kill me?"

"Money," she said, barely able to speak. "My family is poor. My sisters will have to become prostitutes if we don't find more money."

"Where is the money?"

"Hidden in my bed."

"Send someone to find it," she told Du Mu. He gestured. Two guards left the room. Jing leaned forward. "Who gave you this money?"

"A man. He wore a hood and kept his face hidden. He came to the wall and gave me coins. He gave me the poison to spread on the pillow. Have mercy, my Lady, in the name of the Goddess of Compassion whose devotee you are. Please don't have me crucified."

"You will die, you traitorous little—" Du Mu stopped, not wanting to use vulgar language in front of the princess.

"She did this out of concern for her family," Jing Li replied. "For this reason, I ask that you spare her life—and give her to me for the task I have in mind. If she lives through it, she will redeem herself."

Du Mu spread his hands, his eyes full of malice at the servant girl, mouth tight, but acquiescence in his manner. He had understood it was a command.

"You should appreciate that the Princess is merciful," he said, fighting to control his anger. "If this were my decision, your immediate future would not be a pleasant one. But I defer to her judgment. You belong to her now."

"What is your name, girl?"

"Soong, an it please you, my Lady."

"I want you to go and bathe. I detect from your smell what happened to you. This often happens when we are terrified. When you finish bathing, wait for me in the bath chamber."

She left, accompanied by guards. After a moment, the chief servant returned with a bag of coins he had found in Soong's mattress.

"Spread them on the table," Chen ordered.

The servant opened the bag and poured out its contents. The horde covered the entire tabletop. Chen recognized the coins of the realm but also saw ones imprinted with eagles and the faces of Europeans.

"German, British, American," Chen said, running his fingers over them. "These are from inside the compound. Someone there knew we were coming."

"I don't know how that could be," Du Mu said. "Only I knew your identities or that you were coming here. Surely you don't suspect *me* of treachery."

"We know you for an honorable man. There has to be another explanation. The coins are various. Whoever delivered them to the girl took up a collection, which shows their resources are limited and that they can't get out of the compound—though they seem to have an intermediary, someone from the outside who is able to communicate with them and who received this payment to pass on to the girl." He looked at Du Mu. "We need to move quickly. This plot failed, but if they have successfully infiltrated your staff, we are not safe here."

"I am ashamed beyond my ability to express it," Du Mu said. His eyes glistened with tears.

"This treachery is only one effect of a disease deep in the body of our nation. If we can break the resistance of the foreigners in the embassy compound by destroying the relief convoy coming to them, the disease will be purged."

Du Mu nodded and bowed.

o   o   o

Princess Jing Li walked into the bathing chamber. Soong stood by the side of a tub. The air, steamy, filled Jing's lungs and made her feel more purged of the poison that had invaded her body. Soong had wrapped a towel around herself.

"Drop the towel," Jing said.

Soong let it fall to her. Jing assessed her. She was a strong girl with wide, firm shoulders, well-developed ribs, a flat stomach, powerful thighs, and muscular legs. She had small breasts and a small, neat triangle of black hair where her legs met.

"Do you desire me, my Lady?" she asked, looking up and attempting a smile.

"My desires do not so tend," Jing said. "Are you used in this way here, Soong?"

"Sometimes. It is not a thing I in which take pleasure, but when a highborn lady who is the Master's guest demands it of me, I have no choice but to obey."

"Well, I don't have that in mind. I only wanted to see your body so I could assess your level of strength. You are a strong." She did not reply but dropped her eyes modestly. "You're from a farm?"

"Yes."

"I can tell you've worked hard and eaten wholesome food. If you're a woman from this area, you must know the use of the staff."

The girl did not reply.

"Do you?"

"Yes, my Lady. I hope this does not displease you."

"Quite to the contrary. Get dressed and meet me in the courtyard. I'll tell your master to permit you to wait there. Remember you are my slave now."

"I will obey you, Princess Jing." And forgetting she was naked, Soong made a bow, bending her slender body low, her hands at her sides. Jing thought her bow was one of the loveliest things she had ever seen.

She went upstairs and drank a potion the doctor had prepared, instructed the guards to fetch a wooden staff and then went down to where Soong was waiting. As always, guards stood near her. Jing nodded. She looked lithe and trim in pants and a smock. A guard handed the staff to her.

"You were taught to fight with a staff because of predatory animals and predatory men. Is this correct?"

"Yes, my Lady. Wolves and wild dogs would attack our animals when we led them out to pasture. And the men would sometimes assault us if they caught us alone in the open."

"I'm going to act as if I were one of those men. I want you to defend yourself when I try to throw you to the ground. Don't be afraid to strike me. In fact, I want you to hurt me as much as you are able. If I don't think you can defend yourself, I will return you to your master, Du Mu, and you will die a painful, shameful death. Staff up! Prepare to defend yourself."

The girl lifted the staff to the *en guarde* position, instincts kicking in. Jing knew she could not afford to make it easy on her. She came at the young girl as swiftly and deceptively as she knew. Soong swung her staff, missed, whirled, ducked, and swung once again, striking Jing on the knee. When Jing recoiled, Soong brought the staff hard on her ribs, knocking her to the ground.

She knelt, horrified.

"Please, Princess Jing, don't be angry with me!" she pleaded.

It took a moment for Jing to get her breath. She made gestures to show all was well. When she could speak, she said, "You defend yourself well. I'm pleased. Come with me. We'll be leaving the compound shortly."

They walked back inside Du Mu's massive home. Soong carried her staff.

O O O

"The figure of the Weather God sits above the shore," Du Mu said to Cheng. "People think it is merely an icon. It is, in fact, the entrance to a device that controls the underground water of this region and can bring a tsunami against the foreign fleet headed our way."

"How is this possible?"

"I would say by magic, but it is in fact by knowledge. He has somehow tapped into the heat deep in the earth and can control it. He uses this energy to draw up seawater and fill the pool around the Weather God. There are also reservoirs carved into the hills that rise up behind the structure. He can release the waters all at once. The force of its fall creates a massive wave."

"Any weapon must be proven for its temper and trueness. Has this device been demonstrated to work?"

"The Japanese sent ships here five years ago with the intention of seizing this harbor and setting up one of their 'spheres of influence,' as they call them. The Weather God did not make a tsunami at that time but created waves so high the Japanese gunboats could not maneuver and could not fire their guns. They abandoned the attack. This was in the early stages of construction, when the device did not operate at full capacity. Now construction is complete. The device has been tested. We used old wooden ships, and the wave this machine produced rolled over them and sent them under. Shao Jiazhen, though, is the only one who knows how to operate it. That is why he must be freed.

Chen ran his gaze over the complex, huge and impressive. The figure of the Weather God—massive and made of iron covered with ceramic—rose out of a pool. Probably fifty feet tall, its benevolent face reminded Chen of the god of Good Fortune. The statue stood in the middle of a long wall of red brick that went all the way down to the narrow strand of beach that met the sea below it. Chen thought it might be a low-budget replica of the Forbidden City. A complex of temple-like buildings and a citadel with cannon ports stood at one end of the wall that enclosed the reservoir.

"Are any of the foreigners aware of the structure's function?"

"I don't think so. But if they get near enough to shell the complex, I think they might destroy the machinery. They probably see the buildings and the wall as a good place to mount guns."

Chen's mind quickly reviewed the situation into which he would soon plunge. European nations, taking advantage of political disarray and bolstered by their superior technology, had made incursions into China. They set up their "spheres of influence," mostly ports where they could export goods and bring opium into the country. The people resented their intrusion and their efforts to make money through the opium trade. Eventually a rebellion broke out. The "harmonious fists" began attacking and harassing foreign elements. The attacks had escalated into full-scale revolt. In Beijing, the Boxers (as the foreigners called them) had taken control of the city. They had driven the European and Japanese contingents—diplomatic staff, missionaries, international workers—into the embassy compound. Strong contingents of troops, heavily armed, protected them, but they were running low on food and ammunition. The relief convoy from their various supporting countries had drawn near. It carried additional troops, weapons and supplies. This is what Du Mu and his confederates wanted to stop so the rebellion could achieve victory.

"We'll see," Chen said, breaking out of his revelry. "The best thing would be for us to leave now. We don't have much time."

"That girl should die. I should make an example of her."

"You'll have to take this up with Princess Jing. We'll return to your estate and depart from there. I think all our equipage is in order."

They rode the two miles back to Du Mu's estate where Jing and Soong waited, both dressed in fighting clothes. Du Mu frowned when he saw Soong. She blanched, fearing her former master might still punish her with torture or that perhaps Jing would change her mind and deliver her over to him. Jing put her hand on Soong's shoulder.

"This young lady will be a valuable ally to us," she said. "She will aid us greatly when we infiltrate the complex."

"What is the position of the European flotilla? Is there word on it?"

"They will fuel in Japan and, after that, make a course directly for us. They will arrive within the week."

"Then we need to begin our journey."

They slung on their packs and departed, beginning their trek to the Forbidden City. It was too dangerous to ride horses, so they went overland.

O   O   O

They went at a quick pace. Soong puffed and panted but kept up. When they stopped to rest, she took off her pack and lay down, often falling asleep. When roused, she got up and marched. They walked until darkness, stopped and made camp. Jing put rice on to boil. Soong fell asleep again. Jing woke her.

"Eat," she said. "We will rise at dawn and see how much distance we can cover tomorrow. We don't know what we're up against, and once we do free Shao, it will take a couple of days to get him back. It is vital we move and as quickly as possible. Eat and then you can sleep."

Soong ate rice and vegetable fritters, rolled in her blanket, and was oblivious until the first grey light of morning graced the sky. They started out early and made good progress, so that by the end of their second day, they arrived at the villages and farms that serviced the capital city. They ate at an inn and took rooms. Jing would sleep with Chou, but before she left Soong in her tiny cell, she knelt by her bed.

"Tomorrow," she said, "you and I will infiltrate the compound. Something you must know, Soong, though perhaps from your experience as a servant in Du Mu's household you know this already."

She paused. Soong looked at her with big, expectant eyes.

"Your womanhood," she continued, "is like a golden sword. It is a beautiful treasure, but there are times when you must use it to protect your life or the lives of others. I began as a warrior in the tradition of Mulan. I fought many years as a chaste maiden, but I soon realized this was both impractical and distracting to my subordinate officers. I went home for the winter, let an old boyfriend take my virginity and ... well, shall we say, *break me in* a little. When I returned to the field in the spring, I began to have liaisons with my officers. It worked marvelously. It made them more loyal and more skillful at fighting. They competed to demonstrate their valor, loyalty, and courage. I did not let any outstanding display of any of these things go unrewarded. It has been so to this day. You told me you were required at Du Mu's estate to service women—men, too?"

"Yes, my Lady. More men than women."

Jing smiled and patted her shoulder gently.

"The things we will do, we will do together. I will never ask you to do anything I will not do myself. Sleep. I will tell you what our plan is when we arrive at the embassy complex. But for now"—she took out a phial—"drink this in the morning. It will prevent you from getting pregnant." Then she held up a glass container. "Also, anoint your secret parts with cream in this jar. It will also act as a contraceptive and as a lubricant."

Soong nodded. Jing left and went to sleep with Chen Hao. In the morning they ate and made their way into Beijing.

O   O   O

The city looked like a city under siege. Gutted buildings rose. Gangs of armed soldiers patrolled the streets. They passed a burned out church. Dozens of bodies lay on the ground around it. A white man in a Christian priest's clothing and two Chinese men had been hanged from the lintel above the entry.

The soldiers gave them looks, but they recognized Chen as a man who bore arms and did not challenge him. The three of them came near the compound. Chen talked with the commander of the Boxer force guarding the east side. After a parley, he nodded to Jing and went his way. She and Soong changed into the coarse, ragged dresses they had purchased in a tiny village early that morning, took off their shoes, rubbed dirt on their hands and faces, and crossed the hundred yards that separated the Chinese and American troops.

As they drew close to the compound, Jing noted the damage done by shelling. Some of the buildings smoldered. As they approached the trenches, sentries came into view. The blue uniforms told her the men defending the parapets were Americans. As they came closer, the soldiers—there were six of them—leveled their rifles. One of them stood up and held a pistol.

"Stop where you are," he said in Chinese.

Soong halted, but Jing walked a few steps closer. His hand tightened on the revolver.

"Please, sir," Jing said, "hear as I speak." She deliberately made her English, which she spoke fluently, sound clumsy and rudimentary. "Please hear our words."

The soldier relaxed just slightly.

"What is it you want?" he asked in English.

"We are hungry."

"So are we," he replied, a smile playing on his lips. The other men lowered their rifles, smiled and chuckled.

"We will pay for food," Jing said, and then she lifted the hem of her dress, pulling it up past her waist. Soong blinked in astonishment and then followed suit.

The soldier stared a moment and then grinned.

"Well now. You have a kind of currency that is legal tender anywhere." His men laughed. "I think we can give you some food. Come on."

They dropped their garments and climbed the soft mound of earth in front of the trench. The American soldier offered Jing and then Soong his hand.

"We only ask that you feed us first. We are very hungry."

He turned to a black soldier. "Hobbs, go get a couple bowls of rice—and whatever else they have."

The man scurried off. The American looked Jing full in the face.

"Where did you learn to speak English?"

"Missionary school, my sir."

Her father had insisted she learn the English tongue so she could negotiate for him. Since both the British and the Americans spoke that language, it seemed the most sensible one to learn. She had studied with missionaries and private tutors.

"I don't think the missionaries would like what you're doing now."

She did not respond. Hobbes came back with two tin plates heaped with rice and some sort of bread. The man who seemed in charge nodded, and he handed them to Soong and Jing.

"Eat while we get things ready. My name is Sergeant Kelly." He walked off and began talking with a group of men who listened to him with eager surprise.

"Eat like you are starving," Jing said. Soong looked at her and began to wolf her food. Kelly came back over.

"Sister," Jing said in Chinese. "Do not eat so fast. Eat slowly so it will do your stomach good."

Soong looked at her, not comprehending, and then realized it was part of the ploy. She took smaller portions and chewed more slowly.

"She's your sister?" Kelly asked in English. As Jing had suspected, he knew Chinese fairly well.

"Yes, my sir. We have not eaten in many days."

He looked at Soong. "How old is she?"

"Sixteen year."

He pondered and then went off. They finished their food and stood. Jing went over to Kelly.

"We are ready, my sir. We will pay for the food you gave us."

He led them to a tent and told them to stand by the door, showing familiarity with local practices and how prostitutes advertised in China. After a while a group of five men appeared.

"Only five?" he asked.

"A lot of the men got religion hanging around the missionaries," Hobbes smiled. "I put the word out, but these are the only ones who showed up."

"Well, let's get going then."

Hobbes was the first. He picked Soong and took her into the tent. The next three wanted Jing. Number five took Soong. Kelly, who was last, picked Jing. When they had finished, the two of them came outside the tent. Kelly gave them a loaf of yeast bread wrapped in cloth.

"Here. This is for you," he said. "If you want to come back in a couple of days, we'll have more food for you. But be careful. The Boxers will kill you if they find out you've been here."

Soong nodded. An awkward moment passed and then Kelly said, in Chinese, "Go home."

He turned. Jing glanced at Soong and motioned, pointing for Soong to get behind her and stay close. Jing followed Kelly, making no noise as she stepped behind him, less than a foot away, shadowing him as he crossed the common and went into one of the buildings. He neither heard, saw, nor otherwise sensed the presence of the two women. The other soldiers, vigilant at their posts, did not look back. When Kelly went into a door, Jing broke off from him, Soong following her, and hurried around the side of the building he had entered. She and Soong slid into a shadowy alley between two large structures.

Soong looked at Jing with wide eyes. "How did you do that, my Lady? Was it magic?"

"Not magic. I simply got in his blind spot. If you stalk a person from behind with a certain approach, they cannot see you. If you're quiet, they will not detect you at all. It was stealth, not magic. It is exhausting, though. Sit. We need to rest."

They rested a few moments in the cool and dark. Jing looked around and saw a bundle lying at the opposite end of the corridor. She smiled. Chen had penetrated the compound as well. She retrieved the bundle. "Change," she told Soong. Beside the bag containing their clothes she saw her weapons array—sword, dagger, throwing stars, Soong's staff. She stood guard as the girl changed clothes. Jing dressed and cautiously stepped out into the sunlight.

"Hold where you are," a voice said.

She turned. It was Hobbs. He pointed at revolver at her.

"What are you doing here? Where did you get those clothes?" he saw the dagger hanging on her belt. Before he could speak, the gun few from his hand. Jing heard a thump and Hobbes crumpled to the ground. Soong stepped up, staff at ready. Jing felt the fear and tension go from her. She smiled.

"Thank you, Soong. Let's get him back in the alley before someone else sees us."

They dragged him back into the space between the two buildings. "Will we kill him?"

"Remember what Sun Tzu taught us. Killing is not the primary thing. It is better to keep a city intact than to destroy it—and so with the life of a human. He will be out for a long time. Let's bind him."

They tied him up and put him in the recesses of the alleyway. Soong wondered if they would take his pistol, but Jing told her no.

"Using it would violate the spirit of our endeavor. We need to move quickly. Come."

The two women exited the corridor by the back way and went on toward the American complex.

o   o   o

Chen moved through the shadows, looking for where Shao might be held prisoner. So far he had encountered no one, though once he heard a large group of people singing songs—probably a worship service, he thought, which would cut the number of people roaming through the building. He stalked the empty corridors until he came to a floor covered with bright colored tile. He stopped.

He waited. The floors in the building were wooden. The design of manufacture of the tile was undoubtedly Chinese. Chen scanned the area. The tile covered a rectangular space about twenty feet wide and twice as long. Across the tile space he saw a door. In front of it stood one of those sculptured soldiers the ancient emperors placed to guard their tombs. He noticed it carried a real sword in its stiff clay hands. Puzzled, he stepped on to the tile.

To his astonishment and fear, the ceramic figure gripped the sword and assumed the stance of one ready to fight.

He stepped back, not trusting his eyes. The figure remained at ready as Chen stepped over to the left, not touching the tiles. The figure did not follow him, nor did it turn its head. At the far corner of the tile rectangle, he stepped on it once again.

The figure turned to face him. He understood that it was a machine—a contrivance of amazing ingenuity. And he knew only one man in the world would have the skill to construct such a thing. Shao Jiazhen would be found just beyond the door. He was being guarded by a device of his own making.

Even a device could know defeat, Chen thought. He took a step toward it. It advanced, lowering its sword. He took out a throwing star and launched it at the thing's head. It hit square but glanced off. The figure did not move. He hit it again, aiming for its stomach. The throwing star skidded off, doing no damage.

He swung his sword. It hit the figure but turned under, not biting, not doing any damage. The figure swung at Chen, who ducked and felt the blade pass close to his face. He sprang back. The figure retreated to a defensible position, still at ready, its unseeing eyes fixed on a point beyond the wall.

Chen licked his lips. Shao had designed the contrivance to defend the door. Besides providing it with motion, he had covered it with material so hard and smooth it deflected any object that came against it. He pondered, studying the thing. Where would it be most vulnerable? He noticed its hands.

Its hands did not reflect light as the remainder of its shiny body did. They looked unglazed. Time was as much his foe as the machine. He had to act quickly and decided to proceed on this hunch, hoping his assessment was accurate.

When he stepped on to the tile, the figure came toward him, lowering its sword. Chen took out a throwing star and aimed it the statue's right hand. He heard the sound of a plate breaking and retreated to see what he had done.

The covering on the figure's left hand finger had broken off, revealing a framework of iron with intricate pulleys and wires. He reached in the pocket of his smock and pulled out two more throwing stars. In an instant he broke the ceramic covering on both its hands.

This did not stop it. The thing still gripped its sword, but Chen could now see the mechanism that enabled it to grasp a weapon.

Chen went on the tiles and lunged. The machine-soldier swung with lightning speed and sliced his leg below the knee—not a life threatening wound, he knew, but one that would soon disable him. He stepped back. The figure withdrew. He suddenly sprung and contacted its left hand with the full force of his sword.

The thin metal yielded to the blow. Chen sheared off three of the device's fingers. It went still, but, at the same time, something wrenched Chen's sword from his hand.

Silence fell. Chen stood unarmed in front of the disabled manikin. When he felt sure the contrivance was completely dysfunctional, he bent down and tried to pick up the sword. He could not make it budge; it stuck to the floor by some magical spell. He also felt something pull at the dagger on his belt. When he walked off the tiles, the pressure ceased.

He had to find Shao, he decided, even if looking for him would mean abandoning his primary weapon. He walked toward the door. The pressure pulled at the dagger as before, but he managed to keep it from flying to the ground. He turned the handle.

The room contained what Chen took to be inventions—half-finished machines, two more terra cotta soldiers not yet entirely covered with tile, their gears and pulleys visible. He strained to hear. He heard footsteps.

He had expected that Shao Jiazhen would be old. He connected age with wisdom and skill, assuming that only years of study could produce such a mechanical wonder as the thing he had just fought off. Instead, before him stood a man his age—surely not yet forty. Hair thick and black, face and body spare in a healthy way, he smiled on seeing Chen.

"I assume Du Mu has sent you here?"

"He has. You are Shao Jiazhen?"

"I am he."

"I am Chen. We have come to rescue you."

"We? There are more of you?"

"Two more. We have a plan to get you out of here and back to Xanting and the Weather God."

"That will be difficult."

"We got in. We'll get you out. I need my sword, though."

"The figure you fought is empowered by loadstones embedded in the floor. You probably managed to shear through its interior mechanisms, which would neutralize its polarity and drain it of energy. But the loadstones would then attract all metal objects to it."

Chen hardly comprehended what Shao said. He looked down at Chen's feet.

"You're bleeding. I'll get your sword for you, but first let me look at your wound. I can probably patch it up."

"You know medicine?" Chen asked.

Shao smiled. "I know everything," he said.

After Shao had sutured the wound, they heard the door handle turn.

O   O   O

Jing licked her lips nervously as Cao opened the door. She had managed to talk their way out of their discovery. When she and Soong had sneaked into the American quarters, they heard voices and the clattering of weapons. She could tell a large force had come against them, no chance of fighting them off.

"Hide our bags and weapons," she told Soong. "Here."

They stashed their packs, Jing's sword and dagger, and Soong's staff. As they finished, a group of twelve soldiers—ten Chinese and two Westerners—all heavily armed, turned the corner. A Chinese man in ornate robes led them.

The man looked them over. His eyes rested on Soong and then he turned to Jing.

"Who are you and what are you doing here? I am Cao Cao, director of internal affairs for this compound. I don't recognize either of you."

"The American brought us here," Jing said, "for the pleasure of the scientist."

He grinned. "Ah, you are the two women from earlier in the day. They said they sent you back."

"They told us to come here—that our services would be needed one more time."

"I see." He scanned their garments. "They told me you were both dressed in rags. Where did you get those clothes?"

"They are the garments of two women who died to disease—or so they told us. They gave us these because they wanted us to look presentable to the Master Shao."

"I see. Your name?"

"I am Shangguan," she lied. "This is my sister." She glanced at Soong who drew two fingers across her mouth—the sign made by people who were mute. Jing also caught a warning in her eyes. "She wanted me to tell you she is mute and cannot answer you if you speak to her. Her name is Lan."

"She is a very beautiful lotus flower." He turned to his guards and dismissed them. "I will take you to where Master Shao dwells. After he chooses one of you, the other can come with me and, when the one he picks is finished, that one may join as well. My guards and I will reward you with food and money. You won't lose for your time."

"We are thankful for your offer, sir."

"Come then."

They had made their way through the American quarters past white women and men in the heavy, odd clothing they wore, the men with their unattractive facial hair, the women with their flowery, billowing dresses. They turned through a series of corridors and came to a colorful tile floor. A statue of a tomb guard, its hands broken to reveal intricate mechanisms, stood near a door. On the floor beside it lay Chen's sword.

The man leading them opened the door.

Once inside, he turned to a man Jing assumed was Shao. She marveled at how young he was.

"Well, my dear scholar," Cao said, "the Americans are grateful enough for your work that they have decided to reward you. Two fine women stand before you—one beautiful and stately, and one a little plum just waiting to be plucked from the bush."

Jing hit him on the back of the neck and knocked him out. He fell heavily to the floor.

"You are Shao?" she asked. "Where is Chen? Is he hurt? I saw he lost his sword."

"I'm here," he said, stepping out from behind a screen. Jing noticed he was limping. Relief flooded over her to see him alive. Soong stepped up.

"This man," she said, "is the man who brought me the coins. I never saw his face, but I know his voice. We met in the dark and he wore a hood. I covered my face with a veil, but he would know my voice. That is why I said I was mute."

"You are a wise young woman," Jing said. She turned to Chen. "You're hurt," she observed.

"I'll be all right."

"We need to hurry. We knocked out an America soldier. He will wake soon."

"I will arrange for you to get your sword back," Shao said. "What plans do you have?"

"Jing and Soong will smuggle you to the door as I create a diversion."

"One man will create a diversion?"

"They don't know I'm only one man."

"You're hurt," Shao said. "You can't fight off the combined forces of the Westerners. Be ruled by me. I think I can help."

He led them into a room and then down a winding metal staircase, outlining his plan as they went. They descended into a large, dimly lit chamber. Shao pulled a lever embedded in the floor. It sent a spark that lit a series of oil lamps around the perimeter.

In the orange lamplight they saw small, squat shapes. They looked somewhat like the ceramic figure Chen had fought, but they were smaller—three feet high, round and squat. They gripped swords with one mechanical limb. The other limb hung free. Chen noticed they were made of metal, not ceramic.

"You all you know your instructions," he said. "Be sure you show terror."

They nodded. Chen had put on peasant dress. Jing and Soong had recovered and dressed in the ragged garments they had worn into the compound. They stored their other garments and their weapons in a cloth bag Chen had slung over his back. His wound had bled through the thin trousers he wore.

Shao told them to stand back. They stepped toward the rear of the room. The inventor went over to a display of buttons and levers. He seized a large lever with both hands and pulled it back.

Chen became aware of energy in the air. It surged, invisible but discernible, traveling in waves, filling the room with its impulses.

The figures clanked upright. Chen heard the noise of metal contracting. The figures stood straighter. At the same time a wide door opened by means of chains. Sunlight filtered into the large space. At a nod from Shao, Chen, Jing, and Soong hurried to the front of the chamber. When the door had opened all the way, they ran out into the courtyard.

They began to scream in terror, catching the attention of the American guards. Kelly turned and ran up to confront them, waving his pistol.

"What are you doing? Halt! Stop!" He spoke in Chinese.

"Demons! Demons!" Jing shouted, pointing back, feigning terror.

As he spoke, a bolt flew through the air and struck Kelly in the side. He fell. Chen never learned if he survived. The mechanical soldiers began releasing missiles from portals in their chests. By now, Chen, Jing, Soong, and Shao had reached the trenches.

The American soldiers had seen Kelly fall and saw the mechanical soldier advancing. As Chen and the others ran past them, pointing back and shouting "Demons" the Americans did not oppose them. They opened fire on the metal attackers. Chen heard the rifles go off, the sounds of more projectiles releasing from the other side, shouts, curses, and screams. The noise of bullets striking metal told him the soldiers were hitting the manikins, but a backward glance told him the machines continued to advance.

Once they were past the trenches, he took a small mirror out of his pocket and flashed it. A flash came in response from the Boxer ramparts.

"Everyone get in single file," he said, "and follow—stay in a straight line behind me."

They fell in, Chen in front, the others behind him. He moved straight toward the flash signal. As they neared the Boxer ranks, the troops opened fire. They left a corridor, though, for Chen and his party. As they ran for cover, bullets whizzed past them like angry wasps buzzing through the air.

They crossed the Boxer lines. A man in a military uniform came to them and bowed.

"I am Yuan," he said. "The commandant is supervising the firing, but I am here to supply you with horses and send you on your way."

Chen nodded. His leg hurt. The sutures had split open and the wound bled badly. As rifles stuttered in the background, two men led four strong, sleek horses. Chen collapsed.

Shao and Jing knelt over him.

"I need to go with you," Chen said, gritting his teeth.

"You are a capable warrior," Shao replied. "If you lose that leg, however, you will not be so capable. I will leave you here in the care of a physician. You must promise me you will not leave until you are well—the physician who cares for you will determine when you are well."

He looked up at Jing. Their eyes met.

"I agree."

"Good. I'll have a potion for you to drink, but we need to get you out of here."

The rifle fire continued as four soldiers appeared with a litter. They carried Chen to a house out of the range of the rifle fire. The others followed. Once inside, Shao conferred with the physician. The doctor cleaned and re-sutured the wound. Shao gave Chen the potion. Within a minute, he was out cold.

○   ○   ○

"He will sleep for at least a day and night with that one," Shao told Jing. "I could tell that in spite of his promise he would be on a horse and heading for Xanting the moment we were out of sight."

"Will he heal?"

"If his wound is properly cared for, yes."

Jing turned to Soong.

"You will stay here and assist the physician. See to Chen's needs and dissuade him from leaving until the doctor releases him. "She turned back to Shao. "We need to go. We have a hard ride ahead of us."

He only nodded.

They mounted the horses and rode until nightfall, fortunately finding an inn. As they ate, Shao told Jing about his ordeals at the compound.

"At first they thought I was only a noble and beat and threatened me, trying to extract money. Then Cao Cao recognized me. They set me to creating an army of mechanical soldiers to attack the Boxers. Due to your intervention, I was able to send them against the international force. They wanted one-hundred. I had only manufactured twenty."

"Will they destroy the foreign force?"

"No. They would have run down rapidly. After twenty minutes, they would go inert."

"But your Weather God device will destroy the fleet of ships they are sending?"

"If we get there on time."

"We will arise at first light. We're halfway there already."

She went to her bedroom. Though she did not believe much in the goddess, she had, in her younger days, dedicated herself to that deity. She opened the widow of her small room and looked up at the moon. It rode in a ship of silver clouds. Stars gleamed through the gaps in the clouds. She closed her eyes and lifted her hands in silent supplication to the Goddess of Compassion for her protection and guidance.

Opening her eyes, she saw three men holding torches ride up to the inn. One of them was the man she had knocked out at Shao's laboratory: Cao Cao.

She grabbed her sword and hurried through the door. No time to change out of her smock, she ran down the stairs and stood at ready when they entered the door.

They burst in. She threw a dart and killed one. The other two took shelter. Cao Cao produced a pistol and aimed it at her.

Jing had never defended herself against a firearm. Chen had taught her how to block a bullet, and the two of them had practiced the technique with him firing—but he had probably gone easy on her. She raised her sword, watching the angle at which Cao leveled the pistol. He fired twice. She crouched and raised the blade. Both bullets deflected off it. She dropped to her knees and flung a dart at Cao, hitting him the shoulder. The third man had fallen down. Jing sprang, somersaulted and landed on her feet, kicking the firearm out of Cao's hand and bringing the blade of her sword against the third assailant's throat.

"I do not desire your death," she said. She reached down with her free hand and disarmed him. "Go. No harm will come to you." He nodded. She lowered her sword. The man scrambled out the door. A moment later she heard the sound of his horse galloping away.

She let herself relax. By now the other lodgers and the innkeeper had rushed downstairs. All were armed. She went over to the innkeeper.

"I'm sorry. These men attacked me. I had to defend myself."

The man squinted. "You are the Princess Jing Li."

"I am she. I am sorry I brought the ill omen of death to your place."

"Ill omen of death?" he repeated, his lip curled in scorn. "I've been paying protection to this bastard for years. He's a ruthless criminal, and his gang of thugs terrorizes everyone on the road from Beijing to Xanting. You are an avenging saint."

Cao Cao was not dead, but he would be soon. Jing used poisoned darts. His death would not be quick or easy. The poison had no antidote, and its effects were irreversible. Fatigue from all she had gone through fell heavily on her. Shao came up to her. He looked down at Cao Cao.

"He will not recover," she said.

Shao nodded. "Should we leave here?" he asked. "We can ride by torchlight."

"I must sleep," she replied. "We'll get up early."

She went back to her chamber. Despite the danger that other members of Cao's gang might arrive, she slept soundly until predawn. She and Shao ate a quick breakfast and headed for Xanting and the shore.

They rode steadily and arrived at the site of the Weather God machine when the sun was still high. Du Mu awaited them with a guard of soldiers in case someone tried to intervene. The three of them entered the area through a door and wound up a series of staircases carved out of rock. They toiled their way upward in lamp lit dark until they came to a platform that looked down at the sea, the shoreline, the Weather God, and the wall around him. She also noticed, from up high, that the floor of the sea below the complex was covered with flat tiles. It made Jing dizzy. The breeze blew full in their faces. Du Mu pointed.

"There they are."

Shao gazed out at the horizon. "Too far off," he said. "We need to let them get closer."

Jing strained her eyes. She saw the ships, white shapes above the blue water. She could see the plumes of smoke rising from their smokestacks. The wind blew her hair in her face. She pulled it back and saw a flash come from one of the vessels.

"They're firing their cannons at us," she said.

Shao nodded. A second later they heard a whistling sound. A violent explosion shook the ground as a shell blew apart a section of one of the buildings on the shore.

"Will they destroy the device?"

"They're not hitting the device. Those buildings are nothing but empty facades. They look like a fortress, but they're hollow. That's what the Westerners will shell, though, so—at least as they think— their landing here will be unopposed.

The ships grew closer. The shelling continued. Deafening explosions went out in profusion. Jing summoned her self-control so she did not appear frightened before the two men. Du Mu winced. Shao stood by placidly. The shelling from the warships soon reduced the buildings on the shoreline to a smoking pile of rubble. The ships had come near enough that she could see the masts and flags. She counted twelve.

She also had become aware of a rumbling sound. The ground under her feet seemed to move. She wondered for a moment if an earthquake had come—if their plans might be ruined by an unexpected natural event. She said nothing. The shaking and twisting sensation continued. She realized in a flash that what she felt was the mountain behind her filling with water.

The ships were now visible, perhaps only a half mile from the shoreline. They had stopped firing their guns. Shao walked over to a wooden trap Jing had not noticed, opened it and walked down a set of ten steps. Jing and Du Mu moved forward so they could see. Another explosion rocked the decoy buildings. Shao calmly seized the lever and drew it back.

A clanging of machinery sounded—a cacophony of metal on metal, of creaking, groaning, grating, the sound of pulleys and leavers, a release of steam, and finally the noise of a cataract more deafening than the Huangguoshu Waterfall (Jing had journeyed there not long ago). The walls and superstructure below the statue of the Weather God fell away, releasing a torrent of cold blue that plunged in a giant mass straight down toward the sea.

For just a second the liquid hung in the air. Then, with a crash like thunder, like landslides, like the days of the gods' judgment, it hit the surface of the sea below them.

The tons of falling water from the mountain sluice struck with such force it heaped the standing water of the shore into a giant column. Jing would have guessed its height as twenty feet. For a moment it seemed to hang there, churning, seething, growing. She wondered if it might collapse upon itself or back on them, but then it rolled seaward, toward the East, toward the shores of Japan and Korea, toward the ships entering the harbor.

She did not see them go under. The wall of water hid their sinking. She only knew that when the wave rolled on out to the sea and disappeared in the distance, all the ships were gone.

The physician had still not released Chen by the time Jing returned to Beijing. He was grumpy but valued his health and mobility enough to obey medical orders. His wound was healing. Soong, he said, had been a good nurse.

The Europeans, Americans, and Japanese were shocked and devastated when they discovered a tsunami had sunk their fleet. A freak occurrence, they reasoned. The besieged garrison in the embassy compound had begun negotiations with the Boxers who had agreed to allow them to evacuate the embassy compound, if they agreed to remove all troops of all nationalities from Chinese soil. Politicians in London, Berlin, Washington, Tokyo, and elsewhere were saying that maintaining spheres of influence in China was costly and dangerous. Their nations, they argued, needed to abandon the venture altogether.

After a few days of rest and quiet, Jing stood on a balcony, enjoying the cool of the night and the spectacle of moon and starlight. Soong came and knelt in front of her. Jing insisted she rise and stand.

"Do not bow to me. You are my sister and my comrade, not my servant. You saved my life. I am greatly in your debt."

"If you are in my debt, repay it by teaching me the arts of war. I want to learn to fight for my people, as you do."

"You're a great warrior already. But go home to your family. Spend a season with them. When harvest time and winter have passed, I will come to your home. We can begin to train."

"Thank you, my Lady. Will you marry Chen?"

"Neither of us can think of marriage now. There is too much to be done. Perhaps someday—at least I hope so."

Soong smiled and took her leave.

Jing looked up. The night sky, she thought, was the garment of Kuan Yin, Goddess of Compassion.

The stars were jewels in her quiet, dark gown.

THE SPIRIT OF THE GRIFT

Sam Knight

Spiritualist and Medium," Georges deciphered aloud. The hand-painted sign was decorated with so many flourishes that the storefront name had been rendered nearly illegible. He turned his attention away from the row of businesses lining the street and grinned at his brother Yves. "I believe we have found our next benefactor."

Yves smiled back. "Mother would be proud!" The two looked nothing alike. Georges was dark haired, dark complexioned, and kept himself immaculately groomed, while Yves had a mop of dirty blond hair, grimy fair skin, and teeth that would make a warthog jealous.

"You really think so?" Georges looked quizzically at his brother. "I mean, we are kind of cheating...."

"Honestly! Worried about cheating the cheaters? How could you forget the look on Mum's face when she realized she had run out of money, giving it away to swindlers like this?" Yves pointed angrily at the little shop.

"Out the way!" a voice cried out behind them.

Yves and Georges hurried out of the cobblestone street just as an ice wagon raced past. Both brothers gestured rudely at the driver who had not only failed to slow, but had flicked the reins to speed the horses up. The improper gesture befit Yves ragged appearance, but it was comical when matched with Georges' pinstriped suit and gentlemanly façade.

"Bastard!" Georges called after the horse and wagon, knowing the insult fell on deaf ears. "I hope your ass freezes to the buckboard!"

"Let it go." Yves patted his brother on the shoulder. Georges could easily work the minor incident up into a major occurrence that would overshadow the next few days. "It's not worth it."

"Still. He's a bastard. Acting like he owns the streets."

"Well, we were just standing in the road gawking like village idiots." Yves's pale countenance went slack-jawed as he made a blank expression at Georges.

Georges reluctantly smiled. "All right, then. Let's go make some money."

"Now yer talkin'," Yves replied in a slurred voice to match his idiot persona. "Oh, wait." He dropped out of character and patted his pockets. "Do you have a kaleidoscope? I don't think I have one on me."

"I've got one. Do you have the ghost-scope?"

Yves rolled his eyes. "I've *always* got that."

"All right then. Again. Let's go make some money."

Georges glanced up and down the street to make sure no more carriages would try to run him over before stepping back out onto the cobblestones. He straightened his jacket cuffs, adjusted his waistcoat, and corrected his posture to be as stiff as possible. He strode across the street with an air of dignity.

Yves followed, slouching and swinging his arms like the hunchback of Notre Dame.

The kingly fashion in which Georges entered the shop was wasted on the unoccupied room. The show Yves put on, attempting to open the door Georges had allowed to shut in his face—by using only the backs of his hands—was also wasted. Neither brother was discouraged in the slightest.

Looking around at the shelves and glass display cabinets full of expensive oils, potpourris, and incense, Georges smiled to himself. This place obviously made plenty of money.

"Ahem!" Georges cleared his throat in the rudest polite way possible.

On the other side of the room, Yves began picking at the seat of his pants with one hand while stretching up on tip-toe to try to reach glass baubles off the top shelf of a display with the other. When no one emerged from the back, Yves went ahead and knocked a few of the curios off.

The resulting sound of shattering glass quickly summoned two people; an overweight middle-aged man wearing standard home-made burlap pants and shirt, and an attractive young woman in a velvety red dress befitting a spiritualist. The man wore a sour look and had a small club clenched tightly in one fist. The woman, wild-eyed, held the top of her bodice together with one hand while frantically trying to button it up with the other.

Georges had a hard time deciding which of the two he most wanted to keep his eyes upon. Fortunately, Yves chose that moment to curl up on the floor and begin wailing like an infant.

Rolling his eyes up toward the heavens, Georges assumed the look of someone so disaffected he might die just to relieve his boredom. "Oh, puh-lease! Not again. Three times in one day is quite enough!"

Georges spun on his heel and marched over to Yves. "Here." He pulled a telescoping brass tube from his coat pocket and held it out.

Yves peeked through his fingers to see what was being offered before he stopped crying. When he saw the kaleidoscope, he snatched at it instantly. Tears a thing of the past, Yves put the tube to his eye and grinned as he looked around the room.

With a heavy sigh, Georges tiredly turned back to the other two people in the room. "I am terribly sorry. I will pay for whatever it is he has broken."

The heavy man's knuckles returned to a normal color as he relaxed his grip on the club. The woman turned her back to Georges and Yves and quickly finished buttoning up the front of her dress.

"I've got it, Papa," she whispered.

The man eyed Georges, then Yves. Yves eyed him back through the kaleidoscope with a silly grin. Grunting, the man returned to the back room.

"Please, sir," the woman called Georges attention back to her, "allow me just a moment to clean up the glass." She bent down behind the sales counter.

As soon as she was out of sight, Yves put the kaleidoscope in his pocket and pulled out an identical looking brass tube, his ghost-scope.

The woman came out from behind the counter with a broom and dustpan and began sweeping up the colored shards from the wooden floor.

Yves followed her every movement with his scope. Georges was hard pressed to keep a straight face as Yves waggled his eyebrows at the young woman's lithe form.

A nearly overwhelming scent of perfumed flowers and fruits filled the air, mixing with a horrid burnt smell.

"Dear God!" Georges covered his nose with the back of his hand. "What is *that?*"

Yves retreated to the farthest corner of the shop and began feigning retching noises. At least Georges thought Yves was pretending.

"I'm terribly sorry, sir!" The woman continued cleaning. "Some of those oils were quite rare and valuable because of their strong scents."

"Hmph!" Georges almost sniffed in disgust, but thought better of it. "*Of course* they were."

With an apologetic smile, the young woman finished sweeping up the shards and took them into the back room. When she returned, she opened windows and used a small wooden stool to prop open the front door.

Yves went back to looking at everything in the shop through his mock-kaleidoscope, although he continued to make quiet gagging noises.

Georges, still holding the back of his hand to his nose, was on the verge of gagging himself. "Perhaps I should return later, after this has aired a bit."

"Oh yes, sir," the woman bowed slightly. "That might be a wise choice."

Georges narrowed his eyes at her. "Are you trying to get rid of me?"

"Oh, no—!"

"Do you find you have difficulty hiding your disdain for my poor brother? Do you think it improper that a wealthy family would keep one if its own around instead of putting him in an asylum or turning him out to the gutter?"

"Sir! I—No!" The woman's face turned red as she became flustered.

"You'll not be rid of me that easily! I came here to speak with the dead, and I'll not leave until I have!"

"Please, sir. This way." She pointed to a wooden door in the back. "We hold our séances back here where the bright of day doesn't interfere as much."

When Georges didn't follow her gesture, she led the way.

"Come, Tomás," Georges said to Yves. "Let us go see if Mummy will talk to you here."

"Mummy!" Yves spoke for the first time since entering the shop. "Mummy, Richie! Mummy!" He jumped up like a child and danced over to hug Georges.

"Yes, Tomás, Mummy." Georges stiffly hugged Yves back for a moment before pushing his brother away again and straightening his jacket.

"Where? Where Mummy?"

"In there, Tomás. In that room. Let's go."

Yves stopped and looked around with a confused look on his face. "No Mummy?" he said to the air. He frowned deeply. "No Mummy!" he told Georges and stomped his foot.

Georges sighed. "Let's go see anyway, Tomás."

"No, Richie! No Mummy!"

"Please, Tomás. Let's go see."

Yves pouted. "Richie. No Mummy."

Georges put his arm around Yves. "Please. For Richie? Come on." He began gently pulling Yves toward the back room.

Georges gave the woman a weak apologetic smile as they crossed the threshold to enter the darkened room. He looked over his shoulder and quietly whispered, "Tomás thinks he can talk to an invisible lady named Angelica, and she tells him things. Right now she seems to be telling him we will not be seeing our mother here."

"The spirits do as the spirits wish, sir." The woman seemed to plead with her eyes. "We will see what we can see."

She followed them in, and the room went dark as she closed the door. A clicking sound repeated three times as she twisted the key on the wall to light the gas fueled sconce. A warm glow filled the room as the flame came to life and revealed the dark red velvet drapes that hid the walls. Mostly filled by a large round table with a glass ball for a centerpiece, the room also held eight chairs, gathered around the table, and a large portrait of a scowling older woman.

"Please, sit." She gestured to the chairs.

Georges led Yves to a chair and put him in it before sitting himself. The woman took a moment to straighten her dress and her hair, and then, with a flourish, she walked around to the large leather covered chair that established the head of the table.

"I am Madame Limatana, and here, in this room, the spirits do *my* bidding." She waved her arms wide and looked upwards with a distant gaze. Yves followed the pretty young woman's every movement through his kaleidoscope so intently Georges began to worry Yves might break character again.

Madame Limatana seated herself in the leather chair and placed her hands upon the table. She began murmuring a rhythmic chant and swaying in her seat while sliding her hands around on the table.

The light abruptly dimmed. The two men could barely make out the woman's silhouette. Yves made appropriate frightened sounds and leaned into Georges for comfort.

The slight glow from the eyepiece of Yves's ghost-scope caught Georges' eye, and he quickly put his hand over it. Yves pulled away sharply, as though he thought Georges was going to take Tomás' precious kaleidoscope away from him, but he had gotten the hint and the scope disappeared into his pocket, hiding the faint luminescence.

"Spirits! I sense your presence!" Madame Limatana opened her eyes and looked around the room. "Reveal yourselves to us!"

The glass globe in the center of the table began to glow a faint blue. Madame Limatana reached out and caressed the ball with her hands.

"I see your mother ..." she whispered breathily. "She is not happy. She has been trying to contact you, but something has been stopping her. I can hear her ... She is saying ... Richie. Richie. Richie." As she whispered the name, it echoed faintly from elsewhere in the room, imitating her tone and cadence. "Richie, why won't ..." Madame Limatana's voice faded out as the other voice grew to a whisper.

"... you listen to me? Richie? Your brother needs you to be strong!" The voice seemed to come from above them. It was just loud enough to be heard, but not loud enough to recognize the identity of the speaker.

Madame Limatana's eyes were focused upward.

Georges pretended to look up as well, but kept his eyes upon the young woman.

"Not Mummy," Yves whispered to himself and cradled his kaleidoscope. "Not Mummy."

"Tomás? Can you hear me, dear? Tomás?" The voice faded slightly, making it even more difficult to recognize. "Are you being good for Mummy?"

Georges saw Madame Limatana do something with her hand next to her ear, and he knew she was ready for the next trick. Under the table, he nudged Yves' foot with his own to give his brother warning.

"Are you ..." The overhead voice faded.

"... being good for Mummy?" Madam Limatana finished the sentence with her eyes closed. "I need you to be a good boy." The chair Madam Limatana sat in began to slowly rise, taking her up into the air with it. It stopped when her knees reached the height of the tabletop. She shook her head from side to side, as though trying to wake up. "Be good for Mummy! Mummy has to go now. Be good!" She opened her mouth and a ghostly white form began to emerge from within her.

Slowly coming out like smoke, the pale form seemed to expand and rise as it materialized from Madame Limatana's body. Madame Limatana's form undulated eerily slow and fluidly, as though underwater, seemingly trying to wake herself up.

"Not Mummy." Yves voice was quiet, yet carried the shrill edge of panic. "Angie says not Mummy."

"Shhh! Tomás. Everything is all right." Georges whispered.

The last of the ectoplasmic form came out from Madame Limatana's mouth, and her eyes flew wide open as she jerked awake and her chair crashed back down to the floor.

"Angie says not Mummy!" Yves stood up angrily. "Angie says man and woman trick Richie! Angie says fake!" He threw his kaleidoscope through the ghostly apparition floating across the room. The brass tube hit the middle of the suspended cloth, tore a hole through it, and continued on into the curtains covering the walls where it hit with a loud *thud*.

"Yi!" A figure cried out and stumbled out from behind the curtain.

Georges stifled a grin. Yves' marksmanship was good.

"What the hell is going on here?" Georges stood up angrily.

"Papa!" Madame Limatana rushed to check on the man who had held the club earlier.

"You have deceived us!" Georges pointed with a shaking finger.

"Fake!" Yves yelled again and pointed at the glass ball on the table. "Fake!" He pointed at the chair Madame Limatana had been sitting in. "Fake!" He went around the room pointing at things, both seen, such as the scowling portrait, and unseen, such as the curtain he pulled open to reveal a woman who looked just like the portrait.

The woman shrieked and covered her mouth with her hands, unable to decide whether to go help the injured man or try to hide.

"Mama! Papa's hurt!" Madame Limatana called to her.

Georges strode over to the gas light on the wall and turned the key, brightening the room.

"Fake!" Yves tugged on strings that pulled some sort of balloon out from behind another curtain.

Madame Limatana's father finally managed to stand upright. A rivulet of blood ran down his cheek from where the kaleidoscope had struck his eyebrow. "Stop," he called out.

"Fake!" Yves pulled a hidden lever and a wind started up, blowing the curtains and the fake ghost with a rippling effect.

"Stop!" The man roared and stomped toward Yves. "Stop!"

Yves fell into a ball where he was and began sobbing loudly.

"How dare you!" Georges approached the man threateningly. "You charlatan! How dare you try to take advantage of us and then yell at my brother as though *he* has done something wrong?" Georges raised his hand as if to backhand the man.

"Stop. Please stop." Madame Limatana put herself between the two men. "Please."

The older woman ran over and protectively placed herself between Georges and Madame Limatana.

Georges lowered his hand and pulled himself up erect, straightening his coat. "You have not heard the last of me. You will be hearing from my solicitor." He stiffly walked over to where Yves was still crying on the floor.

"Sir, please," Madame Limatana followed him, "allow me the chance to explain."

Georges ignored her. "Come, Tomás. Let us get away from this place. I'm sorry I didn't listen to what you said about Angelica. She was right. I will listen in the future. Come on." He held out his hand.

Yves began reaching up, but stopped, his eyes upon the kaleidoscope he had intentionally stomped upon while yelling "Fake!" and exposing the rigged props. His mouth dropped open and his eyes went wide as he pointed at the broken toy. His jaw began working, but no sound came out.

Georges followed Yves pointing finger until he was looking at the glass shards and smashed brass tube. He allowed his own countenance to darken into a hopeless despair. "Oh dear God, no."

Yves let loose with a mighty ear-shattering wail and began crawling toward the broken toy.

Georges blocked his way. He bent down and scooped the man up like a child, holding his crying countenance into his shoulder. He turned, glaring with burning eyes, and hissed. "That was the only thing he had from our mother. It was the only thing that calmed him."

"Sir, I am so sorry …"

He turned his back to them and carried the sobbing Yves out the front door and into the street.

"God Almighty! How much farther? You weigh as much as a mule," he grunted into Yves ear.

"Go 'round the corner," Yves sobbed into his shoulder as he kept an eye on the store's front door.

Georges made his way between buildings, dropping his brother the instant tapped him to let him know they were out of sight.

"Oh, thank God. My poor back."

"How'd it go?" Yves asked. "Did they look worried?"

"Not as worried as I would have liked, but enough I think. You might have ruined it by scoring the man in the eye!"

"Not like he didn't have it coming. He's back there bilking money from poor old ladies who believe in his malarkey. They're not any better than the people who took all of Mum's money pretending they were talking to Father."

"Let's circle to the back of the building and see if we can figure out what they are up to." Georges suggested.

Yves nodded and pulled his ghost-scope out of his pocket. It looked just like the broken kaleidoscope. As they neared the back of the building, he extended the scope to its full length and began looking through it.

"Anything?" Georges asked.

Yves shook his head and passed the ghost-scope over.

Georges held it to his eye and examined the view of the world it provided.

The back of the building became as if nothing more than a yellowish shadow, revealing other, darker yellow shadows within. Georges could make out three figures moving around, and he could even tell which was Madame Limatana and which were her parents, but it was hard to tell what they were doing. The man waved his arms quickly and angrily as the women followed him around the shop, appearing to talk and lay hands upon him to calm him, but beyond the movements of their shadowy outlines, details were lost.

"The walls are too thick." He handed the scope back to Yves. "Did you have any trouble using it inside?"

Yves put the scope in his pocket.

"A little. Not too bad. I could see well enough to find all of their tricks. How long do you think we should wait before we go back?"

"What do you want to try to get? Hush money or part of the business?" Georges' eyes gleamed with excitement.

"I still feel trying to get part of the business will come back to haunt us one of these days. I still think we are better off just taking money and never having anything lead back to us. If someone gets really upset about paying us off every month, they could track us down through a bank deposit."

Georges frowned. "In that case, I say we go back tonight."

"Sir! There you are! Please! You didn't give me a chance to explain!" Madame Limatana had turned the corner and spotted them.

Georges cursed under his breath as Yves quickly pretended to be quietly sobbing.

"Please, come back." The woman hiked the edge of her dress up as she hurried over to them. "Please. I can put this right if you will just give me the chance."

Georges glanced at Yves who was having a hard time hiding a satisfied smirk as the woman closed in on them. Yves nodded slightly.

"And just how do you intend to 'put this right'?" Georges asked.

She stopped and curtsied as she reached them. "I am so sorry about your kaleidoscope," she told Yves, who refused to meet her eyes. "We can see about getting you a new one. Maybe a better one, even."

Turning back to Georges, she bowed slightly again. "Please, sir. Please come back."

Georges sighed exasperatedly. "I will give you five minutes. Come, Tomás."

Yves resisted, shrugging off Georges' hand. "Not Mummy."

"I know. But let's go see what they have to say. Please. For Richie."

Yves reluctantly followed Georges and Madame Limatana back to the shop. He made retching sounds as they walked through the lingering odor of the spilled oils.

Madame Limatana's parents were waiting for them. The man's eyebrow had stopped bleeding, and the blood had been mostly cleaned off his face.

"Sir," began the man, "We are terribly sorry for any distress we may have caused you and your brother. It's just ..." he broke off looking for the right words.

"It's just that you are frauds, bilking good honest people out of their money with your petty lies designed to give them false hope." More bitterness from his own history crept into Georges' voice than he had intended.

"Oh, no sir." Madame Limatana stepped forward again.

"We have found," interjected her mother, "that most people who claim they want to speak with the dead truly do not. They want to feel released of burdens and obligations to the departed, but they rarely want to actually speak with the deceased."

"Which is why we installed our diversions and gimmicks," Papa finished. "To allow us to grant them that peace of mind. But if you truly wish to speak to the spirits of the departed, we can accommodate you." He pointed back to the room Yves had nearly torn apart and eyed Georges challengingly.

Georges hesitated for a moment, but Yves made the decision for him by marching into the room muttering, "Fake."

Georges followed. Madame Limatana was the last to enter the room, closing the door behind her parents as they followed Georges.

Mama seated herself at the head of the table where Madame Limatana had been before. Papa and Madame Limatana followed suit, sitting to either side of Mama, who gestured for Georges and Yves to sit as well.

Yves noisily wiped his nose on his sleeve and climbed into a chair, sitting while holding his knees close to his chest. Georges managed an affect of impatience as he seated himself.

"No need to turn off the lights?" he asked snidely.

"No." The old woman's answer was neither terse nor acquiescing. "The spirits care not." She held out her hands to her daughter and husband, and they took hold of them. Papa offered his hand to Georges while Madame Limatana reached for Yves'.

Yves grabbed the young woman's hand with a silly childish grin that Georges thought was likely less than half faked. With a sigh, Georges took Papa's hand and then took hold of Yves other hand, completing the circle.

Mama closed her eyes and bowed her head, muttering a chant. The room grew cold, and the gas light fluttered although there was no breeze. Her voice took on an ethereal quality, a lilting timbre beyond the capability of a human voice.

"Georges? Georges, is that you?" The voice came from the woman, but seemed to be all around at once. Georges went pale at the sound of his real name.

Yves' eyes went wide and flashed from Georges to the woman leading the séance.

"Oh, my poor, poor little Georges."

As something touched him, Georges jerked upright and pulled his hands back, turning to see behind himself, and feeling the back of his head.

"Yves! For shame!" the voice continued.

Yves nearly fell out of the chair trying to turn around.

"Why do you lead your brother around the country like this? It's not good for either of you. And don't get me started on how you are wasting your father's invention!" The room grew frigid as the ghost scope lifted up out of Yves' pocket and hovered in the air before them.

Yves grabbed at it, but then dropped it on the table, as though he had been burned. Frost rapidly grew like ivy across the brass and filmed the lenses.

"So many good things you could have done with it. You could be helping doctors heal people. You could be letting others see it to learn how to make another. But no. My children use their father's greatest gift to them for petty extortion and cheap thrills with poor unsuspecting women."

Yves face jerked as an audible slapping sound filled the room. His hands flew up to cover his reddening cheek.

"God Almighty!" Georges eyes were wide in fear.

Madame Limatana's hair swirled behind her head as though someone were lovingly stroking it. She was unfazed by the ghostly touch and even gave an appreciative smile to the air above her.

"Lavinia. Boamos." Madame Limatana's parents both looked up. "You do a good thing here. I am sorry my sons have caused you so much trouble. They didn't understand what you do. They will fix everything they broke and pay for everything they can't."

"*Sastimos, Didikai,*" Mama said with a gentle smile.

The wind ruffled Mama's hair and then a cold chill surrounded Yves and Georges. Both of their chairs began to rise into the air and they grabbed the edges for balance.

"Mind your mother, boys," their mother's disembodied voice warned. "Put this right, and get your lives straight before it is too late."

The chairs slammed back to the ground, nearly sending Georges and Yves falling out of them. And then the presence was gone.

Georges' breath came in rapid pants in the silence that followed. Yves scrambled to grab the ghost-scope off the table and held it to his eye, searching desperately for any hidden mechanism that could have lifted his chair.

Madame Limatana and her parents stood up with gentle, yet self-satisfied smiles upon their faces.

"You can start by re-hanging the curtains," Papa told them and left the room, followed by Mama.

"And I'll thank you to never look at me with that scope again." Madame Limatana's cold gaze and tone of voice froze Yves where he was.

Georges shakily got out of his chair and imitated Yves by examining it, but his examination was cursory. "I think that really was Mother," he whispered. "We shouldn't have been doing this. I told you! We were the crooks all along. How many people have we...?"

Yves grabbed Georges' shoulder and spun him. A huge red welt in the shape of a handprint covered his cheek. "If that was really Mother, then why did she slap me for being a Peeping Tom, but not you for blasphemy?"

"I didn't blaspheme!"

"Yes you did." Yves waved his arms angrily. "When I got slapped you yelled out 'God Almighty!'"

A slapping sound filled the room and Yves' head jerked sharply to the side. When he looked back at Georges, he had welts on both sides of his face. He glared at Georges. "Mother always did like you best."

THE HEART OF APPRICOTTA

Mike Cervantes

A Letter from R.J. Bricabrac to George H.M. Entrils, Dean of Anthropological Studies, Interdimensional University:

Dear Sirs,

Thank you for providing me with another opportunity to present my findings. Unfortunately, I'm unable to do so in person, as I've come back from my latest expedition with a bad case of Portal Pox. I'm certain I'll recover in enough time to see you in person soon, but meanwhile, I've been a bit too busy, quarantined in my dormitory while the faculty throw numerous parties around me, so that I may give the disease to the other little scientists.

It's just another one of the many small sacrifices that I, Rufus Jerome Bricabrac, Junior Explorer, Second Class, Undergraduate, Emeritus, of Interdimensional University, enjoys doing for his old alma mater. While I am always the first to admit that my tenure as a full member of the faculty was quite … unavailing, I still work hard daily to uphold the principles of our storied institution, or "Ol' Timesides" as the students like to refer to it.

From the very moment our founder, Professor J. Orenthal Ungrate, invented the Trandimensional and Interdimensional Machine Of Travel For History and Industry, or T.I.M.O.T.F.H.Y. for short, I, and every little wheel involved with the tenure of I.U.

has worked tirelessly to keep a record of geography and history for every little sideways alternate reality that crosses into our stratosphere as a result of interacting with his wonderful invention. I remember being there personally the day the Professor sacked the entire geography department, scoffing at their ridiculous claims that we'd put the frontier out of business, since he had created a machine that could offer us countless, possibly infinite, frontiers to explore.

Ah, Professor Ungrate, may he live forever … And one day perhaps escape the belly of the mysterious eldritch abomination who appeared in the portal and swallowed him whole in a vain attempt to absorb his inner power.

But I digress. One could certainly spend a lifetime explaining our glorious history, but one can also spend a lifetime attempting to add to it, which is precisely what I attempted to do with my latest expedition.

I chose to attempt something that my contemporaries had yet to conquer successfully: a thorough geographical survey of the dark, untamed, center of the continent of Appricotta. Located in universe quadrant 9-611, Appricotta, like our own Africa, is a wild, untamed, wilderness, filled with tall, ungroomed foliage, and any manner of monstrous untamed fauna, the likes of which we'll never see in our own dimension. A contemporary of mine, Hammond Wholewheat, was the last to attempt to explore these treacherous jungles and came back with only these three words to say about the whole of: Appricotta "It's the pits!"

Undeterred by my colleague's negative assessment, I immediately began to set my sights on finding the center of Appricotta. I collected my supplies: food, camping gear, and navigational equipment, as well as my trusty instantaneous daguerreotype maker, able to record images of the continent with a mere shutter click..

Since I am currently not in any way tenured by the University, I had no resources to secure a proper crew, and instead I had to once again impose on the good nature of my trusted manservant Quee-Zay. A native of a savage version of Finland located in universe quadrant 11-11, Quee-Zay is a man who knows no fear. Literally, the concept of fear does not exist at all in his universe. He became indebted to me after I saved him from a rampaging Hunkabeast, and let me tell you, it was a hunk of a Hunkabeast, and he has been my loyal confidant in many an expedition. His skills compliment mine ideally, for as much I am intelligent, sophisticated, and worldly of mind, Quee-Zay is strong, wily, and interested in little besides his own self-preservation.

With supplies at the ready, we immediately passed through the T.I.M.O.T.F.H.Y. and found ourselves at a camp just north of darkest Appricotta. There, we met with the native Gelby tribesmen, who we've become allies with us in the numerous times we've failed to find the center of the continent. We spent our first night in their care, partaking of wine in giant juice-filled gourds and participating in a tribal dance performed by the chief in order to wish us a safe journey. At dawn the next morning, we set on our way while the Gelby stood at the border chanting "Ooba-Toohwa-Nawa," which I understand means "Good luck. You'll need it."

Aren't they sweet?

We began by venturing into the dense jungle, Quee-Zay hacking away at the overgrown foliage with his machete. I had my Instantaneous Daguerreotype machine at the ready, certain we'd reach the vast, uncharted, center of the continent a lot sooner than we expected. But, no sooner had I thought that did Quee-Zay stop dead in his tracks, his spindle-thin body bent over two pairs of dense bushes I couldn't see over.

"What's the matter," I asked of my astute guide.

"Big water," he replied.

I stuck my head into the foliage at Quee-Zay's height and saw that indeed, we had walked a straight line into a steep cliff overlooking a gigantic waterfall. I quickly tossed a rock in order to determine the depth of the drop. To this day I wonder what happened to that rock. Anyway, I reasoned that since there is a waterfall, we must be standing on the very ground upon where the river decides life is no longer worth living. Therefore, we can merely walk along the edge of the cliff towards the waterfall to find a spot to proceed.

The detour took several hours, trudging in an ellipse around the cliff with Quee-Zay still hacking away feverishly at the native plant life. Finally, we could see a clearing. I practically jumped over Quee-Zay's back and ran towards the first thing we'd found in that godforsaken place to resemble a meadow. Eagerly I threw my hands into the river, splashed the water on my face and loudly exclaimed,

"We're free!"

That's when a hundred spears thrust out from the bushes in every direction, stopping just short of my neck. I instinctively began to follow standard "captured by natives" procedure by putting my hands on my head and slowly getting back onto my feet. Standing at my side was Quee-Zay, who was coaxed from hiding by yet more spears.

"We been bought," he quipped.

As we took the long walk back to the home of these ruffians, I got my first good look at them. They looked pretty standard for tribesman, hair bound into braids tied with bones, bones in their noses, war paint across their faces, and nothing to hide their personal shame but a loincloth. That was all pretty standard. Their dark blue fur, white shiny fangs, and claw-tipped fingers, however, were enough to give me considerable alarm.

Once we were led to the center of the village, my eye caught sight of a giant black cauldron right in the center of the square. In any known universe, that spells "cannibalism." Oddly, I didn't feel afraid. Instead, I felt an enormous amount of indignant rage well up within me. I vocalized many times over how much I resented being eaten, and said many things to the effect of "I will not be a feast to these cannibals!" and "Don't these cannibals know they're about to devour a man of true genius?" but unfortunately, as our captors embodied the very definition of "primitive," my words were lost on them.

It wasn't until we began to be lowered into the water filled cauldron that inspiration struck me. I asked Quee-Zay if he could speak to them a few words in Gelby. Quee-Zay did so, and after many words exchanged in the interdimensional tongue, he turned to me and awaited my inquiry.

"So what did they say?" I asked.

"They not like you keep calling them cannibals," Quee-Zay replied "They don't have any interest in eating their own kind."

"If that's the case, why won't they set us free!?" I said, feeling my temper rising again.

"We not their kind."

I endeavored to protest again, but stopped as soon as I felt what could only be the sensation of a heavy pot lid slamming over the top of my head. Fortunately, I was still wearing my pith helmet, or I certainly would have spent the remainder of my soup-like experience as a helpless vegetable. As I sat in the center of total blackness, I allowed serenity to wash over me, and I recalled an important lesson relayed to me by my former professor, Chauncey Putz-Gamey: The best way to avoid cannibalism is to taste terrible.

I instructed Quee-Zay to join me in emptying our pockets for anything foul that might bring negation to our own flavor. I added paprika, fish bullion, removed my socks and underwear and wrung them into the cauldron water. Quee-Zay threw in the milkweed he frequently chews on for indigestion and an enormous cube of saltpeter he wears under his headdress for religious purposes. I came to a conclusion in the moment that perhaps an enormous amount of oxidant into a rapidly boiling cauldron was perhaps not a good idea, roughly around the time the pot began to boil over, blowing the cauldron lid clear off our heads and sending it sailing into one of the nearby thatched huts.

The natives looked oddly at us.

We looked oddly at the natives.

The natives looked meanly at us.

We looked affrightedly at the natives.

Thinking quickly, I informed Quee-Zay to commence "Operation Snail Shell," an improvisational tactic wherein we both tipped over the cauldron until it was standing upside down, then lifting the mouth of the immense appliance over both our heads and carrying it over us as we ran for our lives. It would have been successful, if not for the fact that this particular cannibal's pot was indeed very heavy, and we were only able to lift it waist-high. We nonetheless attempted to make a run, but just as I'd calculated we'd only made it a few steps before we crashed pot-first into a nearby tree.

I attempted to bargain with Quee-Zay to be the first to peek out of the pot to see how far we've gone, but he insisted that he chose paper over my rock, even though it was too dark inside to actually see our hands.

I lifted the mouth of the pot and was met with the sight of the cruelest pair of feet I'd ever seen in my days. These feet belonged to the tribe's chieftain, who I believe was a being composed entirely out of fat, fur, and anger. Quee-Zay's translations relayed to me that our self-interested attempt to avoid becoming appetizing had upset a tribal ritual, desecrated sacred ground, and angered a god whose only concept of mercy is the sending of plagues containing only tiny frogs.

"Does this mean we won't be eaten?" I asked sheepishly.

"They not want to waste the dishes. Now we will be sacrificed to big water." Quee-Zay said with a bit of native exasperation in his voice.

We were tied in a prostrated position against a bamboo raft and carried to a river. We lay completely helpless as the tribal chieftain made a heart-felt plea to his angry god to allow us to be perfectly acceptable in our role as an indecipherable smear on the jagged rocks at the bottom of the waterfall. With a salute, punctuated by a word that sounded like a punch to the stomach in Yiddish, the assembled tossed the raft in the river.

The roaring water at my ears was deafening. I tried to do what I could to signal Quee-Zay but was unable to do anything to outcry the river. I knew that I was on my own at the moment, locked in a battle of wits with a body of rapidly moving water, and currently losing. Things were grim. I had thought for a moment about making peace with my chosen deity, only to conclude that I was in another universe and had no real way of confirming that my chosen deity even existed here.

I reached down to attempt the sign of the cross with my right hand. It was then that I realized that the natives had tied the line binding my right hand somewhat loosely, and whenever I pulled down, the ropes around my left ankle would tighten. I attempted to free myself by doing the inverse: I pushed my right hand into the river water and attempted to wiggle my left ankle free from the slightly slackened vine. Presumably, it worked, and I victoriously lifted my freed left ankle in a 90-degree position from the raft.

That's when I hit the branch.

Indeed, a low hanging tree branch decided to rise in our way the very moment I shook my leg free. When it struck me, the pain was excruciating, but putting that aside in favor of not dying, I crooked my ankle and attempted to bring a stop to the crusading death trap. We were safe, but unfortunately still trapped, as I found myself at a loss to untie myself any further without losing my tenuous grasp on the overhanging tree branch.

I felt the raft rock. I turned my head to see Quee-Zay on his feet with both hands gripping the overhanging branch. At first, I was at a loss as to how he managed to get loose from his bonds, but, remembering what had happened a year ago while nearly burned at the stake in a Boston infested with mad Puritans, (I believe that was Universe 471-88) it's likely that he chewed the ropes off.

Now that I'd stabilized the raft, it was Quee-Zay's job to shimmy across the branch and carry me to safety. It was a slow and sensitive endeavor. He first raised his legs to meet his arms. Then he shimmied across the length of the branch, forcing it to bob up and down and nearly forcing me to lose my foothold on the branch. Once he got to the other side, I felt as good as saved.

Then he made a break for it.

I wasn't offended. I was certain that Quee-Zay was merely interested in securing a more suitable means of rescue.

And that would have been perfectly lovely, if the branch hadn't chosen that very moment to snap.

I sailed through the rough, deadly rapids of the river, foregoing my previous hesitation towards prayer while I was tossed right and left down a path of certain destruction. Not seeing another opportunity to catch myself, or really anything in the face of such a torrential whisking, I attempted to resign myself to my fate. In my panic I struggled to remember precisely what the five stages of grief were supposed to be, so I experienced denial, anger, gassiness, and that strange confusion you get when you feel you've left a door unlocked before finally achieving acceptance.

When the raft slid out of the river, I felt the sensation of flying several miles rapidly downward with the wind whipping across my soggy personage, so quickly I felt my clothing start to dry. Every muscle in my body tied itself in a knot as I braced for impact.

I felt a thud.

I felt a bounce.

I felt a thud.

I felt a bounce again.

I opened my eyes to see that I had landed in the center of a net made entirely out of jungle vines and bamboo posts. As far as I could see over the side of the raft, I could tell that this structure was built to protect anyone from falling into the bottom of the waterfall too harshly. My first instinct was to believe that Quee-Zay had saved my life, but he would not have had the time to run away, descend a cliff, and build this highly supportive structure in the time it took me to make peace with the universe.

My contemplation of this was cut short when the air above me was overshadowed by the tribal chieftan, who, while standing over me, emitted a belly laugh that was so immense it rocked the entire safety net and raft along with it. I was untied and taken back to Quee-Zay's side, and it was relayed to me that this whole business about sending foreign men over the falls was all simply an elaborate practical joke played on, as the chieftan put it, "Any scrawny outsider without the stomach to become a proper meal."

We were escorted back to the village where our comedy act was revered by all the natives assembled. Our clothes were dried, we were fed frozen fruit paste and coconut stalks fried in oil. We were also given a daguerreotype taken of me mid-fall.

We were asked to possibly stay among the tribesmen as honorary spiritual leaders who were tasked with bringing their youthful female charges into womanhood, but, having had enough excitement for one day, we instead opted to return home. After bidding farewell to the tribe, we hiked through the now clean path out of the jungle and returned to the space where the T.I.M.O.T.H.F.Y would lock onto our coordinates and return us to our universe.

I'm reasonably certain that it was the combination of the native food with exposure to the torrential waters that has me in the condition I'm in at the moment. It has hurt me only in that I sincerely hoped to deliver these findings in person, but the need to bathe daily in kelp and be rubbed in goldfish oil has been preventing me to do so. While there's still much more of the continent of Appricotta to explore, I believe that the work I've done on this expedition has moved us progressively forward in our ongoing quest to better understand the wild dimensional continent. I also hope that this excursion has proven that I am worthy enough to once again be tenured by the university and be awarded a crew for purposes of further exploration.

Pretty please with sugar on it?

—R.J. Bricabrac

BUDAPEST WILL BURN

Jonathan D. Beer

To the soldiers that encircled it, the city seemed to be aflame. Dark smoke hung in thick palls, obscuring the churned soil and flickering muzzle-fires that marked the siege's edge, in and amongst what had been the city's southern districts. There was no pause in the crash of cannon fire, the scream of shells and rumble of shot striking hard-packed earth and stone.

Budapest was on the edge of ruin.

The Ottoman army had struck the city with systematic ferocity. Engineers mapped the fortifications while sweating soldiers dug a network of trenches and artillery parks that encircled the southern fringes of the city. Hundreds of cannons, hauled from the famed foundries of Constantinople across the length of the Balkans, were manoeuvred into place in their embrasures.

On the tenth day of the siege the batteries had been unmasked and a storm unleashed against the city. An unending rain of iron shot crashed through the Hungarian defences, unseating cannon and shattering stone. Wide-muzzled mortars lobbed shells over the walls to burst in clouds of shrapnel or alchemical fire.

Behind vast fortifications, the twin cities of Buda and Pest trembled and tore at themselves in fear. All knew that the city's end was near. Exhausted artillerymen and bleeding soldiers felt it through some arcane instinct. Terrified civilians whispered it to one another.

Such slaughter could not be endured; no army, no city, could take such punishment for long. Hungarian privates and generals alike watched the Ottoman lines in resigned, nerve-deadened fear for the inevitable massing of infantry that would precede an assault, an attack that would end with the city in flames.

Behind the walls, sheltered from the siege front but no safer for it, Budapest quaked in terror of what was to come.

O   O   O

On most days Margaret Island was a delight in late afternoon. Broad leaves softened the summer sunlight and cast dappled shadows on the wide avenues of the park. Couples walked arm in arm, happy that the din of the city was barely audible over the Danube's passage. The worst one had to worry about were the groups of raucous students that terrorised the boulevard, on the lookout for unescorted ladies to make sport with until the evening drew in and the band began to lure folk to the pavilion's dance floor.

The sound of cannon fire roared between the trees. Anne-Cathleen Béres closed her eyes and wished with every fibre of her being for it to be such a day.

She stood alone in the shadow of a tall cypress tree to one side of the wide cobbled path that led into Fort Beatrice. At her back the fort loomed, its ancient stone and crumbling mortar offering little sense of surety or sanctuary. Her husband, Sir Gusztáv Béres, was within, in deep conference with the old, medal-bedecked men who commanded the city's garrison. Gusztáv was the Master of the Royal Armoury, a position of fragile influence and wearying responsibility.

Anne-Cathleen had begged Gusztáv to keep her at his side before he left for the meeting, pleading frailty and anxiety that were all too easily feigned. He had acquiesced, as ever, and had dutifully held her hand in a way he thought comforting as their carriage made its way to the ferry that had brought them here.

She glanced around, afraid that she would be seen alone in the park. She scolded herself for the fear she felt. Before Gusztáv's carriage had left their house in Buda, Anne-Cathleen had despatched the scullery boy to find Ábel for her, bribed into loyalty with a fistful of silver forints. Now she waited, afraid for the first time of the subterfuge she had embraced so readily only weeks before.

Anne-Cathleen had met Ábel Valzeck at a dance at the Margaret Island pavilion. He had strode through the cream of Buda's society with a sense of purpose that ill-suited his clearly inferior station, wearing an evening-suit that had seen better days, possibly serving as scarecrow's dress. Her friends, if she thought of the fawning, simpering creatures she was forced to keep company with as friends, had laughed openly at the way he approached Anne-Cathleen to ask, in a prickly, prideful way, for a dance. She had accepted his hand simply to spite the silly girls.

Ábel had danced terribly, but he was an astonishing lover. Although their ages were only a few years apart, Anne-Cathleen found Ábel wondrously simple; the epitome of masculine passion and wonderfully eager to please. His attentions thrilled her jaded spirit; his naïve, impassioned views challenged her cynicism. Ábel embodied the idealistic youth that she had been denied by an early marriage.

He was a radical and a revolutionary, an anarchist of the highest principle. She had laughed at him when he had told her, his voice low and filled with sombre sincerity. That was the closest they had come to ending their affair. Henceforth Anne-Cathleen had carefully made only the lightest of jibes, enough to rile him and give him leave to pontificate and expound in his way. He and his radical friends, his comrades, would topple the Diet; topple the world given the chance. Ábel believed fervently in the Enlightenment ideals of Equality and Liberty, lost in young dreams that Anne-Cathleen could not conjure and barely envied.

Her dreams were much more selfish.

For five long weeks they had met in parks and cafés in Pest, secret trysts that flavoured an otherwise meaningless existence. Then the war had come, and with it the fear. Fear had gripped the streets, driving folk indoors to bar their windows and hug their children. Man-made thunder roared through the city, carrying with it echoes of violence and madness. The war had always been a far-off thing, the army's triumphs and tribulations a source of gossip. To see and hear it first-hand, battering at the gates of her home, terrified Anne-Cathleen to her core.

The sound of footsteps brushing through grass broke her reverie. She turned; Ábel padded through the short grass, wearing long riding boots and a wool coat that was torn and muddy. A pistol hung at his hip, and a white cotton bandage was wound around his blonde hair, almost concealing his left eye. She had never seen him look less like himself. Anne-Cathleen ran to him, surprised to feel tears of concern prick her eyes.

"Hush, Anne, hush." Ábel cooed reassurances, his deep voice momentarily overpowering the distant guns. His arms encircled her tightly, and she felt the weave of his cotton shirt against her cheek.

Anne-Cathleen lifted her face up to look into his and saw nothing but concern for her etched in his features. He was handsome, even with the bandage, with a quick smile and thoughtful eyes beneath a broad, furrowed brow. But for his eyes, Ábel always put her in mind of a farmhand, proud and content in his naïveté. He stared back at her, a reassuring grin failing to hide his anxiety.

Anne-Cathleen squeezed his hand with hers, forcing a smile to her lips. "What happened to you?"

"Nothing, nothing that will not mend." They spoke in French, Anne-Cathleen's native tongue; Ábel took such pleasure in giving her a glimpse of her homeland. She glared at him and raised her free hand to feel the edge of the bandage. He leaned back and relented. "I was set upon in the street, but there is nothing to worry about."

"But you are wounded."

"It's a scratch. Really, Anne, I am fine. Why are you here? You should not be out alone. Why on earth did he bring you here?"

Anne-Cathleen continued to grip Ábel's hand, pulling him into the shadow of the cypress. "Gusztáv brought me because I told him to bring me. I had to see you. The city is panicked; people in the streets have lost all order. The maid told me there have been riots in Pest and that the constabulary house in Józsefváros has been set alight."

"There is worse," said Ábel, his good looks marred by a grim expression. "Food is running out. The markets have not opened since the siege began, and you know what prices were like before the Musulmen closed us up. Gangs are taking over the communal wells and pumps. Neighbours are turning on each other for the basics of life."

"Ábel, you must get me out of the city. I cannot stay here. We must leave, together." The words tumbled out, fuelled by a desperation that she could see pull at Ábel's heart.

His frown softened. "Darling, if only we could. But there is no way for us to leave, no way for me at any rate. Surely he can get you out?"

"I do not want his help," she lied. Anne-Cathleen had asked and demanded and finally begged Gusztáv to find her a place aboard one of his steamers heading up the Danube, or to use his influence to find her a berth on one of the few remaining airships that lingered in the skies over Budapest. He had insisted that she stay with him, refusing to allow any notion that Budapest could fall to enter his mind. "I want to leave with you. Ábel, we can escape together!"

He was not taken in by her obvious manipulation. "Or is it that you need my comrades to help you because your husband will not?" demanded Ábel. Anne-Cathleen felt a roughness in his tone that she had never heard before. Tears, real and unforced, rolled in slow drops down her cheeks.

"I am scared, Ábel. The city is doomed, and we will all die or worse when the Musulmen break in. I cannot die here!"

Ábel grasped her in his arms again, unable to look at the sorrow in her eyes. "You won't!" All hint of his anger evaporated as suddenly as it had appeared. "I swear it, my love; you will not die here."

Anne-Cathleen struggled against his grip, but he held her tightly. Panic that she had contained for days burst free, her reserve breaking down before a man she had known for mere weeks.

"I must get out, please come with me." She sobbed into his chest, soaking his shirt with pent-up emotions. She clung to him, simultaneously craving the physicality of his presence and hating herself for such a self-pitying display.

"It is not up to me," said Ábel after she had subsided. She let go of him and hastily wiped her eyes.

"But I am asking you." She drew herself up, although her eyes were barely level with his chin. "I have money," she said quietly.

"It is not a question of money," said Ábel.

"Then what? Why would they not help us? Why would they refuse you?"

Ábel was silent. Anne-Cathleen said nothing, still embarrassed by her display of fragility. She watched him, confused by his indecision and resistance. He, like Gusztáv, had never denied her anything before.

253

He paced a few steps away from her and looked to the south, towards the sound of cannon fire and death. He looked afraid, if she could credit it. It was an emotion that did not sit well on him; Anne-Cathleen had never seen him struggle with indecision. He had always been resolute, unflinching. Forthright.

He turned to her. "I will do what I can. There is an airship leaving the city tomorrow, the *Artemis*. I, we, have had dealings with her captain. There might be a place on it for you."

She smiled and stepped into him. She pulled his face to hers, magnanimous in victory. His kiss was soft and gentle; sad, even. Anne-Cathleen suddenly felt guilty. "A place for us. You are coming with me."

He smiled back at her.

O O O

The sun set on the eleventh day of the siege, and the Ottoman guns fell silent.

At first none on the Hungarian earthworks noticed, their senses dulled by two days of unending assault. Slow realisation dawned, men noticing the absence of what had been ever-present. Grins and shouted words drifted up and down the walls as soldiers who stood ten metres apart were suddenly able to converse once more.

Darkness came upon the lines in a rush, dusk lasting only moments. The sudden silence from the Ottomans provoked panic amongst the commanders within the city, and the young night was broken by bugle calls for assembly and cries for reports of the enemy massing. There was nothing; no movement in the Ottoman lines, no hint of a reason why they had chosen to halt their systematic bombardment.

As stars began to prick the midnight sky, sentries were stood down and replaced while reserve battalions were allowed to disperse and return to their billets. Opinions were traded as to the reason for the reprieve. The maudlin assumed the Ottomans were so confident in victory they could take their time. The optimistic prayed the Hungarian field army was returning to relieve the city, and the Ottomans were abandoning their short-lived siege.

All took advantage of the silence to claim a night of unbroken sleep.

O   O   O

Anne-Cathleen stood with one hand against the window of her drawing room, her face illuminated by the light of civilisation burning. Budapest may not yet have fallen to its besiegers, but it had lost itself. The city had descended into a madness of its own making.

She was on the top floor of the townhouse, looking out at Buda through a large semi-circle of glass framed by an arch tall enough for her to stand beneath. A thin bench, upon which sat a large carpetbag filled with clothes and her most treasured possessions, ran the width of the window, but she did not feel like sitting. The view held her, fascinating as much as it was terrifying, revolting as it was enthralling.

The window looked to the south, over the deserted streets and the rooftops of Buda. Fires studded the darkness, stark against the vague silhouettes of towers and houses. From her vantage point Anne-Cathleen could see the riverside market square where she occasionally walked. It was full of people, and though night had set in, she could see individuals clearly, their savage stances lit by burning torches and the lamps of a river steamer moored alongside the dock.

The steamer's captain was in a dangerous position. Though Anne-Cathleen could not hear the exchange, she had a fair idea of what was happening. The mob had gathered in the square as night fell, demanding passage on the steamer, and the captain was justly refusing. Anne-Cathleen felt she was watching some grotesque parody of her own emotions play out in the square; desperate fear, the instinctive desire to survive, directionless anger.

She was too far away to discern faces, but she clearly saw a man on the quay's edge draw his pistol. The captain started back, gesturing frantically at his crew. Horrified and utterly impotent, Anne-Cathleen saw the steamer's men pull weapons from their belts. The pistol's muzzle flashed, and a cloud of red erupted from the back of the captain's head. She turned away in disgust, fighting nausea. She looked back. Bright flashes of fire and puffs of powder smoke edged the dock. Many in the crowd were running, fighting against the press to flee the guns of the steamer's crew, but others were shooting or throwing bricks and cobbles.

Anne-Cathleen gripped the back of the bench to keep her hands from shaking. Under the fusillade of bullets and debris, the steamer's crew cut the ropes holding them against the quay. The riverboat began to drift sluggishly away from the shore, the river's current slow to take hold. Anne-Cathleen fancied that she could hear the mob's roar, denied their chance to escape the city. A treacherous part of her sympathised with them, but for the grace of God, and Ábel's love, went she.

All her sympathy disappeared with a single act of cold-hearted savagery.

A few people had tried to leap the growing gap between the dockside and the steamer's low gunwale but had fallen short or were pushed off by the crew as they scrambled for purchase. That alone was a terrible sight, but worse followed. From somewhere within the mob's press an oil lamp arced through the air, crashing against the steamer's smoke stack. Burning oil rained down on the steamer's wooden deck, and the crew turned in an instant from vengeful demons into panicking children.

Anne-Cathleen cried aloud, stunned as more burning torches and oil were thrown onto the riverboat. Such stupidity! Such violence and malevolence of spirit! Anne-Cathleen watched the crew fight the flames, beating with their jackets despite the heat that scorched their arms and faces. She heard in her mind their screams as they died, and the hateful laughter of the mob that had turned to murder out of spite.

Anne-Cathleen turned from the window, unable to watch anymore. The bounds of society and decency were falling away, and the wicked and lawless were boiling out of their rookeries and slums. Worse, Anne-Cathleen knew in her rational way that it was not just the criminal and the destitute that had killed the river men and cavorted in the streets. More terrible were the ordinary people, the clerks and linesmen and dockers that had seen the bonds of discipline fraying and chosen to give vent to their darkest emotions, freed from responsibility and consequence by the city's impending doom.

The Ottomans had sealed the city and let terror do its work.

A loud hammering echoed through the house, making Anne-Cathleen jump. Her gaze jerked towards the study's door at the sound, her mind conjuring a gang of housebreakers and cutthroats hammering at the entrance to her home. A tremor took hold of her hands, and reflexively she cast about herself for a weapon. Her hand brushed against the carpetbag, and she spun to look out of the window once more, the thick fabric's rough touch pulling her senses back to the real. Anne-Cathleen looked down at the street and smiled involuntarily, and her hand grasped the leather handles of her bag.

Ábel stood beside a short two-horse trap, looked up at the face of the house, and his grim, earnest expression brought a surge of relief and happiness to her lips. He evidently did not see Anne-Cathleen at the window, for he stepped towards the house, disappearing from view beneath the portico's roof. Another set of urgent blows rang through the house. Anne-Cathleen turned and ran from the drawing room.

The hallway beyond was dark, its lamps unlit. Anne-Cathleen ran unheeding to the staircase and plunged down. With each step she felt excitement swelling in her breast, the contending pressures of fear, anger, and self-pity evaporating as she came closer to the door, closer to the escape she had craved since long before the Ottomans had come.

She reached the bottom of the staircase and leapt the final stair, buoyed by unfamiliar joy. She crossed the parquet floor of the reception hall with quick strides and heaved open the stout oak door. Ábel was beyond, staring up at the townhouse's face once again. He wore a long dark coat that fell to his knees, and in his hand was a pistol that he clutched tightly. A peaked tricorne concealed his bandaged brow.

At the sound of the door's opening, he looked down and saw Anne-Cathleen. Their eyes met, and she smiled.

"Anne?" Her name carried across the hall, uttered by a thin, nasal voice.

Anne-Cathleen looked away from Ábel and stared at her husband. Gusztáv stood in the archway that led to his wing of the house, a red gown tied loosely about his midriff. He blinked, taking in her bag and coat. "What are you doing?" His tone was of curiosity, not anger, as if her were asking her why she wore blue instead of green to dinner.

Ábel reached out and took her hand. Without a word she stepped over the threshold of the house and ran. If Gusztáv protested, she did not hear him. Their boots kicked up the gravel path as she and Ábel ran hand in hand to the trap. Ábel leapt aboard and pulled Anne-Cathleen up beside him. She might have been laughing as Ábel took up the reins, standing up on the board as if he were a Hellenic charioteer, and with a snap of his wrists set the horses into motion. Anne-Cathleen's bag tumbled from her grasp into the foot-well, unheeded. As the street moved past her she really did start to laugh, huge choking laughs that escaped her mouth as sobs. The doors and windows blurred as she saw the world through tears of joy.

They drove in silence, Ábel sternly fixed on manoeuvring the trap, Anne-Cathleen lost in a world of her own. The gleeful escape from the house, from her husband, replayed over and over in her mind. It was everything she had wished for, and yet it had been so simply done; a single step and she was free. Why had she not done it sooner? Perhaps she was as mad as the crowd at the dock, giving in to abandon and desire with her doom so close.

Ábel did not intrude on her thoughts and took the trap south, obliquely climbing Gellért Hill. As they passed the Mohács memorial park, the slope began to level out, and Ábel eased the horses' pace. He worked stiff joints and sat down in the seat beside her.

Anne-Cathleen slipped a hand into his and kissed his cheek.

"Where are we going?"

A house we use in Újbuda," Ábel replied. He took several deep breaths, though he seemed unaffected by the excitement rushing through Anne-Cathleen. He took his eyes from the road for a moment. "I am sorry, Anne."

"What for?"

"Where we are going, it is not like you are used to. My comrades are not like the men you have known."

"Are they all like you? Sterling, upright, with principles emblazoned upon their breasts?" Anne-Cathleen grinned girlishly at him. Ábel's answer dampened her newfound cheerfulness.

"No. They are not like me."

Ábel guided the horses around a corner. On their left, bounded by stone walls topped with iron rails, was a red brick townhouse of a size with Gusztáv's. Gas-lamps fixed to the brickwork illuminated the darkness, revealing tall windows with veils drawn and ornamental bushes cut back severely against the house. Three men stood in the courtyard, dressed in the same long woollen overcoats as Ábel, all smoking thin cigars and sporting harsh, unshaven faces. Anne-Cathleen's joyful mood wavered.

"You will be safe here, Anne," Ábel said, "but you must do as I say." Anne-Cathleen bridled but was confused by the sadness in his voice. Ábel turned the trap off the street and beneath an arched gatehouse that led into the courtyard. As a boy ran over to take the horses' reins, Ábel looked over at her. "I did not want to bring you here."

Gravel crunching underfoot, Ábel and Anne-Cathleen crossed the courtyard towards the townhouse's open door. As they walked, Anne-Cathleen noticed Ábel carefully interposed himself between her and the huddle of smoking men. She fought the urge to grip his hand tighter and instead held fast to the straps of her carpet bag. She was off-balance and uncertain. The house loomed over her, a dark shape silhouetted against the night sky despite the flickering gas lamps. She could see nothing of the house's interior. The windows that faced the street were dirty, and thick drapes concealed the rooms beyond.

As they reached the portico, a man emerged from the house and stood beneath the doorway. He wore shirtsleeves and braces, standing with exaggerated ease, arms crossed as he leaned against the doorjamb. Black hair streaked with grey fell in greasy ringlets about a lined, pugnacious face. His hands and face were streaked with oil, through which yellow teeth flashed in a predatory smile.

Ábel squeezed her hand as he caught sight of him. "I urge you, say nothing," he whispered.

"My dear madam, welcome!" The man boomed, his voice echoing around the courtyard. "For the life of me I cannot think why it has taken Ábel so long to introduce us!" The man spoke atrocious French in a loud, mocking tone, waving his arms expansively in a derisive gesture of welcome.

Ábel kept walking, almost pulling Anne-Cathleen behind him. They pushed past the villainous man and into the house. He leered at her as she passed, making Anne-Cathleen squirm against Abel's grip. "Oh, yes. Oh, you are a lucky lad," he muttered. Ábel ignored him.

The receiving hall of the townhouse was much like Anne-Cathleen's own. Not her own, she thought with a start; like Gusztáv's. The same parquet floor extended out to the two wings of the house, although it was scuffed and ill maintained. A double staircase climbed each side of the hall, its carpet pattern hard to make out in the gloom. In place of the modern gasolier that lit the hall in her former home, a simple candelabrum hung from the ceiling, its few candles casting a wan light that served only to reveal the dirt and grime that would have shamed any home of hers. Men and women milled about the hall, all staring at her with the same grim, hostile look. A woman with grey hair sat in a thin rocking chair, holding a long and battered rifle.

Ábel headed towards the nearest wing of the staircase, towing Anne-Cathleen behind him. She started to ask something, but a curt "Be quiet!" from Ábel cowed her. She had never seen him so agitated, and the way he gripped her hand was frightening.

She followed him up the staircase and into a small, featureless room at the summit. As soon as she was inside, Ábel shut the door and leaned back against it.

"What is going on, Ábel?" Anne-Cathleen rounded on him, tossing her carpetbag onto an oddly ornate four-poster bed that filled the room. "Why have you brought me here? That man was vile; you should have struck anyone that spoke to me like that. This place is awful!" She spat the words at him, her uncertainty pouring out as anger.

Ábel, far from being chastised, replied in kind. "What do you want, Anne? Do you think I wanted you to see this?" He paced away from the door and sat down on the edge of the bed. Ábel rubbed his face with his hands. "In this world a man like me, with my convictions, cannot choose his comrades. And if you want to escape from here, from Budapest, you will be polite and silent around them."

Anne-Cathleen glared at him. Before she could reply, the door swung open and a man of middling age and fine patrician features entered. Ábel sat up straight, and Anne-Cathleen unthinkingly stepped back a few paces to give him some space in the small room.

"Ah, Ábel. And good evening, Madam Béres." Unlike the brute that had barred their way into the house, he spoke polite, if somewhat accented French, and held himself with a far less barbarian manner. He spoke in a way that suggested he was familiar with Anne-Cathleen, although she was sure they had never met.

"Rikárd. I did not expect you to be back." Ábel sounded far from pleased to see him; if anything he was more anxious than ever.

"Neither did I, but Captain Watson was not in a conversational mood."

"Is everything arranged?" asked Ábel. Anne-Cathleen watched him closely; it was as if Rikárd had Ábel in thrall.

"One berth on the *Artemis*, as agreed. The fee was extortionate." His stare bored into Ábel, who did not meet his gaze. Rikárd turned to Anne-Cathleen. "I apologise, Madam, it must seem that we speak in riddles. Ábel spoke of your desire to escape our ill-fated city. Fortunately, we are in a position to help."

"I am in your debt, sir," said Anne-Cathleen carefully. "As to the question of payment, I will do what I can to compensate any expense you have gone to."

"Your husband is famously wealthy, yes, I know." Anne-Cathleen was taken aback. She tried to summon a response, but the words would not come. "I am afraid Sir Gusztáv's money is of little use in these troubled times. We are more interested in his more tangible assets."

Anne-Cathleen's brow creased in confusion. "I do not understand."

"Your husband is the Master of the Royal Armoury, Madam." Rikárd said, his tone patronising. "He is the possessor of the city's weapons, and for a long while we have had designs on his inventory." Rikárd looked at Ábel, expression blank but eyes wrathful. "I had asked young Ábel to arrange for you to help us. I was very disappointed some weeks ago when he told me that you were ... incorruptible." Anne-Cathleen looked at Ábel, mute horror etched on her face.

"Ábel?"

He could not meet her eyes. She could not believe it, would not believe it. He had made her love him, manipulating her at the orders of this horrible, silver-tongued anarchist?

"I had no idea he had continued his little fling. When he came to us to ask that we help you, he was most contrite. He really does love you, you know. How does it feel to know that that first kiss was by my arrangement?"

Anne-Cathleen threw herself at Rikárd. Her fingernails caught his cheek, breaking the skin. She screamed obscenities as she flailed at him, hatred drowning out the aching sorrow that burned in her chest. She felt hands pull her away from Rikárd, and she turned on Ábel, whirling with a hand outstretched to land with a whip crack against his face.

He stood still, eyes wet but locked with hers. She started to speak, but all that came out was a low moan.

"Anne, I love-"—"

"No!" Anne-Cathleen screamed, another hand flashing at his face.

A pair of hands at her back shoved her forward, and she landed on her stomach on the bed. Ábel drew a fist back to strike Rikárd, but a venomous look made him stay his hand. Anne-Cathleen turned over and hugged her chest.

"You would do well to be more civil, Madam." Rikárd lifted a hand to his cheek. Red stained his fingers. "It is only through my very generous nature that we will keep to the arrangement Ábel made and put you on the *Artemis*. Until the morning, you will stay here."

Rikárd turned to leave, clutching his face. "Good night, Madam Béres."

Ábel ran around the edge of the bed to lean over her, hands outstretched. Anne-Cathleen knocked them away, and he recoiled as if stung. "Anne, I would have told you ..."

"Get out! Get away from me!" She clung to her anger like an anchor. "I trusted you. I left my husband for you! Were you ever going to tell me that it was all a part of your childish politics?"

Ábel said nothing, fighting with his own sadness, but Anne-Cathleen would not relent. "Leave, just leave." She was alone, her marriage abandoned for a lie, and suddenly she was choking on sobs that sounded like screams. Ábel tried to touch her again but she flinched back, hugging her knees to her chest, oblivious to everything but the pain.

O O O

Dawn was met in fear.

The slumbering defenders had been awakened hours before, hastened to order by whispers and kicks passed down the walls. It had been assumed that the Ottoman cease-fire was a ruse to lull the Hungarians into negligence in preparation for a dawn assault. Soldiers greeted the morning in silence, peering out from embrasures and trenches at the lightening landscape, rifles and greatcoats beaded with dew.

The day broke, and with it came the roar of cannon fire, every Hungarian cannon still on its axle bellowing defiance at the Ottoman line.

That line remained resolutely, interminably empty. The Ottoman guns remained hidden behind earth-filled gabions; no assault had come under the last ebb of darkness.

What greeted them, looming in the distance over the southern horizon, was far worse than that.

O O O

The door's hinges creaked as Anne-Cathleen gently pushed it open. No lamps were lit on the landing, and only the sounds of a slumbering house greeted her. She pushed further and stepped out of the bedroom. She clutched the handles of her carpetbag, knuckles white around the leather. She stepped out on to the landing, and red-rimmed eyes stared around the hall.

Nothing moved. The dusty corners of the hall were pools of shadow, the few slivers of wan morning light slipping through gaps in the thick curtains nailed around the windows and through the hemisphere of painted glass that crowned the house's doorway. The rocking chair that had held the grim, rifle-armed woman sat empty on the far side of the hall. Ábel's comrades were all asleep, or at least not busying themselves with noisy night-time activities.

Anne-Cathleen looked back through the door at Ábel asleep in the bed, the sheets typically curled tight about him. He had come back soon after he and Rikárd had left, gushing with apologies and pleading for understanding. Anne-Cathleen had been unrelenting, his pleas breaking on the barrier of her anger. Finally they had both collapsed, exhausted by rage and sorrow and shame. Anne-Cathleen's wounded pride had made her argue about where Ábel would sleep, but in the end, when he had climbed in beside her, she had been too tired to stop him.

Anne-Cathleen started down the staircase, jumping at each floorboard's complaint and the rustling of her dress on the carpet. She tried to look at everything at once; the door, the arches that led to the townhouse's two wings and back into the interior of the house, expecting every time she turned to see Ábel standing at the head of the stairs, watching her. Yesterday, or even just a few hours ago, she would have strode boldly, fears masked by a veneer of arrogance and privilege. Now she walked with a whispering tread, starting at shadows.

She crept to the door and bent to the lock, listening for any sign of a sentry without. There was none, but she did not move. Fear had brought her this far; fear of what the morning would bring, of the machinations of Rikárd and his anarchists, of facing Ábel in the light of day. But she stopped short at the doorway. Beyond were other fears, those that had driven her from her husband's shelter to Ábel's, ignorant of the lie of his love. Her hand wavered in the air, outstretched toward the tarnished handle, hesitating before the choice it represented. Where would she go if she wrenched open the door and fled into the night? She could not, would not, go back to Gusztáv; the joyous memory of the wind in her face as Ábel's trap hurtled away from her home too fresh to betray.

Her hand grasped the handle suddenly. That moment, like all the others, was tainted by Rikárd's vindictive revelation.

But no one in the city would take her in—not now. She saw no chance of escaping the city by her own means; if she had, she would have done so long before.

Options dwindling before her scrutiny, Anne-Cathleen looked back up at the room where Ábel slept. Emotions warred within her, and her grip on the handle shook as she did. Slowly she released it and stood in silence beside the door for long minutes. Then, with the same patience as she had descended, Anne-Cathleen climbed the stairs back to her room.

O O O

A flock of predators bore down on Budapest. Sleek and lethal, their wooden hulls sheathed in plates of iron that reflected bright morning light from their starboard sides. Slim gas chambers studded tall flanks, keeping the colossal vessels aloft while broad propellers drove them inexorably on. Dark-skinned men in fleece-lined coats stared through telescopes, contemplating the doomed beauty of the Hungarian capital spread out before them.

The airship fleet of the Ottoman Empire drew closer, confident in its superiority, stately in its progression through the clear skies. A northerly wind restrained their speed but did little more than give the defenceless city more time to contemplate its fate.

The city was helpless. The few Hungarian airships that remained in the city were cutters and couriers, not warships, and the city's rocket magazines had been depleted countering the enemy siegeworks. Bombardment was the terror of all cities, more horrific than any battlefield for its impersonality, more devastating for the totality of destruction that would scour a city of life. Nations had submitted to occupation and annexation in the face of such a threat.

The Hungarian soldiers fled. Battered, bleeding, deprived of rest and the hope of victory, it was a wonder they had held for as long as they had, but to see death itself unhurriedly approach was too much. They fled in ones and twos, officers doing their best at first to contain the rush but soon joining it. The rout spread along the ramparts, heading not north into the doomed city but east, out toward the sun-baked plains and the hope of surviving the day. Behind the Ottoman siege lines, cavalrymen mounted eager horses and contemplated the sport of the day.

In the skies above them, the airship captains did the same.

O O O

The blade of light crept along the floor. Anne-Cathleen watched it stretch from one floorboard to the next, marking time in the most primitive way she could imagine. Eventually the sliver would reach across the length of the floor and begin climbing the wall. Anne-Cathleen had told herself that once the light reached the wall she would stand up and leave the room. There were many floorboards left to cross before that happened.

Anne-Cathleen lay on her side, completely still. Only the occasional blink to clear her eyes betrayed the fact that she was alive at all. She was dully aware of commotion beyond the door of the tiny bedroom, a great deal of clattering, shouted activity, no doubt in preparation for some nefarious purpose. Anne-Cathleen ignored it; it was beyond her concern. She waited for whatever was to come.

Ábel had said he would return shortly, before disappearing out into the mêlée of the radicals' hideout. The shaft of light had made its way across three floorboards since then, and Anne-Cathleen had not heard his voice amongst the din. What he planned to do with her, what Rikárd—thinking of the poisonous man almost made Anne-Cathleen shriek, but she remained still—had planned for her, she did not know.

Long minutes passed slowly. The beam of white morning light inched further, illuminating the dust and dirt lining the deep grooves of the wooden boards.

The noise from the hall subsided all of a sudden, and she dimly raised her head to listen. A shout, louder and angrier than before, made Anne-Cathleen start. She looked at the door. No one had disturbed her since she had ejected Rikárd; the radicals were as content to ignore her as she was to disdain them.

A fearsome yell answered the shout, and suddenly the tramp of running feet echoed through the house. Heavy, hurried footsteps shook the bedroom's boards, and Anne-Cathleen finally moved, lifting herself up to sit on the edge of the bed. She moved back from the door, which burst open to reveal Ábel, sweat-streaked and wide-eyed.

"Anne, we have to leave, now." The look in his eyes was terrible; Anne-Cathleen drew back.

"No, Anne, we are going!" Ábel shouted, startling her. He reached out and grasped her wrist, hard. She instinctively pulled back, but he pulled her up off the bed despite her cry of protest.

"Ábel, let me go! My bag!" He towed her out of the room, hauling her bodily. "Wait, my bag, stop!"

"We don't have time, Anne. Please trust me!" He did not stop in his headlong charge down the stairs, and Anne-Cathleen stumbled behind him. The hall was empty, deserted by Ábel's comrades at a moment's panicked notice. The thought that the constabulary had come to arrest the whole nest of them flashed through her mind, and she tried once more to pull away from Ábel, who turned, wrathful. "God damn it, woman, don't fight me now! I'll not die here and neither will you!" He heaved again, drawing another cry of pain as they ran out into the morning's glare.

"Die? What's happening Ábel?" Anne-Cathleen no longer struggled against his grip. He didn't reply but swore instead.

The yard had emptied; a black four-horse cab crowded with men and women disappearing from view as they watched. Ábel and Anne-Cathleen chased after it, the sense of panic within Anne-Cathleen made worse by ignorance of what threatened them.

As they passed through the wrought-iron gates and on to the street, Anne-Cathleen heard an odd noise, a *crump*, like a sudden intake of breath. She looked around for the source but was hampered by Ábel's unyielding grip. The sound grew, or rather it rippled, a series of wet *thumps* carrying over the houses. They reached the end of the street and emerged into chaos.

People were running from their homes in terror. Men dragged their wives and their wives carried crying children, all of them scared beyond reckoning. Anne-Cathleen felt their fear feed her own, and she recoiled from the crossroads. Some were carrying bags or boxes, which made Anne-Cathleen think of her abandoned carpet-bag; all that remained of her belongings, abandoned.

She and Ábel plunged into the crowd, Ábel leading the way as they were jostled and pushed aside. They headed across the road, running for another row of townhouses on the far side. A single-horse trap sat idle in the street, its driver anxiously looking back at his master's home.

As they approached Anne-Cathleen realised Ábel meant to steal it, and she pulled up short. He finally let go of her and strode on, hailing the driver with an angry yell. The man turned quickly, and his eyes widened. Ábel produced a pistol from his belt and did not stop walking forwards as he cocked it. The driver's hand went for the whip slung by his seat, and Anne-Cathleen screamed as Ábel pulled the trigger and put a bullet between the driver's eyes. The man dropped like a stone, and she screamed again as dead eyes stared into hers.

Ábel leapt into the trap and mastered the rearing, panic-stricken horse in its traces.

"Anne, come on!"

Ábel jerked the reins, kicking the trap into motion. She stepped back, horrified by the casual murder a man she had loved had committed before her. Ábel leaned out, caught her roughly around the waist and hoisted her into the trap. She kicked and fought him, seeing through tears as the world around her collapsed.

Ábel gave the horse its head, and the trap surged out into the road, narrowly missing a man and his wife on the corner as they turned north. They galloped on, past rows and rows of housing and the streams of humanity that poured from each. Those households whose staff had remained through the siege now lost them, every man and woman seeking safety for themselves first and only. Some tried to waylay Ábel, but he brandished the empty pistol at them as they went by. Anne-Cathleen clung to the trap's board, desperate for an explanation for the chaos that had suddenly erupted around her.

As they left behind the houses of the southern slope and started to climb towards the summit of Gellért Hill, Anne-Cathleen looked back and got her answer.

Budapest was burning.

Anne-Cathleen knelt in the trap's seat and saw a city die in flames. The sweep of the horizon was consumed by fire and black smoke, boiled and churning like a corner of Hell itself. The ruined southern districts of the city were hidden by a wall of choking smoke, but she could see flames racing through the streets of Csepel and gardens of Budafok. Across the river Pesterzsébet was too bright to look at, an ember glowing with the ferocity of the sun, radiating heat and devastation. Church spires and mosques, factories and villas, all burned and died, collapsing under their weight as the inferno devoured their foundations. Anne-Cathleen saw tiny groups of people running, confused and terrified, and she tried to turn away rather than see the horror of families fleeing nature's own fury unleashed.

It was a fury unleashed by a flotilla of hovering airships, their outlines wavering through the scorching air. The Ottomans had turned man's primordial fear against Budapest, and Anne-Cathleen heard herself spitting curses and hate at the vast engines of death that even now rained curtains of liquid flame on as-yet untouched corners of Pest. She screamed vows of vengeance and pleas of mercy into the sky, hating them for the destruction they had wrought on her life.

Ábel kept the horse trotting up the hill and gently moved his hand to Anne-Cathleen's shoulder, turning her away from the scene of a dying city. She slapped away his hand and slumped into the seat.

Ábel negotiated the trap up the switchback road that led into the memorial park at the Hill's summit. Anne-Cathleen looked at him for the first time since he had plucked her kicking from the bedroom. She saw the tears that stung his eyes and the tortured set of his mouth, clamped shut to keep in the same cries that she had vented. One shaking hand started to reach out to his, but when his hand moved to grasp hers she jerked back, and a fresh wave of tears rolled down Anne-Cathleen's cheeks.

They turned another corner, and the summit was finally in sight.

"What now?" asked Anne-Cathleen. The words came out as a croak.

"Now," said Ábel, turning to look at her, "we live."

Hanging in the sky over the memorial park was an airship, its keel almost touching the treetops. Anne-Cathleen almost screamed at the sight of it, expecting Ottoman soldiers and the snap of rifles, but Ábel grasped her hand quickly and stifled her alarm. This airship was different from the ghostly rapiers that were killing Budapest; blunt and narrow, with a pair of squat gas chambers fixed to the fore and rear of each flank. Painted across the shallow curve of its bow was a single word.

Artemis.

"Come on, move yourselves!" The call was urgent, not welcoming. Ábel slowed the trap, and Anne-Cathleen half-jumped, half-fell from the trap's board as if commanded. Ábel ran to her side, and she let him help her towards the underside of the *Artemis* as her limbs suddenly went slack. Over the side of the airship came a pair of ropes, tied about their ends in quick loops. Anne-Cathleen did not want to speak, for fear of undoing the miracle that Ábel had conjured.

"How?" The word slipped out regardless. Anne-Cathleen's head swam; too much had happened to her in the last day for her to be certain of anything anymore.

"Later," said Ábel. "Get in." Ábel helped her slip the looped rope beneath her arms and around her chest then did the same to himself. The ground fell away from Anne-Cathleen's feet, and for a moment she felt dizziness threaten to overtake her.

And then she was aboard the *Artemis*, a smooth wooden deck beneath her hands and feet. A man was beside her, dark-skinned hands gently moving her up to sit with her back against the gunwale. Despite the sudden urge to fall asleep, Anne-Cathleen reached up a hand and was helped to her feet by the airman. Ábel was beside her, embracing the huge tattooed man who had shouted down to them. Still dizzy, Anne-Cathleen stepped away from the gunwale and into the lee of the airship's quarterdeck. The trembling in her limbs returned again, and she slumped back against the wood.

Ábel walked over to her and laid a hand on her shoulder.

"Stand up, Anne. Don't worry, we're safe now."

For a moment Anne-Cathleen contemplated pushing his hand away, remembering the awfulness of the last place Ábel had claimed was safe for her. But instead she reached up and gripped his hand, tired of the hate in her mind, longing only for an end to it all.

Together Ábel and Anne-Cathleen walked to the *Artemis's* gunwale. The airship was climbing quickly, putting its stern to the Ottoman airships and the devastation beneath them. To the north, above Buda, she could see a few other airships rising in to the sky; the lucky few, like her, escaping the slaughter of a city. She wondered if Gusztáv was aboard one of them.

Ábel put his hand beside hers on the rail, and she did not pull away. She felt like she was back on the bed in the radicals' den, letting the world move around her. She knew nothing of this ship, its people; even the man she stood beside, not in her heart. Below her, the place she had never called home perished in flames, but she could think of nowhere else she wanted to be.

Anne-Cathleen stood at the *Artemis's* railing and watched Budapest burn.

About the Authors

Cayleigh Hickey

Originally from Madison, Wisconsin, Cayleigh Hickey is currently living in Minneapolis, where she is pursuing a degree in English and French at the University of Minnesota, while trying to find time between classes to work on her first novel.

Aaron Michael Ritchey

Aaron Michael Ritchey is the author of *Long Live the Suicide King*, a finalist in the Reader's Favorite contest. Kirkus Reviews calls the story "a compelling tale of teenage depression handled with humor and sensitivity." His debut novel, *The Never Prayer*, was also a finalist in the Colorado Gold contest. His forthcoming works include a new young adult novel from Staccato Publishing and a six book sci-fi/western series from WordFire Press. In shorter fiction, his G.I. Joe inspired novella was an Amazon bestseller in Kindle Worlds and his story, "The Dirges of Percival Lewand" was nominated for a Hugo. He lives in Colorado with his wife and two goddesses posing as his daughters.

For more about him, his books, and how to overcome artistic angst, visit www.aaronmritchey.com. He's on Facebook as Aaron Michael Ritchey and he tweets—@aaronmritchey.

J.M. Franklin

J. M. Franklin, a current resident of Denver, CO, spends her free time crafting stories of adventure and mayhem. She has been published in the short story anthologies *Penny Dread Tales* Volumes I and II, and is the author of the forthcoming *Tunnel Rat* series. She can be contacted at JMFranklin.com.

Gerry Huntman

Gerry is a writer based in Melbourne, Australia, living with his wife and young daughter. He writes in all genres, and most sub-genres, of speculative fiction, with a leaning toward dark tales. Recent sales include *Aurealis Magazine*, *BLEED* charity anthology, *Night Terrors III* pro anthology, and *World of Horror* pro anthology. He is publishing a young teen fantasy novel, *Guardian of the Sky Realms*, in 2014 (Cohesion Press).

Laura Givens

Laura Givens is a Denver based author and artist. Her art has graced the covers of numerous publishers' books and magazines. She has provided illustrations for *Orson Scott Card's Intergalactic Medicine Show, Jim Baen's Universe, Talebones, Science Fiction Trails and Tales of the Talisman*. Her work may be viewed at www.lauragivens-artist.com. She has sold stories ranging from zombie tales to space operas and weird westerns. She was co-editor and contributor to *Six-Guns Straight From Hell*, a weird western anthology, and is art director for *Tales of the Talisman* magazine.

Keith Good

Keith Good abhors author biographies and therefore redacts the following:

Born in the upper regions of the Lunar Sea, he holds several world records for Peach Pit Spitting. President of the prestigious Bloody Yanks Band, this text is absolutely meaningless, keithisgood.blogspot.com. Another block of meaningless text, the secret of life is home roasted, fresh ground coffee.

A previous draft of *American Vampire* appeared online at www.yesteryearfiction.com.

Quincy J. Allen

Quincy J. Allen, a self-proclaimed cross-genre author, has been published in multiple anthologies, magazines, and one omnibus. Chemical Burn, a finalist in the RMFW Colorado Gold Contest, is his first full novel. He made his first pro-sale in 2014 with the story "Jimmy Krinklepot and the White Rebs of Hayberry," included in WordFire's *A Fantastic Holiday Season: The Gift of Stories*. He's written for the Internet show *RadioSteam* and his first short story collection *Out Through the Attic*, came out in 2014 from 7DS Books. His military sci-fi novel *Rise of the Thermopylae* is due out in 2014 from Twisted Core Press, and *Jake Lasater: Blood Curse*, a steampunk western fantasy novel, is due out in 2015.

He works part-time as a tech-writer by day, does book design and eBook conversions for WordFire Press by night, and lives in a cozy house in Colorado that he considers his very own sanctuary— think Batcave, but with fewer flying mammals and more sunlight.

David Boop

David Boop is a Denver-based speculative fiction author. In addition to his novels, short stories, and children's books, he's also an award-winning essayist and screenwriter. His novel, the sci-fi/noir *She Murdered Me with Science*, debuted in 2008. Since then, David has had over thirty short stories published and two short films produced. He specializes in weird westerns but has been published in many genres including media tie-ins for *Green Hornet* and *Honey West*.

2013 saw the digital release of his first Steampunk children's book, *The Three Inventors Sneebury*, with a print release due in 2014. David tours the country speaking on writing and publishing at schools, libraries, and conventions.

He's a single dad, returning college student, part-time temp worker, and believer. His hobbies include film noir, anime, the Blues, and Mayan History.

You can learn more on his fanpage:
www.facebook.com/dboop.updates
Or on Twitter:
@david.boop.

J.R. Boyett

J.R. Boyett was born on a rural island in the Puget Sound and spent much of his youth in the heart of Dixie. He enlisted in the U.S. Army at the age of 17, where he served for 5 years before suffering a career ending injury. In 2010 he received his Bachelor of Arts from Pacific Lutheran University and is currently pursuing a Master of Divinity at Fuller Theological Seminary.

A Philosopher and Theologian, J.R. Boyett follows in the long tradition of using fictional narrative to not only entertain the reader, but to examine essential questions about ourselves and the world in which we live.

Vivian Caethe

Vivian Caethe is a writer, editor and general miscreant. When not editing, she writes across all genres of speculative fiction, and especially loves weird westerns and science fiction. While doing all of these things, she drinks copious amounts of tea, which she's told will help her retain her sanity. So far she's not convinced. But she's too wired to really tell.

Aaron Spriggs

Aaron Spriggs is a living model of an electron. You either know what state he lives in, but not his income, or you know his income but not which state he currently resides in. I'll tell you this much, he's in Denver, Colorado these days.

Aaron has published a few short stories and several poems and is sitting on a few novels, like everyone else. His fixation is on steampunk, but has written the entire gamut of genres including horror, fantasy, and creative non-fiction.

Entomologist by day and poet/musician by night, Aaron has gone on several musical tours around the USA and is in that rare animal—a signed band. He plays trumpet poorly and theremin passingly (one of the world's only mobile theremins, so no one knows where or when he'll show up). During the heat of summer, Aaron can be found at Burning Man every year.

Peter J. Wacks

Peter J. Wacks was born in California sometime during 1976. He has always been amazed and fascinated by both writing and the world in general. Throughout the course of his life, he has hitchhiked across the States and backpacked across Europe on the Eurail. Peter writes a lot, and will continue to do so till the day he dies. Possibly beyond. Peter has acted, designed games, written novels and other spec fiction, and was nominated for a Bram Stoker Award for his first graphic novel *Behind These Eyes* (co-written with Guy Anthony De Marco). Currently, he is the Managing Editor of Kevin J. Anderson & Rebecca Moesta's WordFire Press.

David W. Landrum

David W. Landrum has published speculative fiction in numerous journals and anthologies. His novellas, *The Gallery, Strange Brew,* and *The Prophetess,* and his full-length novel, *The Sorceress of the Northern Seas* are available through Amazon. A novella titled *The Sorceress of Time,* which features the Princess Jing Lin, from "The Weather God" as its main character, is forthcoming from Eternal Press.

Sam Knight

A Colorado native, Sam Knight spent ten years in California's wine country before returning to the Rockies. When asked if he misses California, he gets a wistful look in his eyes and replies he misses the green mountains in the winter, but he is glad to be back home.

As well as being part of the WordFire Press Production Team, he is the Senior Editor for Villainous Press and author of three children's books, three short story collections, two novels, and more than a dozen short stories, including a Kindle Worlds Novella co-authored with Kevin J. Anderson.

A stay-at-home father, Sam attempts to be a full-time writer, but there are only so many hours left in a day after kids. Once upon a time, he was known to quote books the way some people quote movies, but now he claims having a family has made him forgetful, as a survival adaptation. He can be found at SamKnight.com and contacted at Sam@samknight.com

Mike Cervantes

Mike Cervantes is a graduate of The University of Texas at El Paso with a degree in Creative Writing. He is a participant in many of Denver's local steampunk and creative writing conventions and conferences. He is currently writing an ongoing series featuring the adventures of *The Scarlet Derby and Midnight Jay*, which you can find online at http://thescarletderby.tumblr.com.

Jonathan D. Beer

Jonathan D. Beer fancies himself a writer of science-fiction and fantasy, and spends much of his time exploring the alternate-history 1840s glimpsed in "Budapest Will Burn." He lives in Kent, United Kingdom, with his girlfriend, a requisite pair of cats, and a pair of rats who are just along for the ride. You can read more of his tortured prose at www.jonathandbeer.com.

Additional Copyright Info

OTHER WORDFIRE TITLES

Our list of other WordFire Press authors and titles is always growing.
To find out more and to see our selection of titles, visit us at:

wordfirepress.com

OTHER PENNY DREAD TALES

Penny Dread Tales Volume I
Gears, Coils, Aether & Steam

Penny Dread Tales Volume II
Phantasmagorical Calliope of Clockwork and Steam

Penny Dread Tales Volume III
In Darkness Clockwork Shine

Penny Dread Tales Volume IV
Perfidious and Paranormal Punkery of Steam

Made in the USA
Middletown, DE
18 August 2015